MALICE IN MALMÖ

Torquil MacLeod

McNIDDER & GRACE CRIME

Published by McNidder & Grace
Rosedale
Llangyndeyrn
Kidwelly
SA17 5BN
www.mcnidderandgrace.co.uk

Original paperback first published in 2019
©Torquil MacLeod and Torquil MacLeod Books Ltd
www.torquilmacleodbooks.com

This book is a work of fiction. Names, characters and incidents
are either the product of the author's imagination or are used
fictitiously. Any resemblance to actual persons, living or dead, is
purely coincidental.
Torquil MacLeod has asserted his right to be identified as the author
of this work in accordance with the Copyright, Designs and Patents
Act 1988.
A catalogue record for this work is available from the British Library.

ISBN: 9780857161871

Designed by Obsidian Design

Printed and bound in the United Kingdom by
Short Run Press, Exeter, UK

To Fraser and Paula, and Calum and Sarah. With love.

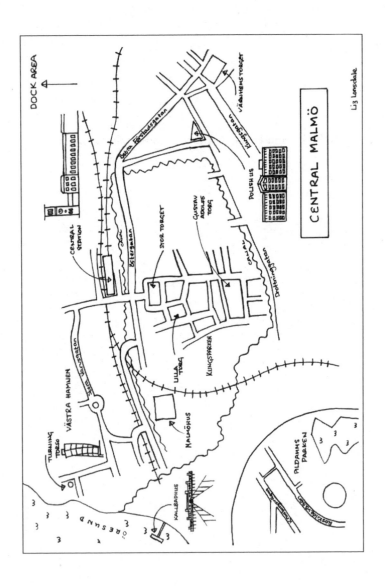

CENTRAL MALMÖ

Liz Lonsdale

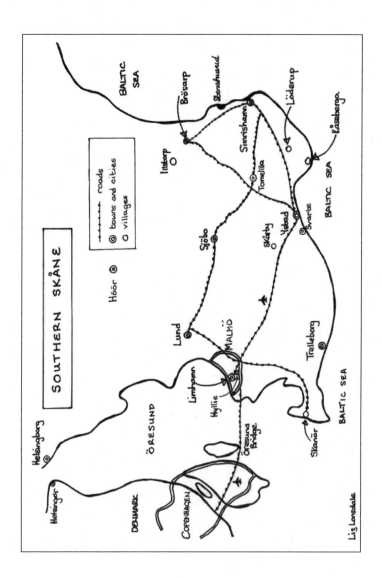

SOUTHERN SKÅNE

roads
towns and cities
villages

Liz Lonsdale

PROLOGUE

Eila knew she had been chosen because she was a girl. And pretty. It wasn't due to any great insight on her part; she was only six. Anders had told her. He knew these things because he was eight. Not that it made her feel any better. Nothing could compensate for the bewilderment and misery she had experienced at being wrenched from her home and loving parents and hastily despatched like a parcel to a foreign land. From what she could now remember, her life had been happy. Her mother and father had cared for her, though she'd sensed that they'd been behaving differently in the weeks before she'd left their small apartment. There'd been a number of hushed conversations. People called Russians were mentioned a lot. And then they appeared in the sky. And there were the peculiar and frightening sounds of wailing sirens, loud explosions and crackling fires in the buildings not far from their home. The faces of the people in the streets looked different, too. It was her first recognition of fear.

During the nights before the awful day of her departure, lying half asleep in her tiny bedroom, she could hear her mother crying through the thin wall. Her father, who had worked in an office in the centre of the city, usually left in an aging suit after breakfast. One day, he suddenly appeared in a new uniform. Eila had been startled at first but strangely thrilled. She thought he looked ever so handsome. Not that her father seemed pleased – or proud. He wore a glum expression, which wasn't like him at all. The evening before he left, he came into her bedroom to read her a story. When he'd finished, he hugged her like he'd never done before. She thought he might be sobbing, as his shoulders heaved gently as he clasped her to his chest. After saying goodnight, he hung around the door. She could still remember his silhouette hovering there for a good few minutes. The next morning, he was gone. Her mother said he'd been called away to fight the Russians. Again, she didn't understand why these people were being so horrible and why her father had to go and fight them. When they'd gone for a walk in the park later that day, Eila had picked a yellow flower to give to her mother to try and cheer her up. It had only made her weep more. Eila felt awful because she thought she'd done something wrong.

The night before she was taken to the big railway station with the two huge, scary figures either side of the entrance, her mother had packed a suitcase with her things in it, including her favourite doll. Eila assumed that they were going on a holiday, as they'd packed the same suitcase last summer when they'd gone to the lake. That had been fun. Her father had smiled all week, sitting at the edge of the water smoking his favourite pipe. When it came to bedtime, her mother told her to get into the big bed in her parents' room. That was exciting. She'd never done that before. She'd woken up when her mother came in. Her mother had snuggled up to her and she'd fallen asleep in her arms.

When they got to the station, there were lots of other children of all ages gathering with their parents. She was still puzzled as to why her mother hadn't brought her own suitcase. None of the parents seemed to have suitcases – but all the children did. Eila began to panic as her mother shoved her towards the line of children.

A large lady, who smelt of mothballs, grabbed her arm. Her mother was holding a handkerchief to her eyes and her own tears started to flow as she realized something was terribly wrong. She broke free of this woman and rushed back to her mother. They hugged tightly. 'I'm so sorry, my darling,' her mother kept saying over and over again. The large lady, in her bulky, hairy fur coat, looking like an ogre from one of the stories her father used to read to her, roughly prized her away. Eila was now screaming, and the large woman told her to calm down and be a good girl. When she turned to call out to her mother to save her, all she could see was her back as she scurried away.

That was over a year ago. Now she was in a place called Sweden. She was living with Anders and Isabell and their parents. It had been so hard at first. They spoke a funny, half-familiar language, but she gradually began to understand it and to speak it herself. She had been taken to the same school as Anders, where some of the other children had said horrid things to her because she was a Finn. They made the word sound as though it was a disease. They laughed at her attempts to speak Swedish. Often Anders joined in. She could feel that he wasn't happy to have her around in their grand home in the country. Eila tried to keep away from him as much as possible. Isabell was totally different. She was just a few months younger than Eila, and they played together a lot. Isabell was Eila's only friend in the world. She was sweet and blonde and had sparkling, blue eyes. Anders often reduced those beautiful eyes to tears with his nasty jokes and bullying behaviour. His parents never seemed to scold him. He was their favourite. His mother's favourite, anyway; Anders' father was rarely at home. He was an important businessman, and he left for work in the nearest town early each morning. Often, he was away for days on end 'on business'. Eila couldn't understand why he wasn't fighting like her father was having to. Then again, no one seemed to talk about Russians in Sweden.

The most exciting thing to happen in her life was a letter arriving from her mother every two or three weeks. These letters were written in Swedish so Isabell's mother could read them out to her. Mamma always said the same thing: everything was well; her father was still away, but she was sure he would be fine. She said how much she missed her little girl, which would bring Eila to the edge of tears, though she tried not to cry in front of Isabell's mother. Then Eila was allowed to keep the letters, though she couldn't really read them. She kept them under her pillow so that when she was asleep, she was close to her mother and father. Then one day, she found that the letters had gone. Later, she found Anders in the garden. He'd lit a small fire and Eila realized that he was burning her mother's letters. As she tried to save them, he pushed her roughly away and laughed. Isabell shouted at her brother, but he ignored her. When the flames died down, he walked off to the house, still laughing. Eila ran and hid behind the wooden summer house and curled up into an unhappy ball. How could he do such a cruel thing? Isabell found her and tried to comfort her, but Eila's sense of loss was deep. Even at six, she felt a great well of loneliness.

Then, the terrible day. It was a month later, just after midsummer. The family had friends over for Sunday lunch, and the children were sent off to play in the garden as soon as the meal was drawing to a close. Eila remembered the flowers were at their brightest and the leaves on the trees were still at their most brilliant green. After her early life in an apartment, she'd learned to love this beautiful garden and the natural world that had only been fleetingly available to her in the park at home and her family's annual trip to the lake. Here, she could enjoy it every day. Her hobby was pressing flowers, and Isabell eagerly helped her pick them for a while until she grew distracted and ran off to find Anders, who hadn't been in a good mood after the adults had sent them packing from the house. When Eila had finished gathering her flowers, she looked around for Isabell. The afternoon sun was hot, and she wandered over to *the shade of the two old oaks in the middle of the garden. One had a tree house built into the branches with a rope ladder dangling from it. It had been made specially for Anders that spring. There was no sign of either Isabell or Anders. Then there was a heavy rustling of leaves above her head. She squinted up. The next moment, a shock of fair curls and a flailing of limbs crashed past her and hit the ground with a thump. She dropped her flowers in fright. They fluttered to the ground, and some of them wafted over the motionless form of Isabell. Eila stood rooted to the spot, unable to understand what she had just seen. Then she sank to her haunches and tentatively reached out for the strands of hair that shimmered on the green grass. She looked around helplessly. Then she felt the first hot tears of despair slipping down her cheeks.*

CHAPTER 1

Bernt Hägg was happy with his pace. Brisk but not flat out. He prided himself on his level of fitness despite the fact that he had slipped into his fifties a month ago. He could pass for someone a lot younger, and many of his female colleagues were genuinely surprised to discover he had reached his half century. And this had pleased him ridiculously. Even more so because he felt his wife of twenty-three years no longer appreciated him as much as he thought she should. And that was another reason why he left their apartment at six every morning to do his forty-minute run; early-morning pleasantries with Petra were becoming more and more of an effort. A quick shower followed by a swift breakfast, and he was out of the family home by half past seven on his way to the office. This routine also meant he could avoid his two teenage sons before they emerged for school. He had been so keen to have a family when he'd first married. But he hadn't factored in the probability that they would turn from lively, interesting youngsters into self-absorbed, thoughtless, slightly terrifying adolescents. They seemed to swing between listlessness and aggression, and he realized that his control over them was waning. He was no longer the centre of their world, and he felt he was becoming an unwanted appendage in their lives, until they wanted money, of course. Petra undermined his efforts to stand up to them and he invariably ended up forking out just to keep the fragile family harmony from crumbling.

Out on the virtually empty streets of Malmö, he could escape into a world of his own; create his own rhythm. He could resurrect the dreams he'd had as a young man and pretend they could still be fulfilled – a career that mattered; a home life that fitted the mellower Sweden of his youth; even some sporting success. He'd always been a good runner and a passable handball player. In his mind, he could still be someone people looked up to. Admired even. Taken notice of at least. One day...

The route never varied. He always aimed to cross the canal on Fersens bridge at around 6.30. And then it was only ten minutes to the entrance of his apartment block. Today was a crisp, late-March morning, and the sun was beginning to cast early shadows from the buildings he trotted past. Coming up on his left was Kungsparken. The first spots of spring colour were emerging from their winter hibernation, though it would be some weeks before the trees came to life. As a Swede, he was grateful for any signs that summer would eventually return. Bernt Hägg slowed his pace as he approached the crossroads at Regementsgatan. One car glided by before he launched himself over the road and closed in on the bridge. He glanced at his watch – 6.29. Perfect timing. As he crossed the bridge, out of habit, he glanced to his right towards Gamla Kyrkogården cemetery. Beyond the tree-lined avenues, guarding the grave stones of the great and the good of Malmö's past, was the Gustav Adolfs torg. The cemetery was always deserted at this time of day as it didn't open its gates until 7.15. Suddenly, he broke his stride, and by the time he'd reached the other end of the bridge, he'd stopped altogether. Surely he was mistaken! There was a large bundle of something on a bench next to the high hedge that encircled the maintenance area. But he could have sworn he saw it move! Though he was loath to break his routine timings, he found himself drawn back to the gate of the cemetery. He hopped over the fence and made his way carefully along the pathway. To his right were a couple of family plots surrounded by low, intricate cast-iron fencing. As he approached the bench, he could see that the bundle was wriggling. Bernt now made out a human figure, its face completely covered in a hood of some kind, its ankles bound, and its hands tied behind with black tape. The person was completely trussed up, but renewed its wriggling on hearing Bernt's footsteps on the cinder path. A mumbling noise emerged from under the dark cloth hood, which resembled a cushion cover.

Bernt Hägg tentatively approached the figure and carefully lifted the hood. A face appeared, the mouth covered in black gaffer tape. The frantic eyes of the man implored Bernt to peel the tape off. Bernt found his fingers shaking as he tried to find the edge of the tape. After a few seconds of fumbling, he ripped it off, and the man gave a sharp cry before gulping in the fresh air. There was something about the man that Bernt found familiar; he racked his brains but couldn't come up with an answer.

'Thanks,' the man gasped.

Bernt could only nod mutely. The experience was so bizarre. They weren't going to believe this when he got to the office.

'Could you untie me?' the man said, breaking Bernt's momentary reverie.

'Sure.' Bernt went round behind him and began to unpeel the tape that was binding his wrists together and to the back of the bench. As he was wrestling with the sticky bonds, he asked the obvious question 'What happened?'

'Kidnapped. I was kidnapped.'

It was the voice. That smooth growl that he'd heard on television interviews. And, looking at the face that he now placed from the business magazines he'd pored over in the office, Bernt knew who the man was.

CHAPTER 2

The monotony was broken by Pontus Brodd rustling his newspaper, accompanied by a chuckle. He shook his head. 'He's done it again!' There was admiration in his voice.

Surveillance was bad enough at the best of times, but having to spend hours on end cooped up in a car with Brodd was not Inspector Anita Sundström's idea of a fun experience. She suppressed a yawn, took off her glasses, placed them on the dashboard and rubbed the bridge of her nose. She caught herself in the rear view mirror and winced. The crow's feet around her eyes were much more noticeable these days. And they weren't the only lines that were causing concern. Her neck was no longer as smooth as it had been. She didn't even want to think about everything sagging south of the shoulders. Things weren't as firm as they used to be despite regular runs round Pildammsparken. She was feeling old. She'd be hitting fifty in a year and half. Then it was definitely downhill all the way. Sitting here in a stuffy car wasn't improving her mood. They'd been surveilling the 1950s brick warehouse for four hours and nothing had happened. Nothing had happened yesterday, or the day before that when the supposed raid on the warehouse stuffed with lucrative electrical goods was actually meant to have taken place. The tip-off had been way off the mark. On the first night, Chief Inspector Moberg had turned up himself to oversee the operation. It had occurred to Anita that they'd been deliberately sent on a wild goose chase and that Moberg's anonymous source was using this as a distraction while the job was happening elsewhere. Of course, this suggestion hadn't gone down too well with Moberg, who was becoming increasingly irascible of late. His temper had always been quick to surface; now the team were constantly walking on eggshells to prevent the rumblings turning into an eruption. As it turned out, Anita's theory hadn't been right either. There had been no reports of any other warehouse raids. Another waste of time.

She glanced across at Brodd. His eyes were screwed up, reading his newspaper by the light of his mobile phone. How she wished she was with her young colleague and friend, Hakim Mirza. But that had all changed six months ago. The case they'd been working on had involved slave labourers and had ended in an exchange of gunfire, resulting in Hakim's recently engaged fiancée, Liv Fogelström, receiving a bullet wound. It had left her paralysed from the waist down. Hakim had blamed Anita for Liv being at the scene of the shootout as she should have been off duty that night. Anita couldn't escape the fact that she had instigated it, though Liv had been more than willing, and her professionalism couldn't be faulted, saving the life of the young man she was there to protect. But that hadn't washed with Hakim who, Anita realized, needed a scapegoat. He'd hardly spoken to her since, which made it awkward as they were serving in the same team. Now she tended to be paired with Brodd, while Hakim made it obvious he'd rather work with Klara Wallen, the fifth member of the Skåne County Criminal Investigation Squad.

The last six months had been hard for both Liv and Hakim. They were still determined to get married. Confined to a wheelchair, Liv was living with her brother in his family bungalow near Helsingborg, while Hakim had moved back in with his parents. This was so that he could save the money which, combined with Liv's compensation when it came through, would enable them to buy and adapt a house that would accommodate

Liv's needs. Any of Anita's offers of help made to Hakim had been rejected. She could understand, but it didn't make her feel any better.

Anita reached over and picked up her glasses and slotted them back on. She noticed a familiar face in Brodd's newspaper. It was a presenter from some popular kids' show, though she couldn't remember his name.

'I don't know why you read a rag like *Sanningen*,' she said, staring across the quiet street at the darkened warehouse. 'The Truth, my arse.'

'It's great. Especially The Oligarch. He's just sown up Jimmy Brantling.'

Now she remembered. He was the over-the-top guy with wacky hair and colourful clothes who enthusiastically leapt about a lot. She had found him profoundly irritating, but children seemed to adore him.

'Don't tell me The Oligarch has entrapped him! How did he do that? Half the things he does can't be legal.'

'He posed as the commissioning editor for some Lithuanian TV station that wanted to take Brantling's show. Promised big bucks. Could be syndicated in all the Baltic States; and also claimed he had contacts in Germany: the biggy! Jumping Jimmy fell for it and ended up having too much champagne. Drugs appeared. He's caught on camera snorting. But the funniest thing is that he told The Oligarch that he hated "bloody kids".' Brodd couldn't help chortling. 'That's him finished.'

'It doesn't seem fair that he tricks people into doing these things,' Anita protested half-heartedly.

'He doesn't just go after celebs. He's done some serious investigative reporting. Like that business fella who was caught insider trading. Corrupt. Didn't entrap him. Just good journalism.' Anita wasn't sure if Brodd would recognize good journalism if it leapt off the page and grabbed him by the throat. 'A number of dodgy types have been caught and put away because of him,' Brodd concluded firmly.

The Oligarch was well-known in Sweden, though no one had any idea what he looked like. His bye-line photo was a silhouette and he'd never appeared on camera as himself. As far as Anita could gather – though she'd be the first to admit she wasn't particularly interested – he often posed as a rich Russian of some sort, duping his victims into confessing things that would wreck their careers. Hence his self-styled nickname. Anita assumed he must be Russian or from one of the old Soviet-controlled states.

Anita took out the flask she'd brought along and poured the remains of her coffee. She didn't offer Brodd any of the dregs; he liked to buy his caffeine fix from a late-night café on the way to the industrial estate to have with his large Marabou fruit and nut chocolate bar. In fact, he'd gone through two bars that night, and the yellow wrappers were stuffed near the gear stick. Anita took a sip, and the warmth in her throat made her feel better. She would give it one more hour then they'd call it a night.

'I've got to go and pee,' Brodd announced as he put down his paper.

'Do it quietly,' sighed Anita. 'And out of sight.'

Brodd eased his gangly frame out of the driver's side of the car and shut the door as soundlessly as possible. It still made a metallic thump, which broke the still night air. Not that it really mattered as there was no chance of anything happening tonight. Anita just prayed that Moberg would admit defeat and call the whole thing off. It would be a relief not having to spend another night stuck in close proximity with a shiftless colleague who liked nothing better than to eat Indian food every evening and was prone to fart when bored. (Inevitably, the window would have to be opened, letting in the cold night air and souring Anita's mood even more.)

Leaning back against the headrest, Anita let her mind begin to wander again. It settled on the other problem in her life – Kevin.

Kevin Ash, detective sergeant of the Cumbria Constabulary in north-west England and long-distance lover. That arrangement suited Anita perfectly. The only problem was that Kevin had flown over to Malmö to stay with her two months before and was still ensconced in her Roskildevägen apartment. Right now, if not fast asleep as she should be, he'd probably be glued to some Swedish TV programme, mindlessly not understanding a single word. His continued presence was causing friction. She had to curb her irritation because she knew it was her fault that he'd decamped into her precious space and showed little inclination to move. The reasons that she hadn't shown Kevin the door were due to a mixture of wavering affection and growing guilt. The previous year, she'd asked him, as a favour, to go to London and find out information about a man who was running a British slave gang in Sweden. Kevin had successfully unearthed the intelligence that was key to the success of the investigation despite being warned off by a senior detective of the Metropolitan Police. The fallout from the arrest of the gang leader was that a number of Met officers were discovered to have been on the villain's payroll, and heads rolled. The fact that the process had been instigated by a fellow policeman hadn't gone down well among the close-knit brotherhood of corrupt coppers. Unfortunately for Kevin, the chief constable of the Cumbria Constabulary happened to be a former senior officer at the Met. Under the pretext that he had mishandled an ongoing investigation into a Lake District hotel scam, Kevin had been put on indefinite 'gardening leave'. With time on his hands, Anita had asked him over to Malmö. He was still here.

Anita would leave for work with Kevin curled up on the day bed in the living room with his second mug of Lipton's breakfast tea clutched on his lap. Every day, he would watch in weird fascination the morning magazine shows with the ever-smiling, clean-cut presenters enthusing over everything from fashion to fancy new recipes. More worryingly, he was also into the kids' channel and particularly liked *Elias och räddningsteamet* with its talking rescue boats. He said he watched it because Anita's one-and-a-half-year-old granddaughter, Leyla, was into it – Anita was pretty sure she wasn't. *Antikrundan, Sveriges mästerkock* – nothing passed Kevin by (despite purporting not to like their British counterparts *The Antiques Roadshow* and *Masterchef*). Anita had asked him why he watched so much Swedish television. He replied that it was a way to learn the language. The fact that he still only used *hej* and *tak* made Anita think that his Swedish linguistic skills had plateaued early. Luckily for him, there were also plenty of British and American programmes to keep him happy (subtitled for Swedish audiences), so he could still catch up with *Midsomer Murders, Murder She Wrote* and *Escape to the Country*.

Another unhealthy obsession was for drinking frightening amounts of Offesson's coffee and, more alarmingly, an addiction to falafels, a popular Malmö dish. To Anita's horror, he didn't eat anything else for a fortnight. She'd managed to wean him off with her own far-from-imaginative cooking. While she was at the polishus, Kevin would make a daily pilgrimage into the city centre and park himself in Lille Torg. In Malmö's hippest square, he liked to sit in its most off-beat café, Folk & Rock. It was cluttered with mismatched furniture and adorned with CDs and posters of a generation of musicians that Kevin grew up with. It seemed to come with its own beggar, whom Kevin had befriended. He said he wasn't used to seeing people actually begging inside cafés and shops. Anita thought the main attraction was probably the lively group of young women who served behind the counter; the tall one with the John Lennon spectacles being a particular favourite. They all spoke excellent English. Though she didn't for one moment think that Kevin would stray. He was like a faithful puppy, and she knew he was passionately in love with her. The fact that she couldn't return that depth of feeling was another barrier between them. Their previous arrangement of meeting up three or four times a year had been ideal as far as she was concerned. It was fun; the sex was lively after prolonged periods of celibacy, and afterwards she could return to the normality of her own space with her family close by. After missing having her son Lasse around when he moved out to live with Jazmin, she had gradually got used to having the apartment to herself. She had total freedom to slob around as much as she wanted. She didn't have to think about the needs and sensibilities of a co-occupant. Roskildevägen was her haven and symbol of independence. A moping, love-struck Kevin seriously compromised all that. It led to arguments, after which she would feel remorse. She had even resorted to ploys to get him out more. She'd introduced him to her local pub, The Pickwick (now he spent a lot more time there than she did, having become very friendly with the barman, Matt, a fellow Brit) and, mindful of his pet passion, she'd sent him off exploring local historical sites. She'd even managed to get him up to Stockholm for a few days, which gave her much-needed respite. And it wasn't as though he didn't try to help: he was constantly tidying up (he'd put things away in logical places, which meant that she could never find them again – that was profoundly infuriating); he babysat for Lasse and Jazmin and obviously loved little Leyla and he bonded with Lasse over football and visits with him to the sauna at Kallbadhus. It's just that he was under her feet at a time when she didn't want any added pressure to a working life that was stressful enough.

Basically, she knew Kevin was bored. Without his job he felt emasculated. He had no sense of worth. She had spent enough time sitting with shrinks to know that he was depressed, though he would never admit it. And she knew that it was all down to her manipulation of a man who loved her to get a result in an important case. She hadn't foreseen the consequences. Now she was paying the price.

The car door was wrenched open, and Brodd lowered

himself into the driver's seat, slightly out of breath. 'Someone's coming.'

Anita was immediately alert. She sat upright. She gently pressed the button for the window, which slid noiselessly down to about halfway. She could hear a vehicle.

'Should we call for back-up?' Brodd whispered, still trying to control his breathing.

'Just wait.'

Where their car was tucked away, they could only see the warehouse straight ahead and the approach from the right, which was the road into the industrial estate. The oncoming vehicle was coming from the left. Could the gang have laid low somewhere else on the estate for most of the night so they wouldn't be spotted coming in? Anita could feel Brodd tense beside her.

Then a van appeared. In the subdued light, it looked blue. There was only the driver visible. It slowed down as it passed them, which made it all the more suspicious. Casing the warehouse? Then the driver turned and gave them a cheery wave. Brodd found himself waving back until he caught Anita's scowl.

'Someone from a night shift?' he suggested apologetically.

Anita watched the van disappear round another building. 'As everybody seems know we're here, I think it's time to go home.'

CHAPTER 3

Anita arrived at the polishus early in the afternoon. After their abortive surveillance, she'd gone home and flaked out for a few hours. When she'd got into the shower, still half asleep, she discovered that Kevin had bought a new shower gel. It irked her unreasonably. It was inconsequential, but she always purchased the same brand. She liked the smell. This one was a strange, slime-green colour, the odour was oddly antiseptic and it didn't lather smoothly. She knew he was trying to do his bit by getting the shopping in. But it was little things like this that she found trying. Maybe she was just tired after three nights sitting in a car with Pontus Brodd, and frustrated that they'd wasted their time on an unfounded tip-off. She'd found herself criticizing the new shower gel instead of thanking Kevin for preparing a late breakfast for her. That tiny complaint had escalated into a full-scale row about how his help around the apartment wasn't actually helping. When she tried to apologize by explaining her tetchiness was down to the situation at work, he'd retorted angrily that at least she had fucking work to go to. He'd stormed out of the apartment shortly afterwards.

She'd hardly had time to settle down to write the report on their efforts of last night when Klara Wallen popped her head round the door. To add to the poor atmosphere within the squad, which Anita recognized hadn't been helped by her own actions, Wallen wasn't one to lift the mood. Since her move to

Ystad with her partner, Rolf, who'd wanted to move back to his home town, Wallen had to cope with a good hour's commute each way. And that's if the trains were running to time; they were no longer as reliable as they'd once been. As Rolf was a man who expected to have a meal on the table when he got back from work and didn't lift a finger to help around the home, tensions had risen. Why Wallen didn't tell Rolf where to shove his meals was beyond Anita. Needless to say, Anita had coped with a number of tearful sessions in the female toilets. Deep down, Anita suspected that Klara was frightened of Rolf. It made her own gripes about Kevin's peccadilloes seem rather pedantic.

'He wants to see you.' Anita didn't need to ask who *he* was. Not another night's surveillance! She would have to conjure up a mystery illness if she was forced to spend any more time trapped in a car with Brodd.

'Sit down, Anita,' Chief Inspector Moberg growled at her when she entered his office. Hugely overweight and with a mop of badly dyed hair, Anita had noted that Moberg's face seemed redder in hue these days. His mammoth appetite was legendary in police headquarters, as was the fact that he'd gone through three wives and at least two live-in partners. Each new relationship produced an ephemeral invigoration before inevitably hitting the rocks, and he would sink into the same self-destructive pattern – eating even more food and drinking even more beer. In the latter capacity, Pontus Brodd played his one useful role within the team: he accompanied the chief inspector on his after-work binges.

'I'm convinced that there isn't going to be any robbery down at the electrical warehouse,' Anita started before Moberg could begin planning any more night-time operations.

'It was a bum steer,' Moberg agreed with a dismissive wave of hand. That was it! No apologies for the interminable hours spent on a pointless exercise. 'No, forget that one; we've got something more concrete to occupy our time. A kidnapping.'

'A kidnapping?'

'Yes.' Moberg was surprisingly relaxed about it. The last time there had been a kidnapping some ten years before, there had been frantic police activity. However, the perpetrators had been amateurs, and they'd been easily caught.

'Who is it?'

'Mats Möller.' The name rang a vague bell, but in what context Anita had no idea. 'He's one of the new breed of sexy business people who make their money confounding ordinary folk like us with technology.' Exactly the type Moberg would normally have no time for.

'Dot com sort of thing?'

'Not exactly. Came up with some clever computer software program that can be used as a diagnostic tool in trucks and vans and things like that. He's made his fortune from the motor and haulage industries. I don't really understand it other than it makes running fleets of vehicles more efficient because they can identify any faults very quickly, fix whatever and get them back on the road. Saves millions. And it's made Möller millions.'

'Which makes Möller a juicy target.' It now dawned on Anita who he was, and she remembered that she'd seen him on the television talking to a group of young entrepreneurs. The gist of the discussion had centred around Möller's genius, and he'd said nothing to contradict that assessment.

Moberg leaned forward, which had the effect of putting an enormous strain on his shirt buttons. 'Exactly.'

'When was he taken?'

'Friday night.'

'Why haven't we heard about this before? He must have been missing for four days.'

Moberg spread his chunky fingers out on his desk top. 'No, he's not missing. He turned up yesterday in Gamla Kyrkogården, tied to a bench. His ransom has already been paid.'

'So, what are we meant to do?'

'The commissioner wants us to investigate. But quietly. No fuss. No press. And that's how Möller wants it, too. Something like this is bad for the reputation of the city. Doesn't look good if one of our most high-profile businessmen gets kidnapped. As it's obviously been carried out very slickly, the worry is that whoever is behind it might strike again.'

Anita nodded. She could see the logic.

'So, we're going to see him now.'

'We?' Anita queried. It was rare these days for Moberg to get off his large backside and move from the sanctuary of his office.

'Yes, *we*,' Moberg barked. 'I'm still capable of asking a few bloody questions!'

CHAPTER 4

Anita drove, though she found it difficult to manoeuvre the gears as Moberg spilled out of the passenger seat and invaded her driving space. It was only a short journey, but it made Anita realize how much Malmö had changed in a relatively short time. They passed the Central Station, recently transformed into a modern transport hub with an airport-like concourse of shops and eating places. Anita followed the road round to the left. On her right was the Inner Harbour. What she still thought of as the *new* university building had once stood alone. Now it was wedged in among a phalanx of contemporary structures. Many were part of the expanding university while others were office blocks. To the left was Malmö Live, described as an *Event Centre*. This strikingly modernist interconnected group of red, gold and white cuboid blocks of differing heights and orientations – consisting of an impressive concert hall home to the Malmö Symphony Orchestra; a conference centre; an hotel, offices and housing – had changed the city's skyline. Not all the designs were to her taste, but she was proud of the way Malmö was growing up and starting to replicate its sophisticated cousins, Copenhagen and Stockholm.

Another quick right turn, and Anita took the car beyond yet more university buildings and into Bassängkajen before parking it facing Södra Varvsbassängen, the southern basin. This large expanse of water had been the centre of the famous Kockums shipyards. Years ago, this mainstay of Malmö's commercial activity was a place of industrial bedlam. Now the cranes were long gone from the basin and massive redevelopment was taking place. Across the water, some of the old, mid-19th-century, red-brick buildings still stood, as did the Kockums headquarters towering behind them, keeping a paternal eye on the operation below. Opened in 1958, it had heralded an exciting new age that would be curtailed by the swiftly assembled Japanese and Korean ships of the 1970s. Coming from Malmö's most famous business family, Frans Henrik Kockum had closed down the original tobacco factory in 1825 because he had seen the potential of the new railways. He started producing wagons. This expanded into ships in 1870. Sadly, the last vessel left the basin in 1987. The company returned to its core railway wagons business before eventually leaving the city for Trelleborg only a handful of years ago. As Anita looked along the waterfront to the funky, tall glass building that housed Mats Möller's enterprise, she realized that it was men like him who were perpetuating Kockum's legacy.

Before leaving the polishus, Wallen had quickly filled them in on what she could find out about Mats Möller after a quick internet search. He was a thirty-five-year-old bachelor who had come from Eslov in Skåne. He'd gone to university in Lund for a couple of years before dropping out when his 'great idea' was turned into a fledgling venture. He'd started out with two employees and now had over a hundred, all housed in the glass complex that Anita and Moberg were now walking towards. He'd had *MM Hus* purpose built and had incorporated a penthouse apartment at the top, so he lived above the shop. Despite making occasional appearances on television, he'd managed to keep his private life out of the press, though it was rumoured that he had a house in Morocco, where he would escape the clutches of the Swedish winter.

As they approached the five-storey *MM Hus*, Anita and Moberg could see people at workstations on the first few floors through the wide, plate-glass windows. The fifth floor, however, though mainly glass, reflected the day's dull light without exposure to the outside world. Möller guarded his privacy.

Anita surveyed Möller's kingdom. For the time being, it stood alone, though she suspected that wouldn't remain the case for long with the massive amount of development going on all around the basin and the surrounding streets. Soon there would be no gaps between *MM Hus* and the large Lantmännen flour mill with its cylindrical silos further along the quay. In front of *MM Hus*'s main entrance, a few expensive cars were parked, and there was the usual rack of bicycles. But this wasn't Moberg and Anita's way in. Moberg had been given instructions to go to the back entrance and press the buzzer. Möller wanted to see them in his apartment. Anita thought that if this was the spot where he'd been snatched on Friday evening, then it was quite possible that nobody would have been around to witness it. The plain metal door looked like a service entrance and not one leading to a luxury apartment. The buzzer didn't even have a name next to it, though the visual intercom was obviously of the highest spec. Moberg poked the buzzer with his finger and spoke brusquely into the grill.

'Chief Inspector Erik Moberg and Inspector Anita Sundström.'

They heard the door click and Moberg pushed his way into a corridor. At the far end was a set of metal doors and a lift button. To the deliberately drab exterior of the corridor, the lift was a complete contrast. It felt light and airy with its mirrored walls, light-oak hand rail and carpeted floor. There was only one button – the lift only stopped at the top floor.

There was a hint of a hiss when the doors opened and they found themselves walking into a spacious room with massive picture windows. You might not be able to see in, but you could certainly see out. The vista wasn't spectacular, as too many apartment blocks had sprung up in Västra Hamnen to see the Sound properly, but it had an uninterrupted view of Malmö's iconic Turning Torso. This was the beating heart of modern Malmö. The décor, however, didn't entirely conform to the cool Swedish image. The room did possess some of the spare design that was regarded as a Scandinavian trademark – stark white chairs and low-backed sofas – but in sharp contrast with the contemporary look were rich, heavily patterned Berber rugs on the floor, brightly decorated tin-glazed pottery on the shelves and a hand-carved, intricately detailed, wooden screen dividing the room; evidence of the owner's visits to Morocco.

The owner himself, who came to greet them, was tall with light-brown hair scraped back into a man bun, a neatly clipped hipster beard and dark, piercing eyes. He wore blue jeans and a casual green shirt. His smile showed a gleaming set of teeth. Anita thought he'd recovered from his ordeal rather quickly.

'Thank you for coming.' Möller firmly shook each of their proffered hands.

They took their places on a sofa. Anita wondered if the thin legs would support Moberg.

'Can I offer you a drink?' Möller asked as he went over to a sleek white table sporting bottles of spirits on an Arabic silver tray.

Anita could see that Moberg was tempted before gruffly declining. Möller poured himself a whisky.

He gave a shrug as he came back over to them. 'I've needed a few of these since yesterday.' He sat down opposite them in a low-slung chair, his knees drawn up like twin peaks in a mountain range. He placed his glass on the right-hand peak.

'I need you to take us through everything that happened to you from Friday until you were found in the cemetery,' said Moberg, getting straight down to business.

Möller took a thoughtful swig of his whisky.

'It was about half past nine, Friday evening. I took that lift,' he said, indicating the one from which they had just emerged. 'That's for the apartment. I have another one that goes to the offices below. As I came out of the back door, I was approached by two men. I thought they were lost and were going to ask for directions. The next thing I knew, they had grabbed me and hauled me over to a van–'

'Colour?' Moberg interrupted.

'Erm... green, I think. It was difficult to make out in the dark.'

'And the men?'

'It was so quick. One was totally bald. The other... short cropped hair.'

'Ages?'

The eyes opened wide as though appealing for help. 'Anywhere between thirty and forty. Then again...'

'We can show you photos later,' Anita put in helpfully. 'You might recognize them.'

'And then what?'

'I was bundled into the back of this van and they put a hood over my head and tied my hands behind my back.'

'Did they speak to you?'

Möller shook his head. 'Not then. Later on. One of them spoke in English.'

'English?' Moberg queried.

'Yes. But he wasn't English. It was with an accent.'

'Where from?'

'I'm not good at that sort of thing. If he'd spoken Swedish with an accent, it would have been easier to pinpoint. He might have been Slavic or something like that. Definitely not Scandinavian.'

'Eastern European?'

Möller rolled his eyes hopelessly. 'I'm sorry. I was shaken. And frightened. Before the hood went on, one of them had a gun.'

'What sort of gun?'

'To me a gun's a gun. A handgun of some sort.'

'Right, so you're being driven in the van. How long were you in there for?'

Möller retreated into his whisky. He'd seemed so calm when

they'd entered his apartment but as Moberg probed, Anita could see that he was finding it hard to revisit the events of the last few days. 'It seemed like a long time. In truth, it may have been only fifteen to twenty minutes.'

'So, somewhere in the city or very close?'

'I suppose.' Möller drained his whisky and winched himself out of his seat and went over to the tray for a refill.

Anita could sense that Moberg was itching to take up Möller's offer of a drink, but he kept himself in check.

'What kind of place did they take you to?'

'I think it was old. It smelt old; you know like a deserted place. It echoed. After they'd left me for a while, I called out. My voice echoed. And, yes, it stank of oil. As though it was in the very fabric of the building; oily and musty.'

'Could be a warehouse,' suggested Anita. 'Or a disused workshop or garage.'

'I did hear traffic. Heavy vehicles mostly.' Anita could see Moberg weighing this up. An industrial estate or perhaps the docks? There would be a great deal of searching ahead for the team.

'So, you're trussed up in this place. Did they make clear what they wanted?'

Möller returned to his seat. 'Not straight away. I was losing track of time. They fed me at least four times before anyone spoke to me.'

'What did you eat?'

'Pizzas... falafels...'

'Did you get a better look at them when you ate? Someone must have brought in the food?'

'No. I think the two guys that picked me up came in. They wore balaclavas. Black. One held a gun while the other untied me and they watched me eat.'

'You must have got a view of your surroundings then,' said Anita.

'It was dingy. No light was coming into the room. I wasn't aware of any windows. The place just felt big; as though I was in a corner.'

'How did you see to have your food?'

'The guy with the gun had a torch in the other hand. He made sure I knew he was armed. Then he pointed the light at me while I was untied and ate. And while my hands were loose, I was allowed to pee and shit in a bucket. They kindly emptied it for me,' he added sarcastically.

'Basically, they waited before making any demands?'

'I presume they were trying to disorientate me. It sure as hell worked. And with no one actually speaking to me, it freaked me out. I didn't know whether I was coming or going. I just wanted to get out of there with my life. Sod the cost.' The whisky came to his aid again. He dried his lips with the back of his hand. 'All the time I was in there, I pretty well knew what they were after. I'm a rich guy.'

'And then they made their demand?'

'They came in. Three of them. The two originals and some new guy. Still had their faces covered. It was the new one who spoke, again in accented English. He made me a very simple offer. I pay them money or they would kill me. He didn't beat about the bush. He had a computer with him. Either I sign money over to them or his friend would put a bullet in my head. There was none of this "we'll leave you in the dark for a few more days and you can think it over" nonsense. I had five minutes. If I didn't pay up, they weren't going to waste any more time on me.'

'So you paid up?'

'What do you think?' The first flash of anger. 'Of course I bloody did! I wasn't going to call his bluff. Would you?'

Moberg wasn't going to give him the satisfaction of an opinion.

'Carry on.'

'I was to use the computer to transfer money from my various accounts into one single account. Then he gave me a number and a code to transfer the money to him.'

'How much?'

'I'm not telling you that.'

Moberg sat upright and stared hard at Mats Möller. 'Look, if you want us to retrieve your money, we need to know how much we're looking for.'

Anita was nonplussed by Möller's reaction. 'You'll never find it,' he scoffed. 'What do you think I've been doing from the moment I got back here? These guys knew exactly what they were about. They nearly cleaned out my personal funds, but it wasn't an amount that I would have had to dip into more complicated sources for, like through the company. They weren't in the business of hanging around. The account that I paid the money into – and I made sure I memorized the details – was emptied within minutes. Dispersed to a number of other accounts and then swiftly moved on until it became untraceable long before I was released. These were professionals.'

'In kronor?'

'No. Dollars. It'll be tucked away in the Cayman Islands or Switzerland or Panama. These guys work so quickly that you end up chasing your tail. I won't see that money again. Which is why I don't want this getting into the press or being generally known. It doesn't look good. I have lots of international business contacts. It's all about trust. It might look like someone is targeting MM Data. That would hardly inspire confidence. And all the people downstairs. Good people who don't want to worry about their jobs.'

Moberg pursed his lips. 'That's all very well, herr Möller, but it might be someone "downstairs" who tipped off the kidnappers about your movements.'

'I can't believe that. In any case, I wasn't snatched during business hours. I was going on a social date.'

'What was the social date?'

'Well, not a date as such. But, when I'm in Malmö, I often go over to Copenhagen on a Friday night. Get the train, have a meal, go to a club. Usually stay overnight. Sometimes I meet up with friends, though I hadn't planned on seeing anyone in particular that night.'

'That explains why no one reported your disappearance.'

'No. It was all done over the weekend. All very neat.'

'What about when they released you?'

'I was asleep when they came in. Without a word, they dragged me up, put some tape over my mouth and bundled me into what I assume was the same van and off we went. When we stopped, they took me out. I could hear birds, so I thought it might be in the country somewhere. They tied me up to a bench and then I heard them leave. The crunching on the path. I was aware of some traffic nearby. I tried to shout for help. It was useless with the tape on, of course. I was feeling the cold too, so it was lucky that jogger came to the rescue.'

Möller took another sip of his whisky.

'The kidnappers must have been watching your movements for some time,' said Anita. 'From what I gather, you're often away on business.'

'Yeah. I spend a lot of time in Germany, France and the UK among others. Starting to make inroads into the States as well. I was in Detroit last month.'

'Surely some members of your staff, your PA for example, would know roughly your whereabouts. Certainly when you're around in Malmö.'

'Harriet, my PA, knows my movements for obvious reasons. But she's the only one who does. And I trust her implicitly. No way would she have divulged information like that to another party. She knows I like to keep myself to myself. I have to make public appearances for the sake of the business, but I'm basically a very private person. Harriet respects that.'

'We'll need to talk to her,' said Anita. Möller twisted his face. He didn't like the idea. 'Does she know?'

He shook his head. Then, with great reluctance, he agreed. 'OK. But I'll speak to her first. No one else downstairs, though. I want to keep a lid on this. I know Harriet will be discreet.'

'All right,' Moberg acquiesced. 'Inspector Sundström will come back tomorrow and speak to her.'

'Eleven?' Anita suggested.

'Fine. Make sure you come up here to the apartment. Not the office.'

'No problem. Could there be a personal element to this? Someone you've crossed? An enemy?'

'Business can be cut-throat, but I don't think I've upset anyone enough to warrant them kidnapping me.'

Moberg slowly lifted himself off the sofa with an undisguised groan. Anita also stood up. The chief inspector had obviously got as much out of the conversation as he wanted, or thought useful.

Möller put down his almost-empty glass and followed them towards the domestic lift.

'I believe you have a house in Morocco,' Anita said. 'Do you spend much time there?'

'Quite a lot. It's my escape from work. I've got a place in Essaouira on the Atlantic coast. I do a lot of windsurfing. I kitesurf, too.'

Anita turned to Moberg. 'Maybe that's where herr Möller was spotted as a potential target.'

'No,' Moberg waved her suggestion away before pressing the lift button. 'Herr Möller is well-known here. This is where his profile is highest.' He raised his eyebrows to the young entrepreneur in a manner which suggested that his colleague didn't know what she was talking about. 'My guess is it's some Swedish-based, Eastern European gang behind this.'

CHAPTER 5

'What did you make of that?' Anita asked as they headed back to the polishus.

Moberg grunted. 'Some people have too much money.' It was a typical Moberg comment. It didn't help either. He remained silent until they returned to headquarters, where Anita dropped him off. Since the building of the prosecutors' office and courts next door, the car park had gone, and Anita needed to find a nearby street. It was annoying, and she had started to walk to work more often. At least the exercise was beneficial, though on cold mornings, she jumped on a bus.

Moberg squeezed himself out of the passenger seat and then, with one hand on the roof, he leaned over and shoved his head back in the car. 'I want you to give a briefing to the rest of the team in an hour.'

'What are we going to do?'

'It's up to you. I'm going to get onto Stockholm and see if they've come across any gangs doing this sort of thing.' With that, he slammed the door so hard it nearly came off its hinges. It made Anita start. She stared resentfully after the man mountain waddling towards the polishus entrance. Thanks a million!

The occupants of the meeting room exuded little enthusiasm. Wallen appeared anxious: Anita knew she was worrying about missing her train back to Ystad. Brodd was looking vacant:

he was waiting to snaffle Moberg for a drink as soon as the meeting finished. Hakim was just sullen. Since Liv's shooting, the spark had gone out of him; he always seemed preoccupied. Anita thought it was only natural. She had hoped that throwing himself into his work might take his mind off his worries. It didn't. Maybe because the bright future he had planned for them both had been shattered by the very job they had loved. Moberg was the last to join them. He sat down at the head of the table before nodding to Anita.

She stood in front of an enlarged map of Malmö. She briefly took them through the events as described by Mats Möller and pointed out the locations of the snatching and the dumping. On the map, she had drawn two circles – the inner one indicated locations within a fifteen-minute radius from Mats Möller's apartment and the outer one represented a twenty-five minute journey.

'From what Möller said, he thinks that he was probably held in a disused warehouse or workshop. Now, we've got a number of industrial areas here, from Fosieby and Elisedals on the south side to the docks in the north, and everything in between. Of course, it might be somewhere closer by and they just drove around to give the impression of distance. So, one of our first jobs is to check out all these sites. Find where Möller was held, and we might be able to piece together who used the premises.' She turned to Moberg. 'As for the people who did this, the chief inspector has his own theory.'

Moberg brushed down his wide shirt front. As it settled back against the contours of his stomach, he began: 'My gu... my instinct,' he quickly stopped himself saying *gut* as he didn't want to prompt unwanted sniggers, 'is that it's an Eastern European gang. Or even Russian mafia. This has their stamp on it. I've been onto Stockholm. They've been monitoring gang activities, especially by foreign groups. They agree that this is the type of operation that some of those gangs have carried out in the past.

27

However, the boys up there say that, in their experience, such kidnappings have mostly been internal jobs. That is to say, the victims have belonged to rival groups. It's highly unusual for them to pick on an outsider... an upright citizen with nothing to do with criminal gangs.'

'So, what we also need to do is concentrate on Mats Möller himelf,' Anita carried on when it became obvious that Moberg wasn't going to contribute any more information on the Swedish gang scene. 'Why was he targeted? Is there some reason other than the obvious one – his wealth? If the group behind this isn't one of the chief inspector's gangs, are they simply after the money for themselves, or are they raising funds for a cause? ISIS springs to mind, and Möller does have a home in Morocco, though the man who spoke to him didn't sound Arabic. If it wasn't a specific group behind this kidnap, was it a personal attack on Möller? Has he any enemies? He claims not. We need to look into his business, his finances–'

'He won't have any left!' chipped in Brodd.

Anita ignored him. 'Who has he been dealing with? Is there anything in his personal life that might raise suspicions? What about the Moroccan link – what dealings go on there?' She glanced across at Hakim. 'I think this might be up your street, Hakim.' She gave him a smile, which wasn't returned. 'It won't be easy. He's very private, or so he claims. He doesn't want the kidnap to become public knowledge. His staff don't even know about it. So, no talking to the press.' This was accompanied by a glare at Brodd, who was the most likely to blab.

'The commissioner wants this done with the utmost discretion,' added Moberg fiercely.

'I'm going to see his PA tomorrow,' continued Anita. 'Now, before we go tonight, we'll sort out where to start searching for the kidnappers' hidey-hole.'

'How much ransom did he pay?' This came from Hakim.

'He wouldn't tell,' Moberg said with some disgust. 'Says he

doesn't want it getting out. Bad for business confidence.'

There was half a twinkle in Hakim's eye that Anita was glad to see. 'That's rubbish. It's more likely that he paid most of the ransom out of money salted away in some tax haven. He probably doesn't want us looking into his finances because we might bring in the tax authorities and they'll uncover all his skeletons.' After a pause: 'It's only a thought.'

'It's a good one,' said Anita. 'It might explain his reticence. And if the kidnappers knew about his financial arrangements, it would make their job easier. He did pay up very quickly.'

'He claims that he had a gun to his head.' Moberg even managed a half chuckle. 'That can be very persuasive, too.'

When Anita got home, there was no sign of Kevin. She found herself at a loss: usually he had something organized for an evening meal – making it himself, ordering a carry out, or going out for something. She checked the fridge: not much there. The cupboard was stocked well enough. Kevin had been in charge of the shopping over the last few weeks and had created his own storage system, which was anathema to Anita. With a sigh, she decided it was too much trouble to start anything from scratch, and she took a pizza out of the freezer. It was big enough for two so, if Kevin deigned to return, there would be enough for him. She put the pizza in the oven on a low heat so she had time for a glass of Rioja from the half-empty bottle next to the sink and she retreated into the living room. She switched on the television without even thinking what might be on. It was the usual mindless game show that played in the background most evenings as a substitute for Kevin's endless chatter. She realized that he didn't have many people to talk to and that she was the obvious target for his verbal frustrations. Often, when he started waxing enthusiastically about some historical item that had caught his imagination or some crappy television show he'd just seen or some political shenanigans that were winding him up, she found herself tuning out. Yet, even at his most infuriating, he could find a way to make her laugh, which in itself was annoying. She gratefully took a long sip of wine. This was what normality should be like.

Anita put down her glass and picked up the free paper that loudly clattered through her letterbox each morning at an ungodly hour. Nothing exciting happening in Malmö; just an article on FF's chances for the coming season, which started in the first week of April. Maybe a few matches at the Swedbank Stadium would keep Kevin occupied if he was still around. Part of her wished he would just go. They needed a break from each other; well, she needed a break from him.

As she tossed the newspaper onto the chair next to the day bed that doubled as her sofa, she reflected on Mats Möller's desire to keep his kidnapping out of the press. She also thought it odd that he wouldn't say how much he'd paid out. Maybe Hakim had been right about him salting money away. Or maybe it was a wealthy person's thing – they like you to know they're rolling in it without actually admitting how much 'it' is. They're all the same, she supposed, Donald Trump being an obvious example. She'd found Möller in Sweden's *Forbes'* rich list, but not quite in the same league as Stefan Persson of H&M, the Rausing family of Tetra Pak and Ferring Pharmaceuticals' Frederik Paulsen. Or even Kristina Ekman of Wollstad Industries. That name had given Anita a jolt, as it brought back memories of an earlier murder investigation that had terminated with Kristina's father, Dag Wollstad, evading police capture and escaping to a luxurious exile in South America. Kristina was still running, all perfectly legally, Dag's operations in Sweden. Möller wasn't on the upper echelons of the mega-rich; he was a serious dollar millionaire, not a dollar billionaire. That made him an interesting target for the kidnappers. It was almost as though they were working under the radar. And they could get the money out of Möller without anybody else being involved – no family to consider or relations trying to raise a ransom to meet a deadline, and no old-fashioned money drop or worry about police interference. It would have taken a lot of planning and research – possibly inside knowledge? The effort was worth it. Her instinct was that this gang was long gone and that the chances of apprehending them were slim. The team would simply be going through the motions, which was why Moberg was dumping it on her. He'd shown his face to Mats Möller, but she knew he'd only done that to keep Commissioner Dahlbeck off his back.

Anita had finished her pizza when she heard the front door open. Kevin appeared in the kitchen doorway, slightly flushed. Anita guessed he'd been propping up the bar at The Pickwick. He grinned at her. 'Are you still speaking to me?'

She finished putting her plate and cutlery in the dishwasher.

'It was you that walked out,' she said pointedly as she closed the dishwasher. 'There's half a pizza in the oven.'

'I had a falafel on the way back.' She could smell the beer on him. 'Been to The Pickwick.'

'Drowning your sorrows?'

He plonked himself down on one of the kitchen chairs.

'No. I've been thinking.' He raised his hand: 'And before you say anything, I am capable of thinking sometimes.' Anita didn't know what was coming next, so she sat down at the table opposite him. 'About us.' This sounded ominous.

Kevin glanced around and his eye caught sight of the bottle of Rioja. There was enough left for one glass. Anita watched him get up and find a glass before emptying the bottle. He sat down again and put the wine in front of him, though he made no effort to take a drink.

'I know I've been getting on your tits. I've overstayed my welcome.' Anita didn't know what to reply, so said nothing. 'Yes. I can see that. When you asked me over, I hoped it was more than just pity.' An amused expression crossed his face. 'Or guilt.'

31

He had hit the nail uncomfortably on the head. 'I was hoping to take our relationship to the next level. That's because I'm in love with you, Sundström.' She'd always known it, but this was the first time he'd expressed it. 'After I'd calmed down this morning wandering around Pildammsparken, I went to Folk & Rock. By the way, they've got a great new sticky bun thingy there. Can't remember the name. You'd love it. Anyway, I started to reflect.'

'And you had a few reflective pints at The Pickwick.'

'Of course, no man can cogitate on coffee alone. Anyhow, I concluded that the problem is that I don't have a designated role in this relationship. Neither of us does. We just drift. Sometimes happily, sometimes not. I think we should anchor it. I think we should get married.'

Anita hadn't expected this and found herself looking around for a drink. She grabbed Kevin's glass and took a swig.

'Blimey! Is it that bad? I know it's not the most romantic of proposals. But we're a bit long in the tooth for all the mushy stuff.' His smile was forced now as he awaited Anita's reaction.

'I don't know what to say,' was the only thing that came out of her mouth as her mind did somersaults.

'Look, I've just sprung this on you. It's too early for an answer. I appreciate there are practical problems. I know you'd want to stay here to be close to Leyla. But I may not have a job to go back to if my chief constable has his way. I could come and live in Sweden. It can't be that hard. You all speak brilliant English. Except your mum and your aunt, and I don't think they like me anyway. But I get on great with Lasse and Jazmin. And I love little Leyla. I could get some sort of job here. I wouldn't be hanging round the flat like I'm doing now.' Even Kevin realized he was rambling and stopped talking abruptly. He could see his sales pitch wasn't working.

'I'm sorry, Kevin. I can't. It's not what I want out of life at the moment. I don't want more complications.'

'So I'm a complication?' said Kevin tetchily.

'Sorry, that was the wrong word. It's just that I've got problems at the moment. Work problems. You know all the Hakim business. It's not a good place just now. And you know the stresses of our job.' She held up a warning finger. 'And don't say anything... I feel bad enough about that as it is. I'm messing people's lives up.'

'You wouldn't be messing mine up. I want to be with you.'

Anita leant over the table and took his hand in hers. 'Kevin, I'm very, very fond of you.'

'You don't love me, do you?' he said, trying to pull his hand away.

'I do in my way. But I don't want commitment. I've done that and it didn't work out. You're so different from Björn. And that's a good thing,' she added hurriedly. 'You're not selfish and full of bullshit, though you do talk a lot of rubbish at times.' She squeezed his hand. 'That's one of the reasons I like you. I love spending time with you. We have fun together. But after the last couple of months, I just think we'd never be able to live together.' She let go of his hand. 'I was happy with our arrangement before.'

'Long distance?'

'Yes, I suppose.'

'So that's a *no*?'

CHAPTER 6

They stood awkwardly at the entrance to Triangeln station. The concourse in front of Sankt Johannes kyrka was already filling up with scurrying workers despite the early hour. Kevin was heading for Copenhagen's Kastrup airport. After his failed proposal, he'd booked the next available flight to Manchester. That had been Tuesday night; this was Friday morning. The last couple of days hadn't been easy. They'd managed to avoid each other for some of the time: Anita at work and Kevin saying his farewells to Matt at The Pickwick and the girls at Folk & Rock. Anita had been there when he'd said goodbye to Lasse and Jazmin. They seemed genuinely disappointed he was going and Kevin had given a Leyla a long, giggly hug. Lasse had given his mother a reproving look that said that she didn't know what she was throwing away. Their last evening together had been spent at a Spanish restaurant not far from the polishus. They'd both drunk too much and had ended up making lusty love on the day bed in the living room. But they'd spent the night in separate rooms.

'Let me know you've arrived safely,' ventured Anita, who felt she had to say something.

'Of course. And don't forget to email me. I know you're not very good at that.'

'I'll do my best.'

He wrapped his arms round her and gave her a hug which almost squeezed the breath out of her body. He hadn't mentioned

34

the proposal again and had acted as politely as he could in her company. Typically British, she thought. Deep down, she knew what an effort he had made to ask her to marry him and how wounded he must have been by her rejection. When he let go, she was able to breathe again, though she felt a sudden rush of sadness. Was this really it? Was it over?

'Have you got your coffee?' she asked. It was such a banal thing to say in the circumstances.

'Two packets of Offesson's. You'll have to send me some more when I run out.'

'OK.'

Kevin picked up his suitcase and half turned towards the station. He stopped.

'By the way, I bought some of that shower gel you like. Two bottles actually. They're in–'

'I'll find them.'

Kevin nodded. And with a last glance, he was swallowed up in the flow of commuters descending into the bowels of the underground station.

The walk to the office gave her time to reflect. Not on Kevin's departure and the implications for their relationship, if they had one left that is, but on the kidnap of Mats Möller. Progress was slow, but there wasn't the same urgency as with a live investigation. Searches of disused, industrial buildings hadn't given them any leads as to the location of Möller's captivity. Not yet, anyway; there were plenty more to root around in. And, of course, the circles on the map were only based on what Möller had told them about the length of time he'd been driven in the van. Frightened and disorientated, his estimation might be way out, in which case the search area might be even wider.

What *had* been of interest was Anita's interview with Möller's PA, Harriet Åkesson. Anita had expected someone like Möller to have some eye candy secretary with long legs, big breasts, and a sexy smile to cover up a vacant expression. She soon berated herself for conjuring up such a sexist stereotype when she met Harriet Åkesson in Möller's apartment on the Wednesday. Åkesson wasn't exactly frumpy, but she didn't pay any lip-service to modern fashion. Her clothes were plain and practical. Not a hint of make-up. With greying blonde hair swept back in a severe ponytail, Anita put her at about sixty. Her large round glasses gave Anita the impression of an owl peering into the darkness looking for prey, and she was clearly employed because of her sense, wisdom and efficiency. She answered all Anita's questions in a precise manner. What became plain was her affection for Möller. She was a mother figure who helped order his life and business while being indulgent of his moods and transgressions. She made it clear that she wasn't keen on some of his acquaintances in Morocco. She'd been out there a couple of times and thought they were a bit louche, though she wouldn't elaborate. This made Anita wonder again about the possibility that the train of events had been set in motion by someone or something connected with Möller's Moroccan visits.

Åkesson had already prepared a schedule of Möller's appointments for the last three months and the dates when he was away in Morocco, Dortmund and Detroit.

'Would anyone else know about these movements?' Anita asked as she scanned the list in her hand.

'No. Mats is very good with his staff. They respect him. They love him even. However, he likes to keep things close to his chest. He likes to be in complete control. If I'm honest, he's slightly paranoid about the possibility of competitors gleaning information on MM Data.' That chimed with what Anita had gathered from their meeting with Möller and his reasons for not letting the kidnap become public knowledge. 'Mats makes all the important business decisions himself. Of course, he has an office manager, Christian Frandsen. But that's just for the day-to-day running of matters downstairs and making sure the operation runs efficiently.'

'And would Christian Frandsen know about some of herr Möller's movements?'

'A number of the business trips, of course. And they discuss potential clients. But it's always Mats who drums up new business and keeps existing clients happy. He's good with them face to face,' she said with some pride.

'And what about his private life? Do you act as his confidante?'

'Certainly not,' she answered disapprovingly. 'What he does in his own time, and with whom, is entirely Mats' concern. Though if he wants any advice, he does turn to me.'

'What sort of advice?'

'Nothing of a personal nature, I assure you. It's usually about the company. What I think of certain employees. Have they got the right attitude? Are they happy? Is Christian on top of things? He likes to know what I think of the reports he's asked me to type up. Maybe what restaurant he should take a particular client to...' She sounded indispensible. For a moment, Anita tried to visualize Åkesson as someone who could organize the kidnap of her boss. From a practical point of view, possibly. She was resourceful. She was the only one who knew his routines. She was a great organizer. Motive? Though her appearance was neat, she was not an extravagant person. Anita assumed that Möller paid her well. What would she do with all the ransom money? In her job, Anita got immediate instincts about people. Harriet Åkesson was just as she seemed. Dedicated, loyal, efficient – MM Data and Mats Möller were her life. And at the start of the interview, she had appeared genuinely upset that Möller had been kidnapped and that he could possibly be treated in such an appalling way. Anita could tell that she would be even more protective from now on. Despite that, she'd get Hakim to check out Harriet Åkesson's finances.

Åkesson could think of no one who would want to do Mats Möller any harm and do such a dreadful thing to such a nice young man. Had she been aware of anybody suspicious hanging around the building? Not to her knowledge.

Later that same day, Möller came into the polishus and looked through the back catalogue of obvious suspects. He didn't recognize anyone. Harriet Åkesson's finances turned out to be in order. She was paid handsomely and had plenty of disposable income. She lived alone with two cats near Limhamn, though she had been married and divorced some thirty years before. Ex-husband was dead. She had been Möller's second employee when he'd set up his fledgling business over a decade before. The first one had only lasted two months. He'd been checked out too, just in case there had been an acrimonious departure and he was looking to get even. He was living and working in New York and doing very well for himself. And Moberg's further conversations with Stockholm hadn't yielded anything useful on his Eastern European gang theory. Yes, they did operate like that on rare occasions, but reiterated that taking rival gang members was the norm. And, no, there was no intelligence of any recent activity in the Skåne area. So, as the weekend approached, they had nothing.

Anita hadn't even had time to get a coffee when Moberg came barging into her office.

'Have you fucking seen this?' he said, slamming a newspaper down violently on her desk. His face was beetroot red and Anita worried that his blood pressure would go off the scale.

She stared at the creased copy of *Sydsvenskan*. The front page headline screamed out: BUSINESS MAESTRO MÖLLER FREED AFTER DRAMATIC KIDNAP

'Ah!' was all Anita could offer as she quickly scanned the article while Moberg breathed heavily behind her. There was a photo of Möller taken at some business conference. It was dwarfed by a bigger picture of a man grinning at the camera, sitting on a bench in Gamla Kyrkogården cemetery. It became apparent that this was Bernt Hägg, the man who had found and unbound Möller. He was enjoying his fifteen minutes of fame. The way the article read, you'd have thought that Bernt Hägg had fought off the kidnappers single-handedly and freed Möller through his own brave efforts. Needless to say, there was no comment from Möller, who appeared to have gone to ground. Anita didn't have time to get as far as the paper's speculation as to who had carried out the kidnap.

'The commissioner's gone apeshit. He's shouting at everyone, including me. It's not my bloody fault! Möller's been on the phone in a panic and has gone into hiding. We should have sorted this Hägg halfwit out and made sure he didn't say anything. Why didn't you think of that?'

'What?' Anita was feeling fragile after seeing Kevin off and all the implications of that situation. This was too much. She cracked. 'It's nothing to do with me! You're the bloody boss! You get paid the money; you make the bloody decisions!' Through her fury, she knew that Moberg was only taking it out on her because the commissioner was taking it out on him. The fact was that the whole business was out of their control, though there were a couple of things she'd spotted in the article that couldn't have come from Bernt Hägg.

Moberg scrunched up the newspaper in his massive fist and stamped out of the room.

After Moberg had gone and she'd calmed down, Anita picked up her office phone and punched in a short number. It was answered immediately.

'Pontus. Have you been speaking to a reporter from *Sydsvenskan*?'

'What about?' came the cautious reply.

'How did the paper know where and when Möller was snatched? Or the kind of place he was held?'

'Search me, Anita,' came the innocent reply. Now she knew Brodd had definitely blabbed.

CHAPTER 7

'Are you threatening me?'

He was furious and he was frightened. The confident voice at the other end of the phone continued as though he hadn't spoken. He wanted the voice to stop. How could the man know such things? He tried to interrupt, to suspend the flow...

'Why can't you leave me alone?'

The bastard was laughing; actually laughing. He stood there, paralysed. This couldn't be happening. He couldn't help himself; he kept listening. The receiver was clamped to his ear. Why couldn't he rip it away and silence his tormentor? But the man had hinted at something even darker. He *had* to know if he really knew.

The man's voiced stopped.

'What do you mean you'll be in touch?' he yelled. Why couldn't he just come out with it now so he would know what he was up against?

The line went dead.

He was sweating. The phone felt clammy in his hand. He felt nauseous, desperate. And powerless – the past was written and there was nothing he could do.

Anita drove her car along the slip road and onto the E6. The morning of Thursday, May 4th was brightening up after the heavy overnight rain, though there were still pools of water visible at the sides of the carriageway. Anita was glad to be getting out of Malmö. The fields were emerging from their winter drabness, and yellow bands of ripening rape were beginning to dominate the vista. The optimistic early summer morning didn't improve Anita's mood – she was slightly dreading her trip to Helsingborg. She was skipping work on a mission that she knew she had to undertake both for her own sake and that of the team.

April had been a difficult month. The Mats Möller kidnap investigation had hit a brick wall. Each opening had soon closed. They had found the premises that Möller had been held in, which had caused huge initial excitement. It was a unit down on the docks which had been a workshop for vehicle maintenance, belonging to a company that had closed its doors back in the 1990s. The area had yet to be redeveloped. The workshop had been given the full forensic treatment. Nothing of interest had been noted other than that the kidnappers had broken in to create their hostage base. When forensic technician Eva Thulin's report came in – and it was thin – all she could say in conclusion was that 'these guys are real pros'. The effect was to set Moberg off again on his Eastern European gang theory, though no one was really listening any more. The owner of the premises had been tracked down and didn't even realize it was part of his property portfolio. It had been part of a bigger purchase some years before. No one working in the area had seen anything suspicious. CCTV had shown up a number of green or dark coloured vans passing various points in the area over that March weekend. All except one was traced. That one had a Danish number plate. They tracked it back and discovered it had been driven into Sweden over the Öresund Bridge a week before the kidnap. But there was no record of it leaving the country either by road or ferry. The Danish authorities found that the van had been bought from a dodgy second-hand car lot outside Roskilde. Cash payment. The description of the buyer, though vague, was similar to one of the men who had approached Möller. That was a dead end, too.

In her desperation, Anita's thoughts returned to the tip-off that Moberg had received about the planned robbery of the electrical warehouse. Her original reasoning that it might have been a ploy to send them to the wrong location while a robbery was carried out elsewhere had proved unfounded. Yet now she couldn't help wondering if it was all part of the kidnap plan. A significant number of police officers had been sent to the southern side of Malmö on a fruitless quest while the kidnappers were operating in the northern docks. The call had come in from a pay-as-you-go phone somewhere in central Malmö. Again, a dead end. Even checks at all the nearby surrounding fast food outlets hadn't thrown up clues as to anyone unusual buying in the pizzas and falafels that Mats Möller said he was fed by his captors.

The atmosphere in the office was cheerless. The Möller case hadn't improved Moberg's mood. The press had given the police a hard time, and the commissioner had passed the buck to his senior officer on the case. Brodd was keeping a low profile. Anita had eventually wheedled out of him that he'd been approached by an attractive female reporter who already knew about the kidnap from Bernt Hägg, and Brodd thought there wouldn't be any harm letting slip a few extra details. Klara Wallen had enough of her own problems. Normally, she shared them with Anita in the confessional of the female toilets, but she hadn't been very communicative recently, which Anita took as a bad sign – maybe Klara had had enough of Rolf the Sloth? (one could but hope). And then there was the tension with Hakim. Hence her trip today.

She took the E4 off the E6 and then quickly onto the 111, which skirted round Helsingborg. On the north side, she came to Laröd and found the small estate where Liv Fogelström was living with her brother's family. It was a modern, white, one-storey building. Anita knew that it had temporarily been fitted out to enable Liv to move in. The door was answered by Liv's sister-in-law, who seemed pleased that Liv had a visitor. She was shown through into the small garden at the back, which was mainly patio and a small patch of grass that had a couple of deflated footballs nestling next to what was an attempt at a flower border. The footballs might explain the squashed daffodils. Liv was sitting in the sun in her wheelchair with a laptop on her knees. She, too, greeted Anita with a broad smile, which immediately made Anita feel at ease. She hadn't seen Liv properly since she was in hospital. Hakim had hardly encouraged a visit.

Despite her awful experience, Liv was still as bright-eyed as Anita remembered her. Her blonde hair was now cut a lot shorter, which accentuated her chubby face. And she had put on a bit more weight, understandable with her lack of exercise.

'It's so good to see you, Inspector.'

'Anita, please.' She sat down on a garden chair opposite. She didn't really want to ask but found herself saying 'How are you?'

'I'm fine.' Anita marvelled at how she remained so bubbly. How could someone who had had her life so dramatically changed in an instant be so upbeat? Anita knew how resentful she would be in similar circumstances and how she would rail against the unfairness of it all. Liv closed the laptop. 'I like surfing the net; takes my mind off things. But I'm getting better all the time, though, according to the consultants, I won't be able to use these anymore,' she tapped a leg. 'But what the hell do they know? Anyway, what's happening at headquarters these days? I'm out of the loop.'

'Doesn't Hakim tell you what's going on?' Anita asked.

Liv pulled a face. 'He doesn't like talking about work, after all this. Thinks it will upset me. He's over-sensitive.'

'He doesn't like talking to me much these days, either.'

'I'm sorry about that. I keep telling him it was my decision to be there.'

'He took it all very badly. Not surprisingly, I suppose.' Anita knew she would be just the same – she would have looked around for someone to blame for mucking up her life plans.

'I know. Sometimes you'd think he was the one that got shot!' Liv giggled. Again, Anita was taken aback by her cheerfulness. 'He still respects you.'

'Just doesn't like me.'

'He'll come round. Our marriage plans haven't changed. They're just delayed.'

Liv's sister-in-law came out with a tray on which was the obligatory coffee thermos and cinnamon buns.

'Malin looks after me so well,' said Liv when her sister-in-law had retreated into the house. 'My brother and her have been brilliant. And the kids are great. So funny. But I don't want to overstay my welcome. They've done enough for me already.'

'Are you looking around for a house?'

'Hakim is. Got a couple of possibilities, though they'll need work to get this battleship through the doors,' she said, giving the wheelchair a pat.

Anita took a bite out of her bun, not quite sure what to say to keep the conversation going.

'Leyla's growing,' Liv said before Anita had time to think something up. 'And what a smile! She's beautiful!'

'I didn't realize you'd seen her.'

'Jazmin's been a couple of times.' Anita was surprised that Jazmin hadn't mentioned it, though, on reflection, it might have been in order to avoid any more trouble between her brother and her partner's mother. 'It's nice to get visitors. That's why it's great to see you. Does Hakim know?' Anita shook her head. 'I won't say anything until the time's right.'

'I would have come before, but...'

'I know. It's just I get so bored. There's only so much TV one can watch. Or being glued to this,' she said, glancing down at her laptop. 'I'd like to get back to work at some stage. Even if I can't run around anymore, I can still use the technology; I did enough computer courses before this happened.' She sighed heavily before that infectious smile returned. 'I know it's impossible at the moment.'

'I'm sure something will be sorted out at some stage.' Anita was trying to be encouraging, though she wondered what kind of role, if any, Liv could now realistically play in the force. Before she ventured down that potentially awkward cul-de-sac, her phone burst into life and saved her. 'Sorry,' she apologized as she took it out of her pocket. 'Anita.'

It was Klara Wallen. 'Where are you?'

'Near Helsingborg.'

'You'd better get back as quick as you can. There's been another kidnapping!'

CHAPTER 8

Moberg's face was redder than ever and he wasn't pleased that Anita had sneaked into the meeting late; it had taken her nearly an hour to get back from Laröd. As she took her seat with an apologetic nod, she saw a photo of the victim on the board. A man in his sixties. Thin, fair hair above a confident face; the most prominent feature being the wide mouth which was creased into a pleased grin. Though the image had obviously been taken from a magazine, there was no hiding the sharp eyes. Again, the man was vaguely familiar to Anita.

'This is Peter Uhlig,' said Moberg, pointing a thick finger in the direction of the photo. 'Sixty-three years of age. Married. Two grown-up children. Like Mats Möller, he's a well-known businessman. Yesterday morning, Wednesday, he left his home in Limhamn at six thirty as he does every weekday morning. He drives down to Trelleborg, where his company's head office is on Hamngatan, just opposite the port. But yesterday he failed to turn up for work. The office rang his home to check if he was coming in – he had a meeting arranged for eleven o'clock – but there was no one at home. They thought he must be ill and so cancelled the meeting. His wife, meanwhile, who had been out all day and obviously thought her husband was at work, returned, and when Uhlig didn't appear for his evening meal – usually prompt at seven thirty – alarm bells began to ring and it was discovered that he was nowhere to be found.'

'Did fru Uhlig report it immediately?' asked Anita.

'No. But you'd have known that if you'd been here.' The tone was reproachful. 'As you weren't around, I went down to Limhamn with Hakim. Fru Uhlig said she'd planned to call us when all other avenues had been explored. She didn't want to cause unnecessary fuss. She thought he might have organized a business meeting or gone off for a golf day, as he sometimes does, without telling her. But there was no answer from his mobile. Then, around ten o'clock, she got an anonymous call to say that her husband was being held and that the kidnappers wanted a ransom. According to fru Uhlig, the voice was muffled. It was male and spoke in Swedish, though she didn't think the accent was local.'

'Not in English?' asked Anita. 'Möller's kidnappers spoke English.'

'I've noted that already,' Moberg replied testily. 'Probably something to do with fru Uhlig's age. She doesn't speak English fluently. Their threat would be fully understood in Swedish.'

'That means these people have really done their homework.'

Moberg ignored the comment. 'Anyway, we've got the techies trying to trace where the call was made from. The upshot is that the kidnappers demanded four million euros by next Tuesday, the ninth – that means the Uhligs have got five days to pay up. It's complicated because two of those days are at the weekend, when the banks don't function.'

Brodd blew out his cheeks. 'What's four million euros in kronor?'

'Roughly forty million,' Hakim answered. 'Just as well they don't want kronor. There's probably not that much around in our cashless society,' he added wryly.

'Forty million,' Brodd said, shaking his head. 'Could buy a lot of meatballs with that.'

'It was definitely euros they asked for, not dollars?' queried Anita.

'Yes. That had me wondering. We'll need to look into that. Naturally, they told her that she wasn't to approach the police, or Peter was a dead man. However, after a sleepless night, she decided to call us.'

'Can they raise the money in time?' Wallen asked the question that they were all wondering about.

'They can certainly afford it. But it's spread all over the place apparently. It's not as simple as the Möller case. I suspect that once the perps got hold of Uhlig, they soon discovered they couldn't just quickly transfer the ransom like they'd done with Möller. The problem for them is that though Uhlig is rich and successful, his is an old-established business where much of the money is reinvested in the firm. Talking of which, what have you found out, Klara?'

Wallen consulted her notes. 'As the name suggests, Peter Uhlig is of German extraction. Typical Malmö story. An Uhlig ancestor came across here from Germany because of the herring industry in the 1700s. The family stayed on and thrived. They moved into ship building and then cement, which was huge business at one time. Through the shipping arm, they got into freight. The shipping went after the Second World War, and the cement side of things was bought over a few years ago by the Hoffberg Cement Group. The present owner, Peter Uhlig, decided to concentrate on freight. He moved out of Malmö ten years ago and set up his main depot and headquarters in Trelleborg. He dropped the family name and the company became Trellogistics. It's ideally located for moving whatever to northern Germany, Poland and the Baltic States, and all points beyond. His office is opposite the new Hamngatan 9 complex. He heads off there every morning promptly, except for the odd golf day, usually spent with business contacts. He has two grown-up daughters, neither of whom are involved in the day-to-day running of the firm directly, though both have seats on the board.' Wallen looked over to Moberg. 'That's about it so far.'

'Good.' Wallen was pleased. That was the most praise anybody was likely to get from the chief inspector. 'I think the two daughters on the company board give us an idea why the money isn't readily available. They'll have to pitch in or give the green light for company funds to be used. The kidnappers have made life a bit harder for themselves this time.'

'If they are as efficient as last time, they'll have planned this carefully,' commented Anita almost to herself.

'Probably. On the plus side, we've got time to act. Try and track them down.'

'And when and where do they want the ransom?'

'They didn't give fru Uhlig any information about that other than it needed to be in five-hundred-euro notes put into a certain type of IKEA cool bag.'

'That's very precise.' This was Hakim. Anita avoided his gaze, stupidly feeling guilty for visiting Liv without his knowledge. 'We think they'll only tell fru Uhlig the time and place at the very last minute, when they know the money is ready. That would get round any possibility that she might have informed the police and find us waiting at the drop site.'

'Exactly,' said Moberg. 'Now we need to play this carefully. If we go charging around, we might alert the kidnappers and they might finish Uhlig off – or push up the price. We need to keep this really discreet. And I mean discreet, Brodd.' Brodd looked suitably sheepish. 'We're keeping this kidnap out of the press for the time being. They think we're useless enough after the last one; I don't want them getting any more ammunition. And no one at Trellogistics is to be made privy as to what has happened. Officially, Uhlig's taken a few days' rest. Overwork. Apparently, that's a believable excuse. We can start by nosing around the place they kept Möller. I doubt they'd use the same place twice, but you never know. That's one for you, Pontus. And just before I came in here, I was informed that Traffic have found Uhlig's car near Gessie. Anita, I want you and Klara to go down and take a look. Get a forensic technician to go over the car and see if there's anything useful there. See if there are any tyre tracks from the vehicle they must have taken him away in. Might be the same Danish van we couldn't find before. After that, get down to Trelleborg. One of the daughters,' he glanced down at a note he'd made, 'Ann-Kristen Uhlig, is expecting you. See if there's any angle on the Trellogistics front. Any enemies, rivals; that sort of thing. Unhappy employees. Obviously, don't mention the real reason why you're there to any staff. Routine enquiries.'

Moberg stopped to take a sip of water from a bottle he'd brought in. His breathing seemed uneven. 'I'm afraid you'll need to sit through any CCTV you can get hold of, Hakim. There'll be nothing out in the countryside where he was snatched, but they may have brought him back into town, especially the dock area. Meanwhile, I'll liaise with the family over the money and we'll put someone in the Uhligs' Limhamn home to be there when the instructions come through from the kidnappers. Whatever we do, the chances of finding Peter Uhlig before they call in with the drop site are pretty remote. What we mustn't do is put his life in jeopardy. That said, I want these buggers caught!'

By the time Anita and Wallen had reached Uhlig's car, the morning brightness had disappeared behind darkening skies. Rain wasn't far away. They found a uniformed officer standing guard over a black Mercedes-Benz S500. It was just off the main E6 route to Trelleborg. The car was parked in a tarmacked lay-by close to where a minor road joined the slip road onto the main highway. The lay-by was big enough to accommodate three or four vehicles.

Anita and Wallen got out. Wallen went over to talk to the officer while Anita surveyed the scene. The landscape was very open with flat, expansive fields, though it would be hard for any passing motorists on the E6 to see anything that might have

gone on in the lay-by, as at that point, the level of the main
road was lower and bordered by scrubby trees. There were no
houses or farm buildings that were near enough for the residents
to witness anything. This spot had been chosen carefully. Anita
assumed, though this would have to be checked out, that this
was Peter Uhlig's regular route to work – back roads from
Limhamn and then onto the E6. The kidnappers clearly knew
the route and the time he headed for the office. Would the staff
at Trellogistics know? Surely some of them would. And the
family certainly would. She took one more look round and then
slipped on her latex gloves.

'No external damage,' commented Wallen, 'so it's unlikely
they bumped him off the road.'

Anita opened the car door. The interior was immaculate.
Despite being a couple of years old, it smelt almost new. It was
well looked after; regularly valeted. Anita felt that Peter Uhlig
must be a fastidious man. Everything was neatly in place except
there was no sign of any briefcase or bag. The kidnappers must
have taken whatever he had with him, including his mobile
phone. That hadn't been traced. Records showed that it had last
been used in Uhlig's home at 23.50 the previous evening. The
eight-minute call had been an early-morning one to a customer
in Japan: 6.30 their time. The rest of the car revealed nothing
of any significance.

Just then a van drove up and out jumped a young, tousled-
haired forensic technician whom Anita had not seen before.
He greeted them with a broad grin and a firm handshake. 'Lars
Unosson,' he said by way of introduction. 'What do you want me
to do?' Anita was taken aback by the young man's enthusiasm.
How long would that last? She ticked herself off for being a
cynical old cow.

'We need you to give the Mercedes the once over, though
I doubt you'll find much,' said Anita with a raised eyebrow. 'I
think what's more important is to see if you can find any tracks

of another vehicle. A van is the most likely.'

He puckered his lips. 'At first glance, there doesn't seem much. Trouble is we had heavy rain last night.'

'Try your best.'

He nodded cheerfully and returned to his vehicle to get kitted out.

'What do you think happened here?' Wallen asked.

'They got him to stop somehow. I suspect they simply waved him down. Pretended that they needed help. Then grabbed him just like with Mats Möller. As you say, if they'd tried to block his car or push him off the road, there'd be some damage to his vehicle; it's even neatly parked. And I also think we'd see some obvious skid marks despite the rain. They didn't rush off either. That could have left marks, too. This was very controlled. These guys are good.'

CHAPTER 9

Anita and Wallen headed along the E6 into Trelleborg. They were taking the route that Peter Uhlig had failed to complete that Wednesday morning. On the outskirts of the town, they passed numerous industrial units, one of which was the massive Trellogistics depot. A fleet of light-blue trucks with the dark-green Trellogistics logo emblazoned on the sides was lined up ready to pick up or deliver goods anywhere in northern Europe. The industrial area melded into urban housing the nearer they got to the centre. One of the country's oldest cities, Trelleborg could trace its history back to Viking times. The herring trade with the Hanseatic League had seen it prosper in the Middle Ages. Like the rest of Skåne, it had become part of Denmark for a time before emerging from the shadows in the early twentieth century, thanks to the shipping trade and the railways. In 1909, the ferry route between Trelleborg and Sassnitz on Germany's Baltic coast was established, helping to bring prosperity. It was also the crossing that Lenin had used eight years later on his way to taking control of Russia through the Bolshevik Revolution. Now the port was the second largest in Sweden, and it was a major site for the freight-forwarding industry, in which Trellogistics was one of the biggest players. Yet their headquarters were housed in a modest, squat, brick building with a red pantile roof on Hamngatan opposite the bustling harbours. Not that Anita could see much of the bustle as a thick sea fret had engulfed the huge cargo ships and ferries. Squinting through the wire fencing that separated her from the docks, she could just discern the hulking shapes of the container trucks rumbling towards their waiting vessels. Even the sounds of all this activity were muffled by the fog.

Anita parked her car, acutely aware of what a mess it seemed in contrast to Peter Uhlig's Mercedes. Wallen hadn't said anything, but Anita knew what she must be thinking. Kevin had cleaned it out a couple of times during his sojourn. Maybe she had been too hasty in driving him away.

'I've been thinking about a connection between the two kidnap victims,' Anita said as she pulled the key out of the ignition.

'Other than that they're both stinking rich,' Wallen observed dryly.

'Obviously they have that in common. But Uhlig is in freight. It would be interesting to know if his trucks use MM Data software. Möller's clients are in the automotive industry. Might be a link.'

As they waited in the reception area for Uhlig's daughter, Anita gazed around the walls, which showed the various stages of the Uhlig company history. Old black and white prints of the shipyards in Malmö contrasted with colourful, up-to-date photos of the latest Trellogistics trucks. There were no pictures of any of the Uhlig family over the generations. Business came before ego.

They were ushered into a meeting room. This, too, was functional, with a large pine table surrounded by stiff, upright chairs. No one lounged here. There was a map of northern Europe on the wall. Trelleborg seemed to be at its centre with arrows emanating from the town in all directions. What contrasted with the utilitarian surroundings was the woman sitting on the opposite side of the table. Anita knew that she must be about forty, though she looked anything but. You didn't expect to see someone with long, green-streaked hair in the staid meeting room of one of Sweden's oldest companies. The three nose rings confirmed that Ann-Kristen Uhlig probably wasn't a typical board member of a freight-forwarding organisation. An electronic cigarette protruded from firm lips, but what really caught Anita's attention were her eyes. Accentuated by black eye shadow, they were blue, bold and challenging; similar to the ones in the photograph Moberg had produced of her father. At first glance, she didn't appear like a woman who would collapse in a crisis. Certainly, with her father's life hanging in the balance, she needed to be strong. Vapour escaped from her mouth as she indicated that they should sit.

Anita opened by introducing herself and Wallen and stressing that they were fully aware that all discussions were to be kept strictly confidential. She also explained that they had found Peter Uhlig's car and that they thought he may have been flagged down. When Ann-Kristen spoke, she had a thin, sing-song voice that made her sound more like a little girl than a mature woman.

'That's typical of Pappa. He would have thought nothing of stopping to help.' With a flourish of her cigarette, she continued: 'I've stepped in to keep an eye on the business while Pappa is... well, while he's indisposed. The company is in good hands. There's a good management team here.'

'We're aware that all the staff are being kept in the dark about what's happened–'

'Except the financial director,' Ann-Kristen cut in.

'Oh?'

'For purely practical reasons. The family... well, my sister Birgitta and I are responsible for raising the money. Mamma's so devastated by all this that she's in no state to coordinate things. Birgitta is seeing to the raising of money from our personal sources. Luckily, she has a wealthy husband, which is useful.'

There was a hint of disdain in her voice. 'Frans Losell has pledged his help.' Anita knew the Losell name from the chain of electrical stores. Money marries money in business circles.

'Do you have a husband... partner that can help?' Wallen asked. Anita could tell it was more out of curiosity than garnering information.

'I have money through the family. My wife doesn't.' Anita saw Wallen's hint of a flinch. So did Ann-Kristen. 'Ella may one day, but with a struggling conceptual artist, it's the work that counts, not the financial rewards.' Wallen shifted uneasily under Ann-Kristen's contemptuous gaze. Anita knew that Wallen had unfashionably forthright views on both lesbians and contemporary art, presumably fostered by the loathsome Rolf.

'And your role?' said Anita, drawing Ann-Kristen's attention away from Klara Wallen.

'I'm seeing what we can raise through the company. That's why I have to talk to our financial director, Paul Martinsson.' Ann-Kristen returned to her vaping.

'OK, that's understandable. But we have to ask if there might be anyone in the organisation who has a grudge against your father, or who may exploit the situation for their own financial benefit.'

Ann-Kristen held her cigarette at arm's length. 'I know what you're getting at. Did the kidnappers get inside information on my father's movements? A number of people here would be aware of the route he took to work. It's easy enough to work out. But I doubt there's an inside man... or woman,' she added with a gimlet stare at Wallen. 'He may not be universally loved, but he's respected. He's a good and fair employer.'

Anita knew she couldn't take it any further without alerting the staff to the situation. Maybe when they got Peter Uhlig back safely, they could investigate properly. There *was* a chance that someone on the inside had supplied information.

'Can I ask you if Trellogistics has had any business dealings with MM Data?'

'A connection with the Mats Möller kidnap?' Ann-Kristen might appear flaky, but there was a sharp mind there. 'Trellogistics do use MM Data's software in the trucks. We've had quite a close relationship with them in the last couple of years. Socially, too,' she added. 'Mats came to see Ella's latest installation at the Modern Art Museum in Malmö, and he supports a number of my charities.'

Anita wound up the interview. As she and Wallen headed for the door, the laid-back poise that had begun to make Anita think Ann-Kristen didn't care about her father abruptly changed.

'Please don't let anything happen to Pappa.'

CHAPTER 10

Hakim rubbed his eyes. Two days sourcing and going through the area's limited amount of CCTV footage of vehicles driving in and around Malmö was driving him a little insane. Was this really what a career as a detective was all about? He knew he was the most technically savvy member of the team, but he was always given this job. He knew its importance, of course. It just wasn't exciting. It wasn't even interesting. He yawned and stretched. His arms ached. He stood up and did further stretching. But whatever calisthenics he tried weren't going to make the Danish van appear. He'd seen all sorts of examples of bad driving, haphazard parking, deliberate speeding and near misses. Some had been quite amusing, and he was thinking it might be fun to put a compilation tape together... when he had time.

He went over to the office window and leant his head against the glass. It felt cool. It was sunny outside, and the folk of Malmö were enjoying their Saturday afternoon. It felt like he was the only person working. Construction work on the new apartments just down from the polishus had ceased over the weekend. One more piece of the city disappearing under concrete. His wandering eye fixed on a young couple sitting on the grass in Rörsjöparken opposite. She playfully slapped her partner, who was convulsed in laughter. They looked so happy. Still giggling, she jumped to her feet as he tried to trip her. She ran a few yards away and stuck her tongue out at the young man. Her litheness brought his own situation into sharp focus. His mind was racked with doubts and injustices.

Why had Allah allowed Liv to be shot? Why had Allah let him down? Or had he let Allah down? Was that it? He hadn't been a regular at the Malmö Mosque for some time, much to his father's sorrow. The truth was that he felt uncomfortable there. It was nothing to do with his beliefs, which weren't especially strong. It was more that he felt he wasn't trusted by the other members; particularly the younger men, who regarded a cop with natural suspicion. In some cases, Hakim encountered downright hostility. The Mosque had suffered a number of cases of sabotage over the years and a particularly catastrophic arson attack in 2003. No arrests had been made, and so it was natural that many lacked faith in the police and those in authority.

His father's attitude to Liv had been antagonistic as soon as he had learnt of Hakim's intentions. His mother hadn't been much better, though she hadn't voiced her concerns to him directly. Though they disapproved of Jazmin's relationship with the atheistic Lasse, their attitude had softened when Leyla came on the scene. What annoyed Hakim was that his father wasn't by any means a fundamentalist, nor was he intolerant of the beliefs of others – he had mixed with westerners for years in his work as an art dealer before the family fled Iraq. From what he'd been told, Uday and Amira Mirza had lived a western lifestyle in a smart suburb of Baghdad. Sweden had given them a home and freedom, though their fortunes were never the same again. They were living in Seved, which, as Hakim knew only too well, was on the high-profile police list of fifteen districts throughout the country regarded as 'especially vulnerable areas'. That meant gangs of youths hovering around, drugs openly bought and sold, and the postal company refusing to deliver parcels directly to homes. But now life in Seved was slowly improving; the area being gradually turned around by the community, and his father was playing a small part in this. So why couldn't Uday come to terms with him marrying Liv? Of course, his parents had both been shocked and concerned about the shooting. They made efforts to be supportive of Liv, and Hakim had had to accept an uneasy truce when he was forced to sell his apartment and move back in with them until he and Liv could buy somewhere suitable to live together. Hakim understood the pressure his father was under from members of the Mosque and the Iraqi community and, consequently, his resentment was tempered by that knowledge. Uday was a proud man and didn't want to be undermined by his son. Hakim wished he could be more like his hot-headed sister, who didn't give a damn about what others thought of her and her situation, especially her parents. She just got on with life in the way she wanted to.

Furthermore, Hakim's bitterness spilled over into other areas of his life. Anita, who had been such a role model for him, had been responsible for Liv ending up with a bullet in her. In his more rational moments, he knew Anita calling Liv in that night had been a legitimate professional request and Liv had been keen to help. And Liv had repeatedly said that he shouldn't blame Anita. Nevertheless, he'd been annoyed that Anita had gone and seen Liv a couple of days before without mentioning it to him. Again, he knew he was being totally unreasonable. The fact that Liv didn't lay the blame at anyone's door only made it worse. He was mentally lashing out on her behalf. Why couldn't he be as forgiving as the woman he loved? Maybe he should visit the Mosque more often.

The couple left the grass and walked towards the canal, hand in hand. It was a simple thing that he and Liv would never be able to do again. He pushed his head away from the glass, went back to his desk and stared at his computer screen again. There was the frozen street scene of Amiralsgatan that he had left a few minutes before. He would have to continue his search. Nothing else had emerged over the last two days that had given them any clue as to who was behind Peter Uhlig's kidnap. Unsurprisingly, the gang hadn't used the premises from the Mats Möller job. And Anita and Klara Wallen had drawn a blank at Trellogistics, though Wallen was full of how odd she thought Ann-Kristen Uhlig was. Anita had established a commercial and social connection between the Uhligs and Mats Möller, though they hadn't been able to take that any further either. They'd gone through the list of employees of Trellogistics and MM Data, but no common denominator was obvious. That didn't mean, however, that there hadn't been someone who had worked at both companies in the past. Another of Anita's ideas had also been looked into – Uhlig's son-in-law, Frans Losell's electronics business. His chain of stores was supplied from the electrical warehouse they had had under surveillance when the first kidnap had taken place. This had resulted in another dead end; they could find no connection. And all this negativity hadn't improved Moberg's temper. He was taking it all too personally as far as Hakim was concerned. So, *he*'d better try and find something. It promised to be a long Saturday night.

CHAPTER 11

It was Tuesday, May 9th. Just after 11am. Anita felt tense. It wasn't only because Hakim was sitting next to her in an unmarked police car. She was awaiting instructions from Moberg, who, at this moment, was in the Uhlig family home. Their role was to follow Ann-Kristen Uhlig's car at a discreet distance. The call was imminent. What instructions were the kidnappers going to give? She prayed that they hadn't cottoned on to the fact that the Uhligs had reluctantly, though sensibly, contacted the police. The money had been collected from various sources, and the commissioner had been able to persuade a couple of banks to put it together in physical form – euros. The eight thousand 500-euro notes had been placed in a large, lime-green IKEA cool bag as requested. Why that particular holdall, Anita didn't really know. Maybe the gang had worked out that such a container was spacious enough to carry that amount of cash. And the bags were common enough.

They were parked on the edge of Limhamn. On hearing from Moberg, they would follow Ann-Kristen Uhlig in her father's bulky, black Volvo XC90. Moberg had had a miniature camera installed on board so that they could record Ann-Kristen's journey and pick up any further instructions she might receive over her mobile phone – and hopefully see the kidnappers if they approached the car. Ann-Kristen had been briefed to try and get them within camera range if at all possible, but not to put herself in any danger. She was assured that there would be police officers on hand if any problems arose. Moberg's plan was to be flexible. They would watch the handover of the money and then follow the kidnappers to where Peter Uhlig was being kept. They didn't for a minute believe that Uhlig would be handed over at the drop site. On the other hand, if things went wrong, they would take immediate action and arrest the kidnappers, hoping against hope that the whole affair wouldn't end in bloodshed.

The fact that she had been paired off with Hakim wasn't helping Anita to relax. As usual, he was being uncommunicative. But if things didn't go well, she was far happier having Hakim at her side – Brodd would simply be a liability. Brodd was to be Moberg's driver – the chief inspector wanted to oversee the operation. There were at least three other unmarked cars involved. The silence was broken by Moberg. 'Ann-Kristen's on the move!' he barked over the line. 'But she's in a different vehicle.'

'Not the Volvo?' queried Anita.

'No. The bastards have told her to use her mother's small runaround. It's a blue Volkswagen Golf.' He quickly gave the registration.

'Do they know we're onto them?' Anita asked anxiously. The implications could be disastrous.

'I don't fucking know!' he bellowed back irritably. 'But they certainly know the Uhligs' cars. Ann-Kristen's only got forty-five minutes to get to the site so we haven't had time to change the bloody camera. She'll be passing you in a couple of minutes. She's been told to get to Skårby by noon and wait outside the church for further instructions. Make sure you're not fucking seen – and don't you dare lose her!'

The line went dead abruptly. Already their plans were going wrong, and the pressure was telling on Moberg. Anita had a horrid feeling that things weren't going to get any better.

'Skårby? Why is that familiar?'

'It's just off the E65 before you reach Ystad,' said Hakim. These were the first words he'd spoken since he'd got into the car. 'It's near the Ystad Djurpark.'

She'd been to the wildlife park before. It exhibited everything from emus to elks. Was it chosen because there would be a lot of traffic around at this time of year? And why the church? Would it be the first of many locations Ann-Kristen would be sent to before the kidnappers deemed it safe to pick up the money? Maybe it was a way of testing if there was a police presence.

Any further speculation was abruptly brought to a halt: 'That's her,' said Hakim as he nodded towards the road ahead and a blue Volkswagen Golf appeared with Ann-Kristen in the driving seat. Anita turned on the engine and waited for a couple of other vehicles to pass before slipping into the traffic.

It took fifteen minutes to hit the E65. Anita wondered how Ann-Kristen was holding up. It wasn't an easy thing she was being asked to do. Judging by her consistent speed, she must be coping. With a deadline, it would be tempting to rush in case she didn't make Skårby church by twelve o'clock. Her father's life could depend on her getting there on time. The traffic ahead was steady, so it was easy for Anita to keep an eye on the blue Volkswagen without having to get too close.

Moberg's voice snapped into her thoughts. 'Pontus will get us to the village before you reach it. There'll be another car there too. When Ann-Kristen parks at the church, just drive straight past and then double-back and wait. But be ready – the buggers might be sending her all over fucking Skåne!' Then he was gone again.

Now they could see that Ann-Kristen was speeding up. The situation must be getting to her at last. The E65 constantly changes from one to two lanes and back again, and Anita nearly lost sight of her when they were funnelled into a single lane and a truck nudged in between them. Fortunately, the second lane reappeared and Anita was able to nip past the truck; now she was only two cars behind the Volkswagen. As dark clouds swept across the sky, Anita hoped that the weather would hold; rain would only add to their problems.

'The turn-off's coming up in a kilometre,' said Hakim quietly. There was a huskiness to his voice, which Anita recognized as tension. She was feeling the pressure, too, and her hands felt clammy on the steering wheel. She hoped the kidnappers weren't armed. The likelihood was that they were; a thought that didn't help to settle her nerves. Up ahead, she could see the Volkswagen slowing down and indicating. There was no oncoming traffic, so the Volkswagen crossed over the carriageway and onto a side road. Anita had to wait for an oncoming car before she, too, came off the main highway. There was no vehicle now between her and Ann-Kristen's, though there was a sizeable gap. The road was straight, and they were heading deep into the Scanian countryside with its open, undulating fields and little white houses, randomly dotted here and there like dice thrown on a board. There was a small knoll in the narrow road in front of them and Ann-Kristen mounted the crest and disappeared down the other side. They reached the gently curving summit shortly after and could see the village of Skårby ahead with its squat, whitewashed church set on an embankment.

'No!' she heard Hakim mutter. And immediately she saw the problem. A police officer standing next to his patrol car was waving down the Volkswagen.

'What the hell?' shrieked Anita. 'What are they doing here?'

They could see Ann-Kristen pulling off the road into the lay-by next to the parked patrol car. Automatically, Anita slowed down.

'We can't stop now. Keep driving,' urged Hakim. She knew he was right. They would just draw attention to themselves and further jeopardize an operation that already wasn't running according to plan.

As they drove past, they could see a second uniformed officer get out of the patrol car. They reached another rise in the road and over they went. Hakim arched his neck and looked back. 'Can't see them,' he said through gritted teeth.

Two minutes later, they entered the village with the old church and its impossibly immaculate graveyard on their right. In front of the church was a large parking area, which was deserted.

'What the fuck's happening?' Moberg's ranting voice burst into life. Anita had clocked his car in the archway of a farm entrance opposite the church.

'She's been stopped by a patrol car. Must be out from Ystad.'

'The fucking idiots!'

'They weren't to know.'

The swearing continued until the line went dead again. Anita turned the car at a junction; the road to Sjöbo going in one direction and the way to the wildlife park going in the other. Just before the church, now on her left, and Moberg's car on her right, she pulled into a space in front of a neat little house, next to where a large SUV, presumably the owner's, was already parked. From this ideal vantage point, she and Hakim could see both the church car park and the road leading out of the village back to the E65. She turned the ignition off. All they could do now was wait.

'What a bloody mess,' she said, giving the steering wheel a frustrated thump.

'Why have they stopped her?'

'God knows! Some stupid traffic thing. As though they haven't got anything better to do.'

It was then that she noticed another vehicle parked tightly against the wall of the church hall, positioned at right angles to the car park. It must be Wallen with one of the other officers brought in for the operation. She knew that everyone involved would be on tenterhooks awaiting Moberg's instructions.

'Where is she?' This was Moberg again. His agitation was understandable.

'Wait a minute,' Anita said. A car came over the rise. Disappointment; it wasn't Ann-Kristen in her Volkswagen. 'Sorry. Not her.' She heard Moberg curse again. A Saab packed with young kids and a harassed-looking mother drove through the village and turned off towards the wildlife park.

'Anita,' Moberg said sharply. 'You'd better drive back out and see what's happening. The fuckwits might even be taking her in. And we've only got three minutes left!'

Anita started the car up.

'It's her!' said Hakim, pointing up the road. Ann-Kristen's now-familiar blue Volkswagen was coming over the rise and heading down towards the village.

'She's coming!' Anita's relief was palpable.

'Right, sit tight but be ready to move at a moment's notice,' ordered Moberg.

The Volkswagen indicated and swung slowly round into the car park. Anita could only see the back of the car – the others would have a direct view. She didn't want to move her car any closer as it might attract attention. For all they knew, the kidnappers were somewhere close by watching them watching Ann-Kristen.

After they'd been sitting there for what seemed like eons but could only have been minutes, Hakim sighed. 'What's she doing?'

'I can't tell. The trouble is they might have seen her with the patrol car and taken fright. That might not be good news for Peter Uhlig.'

'They'll either kill him or ask for more money.' This was the nearest they had come to a conversation in months.

They sat in silence for another five nerve-racking minutes. The only interruption was Hakim breaking open a bottle of water. He offered it to Anita first. Though she was parched, she shook her head. Even a drink would break her concentration. She'd already lowered the window in case she could pick up the sound of Ann-Kristen's mobile phone going off. But she was too far away, and the odd car coming past didn't help.

It got too much for her. 'Is there any sign of anything?' she asked Moberg.

'Nothing,' he growled. 'She's just sitting there.'

'Are they on to us?'

'Fuck knows. Look, Anita, wander over to the church. Make eye contact with Ann-Kristen. Anything to see if something's happening.'

'Are you sure?'

'Of course I'm bloody not! Just do it!'

'Not sure this is a great idea.' She opened the door.

'Don't make your pistol look so obvious,' observed Hakim. She took off her holster and handed it over.

'Are you certain?' Hakim queried.

'Don't like the damn things.'

'Be careful.' Was there a hint of concern in his voice?

Anita sauntered up the road and approached the church as though she were a casual visitor. Or that's how she hoped she'd come across. She felt anything but. Her hands were sweating and her mouth was dry. She deliberately didn't glance in the direction of Moberg and Brodd, nor at Wallen's car nestled next to the hall. She waited for a large yellow truck to trundle past before she crossed the road and onto the gravelled car park. A furtive sideways peek at Ann-Kristen didn't resolve anything – Peter Uhlig's daughter was staring straight ahead of her as though in a trance. She could see the mobile phone clutched in her hand. Anita walked through the gates guarded on each side by a short, stone post capped by a ball finial, whitewashed like the church beyond. Her feet crunched on the recently raked gravel path. It was virtually the only sound in a village that seemed devoid of people at that time of day. The burial plots each had low, beautifully clipped box hedging around them and were interspersed with carefully tended flower beds. Anita made her way up the slope to the church with its crenellated tower and red-tiled roof. Its restful simplicity seemed at odds with the complications of the human drama that was being played out in its shadow. Suddenly, Anita heard a car door open behind her and she turned to see Ann-Kristen ease herself out of her car. She caught Anita's eye and shook her head. Then she pulled out a packet of cigarettes and lit up. The situation was obviously too stressful for vaping. Anita could have done with one herself. She squinted at her watch – 12.16. The call should have come through a quarter of an hour ago. Now she was convinced that the kidnappers had been watching and had panicked at the sight of the patrol car. She really feared for Peter Uhlig.

Returning to her car, she exchanged a rueful smile with Ann-Kristen, who was sucking the life out of her cigarette; her green-streaked hair twitching in the breeze. She reported back to Moberg, who fumed a bit more before deciding to sit it out for a while longer.

By one o'clock, dull frustration had displaced anxious anticipation as it became increasingly clear that nothing was going to happen. No call was going to be made; something had gone very wrong. Was it something they had done or something beyond their control?

'OK, that's it.' Moberg broke the silence. 'Let's get Ann-Kristen and the money back to Malmö.'

Minutes later, they were all gathered round the Volkswagen. Ann-Kristen was smoking again, her nerves shredded by the experience. Worry was etched into every feature of her face.

'Why did the patrol stop you?' Moberg asked the question that had been on all their minds.

Ann-Kristen flicked away some ash distractedly. 'Something stupid. They were worried about the front tyres. Looked to be down. Said it was dangerous. The tread was threadbare too.

I promised to get Mamma to sort it out. One of them even blew the tyres up for me. It was just some spot check thing. He apologized for holding me up, but stressed that safety was important.'

Moberg's expression was thunderous, but he managed to keep his temper under control.

'Right, Anita, you take the money back to the polishus. I'll escort Ann-Kristen to Limhamn and report to her mother. Hopefully, they'll set up another drop.' His tone was doubtful.

Anita opened the car boot. Inside was the lime-green IKEA cool bag. It was bulging. Yet when she picked it up, the bag felt light considering how many notes were stuffed inside it. Then she noticed the foot pump next to it.

'Did the police open the boot?'

A long plume of smoke emerged from Ann-Kristen's mouth as she replied 'Yes. The other one got out the foot pump. It's OK, I checked the bag was still there when he'd finished.'

Gingerly, Anita unzipped the bag. She registered no surprise when she saw the contents. She took out a handful of crushed newspaper and held it up so everyone could see.

Moberg gasped. 'Fucking hell! The police car!'

CHAPTER 12

Anita was still in bed when she got the call to go to Östra Kyrkogården, the cemetery just off the Inner Ring Road. Within five minutes, she was out of the apartment and in her car. The seven o'clock news came on the car radio. Though she knew that there couldn't possibly be any mention of yesterday's debacle in Skårby, she held her breath until the headlines had been announced. The team had gathered in silence for a debriefing yesterday afternoon. Even Moberg was subdued, even more so when he was called away to report to the commissioner. No one hung around the office awaiting his return. Anita had escaped to The Pickwick. They had been outwitted by the kidnappers. Whether the gang had been aware of the police presence or not, they had cleverly succeeded in getting clean away with the ransom. Would they bother sticking to their bargain and release Peter Uhlig? Or would they dispose of him? – that was the over-riding fear. However, as Anita drove through the city in the direction of Rosengård, she knew that they had kept their word.

She drove through the gates of Malmö's largest cemetery. Spread over a wide area, it was divided into sections, each enclosed by a shoulder-high hedge. Within each section, the gravelled burial areas were cordoned off by low, neat box borders; Skårby again but on a much bigger scale. Anita made for the two buildings at the far end of the site. These were the twin chapels of St. Gertrude and St. Knut, built in 1943 to a design by Sigurd Lewerentz, who was obviously so pleased with his work that he was buried here. Anita parked her car next to the chapel of St. Gertrude. The portico, with its eight thin, square pillars and its almost-flat roof resembled a veranda and would have looked more at home on the *High Chaparral* than in northern Europe. The plain, rectangular structure behind continued the theme. It was rather a melancholic building, perhaps reflecting the era when war raged all around an isolated, neutral Sweden. But in this morbid place, surrounded by the dead, Peter Uhlig was very much alive.

He was sitting on a bench with two uniformed officers talking to him. One of them noticed Anita and came over to her. Anita recognized Jeanette Malmborg, and they exchanged friendly smiles.

'He was found half an hour ago by someone walking though the cemetery,' Jeanette explained. 'We were the nearest to the scene.'

'Is he OK?'

'Shaken up. Fine otherwise, I think. We've sent for an ambulance.'

'Where was he?'

Malmborg nodded in the direction of the serried rows of hedges. 'Section five. He was tied to a bench and he had this over his head.' She produced a black cushion cover. Not quite square, it was similar to the one that Mats Möller had had over his head when he was discovered. 'As you can see, it's a cushion cover. Not new.' Probably bought for cash at a second hand shop – Myrorna or Emmaus perhaps; that was the conclusion they'd drawn over Mats Möller's improvised hood.

'Did he have black gaffer tape over his mouth?'

'Yes. And wrapped round his hands and feet. The sort that can be bought anywhere. I noticed the skin's red raw on his wrists.'

'From the tape?'

'Looks more like being tied up with rope.'

'Right. Bag up the hood and the bits of tape. Thanks.'

Anita approached the kidnap victim. He still wore his work

clothes, his suit now crumpled and dirty. He was only half the man she'd seen in his photograph: his face was gaunter and his eyes less piercing. But it was also his confidence, so apparent in the picture, that seemed to have been drained out of him; a fact which seemed to make him slighter and smaller. 'Herr Uhlig, I'm Anita Sundström. I'm glad to see you're safe.'

'I want to see my wife, my family.'

'Of course, you will. But first, we need to make sure you're OK.'

'I'm perfectly fine,' he said stubbornly.

The early morning quiet was shattered by the wailing siren of an approaching ambulance.

'You'll be taken to hospital to be checked over. Officer Malmborg will accompany you.' He was about to protest again. Anita's raised hand cut him off. 'I'll inform your wife, and she and your daughters can meet you there.' This seemed to appease him. 'Naturally, we'll need to talk to you in detail about what has happened.'

Uhlig slowly got to his feet. 'First Mats Möller, then me. What's going on?'

'That's what we're trying to find out.' The dubious expression on his face spoke eloquently of his scepticism.

Anita watched the ambulance crunch its way along the gravel drive. Just then, another vehicle arrived. Out of it stepped a dishevelled and bleary-eyed Pontus Brodd.

'Was that Peter Uhlig?' he said, pointing towards the disappearing ambulance.

'Yes. He's OK. I'm going to have a look round here and where he was tied up. See what I can find. Too far from any CCTV, unfortunately,' she said, glancing around. 'At least Moberg will be pleased Uhlig's back safely.'

'Ah, you haven't heard?'

'Heard what?'

'The chief inspector had a heart attack last night.'

CHAPTER 13

He sat bolt upright. He was bathed in sweat. He wiped his eyes, moisture clinging to the back of his hand. The nightmare had been terrible, but he'd woken up to a reality that was even worse. The light was peeping through the curtain, and he looked at the clock: 4.37. He wouldn't be able to drop off again. He didn't want to. He was afraid to shut his eyes. He licked his parched lips. Trembling fingers reached for the water he had by his bedside. His hand brushed the glass and sent it crashing to the floor. It shattered as it hit the boards, and the water snaked over the shiny surface before seeping into the fringes of the rug. He had neither the energy nor the inclination to get out of bed and clear up the mess.

Though he fought it, his mind kept coming back to the phone call; the voice had laid bare so much of his life – but not *that*. Surely, he couldn't know about *that*?

He lay back, his head resting on the pillow, and gazed at the dawn filtering across the ceiling. That feeling of helplessness engulfed him again. What *did* the man want?

The last time she'd been in the hospital was to visit a bed-bound Liv Fogelström. Now it was another colleague. In Moberg's case, it was purely self-inflicted. In that respect, Anita had no sympathy. The warning signs had been there for years, and he'd made no attempt to change his habits. Yet, as she looked through the glass at her boss lying there, surrounded by tubes and flashing screens, in what appeared to be a peaceful slumber, she couldn't help a feeling of sorrow. He had given her a hard time on many occasions and often hadn't shown her the respect she felt she merited. And many of his attitudes and opinions she found unpalatable. But, despite it all, she had a sneaking affection for this bear of a man, who had no social graces whatsoever, but was a cop who was totally incorruptible and always tried to get to the truth even if it meant bruising egos along the way.

That very afternoon, she'd got an inkling of the pressure Moberg was constantly under from those above him in the chain of command. Commissioner Dahlbeck had called her up to his office and told her that, for the moment, she was in temporary charge of the kidnapping cases and that he expected results – quickly. The drop had been a disaster, which he was doing his best to keep out of the press. The force had been made a fool of by these people. And saving face was what mattered most to the Dahlbecks of this world. Anita suspected it was the debacle at Skårby that had pushed Moberg's ticker over the edge. Maybe the heart attack was a blessed relief.

She'd talked to the doctor as she clutched a bag of grapes. 'He's not good at the moment. To be honest, I'm amazed he survived. If the paramedics hadn't got to the fast food outlet quickly, he wouldn't be with us.'

'I think where he had his attack is a clue to his problem.'

The doctor raised a knowing eyebrow. 'Exactly. That body is one neglected temple.'

'He'll pull through, won't he?' Anita asked anxiously.

He glanced through the window at his patient. 'Pretty sure he will. The primary PCI shows disease in all his coronaries. When he's stable, he'll probably have a coronary artery bypass graft. Whatever happens, he'll need a lot of rest and recuperation afterwards – and a totally new diet. One thing is for sure: you won't be seeing him at work for a good while.'

After the doctor left her, she suddenly felt the weight of responsibility that Moberg's absence had generated. The current investigation was now on her shoulders. She had always felt she was up to the task of leading a team and often railed against the decisions of her superiors when she had disagreed with them. Now that she had been thrust into that position, she realized that she had doubts about her ability to cope with the pressure. How would the others react to her giving them instructions? Brodd would be resentful, Wallen would be jealous – and Hakim? Goodness knows what he'd be like given their present relationship. But decisions had to be made and, before coming down to the hospital, she'd got Brodd looking for the police car, and had put Hakim in charge of searching for witnesses to the dumping of Peter Uhlig at the East Cemetery and scanning any CCTV that might show the vehicle they used.

Klara Wallen was waiting in the hospital car park for Anita to return and then they were going to drive down to Limhamn and speak to Peter Uhlig. He had passed a medical examination and had refused any counselling from a family liaison officer or mental health expert to help him deal with the trauma he'd been through. He'd said that being with his loving family was the best way to get over his harrowing experience. Anita realized that this stance could change once the shock of what had happened fully hit him. That's why she was keen to get as much information out of him as possible before he had a setback. Besides, the commissioner wanted her report, pronto.

Anita and Klara were seated in the sun room of the Uhligs' home. Kevin would have called it a conservatory. It was built onto the side of the large 1950s house and had huge picture windows that gave an uninterrupted view of the garden: a sweeping lawn bordered by a number of mature trees. The white décor, beige floor tiles and cream furnishings contrasted tastefully with the vivid orange of the wall which divided the room from the main house. The early evening sun added extra vibrancy, and the whole room was bathed in a warm glow. A sofa ran along the wall at the base of the windows. The seat had little depth and the wooden back was low, thin and uncomfortable; to compensate, there were several plump cushions neatly positioned along its length and it was here, in this restricted space, that Anita and Klara were perched. Above Anita's head, precariously affixed to one of the mullions, hung a painted plate of modern design, which she assumed was the work of Ann-Kristen's wife. Anita hoped the hook was sound. Peter Uhlig was cocooned in a high-backed armchair next to a white pedestal table which sported a lamp with a Chinese blue and white porcelain base, and a large glass of brandy. The latter had been brought in by his daughter, a fussing Birgitta Losell. Uhlig's wife was nowhere to be seen; Ann-Kristen and her partner, Ella the artist, were in the sitting room watching them apprehensively through the glass door.

'I appreciate that this is difficult for you to go through,' Anita opened, 'but the sooner we get as many details about what happened, the sooner we can try and catch this gang.' Anita was hoping that having two women interviewing him would put Uhlig at his ease and make him more forthcoming.

'Do you honestly think you'll find these people?' He was pointing the glass of brandy in their direction.

'We'll do our best. In the meantime, if you want us to organize some counselling, please say. It's understandable given the awful experience you've been through.'

'I have my family,' he said curtly. 'They will see me through, thank you. Talking of which, I've heard from Ann-Kristen about what transpired yesterday. I should be annoyed at your incompetence.' He replaced the glass on the table. 'Actually, I'm relieved that Ann-Kristen didn't have to meet my captors.'

'She was very brave and cooperative.' Uhlig nodded in

agreement. 'Now, can you take us through the events from the morning you disappeared?'

Uhlig's eyes strayed to the garden. 'Yes. A week ago this morning I sat on the patio here having my early coffee. It promised to be a nice day. I was wrong.' He paused. 'I set off for work at my usual time. Usual route. It was as I approached the E65 that I saw a car parked in the lay-by.'

'Make?'

'A Volkswagen. A bit like my wife's except it wasn't in such good condition. And it was silver. The bonnet was up. Two men were looking under it. As I approached, one of them raised his arm to wave me down. I thought they were in trouble.' He gave a hollow laugh. 'I parked behind them and got out. I didn't even have time to speak. I was grabbed and shoved into the back of their car. They put a hood over my head and I felt my hands being tied. And then we left.'

'Did they say anything to you while you were in the car? Or speak to each other?'

'Yes. Briefly to each other.'

'In Swedish?' He shook his head. 'English?'

'I was so bewildered. Frightened. If I had to say... I think it might have been Russian, but I may be completely wrong.'

Anita and Wallen exchanged glances. Moberg's theory might be correct.

'How long were you in the car?'

Uhlig shrugged helplessly. 'I don't know. It seemed a long time. An hour? Maybe more, maybe less.' Anita was doing the mental calculations as to where they might get in that time.

'What then?'

'I was bundled out of the car. And then I heard a metal door being opened. I was pushed inside, and then further in. Then I heard the door clang shut and I was left by myself.'

'Metal door?'

'Yes. When they took the hood off, I realized I was in a

container. I've seen the inside of enough in my time.'

'Container?' Anita mulled this over for a second. 'So we're talking about a port or container yard of some sort?'

'Yes, I think so. I heard trucks passing from time to time. And I heard a ship's horn in the distance, possibly a ferry's. I heard that a number of times.'

'Regularly or spasmodically?'

'Spasmodically.'

'So, we're definitely talking about a port. Malmö's the obvious one, but there's Trelleborg, Helsingborg and Ystad.'

'I'm sure it wasn't Trelleborg,' Uhlig seemed confident. 'I'm used to the regular sounds of the port, working opposite the docks, and it wouldn't take that long to get there.'

'Wherever they took you, they could have driven you around to confuse you,' said Wallen. 'And to confuse us.'

He conceded the point and took solace in another gulp of brandy.

'And how did they treat you?' Anita asked.

'Not well. They took the hood away but most of the time I was tied up to a chair.' He showed them his wrists. The rope marks had bitten deep. 'I was untied to eat. They did feed me quite well though. Decent food, properly cooked.' Anita was surprised by this as she expected kidnap victims like Uhlig would be given basic rations, especially if they were incarcerated inside a container in a port area. 'I had to carry out my bodily functions in a bucket in front of my captors, which was highly undignified.'

The shadows of the trees on the floor were now receding with the dying sun.

'Could you describe any of your kidnappers?'

'When they grabbed me, it all happened so quickly. But I can describe the one who held his arm up to flag me down. He was swarthy. In his twenties, I would say. Medium height; jet black hair. That stubbly look they have these days. Dark eyes. His teeth weren't very good. Whoever brought me my food and emptied my bucket always wore a mask.'

'The only captor you saw was the man who flagged you down?' Anita confirmed.

'Yes. I was in darkness most of the time. Totally disorientated. The man held a torch so I could see what I was eating or doing... well, you know what. The man never said a word even when I spoke to him.'

'Would you recognize the man who stopped you again if you saw him?'

'Yes. I think so.'

'Good. And you say you tried to speak to him?'

'Yes. He was totally unresponsive. I also tried in English once.'

'If he was Russian, he probably couldn't understand you in either language,' suggested Wallen.

'But someone in the gang can speak Swedish,' Anita pointed out, 'the caller to your wife.'

'Well, nothing was said to me that I could understand.'

'No one spoke to you about the ransom? They didn't try and get you to transfer money over the internet?'

'No. I assumed if I was being ransomed that they were dealing with the family.' He stroked his glass nervously. 'But at the time, I had no idea that it was a kidnap. They might have just wanted to kill me.' He stared at Anita, fear flickering in his eyes. 'I just didn't know what they were going to do.'

'So were you threatened?'

'No. Nothing like that. Naturally, I was scared. Cooped up in a metal box wondering what I was doing there. It would have been easier if they'd communicated with me. At least I might have known what was going on.'

Anita crossed her legs and scanned the notes she'd been making.

'Your release. How did that happen?'

'I was asleep. Of course, I had no sense of time in there. So

I have no idea when it was. Two men in masks appeared and untied the rope bindings and replaced them with tape. Then they put tape over my mouth and placed the hood over my head. This really scared me as I thought it might be the end. I was put in a car and driven off. Then I was hauled out of the car. Definitely two people, as each took an arm and guided me. I could feel gravel crunching under my feet. Then they tied my feet to something with more tape, which turned out to be a bench in Östra Kyrkogården. That's how I was found.'

'Timings? How long was the drive and how long did you think you were trussed up in the cemetery?'

'Difficult to estimate. I think the journey to the cemetery was about an hour. Similar time to when I was taken. But please don't quote me on that as I was in a state of panic – I thought they might be taking me somewhere to finish me off. As for the time I was on the bench...erm,' he puckered up his lips '...a good few hours. I remember hearing the birds singing. Dawn chorus. It seemed a lifetime before that fellow came to my aid and got in touch with you. I knew I was outside, but I couldn't shout for help as I had the damned tape over my mouth.' He absently ran a hand over his lips.

'Thank you; you've been very helpful. Tomorrow, we'll get someone down to put together a photofit of the man who flagged you down. At least we know we're dealing with a port area. Of course, they may be long gone, but there may be some clues. There's nothing you remember that was out of the ordinary during your captivity so we can narrow down the location, is there? You're familiar with containers in your business. Anything different about this one?'

'Not really. My space was quite small. They'd put a partition wall in with a metal door in it. I could tell that. My captors must have been occupying the other half. I could hear occasional murmurings from the far side.'

'Anything else?'

'Don't think so.' He was about to pick up his glass again when he stopped himself. 'Well, there was the dog.'

'What dog?'

'One night, I heard this growling sound. I thought it unusual as you don't get many stray dogs in Sweden. They tend to be rounded up. Well, I assume it was a dog, though I was half asleep at the time.'

'OK. We'll let you rest.'

Peter Uhlig stood up at the same time as Anita and Wallen. He fixed Anita with a pleading gaze. 'These people need to be caught, Inspector. It's not a matter of the money, though I realize that's substantial. What they did to Mats Möller and myself is so wrong. You've got to stop them before they do it again.'

CHAPTER 14

It was ridiculous to feel nervous. Yet that's exactly how Anita felt when addressing the team next morning. She'd done it on plenty of previous occasions, but never in the role of officer in charge. It was the sense of vulnerability which she found unnerving. As one of the team, Moberg was always there to shield her from any flack. Now she was acutely aware that she had no back-up from above; just a yawning chasm between her and the top echelons of the force, from which a great pile of the brown stuff could drop in her direction at any moment. Make one mistake, and the commissioner would hang her out to dry. After reporting to Commissioner Dahlbeck on her debriefing session with Peter Uhlig, her sympathy and respect for Erik Moberg was growing by the minute. Dahlbeck had promised that extra resources would be made available, though he was vague about how and when they would be forthcoming. He was worried about the opprobrium he'd receive from the business community if another kidnap took place. He'd left her with the same plea as Peter Uhlig had made the previous evening, though the commissioner's words were couched in a threat – if this wasn't sorted out swiftly, heads would roll. Anita knew whose the first head would be.

'So, that's where we are with Peter Uhlig.' Anita had just given Hakim, Wallen and Brodd a résumé of her conversation with the businessman. 'As you were with me, Klara, have you had any thoughts?' She wanted to be seen to be involving everyone, particularly Wallen, who might prove a disruptive influence if not handled carefully. She could envisage the troublemaking Rolf whispering bitter somethings in Wallen's ear about why Anita had been picked instead of her.

'It's obvious that the location is industrial, probably a port. He mentioned hearing a ship's horn, probably a ferry's, spasmodically. Uhlig didn't think it was Trelleborg. I don't think it's Helsingborg either as the ferries going over to Helsingør run up to four times an hour; hardly spasmodic. There are a few daily ferries from Ystad. However, at the moment, we think...' and Wallen glanced across to Anita for confirmation, 'that Malmö is the most likely. The Finnlines ships come in up to three times a day.'

'Not that we're discounting the other ports,' added Anita, 'but we'll concentrate on the docks here to start with. Sorry, carry on, Klara.'

'If they kept Uhlig here, it follows the pattern of the Möller kidnapping. This gang is thorough and they do their research. What I did think strange was that one of them wasn't worried about being seen by Uhlig. We've now got an impression of him.' She stood up and stuck a photofit that had been constructed from Peter Uhlig's description on the whiteboard.

'Maybe he's just cocky,' chimed in Brodd. 'Thinks he won't be caught.'

'Or maybe he knows that he won't be hanging around long enough to be found.' This suggestion came from Hakim.

'That's a very good thought,' agreed Anita eagerly. She hoped that this investigation would bring her and Hakim closer together, though being over-effusive probably wasn't the best way forward. Even Anita realized her ebullience hadn't sounded right as she received funny looks from Brodd and Wallen.

'You mean they're just going to carry out these two kidnaps and then go elsewhere?' queried Wallen.

'That'll make the commissioner happy,' joked Brodd.

'I think we have to consider this may not be the end,' said Anita firmly. 'If this is a Russian outfit, they might just bring in other personnel for the next job. The man up there,' she said, pointing at the photofit, 'isn't either of the two men described by Mats Möller. Another thing that struck me as strange was the food Uhlig was given. They served up well-cooked meals. Down in the docks doesn't strike me as an ideal environment to whip up quality cuisine. You'd expect them to go out and get takeaways as they did with Möller.'

'Perhaps they were aware of the fact that we checked all the fast food outlets in the vicinity of the Möller workshop. OK, we didn't get anywhere with that; I know the descriptions of the first two guys were too vague. But they wouldn't want to risk the guy up there,' Hakim waved at the photofit on the wall, 'being identified. Making their own food would avoid that.'

'Still a bit of a faff,' said Brodd.

'Attention to detail, I'd call it,' countered Hakim. 'This gang do things meticulously. There are no fingerprints on the hood cushion covers, which are well-nigh untraceable, or the bits of tape, which is sold everywhere. It'll be virtually impossible to discover who purchased either of them. And just look at the way they fooled us with the police car stunt. By the way, it's turned up in a country lane between Rydsgård and Blentarp. Totally burnt out. Forensics will have a go at it but don't hold your breath that anything useful will be found.'

'Do we know where they got hold of the police car?' asked Anita.

'Yeah. It was stolen from the film studios in Ystad. They're shooting a new cop series there. The uniforms, too.' Despite everything, there was a murmur of admiration around the table.

'The police car incident does raise another question. We believe that the gang is Russian or certainly Eastern European. Our fellow here doesn't appear to speak Swedish or English, unless he deliberately didn't speak to the victim; part of the unnerving process. Yet at least one other member of the gang definitely speaks Swedish and/or English. The man who threatened Mats Möller spoke in English with some sort of accent. The man who phoned in the ransom demand to Uhlig's wife spoke Swedish. And then there's the fake patrol officer who flagged down Ann-Kristen. According to her, he spoke Swedish, though she was too flustered to be sure about his accent. And her description is very vague. He was wearing a cap and had sunglasses on. Though she did say he was very well mannered!'

'Well, when you think about it, to do what they're doing, someone has to be able to communicate to get the money out of the victims.' Anita stopped herself complimenting Hakim again.

'The point is, does this gang have Swedes in it, or is it a purely outside operation? If it's the latter, it's going to be a damned sight harder to catch them. But whatever its make-up, are they getting inside help? Which brings me back to the fact that both the victims have done business together and have social connections. And is there someone behind all this who's pointing the gang in the direction of the targets?'

That night Anita left work late. Even Hakim had given up trawling through CCTV footage trying to find the Volkswagen that Peter Uhlig had been whisked away in. Brodd had found out shipping movements in Malmö for the days that Uhlig was in captivity, and this heightened their belief that the businessman had been kept in one of the harbour areas. Then Brodd had gone off to visit his drinking buddy in hospital. Even Wallen had stayed on longer than usual; maybe she was responding to the extra responsibility that Anita was giving her.

A quiet drink in The Pickwick on the way home had given Anita time to momentarily unwind. She had been pleased with the team's efforts, though that had been overshadowed by a call earlier in the evening from an irate Lasse. 'Where the hell are you?' With the sudden taking over of the investigation, it had completely slipped her mind that she'd arranged to babysit Leyla while Lasse and Jazmin went to the cinema. Her apologies and excuses had received a sullen response. He'd finished with 'This was a break that Jazmin really needed.' As Anita stared at her phone after Lasse had rung off, she realized that her son was becoming as good as his father at emotional blackmail. Now she would have a restless night blaming herself for letting him down.

Before leaving the pub, Matt the barman asked how Kevin was getting on. She gave him an evasive answer about him being busy over in Britain. As she walked home, she wished that he was still here. Someone to talk to about work. She could discuss things with him that she couldn't with the team; certainly not now she had such a strained relationship with Hakim. Kevin was good for bouncing ideas off and giving her sensible advice. He understood the rigours of the job. And he'd make her laugh to take her mind off her worries. He'd certainly know how to handle Lasse and smooth that over. Maybe she would ring him tomorrow.

He withdrew his fist. The impact had made the heel of his hand hurt. He hoped he hadn't broken anything. He gulped for air. It took a while for his heart to stop pumping so brutally. He looked down at the man in the chair; relaxed, still holding the sheet of paper between his hands. No movement. No sound of breathing. He didn't care. He was scum; he destroyed lives. But not anymore; now he was dead scum.

He would have to think fast; think clearly. He took a handkerchief from his pocket and switched on the hi-fi system. He found a pop station and turned up the volume. The noise would cover his movements. It was twenty nerve-racking minutes before he was completely satisfied. He'd found a suitcase in a wardrobe, one of several showing signs of wear. The man obviously travelled a lot, spreading his poison far and wide like a Portuguese Man o' War. Donning a pair of rubber gloves he'd found in the kitchen, he'd systematically gone about removing any possible traces of his visit – the police would be chasing shadows. When he'd finished, the man's computer, phones, wallet, all the information that had been pinned to the notice board, some files he'd found in the bottom drawer of the desk – and even the piece of paper the dead man had been holding in his hands – all went in the suitcase.

The music was still playing loudly; it would cover the sound of his retreat down the corridor. With a tight grip on the case, he took one last glimpse at the man in the chair; the eyes staring, the face creased into a look of astonishment. He exhaled slowly. His nemesis was dead.

CHAPTER 15

The weekend came and went. On the domestic front, Anita had made it up to Lasse by babysitting on Saturday night. She paid for their evening out to salve her conscience. And she enjoyed spending time with Leyla, who was now a walking, almost-talking little lady who had fixed ideas about what she liked and disliked. When she wanted something, she would point to it aggressively. When she didn't, she would stand stock-still in the middle of the room with her head fiercely bowed and a deep scowl on her face. Her tiny tantrums made Anita laugh. She could see that Leyla was as strong willed as her mother, Jazmin. There would be battles ahead! But what Anita loved most was the wide-eyed smile she received whenever she saw her granddaughter. Leyla would toddle up to her as fast as her little legs would go, arms outstretched.

Even when she was watching the sleeping child after reading her a bedtime story, Anita couldn't get her mind off the kidnap cases. So far, nothing had given them any clues as to who was behind the snatching of Mats Möller or Peter Uhlig. The gang were good and had made themselves rich out of their efforts. Though there were things that didn't totally add up, she knew the chances of finding them through the normal channels of detection were indeed remote, unless something unexpected turned up. She still couldn't get out of her head the business link between the two men. Was it a coincidence they were targeted? Should they be investigating the cases from a business angle? Was there something in their dealings that made them ripe for exploiting? Who was in their circle? Had they upset anyone to the extent that he or she would have reason to help the kidnappers? The gang certainly knew enough about their victims to successfully deploy their different methods of extortion. But even if the perpetrators weren't receiving inside help, any information might enable Anita to identify possible future targets.

The only problem with this line of enquiry was that Commissioner Dahlbeck had already dismissed the idea. He didn't want any of his officers sniffing around Skåne's high-profile business community. She had been told in no uncertain terms that that was off limits. He didn't want to risk upsetting influential people by having the police digging into their backgrounds. So, she had resorted to a bit of private sleuthing. She'd rung Liv at a time that she knew Hakim wouldn't be around. She remembered Liv saying that she'd been on a number of computer courses and had been keen to get into technical crime before the shooting. That was another thing Liv had in common with Hakim – they were geeks. (Anybody who knew their way round computers and social media were geeks in Anita's book.) Liv had been delighted to be asked to help. She would trawl the internet to see if there were connections that linked Möller and Uhlig to other prominent business organizations and families. Who were their known associates? Who got on with whom? Or, more to the point, who didn't get on? Were there any hostile takeover bids or deals that had gone wrong? Anita suggested it might be worth contacting the business editors of the major regional papers – say she was doing some research. Pretend she's a student. Just make sure she didn't mention any police connection or else they would immediately think there was a story. And that would get back to Commissioner Dahlbeck. Anita left it up to Liv whether or not she told Hakim what she was up to. Heaven knows what his reaction might be!

After a couple of hours' work in the office, Anita had driven down to Östra Kyrkogården again. She wandered around the massive expanse of neatly partitioned burial areas and along the road into the cemetery where the kidnappers must have driven. It was easy to see why cemeteries made such good drop-off points. No CCTV, except at the chapels, and unlikely that there would be anyone around in the small hours. The dumping of Mats Möller had been more brazen as that particular cemetery was in the centre of the city. Östra Kyrkogården was far quieter, with the apartment blocks on the eastern side some distance away through a thick blanket of trees. Was there anything symbolic in choosing burial grounds? Was it a subliminal threat that if their ransoms weren't paid, this is where any future victims would end up? Or was the choice of location purely practical? Anita sat down on the bench that Peter Uhlig had been tied to. Clouds scudded across a grey sky. Summer was still holding its breath. The grave opposite her was for a baby boy. The dates read December 10th, 1958 to March 26th, 1959. Flowers were laid on the gravel in front of it. Were they from his parents, still remembering after all this time? They'd probably be in their eighties now.

Her peace was broken by her phone going off. She took it out of her pocket and saw it was Kevin. She'd hadn't got round to ringing him over the weekend as she'd planned. Since he'd left six weeks before, they'd exchanged a few desultory emails and one awkward Skype. Yet as she gazed down at his name on the screen, she felt a sense of pleasure.

'Hello, Anita!' Kevin's voice was jaunty.

'Hi. I was going to ring you.'

'Were you?' His voice was mocking. 'I haven't rung at an awkward moment? You're probably at work.'

'I'm sitting in a cemetery.'

'Blimey, have things got that bad?' She could tell he was in a good mood.

'And where are you?'

'It's lovely and sunny here so I thought I'd have a day at the seaside. I'm in Morecambe. You remember, I brought you here and we had fish and chips?'

'Yes. The place with the statue of that comedian. What was his name?'

'Eric Morecambe. Like the town. Actually, I'm standing below his statue right now. I'm on the bit where they've inscribed all the famous Morecambe & Wise punchlines. They still make me laugh.'

'I think they're lost in translation. I don't see what's funny about two men sharing a bed together and the taller one slapping the shorter one around the face.'

'I can see I've got my work cut out convincing you how brilliant they were. Many would say they were Britain's greatest comedians. But, strangely enough, that's not why I'm calling. I've got something important to tell you.'

Anita's heart missed a beat. Was this it? Was he going to say that it was over between them? She wouldn't blame him after she'd rejected his proposal. Now that he'd had time to think about their situation, maybe he'd decided to move on. Suddenly, in that moment, she didn't want to lose him. 'What?' she responded cautiously.

'I'm getting my job back!'

'Wow, that's great!' The relief in her voice was palpable. 'How did that happen?'

'Our chief constable is under investigation. It goes back to his time in the Met. I think he's been caught up in the aftershock of the Tyrone Cassidy business. Which, of course, we started,' he added with some pride. 'Anyhow, the bastard is suspended and the deputy chief constable is happy to have me back. Seems he's not sorry to see the back of his boss.'

'That's fantastic! When do you start?'

'There are one or two bureaucratic hoops to jump through

first, but it'll probably be in the middle of June. So I'm going to enjoy myself until then. I'm off to buy an ice cream after this call.'

'An ice cream? A hot coffee's what I need right now.'

'Look, is there any chance you could pop over for a few days before I start? I won't get any holiday for a while once I do.'

'No, I can't. I'm temporarily in charge at the moment. Moberg has had a heart attack.'

'Bloody hell! Mind you, it's no wonder.'

'You could come here.' She found herself inviting him before she'd had time to think it through.

'Are you sure?' he said cagily.

'Of course. You'd have to occupy yourself, though, as I'm pretty busy.'

'That's fine by me.' He sounded genuinely delighted. 'There's always stuff to do. My girls at Folk & Rock.'

'And Matt at the pub was asking after you. And Lasse will be happy you're around. You'll stop me blotting my copybook.'

'If you're *really* sure.'

'I am.' She knew she needed someone at home to unburden herself to after the strains at work.

They made quick arrangements as to when he'd fly over and the call ended with Kevin jokingly promising he wouldn't ask her to marry him. She was still smiling when she put her phone away. Maybe her private life could get back to the status quo she'd enjoyed before.

Almost immediately, the phone sprang into action again. She frowned as she saw Hakim's name. Had he discovered something?

There was no preamble. 'Anita, you need to get yourself over to Västra Hamnen straightaway.'

'Not another kidnap?'

'No. A murder.'

CHAPTER 16

Västra Hamnen had developed so quickly over the last few years. Every time Anita came out this way, there were even more apartment blocks, intimate courtyards surrounded by cleverly designed houses, cafés and restaurants, all dominated by Malmö's feature landmark, the Turning Torso. The apartment that Hakim had called from was right on the seafront. The heavy drizzle that was now coming down obscured the view. From walks along the shoreline on sunny days, Anita knew how dramatic the vista could be – Denmark was just across the water, the higher buildings of Copenhagen on the skyline. Normally, in the distance, the Öresund Bridge would be clearly visible, though now, like an artist's first tremulous sketch, only the faintest outline could be seen. Even the nearer Kallbadhus, perched nonchalantly at the end of its pier, was almost lost to sight. Not a day for naked bathing!

The apartment block she stood in front of was four storeys high. The building was white with an enormous expanse of glass so the residents could enjoy the panorama. The three upper storeys had balconies that jutted out from the main structure as though straining to get closer to the sea. On either side of the block were others of differing colours, shapes and sizes, all running in a straight line along a decked boardwalk, which was now wet and gleaming. A couple of ducks were enjoying the weather. It was a nice place to live as long as you weren't being murdered.

The main door to the block was open as police officers and forensic staff came and went. Anita made her way to the second floor. At the door of one of the apartments was Hakim. 'A neighbour alerted us as the radio had been playing all night, which was unusual. When he came to complain, there was no answer. The dead man's in here.' Anita slipped on a pair of latex gloves as she followed him inside and along a corridor to the living room, which overlooked the sea. Even before entering the room, she could hear the constant whirring of the forensic photographer's camera as the crime scene was being recorded for permanent documentation. The room was spacious, a fact accentuated by its lack of furniture. There was a single blue sofa opposite a large, wall-mounted television, and a compact hi-fi system, which presumably had been the source of the loud music. The television was the only thing on the walls – no pictures or photographs were to be seen. On a wooden coffee table was a single glass with unfinished whisky in it, a ceramic ashtray with two stubbed cigarette butts, and a book. There was only one chair in the room, of the same design as the sofa. Behind it was a white bookcase. It was in this chair that the victim sat; wide, staring eyes focussed on Anita. The frozen expression of puzzlement on his face made her flinch. It wasn't immediately clear what had killed him, though directly above his head, seemingly touching his scalp, was the business end of a reading lamp, bent gracefully over on its stand like the neck of a swan. It was as her gaze became fixed on this object that Anita noticed the dried blood which caked the stubble around the man's crown. He was sitting with his hands in the pose of holding a book, except there was no book. He was wearing light-brown shorts, a red T-shirt and flip flops. A white-suited forensic photographer was busily snapping away under the instructions of Eva Thulin. Anita was pleased to see her. If this was the first murder case she was going to be in charge of, she needed all the help she could get – and it didn't get any better than Eva Thulin.

They exchanged friendly glances.

'What's happened here?' asked Anita.

'Well, I didn't think reading could be so dangerous,' Thulin commented wryly.

As Anita peered closer, she could see that part of the lamp was embedded in the victim's head.

'That's right,' said Thulin. 'This bendy lamp has a short but strong metal rod attached to the shade. It's for adjusting the angle or height when you're sitting; you can just pull it down by reaching above your head. It appears that the victim was sitting underneath it when the perpetrator smashed the lamp down and the rod penetrated the cranium, just like a stiletto. It probably didn't cause instant death, but he would have lost consciousness before dying.'

'So, one blow?'

'With the right amount of force.'

'Man?'

'Not necessarily. Just someone strong enough to jam that down with their palm or their fist. And it appears this poor guy wasn't expecting it, as he's just sitting there. The head's not tilted round as though he'd heard something that disturbed him or worried him.'

Anita looked closer and then stepped back. 'Either someone's sneaked up behind him or someone was here that he didn't think was a potential threat.'

'Makes sense to me. There's no sign of forced entry. It's up to you and Hakim to work out which.'

Hakim pointed to the victim's hands. 'It looks like he was reading a book.' He nodded at the one on the coffee table. 'If the perpetrator took it out of his hands, it might have his fingerprints on it.'

Thulin shook her head. 'I don't think it was a book.' She picked up a small evidence bag and produced a tiny sliver of paper. 'This was still in his left hand. Unfortunately, there's nothing on it. It looks like part of a piece of paper he was holding. Maybe that's what he was looking at when his killer struck. Then the killer must have taken it away as the victim was dying. It's not here anyway. Whatever was on it may have been the reason for his death.'

'Time of death?'

'Roughly between ten and twelve last night.'

'That fits,' said Hakim. 'The neighbour said the music started before half ten. It was just after he'd started watching a film on TV.'

'When you've finished with the body, you'll give the place the once-over?'

'You know me, Anita. We'll not miss a thing. So don't make a mess before we've had time to go over everything.' Eva talked as she continued feeling her way round the dead man's body. 'Makes a change not having Chief Inspector Moberg charging in and trampling all over the evidence.' She squinted up at Anita. 'How is he, by the way?'

'Pontus Brodd reported that he's getting better. He's sitting up and talking. Well, sitting up and complaining.'

'Just wait until he sees their dietary recommendations. That'll give him another heart attack,' Thulin laughed as she returned to her probing.

Anita went over to the windows and gazed out over the water. If anything, the weather had got worse and was set in for the day.

'Do we know who the victim is?' she asked Hakim.

'According to the name on the front door, he's called Mikael Nilsson.'

She returned to the coffee table and bent over to scrutinize the book. 'Does that look Finnish to you?'

'Yes. Some of the books on the shelves over there are, too.'

'Must be able to understand Finnish. Do we know anything else about him?'

'The neighbour who reported the music said he didn't know anything about him, other than that he wasn't often here. And he was usually very quiet. Kept himself to himself. That's why he thought the music playing loudly all night wasn't normal.'

'Do we know what Mikael Nilsson did?'

Hakim motioned that Anita should come with him. He took her into a small room that was obviously used as an office. There was a desk and swivel chair. On the desk, there was a large printer, assorted pencils and biros in a desk organizer, and an open, half-empty packet of cigarettes along with a well-stocked ashtray. Everything was presided over by an anglepoise lamp, which was still on. A couple of shelves each accommodated a row of upright wooden box files containing magazines; on another there were about twenty books. In one corner of the floor was a pile of newspapers. On one wall, above an empty wastepaper basket, was a large cork notice board. But it was what wasn't there that immediately struck Anita the most – there was no computer for starters. And it was obvious that whatever had been pinned to the notice board had been torn off in a hurry. Little bits of paper were still attached to the multi-coloured drawing pins.

'Have you found a mobile phone?'

'Not yet,' answered Hakim. 'If the computer's gone, it's unlikely that the killer would have left the phone.'

Anita bent over one of the box files and picked out a magazine. It was a trashy one full of celebrities. So were some of the others. In the next container, there were more sober business publications.

'His reading matter is pretty eclectic,' she observed. She flicked through the pile of newspapers. 'I wonder what he did. Without his computer, it's not obvious, though it looks like he worked from home.'

'Only part of the time. The neighbour said he wasn't around much. Away for weeks at a time.'

'Salesman?' Anita offered as she pulled open the top drawer of the desk. It was full of office paraphernalia: rubber bands, staples and the like. The next drawer contained a pile of unused printing paper. The third drawer was slightly open. She eased it out gently. It was empty.

'I wonder if our murderer cleared out whatever was in here. I thought there might be some files or USB sticks to back up work on the computer.'

'He probably used iCloud or Dropbox.' This was beyond Anita, too.

It was at this point that Anita nearly told Hakim about the research she'd asked Liv to do. Then she thought better of it. He hadn't wanted Liv to think about police work and might blame her for getting his fiancée involved again. And though he was speaking to her because he had to, his manner was still cool; professional, without the sense of camaraderie they'd previously shared.

'Nothing much in the kitchen. Liked his coffee though. There must be a dozen packs of Offesson's in one of the cupboards: every blend you can think of. Most people tend to stick to one or two of their favourite ones.'

'Maybe he's a coffeeholic. Most Swedes are.'

'And there's only one dirty plate in the sink, so he didn't share a meal with his visitor.'

'Though I think Mikael Nilsson probably knew his killer. Let him or her in. Didn't think he or she was a danger or else he wouldn't have been murdered the way he was.'

'He might have known him, or her, yet he didn't offer them a drink. Unless we find prints on the glass other than Nilsson's. But that would just be too careless. So it was unlikely to be a social call, even at that time of night.'

'The murder can't have been premeditated. No one plans to kill someone like that. It was opportunistic.'

'There's one more thing you should see, though,' said

Hakim. Anita followed the gangly, young officer out of the study and into a bedroom. It, too, had minimal furniture: a double bed, a bedside table and a long, built-in wardrobe. The only indulgence was a smaller, wall-mounted television.

Hakim opened the wardrobe. It was packed with suits and shirts. At the bottom were a couple of suitcases and a cabin bag.

'So, we think he travelled a lot. Any sign of a passport?'

'Not yet. Can't find a wallet either.'

'And I don't suppose this building has CCTV?'

'You suppose right. But look what I've found.'

There was something glinting behind one of the cases. Hakim lifted the case out.

It was a small safe. Anita knelt down next to it. It was like one of those safes found in hotel rooms. It was locked. 'I wonder if our murderer missed this. Better get it back and find someone smarter than us to open it. And get Brodd down here to talk to the neighbours and see if anybody heard or saw anything. And, of course–'

'Find any CCTV.' It was like the old Hakim, reading her mind.

'If any exists. Not that sort of area,' she said, giving him an apologetic grimace. Was this the first hint of a thaw?

Anita stood up slowly. She felt a twinge in her knee. She hadn't been running around Pildammsparken as regularly as she should have been. 'I'd better get back to headquarters and alert Commissioner Dahlbeck. Where's Erik Moberg when you need him?'

CHAPTER 17

Erik Moberg was sitting up in bed like a beached whale when Anita entered his room. A nurse was tidying his bedside table and clearing away his meal tray, so Anita hovered in the doorway. Moberg noticed her.

'Save me from this woman!' he appealed to Anita.

'Now you just do as you're told, Erik,' scolded the nurse. 'You must eat what's good for you.'

The nurse flashed Anita an exasperated what-can-you-do-with-him? frown as she left the room.

'Well, you seem more like your old, cantankerous self,' Anita commented as she approached the bed. Again, she had a bunch of grapes, which Moberg pulled a face at. It was a cover. She slipped him a bar of Marabou chocolate. 'If this is discovered, I'm denying any knowledge.'

Moberg gratefully slipped the chocolate under his pillow. 'After lights out.'

Anita pulled a chair across and sat near the bed. 'Are you feeling better?'

'Tired. Bored. *Hungry.*'

'Are they not feeding you?'

'Bloody rabbit food. I hate anything green.'

'That's why you're in here.'

'Don't you start! Anyway, cut the crap. How's the Uhlig investigation going?'

'A blank so far, other than we suspect he was held somewhere in a harbour area, and that you might be right about an Eastern European gang – or Russian.'

'I knew it!' That bucked him up.

'I've got Klara overseeing that case as we've got ourselves a murder.'

Moberg's eyes lit up. 'Tell me more.'

'Look, you should be resting. The last thing you should be doing is thinking about work.'

'Give me a break, Anita. That's all I've got.' It was only later that Anita reflected on what he'd said and realized how poignant it was.

'It's a male, about fifty, called Mikael Nilsson. He was in his apartment in Västra Hamnen. He was killed with his reading lamp.' Anita quickly explained to a goggle-eyed Moberg how that was possible.

'That's a new one on me.' She could see he was enjoying himself and was showing more enthusiasm than he had done for a long time. Maybe because he wasn't shouldering any responsibility.

'We don't know what Nilsson did but we do know he was away from his apartment for periods of time. We haven't enough to build up a picture of him yet, let alone who might have wanted to murder him. But it does appear that it wasn't premeditated and that it was someone he knew as there was no sign of forced entry. Where he was sitting and the way he was killed shows he wasn't afraid of his visitor. Whoever did it took his computer and phone. Files too, possibly.'

'Have you talked to the neighbours, nearest businesses, got CCTV, checked with the tax people–'

'Enough!' Anita said. 'It's not your case. You get yourself better.'

He held up his hands in a gesture of defeat. 'You'll come back and let me know how things are going, on both cases?'

Anita had never heard him plead before.

'Yes, I will. I'm glad other people's problems are cheering you up.' Anita stood up and put the chair back. 'Anyway, I'd better get on.'

When she reached the door, Moberg asked: 'Are you managing with Commissioner Dahlbeck?'

'Yeah. He's been OK so far. Seems happy for me to run both investigations.'

'Be careful, Anita. He'll shaft you if it's expedient. Just watch your back.'

The next morning, Tuesday, Anita had two meetings scheduled. First, she was going to speak to Klara Wallen about any further developments in the Peter Uhlig kidnap. Then the rest of the team were going to gather for an update on the Mikael Nilsson murder.

Wallen came into her office at eight. Anita was delighted yet surprised. Getting a commuting Klara in that early was quite a feat. Yet she was an unrecognizably energized Wallen. The fact that she was virtually in charge of the Uhlig case had given her confidence a huge boost.

'Who's making Rolf's breakfast this morning?' Anita couldn't help asking before she had time to check herself. Wallen didn't take it the wrong way.

'The miserable sod can make his own breakfast. He'll just have to lump it.' Anita stifled a 'hooray!'.

Over coffee, they went through what was known. The likely location of Uhlig's captivity, the silver Volkswagen he had been abducted in, the likelihood of the kidnappers being Russian, and the limited forensic evidence.

'The cushion cover is a popular make. It's impossible to trace as it was probably bought second-hand. The gaffer tape is also incredibly common. That particular kind is available in most parts of Europe. And, sadly, neither had any prints on.

Gloves must have been used. The Volkswagen has come up zilch so far. Pity Uhlig didn't get the registration. The only sightings on CCTV have been followed up, and none are what we're looking for. We're trying to trace all that type of Volkswagen Golf in southern Sweden. As for the phone they used on the day of the drop, the call was made in Malmö in the vicinity of the Swedbank Stadium. Untraceable, as it hasn't been used again.'

'The photofit?'

Wallen produced the photofit of the young man that Peter Uhlig had described. 'This is going out in the next couple of days. No one in here recognizes him from this. And Uhlig didn't pick out any of the mug shots I provided of known felons. We may have to go the Interpol route. I'm starting to think we really are dealing with an Eastern European gang.'

'Thoughts about your next move?'

'Just carry on. We've got some extra manpower on it.'

'The commissioner has come good, then.' Not that Anita had been told.

'We're coordinating a search of the harbours to try and find where Uhlig was held. The Ystad and Helsingborg stations have sent officers to scout around their dock areas for a likely spot. Might give us something.'

'They didn't leave us anything in Möller's hidey-hole.' Anita sighed. 'And I'm still puzzled by the food Uhlig was served up.'

'They'd want him well-fed. He was a four-million-euro asset.'

'That's not the point. The guy was in a container, presumably in some yard or other. You're trying to keep a low profile: it's not easy to conjure up decent meals. In practical terms, where do you prepare them? And I doubt if being a gourmet chef is a qualification for being part of a kidnap gang. Besides, you need to go shopping for the ingredients. That means going out and being seen. I know it sounds daft, but ask Uhlig exactly what he was given to eat.'

Wallen pulled a face. 'OK, you're the boss.'

'Less of the sarcasm, Inspector Wallen. One other thing I'd better tell you. You know the commissioner dismissed my idea of looking at the kidnaps from the perspective of the wider business community?' Wallen nodded. 'Well, I'm getting some private snooping done. I've enlisted Liv Fogelström to do some internet searches and make a few calls.'

'Hakim's Liv?'

'Yes.'

'Does he know?'

It was Anita's turn to pull a face. 'Don't know. I'm not telling him.'

Before Wallen left, Anita brought up one last point. 'Something else that's been nagging me is the fact that Möller's ransom caused him some personal financial pain, yet didn't seem to impact on his business. With Uhlig, according to his daughter Ann-Kristen, his ransom created real problems as they had much of the capital needed tied up in the business.'

'Maybe there wasn't another suitable target like Möller. I think you're reading too much into it, Anita.'

'Maybe.'

The second meeting was attended by Hakim and Brodd. Anita had anticipated the usual tension with Hakim. Fortunately for her, he was in full professional mode.

'We didn't have much luck with the name Mikael Nilsson through official channels. There are quite a lot of them around and none seemed to fit our man. However, there was a reason for that: he's not Mikael Nilsson.'

This took Anita by surprise.

'This is what we found in his safe.' With a dramatic flourish, he produced a fistful of passports. 'Six passports.' He laid them out like playing cards in a neat line on the table in front of Anita as though he was about to set up a game of patience. He picked the first one up. 'Swedish. Mikael Nilsson. Fake.'

He passed it over to Anita, who opened it up. The photo only had a vague resemblance to the murder victim. The short, dirty-blond hair of the man in the apartment in Västra Hamnen had been replaced by a slightly longer, browner, thicker thatch and matching moustache.

'So who is he?'

Hakim picked up a Finnish passport. 'Sami Litmanen.' He handed it over to Anita. The photograph showed a younger version of the man she had seen with a lamp clamped to his cranium. The unsmiling face was slimmer, the lips taut, the blue-grey eyes unflinching.

'He's Finnish,' Brodd remarked with some contempt. 'Another knife-carrying drunk.' He was trotting out the clichéd view older generations of Swedes held about the Finns.

Hakim ignored him. 'That explains the Finnish books at his home. He's also got a newer, Swedish one.' He swapped passports with Anita. The face was slightly puffier and the short, dirty-blond hair was receding at the temples. The gaze had a hint of self-satisfaction. This was definitely the man she'd seen yesterday. 'Both these passports are real. That's been confirmed. Sami Litmanen became a Swedish citizen last year. He owns the apartment, but doesn't have a car. No Swedish licence anyway. Born 10th July, 1966 in Helsinki. So that makes him fifty.'

'What about the other three passports?'

'There's a Russian passport in the name of Alexei Gagolin. Again, his appearance is different.' In this one, Litmanen wore a hipster beard and had raven hair. 'And in this Lithuanian passport he's Joris Rimkus.' The curly, blond hair was over his collar. 'Finally, there's an Erkin Akhmetov from Kazakhstan. According to the internet, Akhmetov is the most common surname in Kazakhstan.' The hair was tinted grey, as was the goatee beard: a fresh touch.

'He does a neat line in disguises,' said Anita, still taking in the older incarnation of the murdered man.

Brodd picked up the Russian passport. 'That name's familiar, but I can't for the life of me think why.'

The usual ineffective Brodd contribution, thought Anita irritably. 'What do you make of all these?' she asked, her hand sweeping over the multi-personality that was now Sami Litmanen. 'Points to criminal activity of some sort? International drug dealer? God forbid, a terrorist?'

'I can't say,' replied Hakim. 'I've had them checked out to see if they were obtained through legal channels. Other than the ones in his real name – and we assume it's his real name – the others wouldn't pass muster going through a conventional airport security check. They look genuine enough, but would be immediately detected, so I'm reliably informed.'

'So he couldn't use them for travel?'

'No.'

'Which begs the question: why have them?'

'I don't know. Possibly to prove he was who he said he was at the time. Useful in foreign hotels, that sort of thing.'

'Sounds like a bloody spy to me,' said Brodd.

The thought of getting caught up with the security services again wasn't a pleasant thought for Anita. It hadn't worked out well the last time she'd been entangled with those shadowy figures when dealing with the death of Albin Rylander.

'Conman?' offered Hakim.

'I would have thought he'd have a plusher apartment if he was conning people. It was all a bit low key.'

'Maybe he was a crap conman,' smirked Brodd.

'OK, let's dispense with the speculation. At least we know *who* he was even if we don't know *what* he was. Let's stick to what we know. Someone entered his apartment possibly around ten. The music came on at about ten thirty, according to the neighbour you spoke to, Hakim. Why the music?'

'To make the neighbours think Litmanen was in? Cover up

any sounds that might give the murderer away while he was searching the apartment?'

'Litmanen probably knew his assailant. He wasn't a perceived threat. And the murderer took advantage at that. What made him or her act?'

'Whatever Litmanen was holding in his hands?' Hakim suggested.

'Very likely. Was he holding something that threatened or endangered his visitor?'

'The murderer made sure there was no trace of a connection by taking his computer, phone, etcetera.'

'Pontus. Any luck with the house-to-house?'

'Not really,' Pontus drawled. 'Not many people had actually seen him around. But I did go to the café on the corner. According to one of the staff, Nilsson... sorry Litmanen went in there for his breakfast when he was around. He wasn't chatty. "Polite" and "aloof" were the words she used. Never spoke to the other regulars. Always had a wad of newspapers with him. Would spend about an hour combing through them.'

Just then there was a knock on the door and Eva Thulin came in.

'Hi, Eva.' Thulin returned a weary smile. She'd been putting in the hours. 'Coffee?'

She shook her head vigorously. 'No more. I've done enough to boost the Brazilian economy in the last twenty-four hours.'

'Have you anything for us?'

'I haven't much to add to my initial observations yesterday,' Thulin said, taking her seat at the table. 'The victim had his head pierced by the metal rod on the lamp. It penetrated the cranium and caused injury to the vascular spaces and the consequent raised intracranial pressure led to a loss of consciousness and coning of the brainstem. He wouldn't necessarily have died instantly. Not very nice.'

'Would the perpetrator have blood on him?'

'Some, possibly. Not a huge spatter; possibly on a wrist or cuff. Not enough for anyone to notice when he or she left the apartment. There's no evidence the kitchen sink or basins were used to clean up.'

'You're still not discounting a woman?'

'If she was strong enough and determined enough.'

'Lover?' Hakim suggested. 'Could the fragment in Litmanen's hand have been from a letter? A love letter?'

'It wasn't from a letter,' Thulin was implicit. 'It was from the same ream of paper that he had in his printer in his office.'

'He might have printed out an indiscreet email though.'

'Of course,' Thulin conceded.

'Which would also explain the disappearance of his computer and phone.' Hakim was becoming enthusiastic, and Anita wasn't going to discourage him. 'Whatever he did: conman, drug runner, whatever, the motive might simply be a lover's quarrel. A married woman?'

'If it was a woman, a lover, don't you think he'd have poured her a drink?'

'That's a valid point, Eva. But Hakim's suggestion opens up another possible route to investigate,' said Anita. 'Anything else?'

'Well, he was the only one drinking. We've checked the whisky glass and the cigarette butts around the apartment – only touched by the victim. However, his are not the only fingerprints in the place. It had been well cleaned very recently–'

'By the murderer?'

'Cleaned as in furniture-polish clean. Dusted. Shower scrubbed, toilet sparkling. Either your man was incredibly domesticated or he had a cleaner. Anyway, there is a set of prints other than the victim's. And they're not on the database.'

'Right, we need to ask around. If there's a cleaner, talk to all the agencies in town.'

The rest of the meeting lasted a further fifteen minutes. As they were breaking up and gathering notes and files, Brodd suddenly burst into life. He clicked his fingers loudly and jumped to his feet.

'Now I remember! Alexei Gagolin.'

Anita, Hakim and Eva Thulin stared at him in bewilderment.

'I know who Sami Litmanen is!'

CHAPTER 18

'The Oligarch!'

'The guy who writes for that sleazy *Sanningen*?' spluttered Thulin, almost halfway out of the meeting room door. 'He's a shit-bag.'

'Are you sure?' asked Anita, who was always sceptical of Brodd's offerings.

Brodd was frantically flicking through his phone. 'There! It's on YouTube.' He held up his phone. On the screen was grainy footage, obviously via a spy camera, showing a neatly dressed man sitting on a large sofa in what appeared to be a luxury hotel suite. An unseen man opposite him was talking in English with what sounded like a Russian accent: 'Don't be so formal, Claes. We're friends now. No more Mister Gagolin. Call me Alexei.'

'Is that Claes Svärdendahl on the sofa?' Hakim asked.

'Yeah. The morning TV presenter. Squeaky clean until this,' Brodd said with undisguised relish.

As they watched, the conversation topic became unsavoury: girls, and what Alexei liked to do to them. Claes Svärdendahl responded to the comments in like manner. Then the clip stopped.

'Svärdendahl got in deeper. Or rather, The Oligarch pulled him in deeper. Ended up with a couple of prostitutes in the room. There were photos in the paper, though not footage like this, unfortunately.'

'I know he was married,' said Thulin. 'Big on family values.'

'Well, it destroyed his career,' Brodd said with finality, clicking off the footage. 'And he wasn't the only one either.'

Thulin raised an eyebrow. 'I think, Anita, you'll have a list of suspects as long as your arm. Good luck!'

It wasn't until the next day that they had compiled a list of those potential suspects. Brodd's avid readership of *Sanningen* had proved invaluable. After more internet searches had backed up his assertion that Sami Litmanen was none other than the infamous Oligarch, Anita had had a meeting with Commissioner Dahlbeck. He had been horrified that such a person had been found dead on his patch. 'Wouldn't you think someone as despicable as that would be living in Stockholm?' It was a question that Anita and the team had already asked themselves and couldn't find an answer to. He demanded that Anita keep the fact that the murder victim was The Oligarch out of the press. 'You know, the usual line. Looking into the death of a middle-aged male; suspicious circumstances; investigation at an early stage. Keep details to a minimum. If the media get a whiff of this, we'll never get them off our backs.' That was a given. Over the years, rival newspapers and broadcasters had tried to reveal the identity of The Oligarch, but all had failed. No one knew what he looked like. And he had obviously been very careful: there had been no photos of him in his apartment.

Now Anita found herself in the unusual position of letting Pontus Brodd do the briefing. He was the team's acknowledged expert on The Oligarch. With Klara Wallen now occupied with the kidnapping cases, Anita's small team was complemented by Inspector Bea Erlandsson. Anita was delighted to have the petite detective on board. When Erlandsson had been part of the new Cold Case Group, together they had helped solve a twenty-year-old murder case, much to the chagrin of the team's leader, Alice Zetterberg, an adversary of Anita's since their shared days at the

Police Academy in Stockholm. A vengeful Zetterberg, who had been publically humiliated at a press conference after the arrest of the wrong suspect, soon retaliated by manoeuvring Erlandsson out of the Cold Case Group. Anita had wondered if Zetterberg's decision had an element of sexual discrimination to it as well – young Bea Erlandsson was a lesbian. All that concerned Anita now was that Erlandsson was a good officer who wouldn't have to worry about being intimidated by Chief Inspector Moberg.

On the whiteboard was an enlarged photo from Sami Litmanen's Swedish passport. Next to it were the photos from his other passports, and the silhouette of the journalist used in *Sanningen* to accompany his articles; his anonymity being one of the trademarks of his success. Underneath Litmanen's many guises, there was another row of faces – those of his victims, some familiar to Anita, some not.

'OK. Here at last is The Oligarch unveiled! What wouldn't the Swedish media give for that photo!' Brodd was enjoying his moment in the limelight. Anita frowned; she knew Brodd of old. If that photo found its way into the press, she would descend on him like Vidar, the Norse god of vengeance. 'He's worked for *Sanningen* for nearly a decade and, as you can see, he's accumulated quite a prestigious gallery of victims, from television personalities and politicians to sportsmen and businessmen. We don't know exactly when he came over from Finland, or why. What we do know is how successful he was at catching people out; ruining careers, relationships – some people even ending up in prison.'

'Through entrapment,' said Erlandsson with some feeling.

'He would call it subterfuge. Whatever the morality of his methods, he achieved fantastic scoops and brought down all these people here on the board. Some may have deserved it, some not. Depends on your point of view. In theory, every one of them has a motive.'

Brodd handed out a typed list of The Oligarch's marks.

'I thought this might be handy as a guide to have with you.'
Anita glanced at the list:

Jimmy Brantling, children's television presenter
Kurt Alkeborn, footballer and football manager
Britt Rosengren, soap star
Nils-Åke Rydén, businessman
Folke Allinger, politician
Claes Svärdendahl, television presenter
Absame Madar Geesi, boxer

'Though I've put down their professions, if I was being more accurate, all should have "ex" in front of them,' joked Brodd. 'The Oligarch saw to that.'

'Why this seven in particular?' asked Anita.

'They're the most high profile, so they had the most to lose. Of course, there are others, but me and Bea,' he smiled across at Erlandsson as though she was his new girlfriend, 'have been able to discount some of the others. These are the ones we need to check out first.'

'All yours, Pontus.'

Brodd stood up straight and puffed out his chest.

'Jimmy Brantling is the latest victim. Or last, I suppose. Popular kids' presenter – wacky Jumping Jimmy – who confessed on hidden camera that he couldn't stand kids. Litmanen had filled him up with recreational drugs so he'd be in the mood to say anything, whether he meant it or not. Litmanen was posing as a Lithuanian television executive keen on using him on a new show over there with the promise of more work throughout the Baltic States. Claimed he had contacts in Germany as well. Jumping Jimmy jumped at the chance of extra exposure and extra dosh. Two meetings took place in top-end Stockholm hotels. The "confession" happened at the second meeting. He was immediately sacked after the story broke in *Sanningen*.'

'And the Lithuanian television executive was called Joris Rimkus?'

'You've got it.' Brodd took a swig of water before continuing. 'Kurt Alkeborn was a footballer.'

'He was a good defender. Played at Malmö FF for a time.' Erlandsson was staggered that Anita would know anything about football, but didn't say anything.

'Yes. His career took him to Holland and then Italy briefly in the nineties. After he finished playing, he came back here to Sweden before going into coaching, and then management. Did very well. A spell in England really raised his profile, and three years ago, he was on the verge of taking over the Swedish national team when The Oligarch struck. Litmanen really did pretend to be an oligarch for this one. A rich Russian who was thinking about buying Hammarby in Stockholm. Claimed he had the money to turn the club into Sweden's biggest and best. They've underachieved for years and have only been Swedish champions once in their history, in 2001. He wanted Alkeborn to advise him and offered him a lucrative deal as a consultant. Alkeborn agreed but asked The Oligarch to keep their financial arrangement hush-hush, as the Swedish Football Association might see this as a conflict of interest. He didn't want the prospect of becoming Sweden's national manager to be jeopardized. During two meetings in London, The Oligarch agreed to Alkeborn's terms. That was bad enough, of course. What made it worse was, over a few celebratory vodkas, a well-oiled Alkeborn, who was known to like the occasional tipple, started to come out with scurrilous stories about other footballers and managers, including some of the Swedish players he would soon be managing. Needless to say, Kurt Alkeborn is out of work at the moment.'

'And Britt Rosengren?' Anita knew how popular she'd been. Though she'd never seen her act in her popular soap, she'd caught her a couple of times on chat shows. Besides being very attractive, she'd come across as quite self-deprecating, which had appealed to Anita.

'Ambition was her downfall. She must have been one of the highest-earning actresses around. The Oligarch pretended to be a Swedish, British-based talent scout for one of the big Hollywood studios. He claimed he was responsible for looking for new actors in northern Europe, mainly Scandinavia. Two meetings again. The first in London, the second in Stockholm. How could she resist the lure of Hollywood? They had indulged in a little bit of cocaine in London, which The Oligarch had supplied. She probably took it to fit in. When the meeting in Stockholm was set up, he asked her if she could get hold of some coke and bring it to his hotel, as he didn't want to risk bringing any into the country himself. She hadn't got any herself as she wasn't a user – that's certainly what she claimed later – but got a friend in the business to supply her with some, which she gave to The Oligarch. Next thing she knows, she's splashed across the front page of *Sanningen* as a drug addict and dealer. She was lucky to escape a prison sentence. No one will touch her now, of course.'

'That's awful,' said Erlandsson.

'Her own fault.' It was clear that Brodd had no sympathy for the actress.

'He certainly seemed to have had an instinct for his victims' weaknesses, and then known how to exploit them.' Hakim was shaking his head. Anita wasn't sure whether it was out of grudging respect or horrified disapproval.

'OK, our next victim is in prison, or was until a week ago. Nils-Åke Rydén was a businessman from up north in Umeå, who originally made his money in timber. Then he successfully diversified before becoming a bit of a stock market guru. Held seminars for potential investors; that kind of thing. At a cost to the punters, naturally. The Oligarch got him on insider trading by posing as a rich Russian investor. Rydén gave him tips he shouldn't have known about. This wasn't a case of entrapment;

Rydén had been doing it for some time.'

'So he was a *real* criminal, albeit a sophisticated one,' commented Hakim.

'Yep. That's why he ended up inside five years ago. But as I said, he came out last week. He needs to be traced.'

'Presumably they all do, and their movements accounted for at the time of the murder.'

'That's my next task, Boss.'

'Just stick to Anita, please.' She felt uncomfortable with the elevation. Besides, she'd always loathed the expression 'boss'.

'Right B..., Anita. Next up is a real beauty. And another that ended with a prison sentence. It was one of Sami Litmanen's early scoops. I don't know if you remember an ultra-right-wing group called White Justice?'

'Yes. Nasty bunch, I remember. Anti-everything. Often violently.' The thuggish, square face and tattooed neck on the board didn't look like they belonged to a man who would take any prisoners.

'They've since disappeared into the woodwork or, in some cases, blended into the Sweden Democrats in an attempt at respectability.' Hakim gave an exaggerated 'humph'. 'Well, in the noughties, Folke Allinger was an up-and-coming member of White Justice. He had his eye on the leadership, but his way was barred by a guy called Hans Leonardsson. In 2007, Sami Litmanen enters the scene, posing as the leader of a small Finnish neo-Nazi group. Basically, to cut a long story short, Allinger tried to hire his new Finnish friend to bump off Hans Leonardsson. If it was carried out by another group, Allinger could distance himself from the murder. Then they would join forces with Litmanen's fictitious bunch and form a bigger, trans-Scandinavian group, very like today's Nordic Resistance Movement. After the story ran, Allinger did a bunk. He was caught trying to hop on a ferry to Germany in Trelleborg. Litmanen's in-camera testimony ensured Allinger got eight years. Got out a couple of years ago.'

'He sounds a good candidate,' said Hakim. 'He's the only one so far who's contemplated murder, though you'd think he might have struck earlier.'

'Could have taken a couple of years to find Litmanen,' commented Erlandsson.

'And he certainly had plenty of time to think about revenge.'

'That's what I was thinking,' Brodd agreed. 'Well, now we go from the beast to the beauty – Claes Svärdendahl.' He was a pretty boy with an unblemished face. The smile displayed gleaming white teeth with the trademark gap. Anita was familiar with him as she'd sometimes seen him on his morning show after a late-night shift, horribly bright and breezy when she, clutching her first strong coffee, was still trying to come to terms with the new day. His cheeriness wasn't infectious, just irksome. But he was loved by a legion of women, even though he was married and lived, by all accounts, an idyllic, wholesome Swedish life. He had a family apartment in Stockholm and a summer house on one of the archipelago islands so favoured by residents of the capital as an escape from the rigours of their daily routines. She recalled, without remembering the exact circumstances, that there had been a fuss when he was whisked off the airwaves. Brodd was about to enlighten her.

'It turns out that Claes Svärdendahl's weakness was prostitutes. The clean-living presenter with the beautiful wife and three perfect Nordic kids liked a bit of rough stuff on the side. Not that the beautiful wife knew any of this until The Oligarch informed the world. And when she did find out, there was none of that standing-by-her-man nonsense. She grabbed the three perfect Nordic kids and left.'

'So how did Litmanen set that one up?' Anita enquired.

'Again, a rich Russian. You saw him in that video clip. He told Svärdendahl that he was involved in *Russia Today*, the international English-language news service. The Oligarch said he and a consortium of Russian businessmen were setting up a new television company to complement *Russia Today*, which would have more magazine-style shows. As Svärdendahl's English is virtually perfect, he was going to host the morning programme. Big name guests, big exposure and big money. What wasn't there to like? The first meeting took place in a Stockholm hotel early last year. Once he'd got Svärdendahl hooked, he invited him to St. Petersburg in September. There was nothing rushed about this trap. Put him up at a fancy hotel, showed him the sights and brought in a couple of prostitutes to keep him company. He likes a bit of sadomasochistic fun – obviously his beautiful wife didn't spank him at home. So, Claes Svärdendahl was literally caught with his pants down. Not that he went without a fight. When the job and the wife went, he marched round to *Sanningen* to find The Oligarch and threatened to kill him. Litmanen was nowhere to be seen, of course. The editor had to call the police and have Svärdendahl escorted from the premises. Not an uncommon occurrence at *Sanningen*.'

'Is Svärdendahl the only one who actually threatened violence?' asked Anita.

'No. Which brings me to our last leading suspect: Absame Madar Geesi. Better known simply as Absame, the Somali name for *The Great One*. Absame's parents came from Somalia to Malmö when he was three. Typical immigrant story. Only way out of Rosengård was sport or crime. In Absame's case, it was both. He was a talented boxer, who was picked up by a local trainer called Bogdan Kovać. Kovać ran a small club to keep kids like Absame off the streets. It worked, and Absame moved onto the straight and narrow after some early scrapes with the law: petty theft, joyriding, usual stuff. Absame began to attract attention and turned professional. Boxing's not particularly popular over here – except when Ingemar Johansson was world heavyweight champion back in 1959.'

'I thought boxing was banned here in the seventies,' interrupted Anita.

'1970, to be precise. The ban was lifted in 2006, but with time restrictions on bouts. That's why Kovać had to get Absame fights abroad – in Spain, France, Britain, and in his native Serbia.'

'Like Badou Jack.'

'Who's Badou Jack, Hakim?'

'He's the world super middleweight champion. He's Swedish but fights out of Las Vegas.'

'I hadn't got you down as a boxing aficionado.'

'I'm not really, but I read the newspapers – with the exception of *Sanningen*.'

'As I was saying,' Brodd continued, 'Absame was building a good reputation and got a shot at the European middleweight title in 2014. He beat a German named Gunther in front of his home crowd in Berlin. Now he had a chance to make some real money and there was talk of a tilt for the world title in a year or so. Bought himself a smart place in Stockholm. When he started flashing the cash and overdoing the bling back here in Sweden – and attracting attention by being on the front pages as well as the back, The Oligarch noticed. Suddenly there was interest from wealthy Kazakh fight promoter, the one and only Erkin Akhmetov.' Brodd nodded in the direction of Litmanen's Kazakhstan passport photo. 'Said he could double Absame's earnings and get him an early shot at the world title. Though it probably turned Absame's head, it was Bogdan Kovać who was the boxer's undoing. I'm not sure how Litmanen did it, but he got Kovać to admit that he had supplied Absame with steroids in the early days and performance enhancing drugs after he'd turned professional. Litmanen got this confession out of Kovać while visiting Absame's training camp in Austria. Once the front page of *Sanningen* screamed out that Absame was a drugs cheat, his career was finished. He received a lifetime ban in 2015. He protested his innocence and said that he'd just taken what Kovać had told him to take: he didn't know they were illegal substances; thought they were harmless medications. Needless to say, he also went looking for The Oligarch, promising to tear him to pieces if he ever got hold of him.'

'Do we know where he is now?' This appeared to be the first one with a Malmö connection.

'Yes, we do. He's back here. He's now muscle for Dragan Mitrović.' Anita had never actually come across Mitrović but knew he was well known to the police. Officially, he ran a couple of nightclubs and some gyms, though his main business was drugs and prostitutes. He'd never been caught; he was too clever for that. Anita suspected that he had someone in the polishus who tipped him off before raids. Nothing was ever found in his clubs. Given the circles Mitrović moved in, someone like an angry ex-professional boxer was useful to have on the payroll. 'It may not be a coincidence that Bogdan Kovač disappeared off the radar shortly after Absame began working for Mitrović. Anyhow, Absame lives in an apartment in Apelgården.' Brodd stopped talking then winced sheepishly. 'That's it.'

'Thank you, Pontus. Good work.' Brodd beamed with pleasure. Anita suspected no one had ever said that to him before. 'That's given us a lot to digest.'

'It strikes me,' said Hakim, 'that Litmanen started out as a campaigning journalist and went for legitimate targets before he slipped into stitching up celebrities. Easier and higher profile, I suppose.'

'Doesn't make him any more laudable. He spread misery,' Erlandsson said with feeling.

'OK, we're not here to judge,' said Anita firmly. 'We're here to catch a killer, irrespective of how we feel about the murder victim. Firstly, we're going to have to check out the whereabouts of all these people on the day of the murder. I expect most of them live in Stockholm, so it should be easy enough to discover if one of them took a trip to Malmö around the time of the killing. We also need to discover more about Sami Litmanen. Why was he living here and not in Stockholm, where most of his targets lived and worked? What was he working on at the moment? That might be important given that his computer and phone are missing. I think a trip to see the editor of *Sanningen* might be a starting point.' Anita gazed at the eclectic collection of potential suspects. 'One thing that may discount a number of these people is that they wouldn't know where he lived. We were surprised that he was in Malmö. I'm sure some of them would be too.'

'Which puts Absame at the top of the list,' said Brodd. 'He lives here. He may have seen Litmanen and followed him. Or he may have got Dragan Mitrović to find him for him.'

'You could be right, Pontus. I want you and Hakim to have a word with him. Pull him in if he's being uncooperative.'

'We might need boxing gloves!'

'You've got a pistol.'

CHAPTER 19

Anita unscrewed the cap from the bottle of wine. Her head was buzzing and she didn't care what sort of wine it was as long as it was red and it was alcoholic. She sank down on her day bed and stretched out her legs on the coffee table. It was Thursday night and she had an early flight the next morning. She knew she should be giving the apartment a quick dust and tidy as Kevin was due to fly in on Saturday, and she wasn't coming back from Stockholm until the same day. When she'd invited him back, there hadn't been a dead investigative journalist to worry about. Now she had her hands full, and the timing couldn't be worse. She had half thought about putting him off, but knew how disappointed he would be. Besides, he could do the cleaning, have a meal ready for her when she got home and put up with her moaning about work. The perfect, temporary house husband. And he could warm her bed. At times of stress, it helps to have the close proximity of someone you had affection for, and trusted.

She idly picked up the television remote. She held it in her hand for a few seconds before putting it down again. She wanted to avoid the chance of seeing herself. Earlier in the day, she had given a brief statement to the media saying that the police were investigating a suspicious death but that the investigation was at an early stage. She wasn't in a position to give them further details. She could just imagine the fun they were going to have once they eventually discovered how Litmanen was killed. She omitted to say that they were exploring a number of leads, and that some of those leads had come to nothing over the last thirty hours or so. Jumping Jimmy Brantling had been drunk in a Stockholm bar on the night of the murder. That was easy to corroborate as his rowdy expulsion from the establishment had reached the newspapers. Actress Britt Rosengren had been traced to her mother's home in Västerås, where she had been living since her sacking from her soap opera and her work had dried up. The night of the murder she was helping out at a community theatre a hundred kilometres west of Stockholm. And Kurt Alkeborn had the best alibi so far. He was in South Africa trying to resurrect his football managerial career in a country where he hadn't yet slagged off any players or officials. Businessman Nils-Åke Rydén hadn't been found yet, so Anita had decided, while in Stockholm, to call on Claes Svärdendahl, who had been suspiciously evasive about his movements after Erlandsson had tracked him down and called him. Absame hadn't been at home when Hakim and Brodd had paid a visit to his apartment in Apelgården. Neighbours said he was around but hadn't seen him for a couple of days. One positive was that Folke Allinger lived somewhere in Skåne. He would receive a personal visit when they found his latest address.

And the fingerprints that Eva Thulin had found in Litmanen's apartment *did* belong to a cleaner. The Spanish woman had been questioned and had confirmed that she'd cleaned the place on the Friday, two days before the murder. Litmanen had been going out as she arrived. She confirmed that he was often away, though he liked to have the apartment regularly cleaned even if he wasn't around. She also confirmed that he had a laptop computer and mobile phone. She'd seen him use both.

All this Anita had reported to Commissioner Dahlbeck before he left work in the late afternoon for a game of tennis. Though in a hurry, he'd seemed pleased with their progress and said that

she was handling the dual investigations 'competently'. After her
second glass of red wine, she wasn't sure if 'competently' was a
compliment or a criticism. But he'd definitely been happy about
her appearance in front of the cameras. She'd given nothing
away. She had even referred to the victim by the Swedish name
that Litmanen had on his apartment door so they wouldn't get
a sniff of him being Finnish; that would have given them a bone
they'd have quickly got their teeth into.

Anita stirred herself and made her way into the kitchen.
She knew she should have something to eat and then pack a
bag for her Stockholm trip. As she opened the fridge to peruse
its contents, her mobile phone rang in the living room. It was
probably Kevin. As she wandered through, it occurred to her
that she hadn't got any food in for him. They would have to
have a carry-out on Saturday night.

'Hi!' she called breezily into the phone.

'Is that Inspector Sundström?'

'Yes,' she said warily.

'It's Martin Glimhall.' She knew immediately who he was
– a crime reporter from one of the local papers. She'd known
him for some years. 'I was there when you made your press
statement this afternoon.'

'I saw you.'

'I got the feeling that there was more to it. I know the name
Mikael Nilsson was on the victim's door, but I can't find out
anything about someone with that name in that part of Västra
Hamnen that fits your description of the deceased.'

'You'll have to look a little harder then.'

She heard him laugh at the other end of the phone. 'I think
there's something more than meets the eye here, Anita. Surely
you can give me something. Off the record.'

'*On* the record, Martin, I've got nothing to add. It's too early
to release details. We don't want the investigation compromised.'

'Come on, Anita. I know you. Remember, I was there when

you shafted Alice Zetterberg at her press conference last year.'

'I didn't shaft her. I would never do that to a colleague.'

'Oh yeah. I saw your face when she had to backtrack. The word is you're not pals.'

'I don't know where you get your information from, Martin. We were friends years ago.'

'That's fine by me. I just thought I'd ask you first. Now I'll just have to go and speak to your "friend".'

'Why would you speak to Alice Zetterberg? She's nothing to do with this case.'

'Whatever.' Then he was gone.

Anita returned to the kitchen. Martin Glimhall must have got his wires crossed, or else he was trying to wind her up so that she'd spill some information. Bloody journalists were always stirring things up. And she was going to meet another one tomorrow. She'd fixed up to see *Sanningen* editor, Elin Ljung, at eleven o'clock. She had to admit she'd been surprised to learn that a woman was at the helm of such a sleazy publication. And it was telling that Ljung's response to being contacted by the police was a resigned 'who have we upset now?' Anita hadn't elaborated, other than to say it concerned one of her reporters. It was clear that the paper had no idea that Sami Litmanen was dead. It was likely to come as a nasty shock.

CHAPTER 20

Anita took a taxi to Malmö Airport, which was half an hour's drive east of the city. The taxi was a precaution in case she slept in, which of course she didn't. She always found it difficult to sleep when she knew she had to travel the next day or had an important meeting; she'd been awake for half an hour before the alarm was due to go off and had showered at five. This was going to be a critical day. She hoped that she would learn a lot more about The Oligarch.

The Indian taxi driver had been chatty when she got into his cab and she'd made a half-hearted attempt to sound interested in the conversation. Before they'd left the city limits, he'd told her all about his family and that he came from Chandigarh in northern India and how much she would like it as it was a modern town with wide streets. So sophisticated, like Sweden; that's why he felt at home here, though he wished it was a bit warmer. By the time he turned off the E65 to head to the airport, they were sitting in silence. It had begun to rain as they were passing Svedala. Anita's mood, however, was far from dreary; she felt excited and stimulated by the prospect of taking a lead in this case. Commissioner Dahlbeck's backing was giving her the self-assurance to make decisions and direct the investigation with confidence. With no Moberg breathing down her neck, she was experiencing a sense of freedom she wasn't used to.

Malmö Airport, with its sleek, low, bright-yellow frontage,

had been built in the early 1970s, though it had had a makeover ten years ago. It loomed through the taxi's windscreen as the wipers fought against the rain. Anita liked it. It was small, provincial and intimate, unlike Kastrup with its huge, soulless concourses and over-priced shops and eateries. Nor did it have the heaving crowds of passengers; here you were a person, not a number. Malmö's direct routes were restricted to a few internal destinations, some places in Eastern Europe and a handful of holiday hot spots. More importantly, there were frequent flights every day to Stockholm. Anita's 7.30 Norwegian Air flight to Arlanda would only take an hour and five minutes. She bought herself a coffee from the 7-Eleven and watched her fellow travellers gathering: inter-city commuters, business people and others heading for a weekend break or a day trip to the capital. She didn't envy the commuters. Her job might be demanding, frustrating, often boring and sometimes even dangerous, but she wasn't a slave to routine.

The weather was clearer as she watched the countryside get sucked in by the train from Arlanda Airport to the centre of Stockholm. Soon the farms and fields and trees were swallowed up by the urban sprawl of the capital's outskirts. She hadn't eaten on the plane so she decided to grab a bite at the Central Station before walking in the direction of Gamla Stan. Having bolted down an indifferent sandwich, she headed out of the station. She reached the water's edge and passed the Vasä bridge, which links the modern city to the old medieval heart of Stockholm across the Norrström. She cut along Fredsgatan, which was the next street back from the waterfront. *Sanningen's* offices were located in a solid, red-sandstone, turn-of-the-19th-century building that had been given a modern make-over with a high, glass-panelled entrance. Above the desk in the airy reception area was emblazoned WE ALWAYS FIND THE TRUTH in gaudy red letters. At what cost? thought Anita. An unsmiling receptionist said that Elin was waiting for her and that Anita was to take the lift to the third floor.

Anita wasn't sure what she thought a female editor of a sleazy tabloid rag should look like, but it certainly wasn't the small, middle-aged woman that greeted her near the entrance to the lift. Anita knew that Elin Ljung was forty-five, yet her shoulder-length hair was already going prematurely grey (which she did nothing to disguise) and her face was thinly lined – maybe the result of her highly pressured job. She wore minimal makeup, and barely nodded to the latest fashions. But the brown eyes were fiery and determined; Anita found them disconcerting, even a little frightening. She could imagine what useful weapons they were when Ljung was making the tough editorial decisions which were part of her everyday life. The smile that greeted Anita, however, was a surprise and didn't show any of that world-weary intolerance she'd so often come across when dealing with the press over the years.

Before taking her into her office, Ljung politely asked Anita if she'd like a coffee. The office was a high-ceilinged room with copies of *Sanningen's* more sensational front pages splashed across the walls. Anita spotted both Jimmy Brantling and Claes Svärdendahl among them. On the wide desk sat a massive computer screen next to an open laptop, and a huge television dominated one corner of the room. The news was playing silently. While Ljung retreated behind her desk, a young man brought in a couple of coffees and plonked them down. He exchanged a bashful smile with his editor. 'He'll go far if he plays his cards right,' she said with a glint in her eye after he'd closed the door. Anita didn't think she was referring to his journalistic skills.

'So, how can I help the Malmö police? You're a bit out of your patch,' Ljung added as she swung back and forth on her chair.

'I want to know about Sami Litmanen.'

Ljung immediately stopped swinging and sat bolt upright. 'How do you know about Sami?'

'We know that Sami Litmanen is The Oligarch.'

Ljung gave a low whistle. 'There's only a trusted handful of people in this building who know that. What's he done to come to the attention of the police?'

'He hasn't done anything. Someone did something to him.'

'Is he injured?' Ljung's concern sounded genuine.

'I'm sorry to have to tell you that he's dead.' Ljung's face went white. 'He was murdered on Sunday.'

'Murdered?' She was seriously shaken now. Anita took a sip of her coffee to allow Ljung to take in the news. She had just lost her prize newshound – permanently. 'How come we've heard nothing about it?' Her journalistic instincts had quickly returned.

'We're keeping it quiet at the moment, so make sure nothing appears in *Sanningen* yet.' It was a threat, gently delivered.

'Of course, we'll cooperate fully. But when the story breaks, I would appreciate it if we could get in there first.'

'We have a deal then.'

'Can you tell me how he died?'

'No.'

'A hint? Off the record?'

'Sorry.'

'If you're being so cagey, it can't have been nice.' If Anita hadn't known better, she would have sworn that there was a hint of suppressed excitement in Ljung's voice. 'Do you know who killed him?'

Anita's eyes swept round the walls. 'Maybe someone up there.'

Ljung's eyes followed Anita's. 'You think it's one of the people Sami's exposed?'

'It's an obvious starting point, though we're not ruling out anyone at this stage. It would help if we could learn a bit more about Litmanen. He's a shadowy figure. He was living in Malmö under another name, Mikael Nilsson. We couldn't understand why he was living there when most of his targets were based up here.'

'For that reason, really. Stockholm may be the big capital city, but in the celebrity world it's a small town. Everybody knows everybody else. Sami could keep out of the limelight in Malmö. He'd come up here in various guises and then disappear again. It was a practical decision, too. Copenhagen's just across the Bridge and he could fly to anywhere he wanted quickly. He often met up with some of the people he was investigating in foreign locations.'

'We found all his passports.'

Ljung gave a little snort. 'We've got more in the office here. He never used them illegally, mind you,' she added quickly. 'Trying to cross borders, that sort of thing. He liked to have them in case one of his targets, or intermediaries in the process of contacting his targets, wanted proof of whom he claimed to be. And I suppose he'd need them for some of the hotels he used. I don't think he actually used them that much. They just seemed to help him get into the role. He had business cards made up, too.'

'We didn't find any of those.'

'He probably destroyed them as he rarely used the same character twice.'

'Can you tell me a bit about him? We've virtually nothing to go on. How long has he worked here? What did he do before?'

Ljung opened up a can of snus and popped a sachet under her upper lip. 'Not exactly sure, though it's probably about ten years. I've been here three. As you must know, he's Finnish. He worked for papers over there for a number of years; outgrew Finland and thought there were better, more lucrative possibilities over here. He was on *Aftonbladet* for a while before moving here. I don't know much about his personal life, though I believe his mother is still alive and is living in Helsinki. He was never forthcoming about that side of things. His work always came first, second and third. He kept his privacy.'

'While invading others',' Anita commented dryly.

'You could see it like that. We see it as getting at the truth.'

'Even if you distort it?' Anita gave herself a mental slap. By letting her feelings show, she was being unprofessional. She wanted information from this woman, not hostility.

Ljung didn't appear to take offence. 'It's just the nature of our business.'

'I get the impression that Litmanen was initially more interested in what I would call "serious targets". People like the unscrupulous businessman Nils-Åke Rydén, and Folke Allinger and all that right-wing stuff.'

'God, he was scum. Yes. He felt strongly about a number of the people he went after.'

'Yet, latterly, he seems to have concentrated on so-called celebrities.'

Ljung grinned. 'Change of direction by the newspaper owners. That's why I was brought in. Sales were going down. The world's become obsessed with celebrity culture, and we're no different here in Sweden. These are the public figures that we talk about, constantly want to read about; many set themselves up as role models. At *Sanningen*, we like to puncture a few of the myths these celebrities create about themselves.'

'Like Claes Svärdendahl over there.' Anita waved at the wall. 'Exactly.'

'We identified an initial seven potential suspects, which are now down to four, whom we think might have good motives to go after Litmanen because of his work on your paper. Claes Svärdendahl, whom I hope to see later today; the boxer, Absame Madar Geesi, who lives in Malmö; and the aforementioned Folke Allinger and Nils-Åke Rydén. I believe Rydén's only recently come out of prison, possibly carrying a mammoth grudge.'

'And Sami was murdered on Sunday? That's the fourteenth.' Ljung swung round on her seat to a pile of newspapers on a table behind. She thumbed through the heap and fished one out. 'Monday's edition.' She flicked it open. 'Page five.' She held it up for Anita to see. There was a typical paparazzi shot of a man, arm outstretched, trying to shove away the cameraman. The photo was slightly blurred. The man appeared to be extremely angry, his mouth wide open in mid yell. 'It was Nils-Åke Rydén's coming-out-of-prison party up in Umeå. We sent along one of our snappers.'

'That was thoughtful.'

'We wanted to see if he was showing any remorse. The shot confirms that he wasn't. The point is that it was on Sunday evening, so you can take him off your list.'

'That helps. Any of the others, or people I haven't mentioned, who might have threatened The Oligarch, or you, or anybody at the newspaper?'

Elin Ljung, twirling a biro in her fingers, looked thoughtful. 'Claes Svärdendahl did come here shouting the odds. You wouldn't have thought he had a leg to stand on. After all, he was caught with a couple of prostitutes.'

'Which The Oligarch had provided.'

'I'm afraid I've got no sympathy. He could have walked out. No one forced him to have sex with them. By all accounts, he was a bit of an athlete.'

'What did he do?'

'Burst into the building demanding to see Sami. Of course, Sami wasn't here. He hardly ever comes into the... came into the office. Didn't like being seen; used a back entrance. Svärdendahl didn't believe the receptionist. Then he came charging up into editorial and starting shouting about how all us bastards had ruined his life. Security removed him from the building after we threatened him with the police. If he'd been caught with prostitutes here and not in Russia, he would have gone to gaol, so he got off lightly. It would have done him good to spend a bit of time behind bars.'

'I also hear that Absame wasn't too happy either. Came in search of Litmanen, too.'

Ljung waved her hand airily. 'That got a bit fraught. He went berserk and smashed up the reception area. Made a good story, though. Fortunately, he didn't get as far as the lifts or he might have done some of us serious physical damage. The police were called. He said he'd kill The Oligarch if he ever caught up with him. I actually felt a bit sorry for him, as it was his trainer who was the real villain.'

'He's disappeared,' said Anita ponderingly.

'Really? What's Absame doing these days?'

'Working for a local gangster.'

'Might be worth looking into that,' Ljung murmured reflectively.

Anita wondered if journalists like Ljung ever switched off. Did they spend their entire lives sniffing out potential stories? Could they have a normal conversation without thinking whether there was something that could be used or unearthed? It reminded her of an insurance salesman she'd come across many years ago who admitted he couldn't meet anyone, even socially, without thinking they might be the source of his next sale.

'I wouldn't follow that story up. Absame's boss isn't the kind of person you should cross. Put it this way: no one's explained the disappearance of Absame's trainer.'

'You can't win 'em all.'

'Did you have any trouble with Folke Allinger?'

Ljung shrugged. 'Before my time. Though I did hear that the then-editor's car was smashed up before Allinger's trial. And a couple of staff got anonymous calls making death threats if Allinger went down. I believe the editor rang up the head of White Justice...'

'Hans Leonardsson.'

'Yes. Anyway, the calls and threats stopped abruptly. Leonardsson was as keen as the paper was to see Allinger put away.'

Anita finished her coffee. She put down her cup and again glanced around the walls and the stories that the Swedish public had been both horrified and exhilarated to read. 'Is there anyone else who's threatened you personally? Or The Oligarch specifically?'

'Not that I can think of. I mean, we do get a lot of horrible things said about us on social media, but that's par for the course: there's a lot of hatred floating around the web. I wouldn't put much store by that. They're only brave because they're anonymous. There's a big difference between sitting down at your computer and composing a nasty tweet about a person and going out to hunt them down and commit murder. Besides, most of the people who might have had a motive to kill Sami through his work on the paper wouldn't have had a clue where he lived. We didn't. All we knew was that it was somewhere in Malmö.' This thought echoed the one that Anita had been wrestling with – how did the murderer find Litmanen?

Hakim returned to his desk with a fresh coffee. He put the mug down and allowed himself a stretch. His body ached. Too many hours sitting in front of a computer screen and making phone calls. However, the coffee was his reward for some success. He'd discovered what rock Folke Allinger was hiding under – his particular rock was in Ystad. Hakim's feeling of satisfaction was tempered by not knowing how he'd react to meeting such an obvious racist. He was about to take his first sip when Brodd came barging into the room.

'Come on! No time for that.'

'What's up?'

'Absame. He's been spotted near the bus station at Värnhem.'

Hakim slung on his jacket and followed a hurried, if ungainly, Brodd down the corridor. The small bus station at Värnhemstorget was only about five minutes' brisk walk from the polishus, straight down Fredriksbergsgatan and a sharp right onto Östra Förstadsgatan. They saved a minute by running. The street wasn't busy, and only a few cars passed them heading in the other direction into the centre of town. Ahead, the square opened up in front of them and a local green bus sat waiting next to the dusky-pink cuboid block that constituted the station. From a distance, Hakim could see a number of people milling around waiting for buses to appear. Brodd had come to a panting stop, his hands on his knees.

'I told the constable who phoned in to keep out of sight. We don't want to scare Absame off.'

'What's he doing here?' asked Hakim, who was also slightly out of breath.

'Drugs. He's not only muscle for Mitrović, he pushes as well.'

'Can you see him?'

Brodd nodded. 'There. With the tracksuit. Hoodie down. Leaning against the wall behind the woman with the baby wagon. He's waiting for someone.'

'I see him.'

'Well, let's go and talk to him.'

Hakim wasn't convinced that just casually walking up to Absame was going to be the best approach, so he was hanging slightly back when Brodd marched off in the direction of the bus station. As Brodd reached it, the green bus pulled away and another approached from Sallerupsvägen.

Absame could smell cop at a hundred paces. Brodd wasn't even that close when Absame's head jerked up, took one look and darted across the road right in front of the incoming bus. The driver blasted his horn. Hakim dashed after him with Brodd flailing behind, caught off his guard by the boxer's sudden reaction. Absame sprinted down Pilgatan and past the old entrance to the *entré* shopping centre, which now resembled a building site. As they ran, Hakim saw Absame throw something away, presumably his drugs. They could be picked up later.

Absame was fitter than Hakim but, as the young detective had anticipated the boxer's escape, he managed to keep up.

Absame dashed towards the main section of *entré*, which was dead ahead. He was making straight for the main door of the glass and polycarbonate block. Three youngsters were coming the other way. Absame burst through them and sent one girl screaming to the ground. This had the double effect of slowing Absame down and opening the way for Hakim to rush through unhindered. Ahead were two escalators surrounded on three sides by an angular water feature. Absame bounded up the up escalator with Hakim in hot pursuit. The three floors of malls were virtually deserted as most of the shops were now empty, except for a few on the ground floor. Hakim knew there wasn't much left on the top two floors other than the bowling alley and the cinema. Absame was showing no signs of tiring, and Hakim was feeling an ache in his side that was fast developing into a stitch. He wasn't sure where Brodd was.

The boxer headed for the second floor. 'Stop!' Hakim yelled after him. It had no effect. Hakim's long legs took him up the escalator two steps at time, yet Absame had already reached the third floor. By the time Hakim got there, Absame had circled round the glass balustrade that fenced off the escalators and was tearing down the corridor towards the cinema entrance. If he got in there, it would be a nightmare to try and apprehend him. Hakim was beginning to struggle and was acutely aware of his footsteps doggedly slapping on the tiles in the eerily quiet, boarded-up mall. Absame was now way ahead of him. He'd reached the entrance to the cinema and was tugging frantically at the doors. They were locked. Absame turned round in desperation. His exit was barred. The only thing to do was to go straight for the cop. Hakim had nearly reached Absame when the boxer came running back at him, fists swinging. Hakim tried to get his pistol out but he was too slow and a fist thumped into the side of his head and sent him spinning to the floor. He crashed down on the tiled surface, his head feeling as though it was about to explode. He groggily saw the boxer heading towards the top of the escalators. He was going to get away! Suddenly, Absame stopped and, despite his throbbing head, Hakim saw him holding up his hands in surrender. Then the reason became clear – Brodd was stepping off the escalator with his pistol pointing straight at their quarry.

CHAPTER 21

'What was Sami Litmanen like? As a person?' Anita asked Elin Ljung. From what they had discussed so far, the real Litmanen had remained in the shadows. 'You must have known him as well as anyone.'

'"Driven" is the word I would use to describe him. As I said before, the job was everything. He wasn't one for pleasantries. It was always about the project he was working on, or the one he wanted to do next. He was serious about everything he did. I hardly ever saw him laugh. He had a slightly weird sense of humour, but that was probably because he was Finnish. I know he liked the odd drink. We always had to have a bottle of whisky in when he paid one of his rare visits. Again, very Finnish. But never too much. I always felt he needed to be in control.'

'Control freak?'

'I'd say so. In his work, he was very thorough. Always did his own research. Rarely did he involve another journalist to help him until he'd come to us with the full story. Then we'd check that everything was correct – and legal,' she added with a bashful smile, '– before giving him the green light to go ahead. His attention to detail was almost like he wanted to master those he went after. Control their fate. When his stings didn't come off – and some didn't for one reason or another – he would disappear for days, weeks. He couldn't cope with failure. He was almost fanatical.'

'And the paper put up with this behaviour?'

'Of course. Sami created many of our most famous scoops. He got well paid for them, too. And many were incredibly expensive to set up, though they were usually worth the investment if we got a sensational story out of it. An Oligarch exposé ensured that sales went through the roof. The owners would put up with anything from him because he made them money. What Sami wanted, Sami got, even if it was hard for the rest of us sometimes.'

'In what way?'

'Sami was uncompromising. He had a temper if he couldn't get his own way or thought our support wasn't a hundred percent.' Ljung pointed at the front page on the wall featuring Claes Svärdendahl with the lurid headline: MR CLEAN LIKES DIRTY SEX. 'That covers up the dint in the wall where Sami threw his whisky glass when I quibbled about some expenses he was claiming.'

'Did you like him?'

'He was a bloody good journalist. I didn't have to like him.'

Anita was still finding it hard to pin down Sami Litmanen. 'He didn't seem to have a life outside his work. You say he was well paid, yet his apartment isn't anything special. Did he have any other homes?'

'Not that I know of, though he might well have had. Maybe somewhere in the sun or back home in Finland.'

'Did he have girlfriends or boyfriends?'

'He never mentioned any, and we never asked.' Yet there was someone he let into his apartment on Sunday evening, thought Anita. 'He never socialized with any of the other journalists or any of the other staff. Journos tend to be a convivial bunch and love nothing more than to swap stories over a few drinks. Not Sami.'

Anita uncrossed her legs. She was starting to feel stiff. She had done a lot of sitting already today.

'Was he working on any current project?'

'Yes, he was.'

'Oh?'

'I suppose it won't happen now anyway. I think he was getting fed up with all the celebrity scoops. Wanted something a bit more meaty. I got the impression that this wasn't going to be a sting operation; more good, old-fashioned investigative journalism. It was all a bit vague, but it was to do with a couple of big players in the commercial world. Household names.' Ljung held up her palms to Anita. 'And before you ask, I don't know what companies or individuals he was referring to. Sami was like that. He didn't want to reveal his hand before he'd done his research and everything was planned out. He was always very cagey in the early stages until he was sure he was on the right track. Then he would come to me and present his findings and how he was going to nail a particular target. I think he enjoyed the reaction of his editors. His work was often amazing, and he liked to spring surprises on us. Well, certainly on me. He got a kick out of my gushing praise, like a boy who's brought his teacher a brilliant piece of homework.'

'Were there any details?' Anita pressed.

'I know there was an international element to it. During our initial meeting, he said that he might have to book long-haul flights. He knew I was keen to keep tabs on his expenses.'

'So outside Europe?'

'Yeah.'

'Did he take any of these flights?'

'Don't know. He'd book them using money in a fund we supplied him with. Accounting would get the receipts for each month and pass them through to me to check. We didn't want him spending silly money.'

'Was he close to completing this particular job? Did he give an indication of a deadline?'

'No. Sami didn't work like that. Jobs could take weeks... months. I think the Nils-Åke Rydén investigation took about a year. He was given as much time as he needed. With this one, I got the impression there was something seriously iffy going on. Not like Rydén's insider trading. Power plays with high stakes. He did mention that there was history between the protagonists.' Ljung fiddled with the snus can as though she was trying to think of something else. Then she gave up. 'Sorry. Not very helpful.'

Anita shifted in her chair. She felt she'd extracted as much as she was going to out of Ljung. 'Thank you for giving up your time, Elin.'

Anita eased herself onto her feet. Ljung did likewise. 'Always happy to help.'

They shook hands.

'One thing. You say he did all his own research. Presumably, he didn't keep anything from his latest investigation here?'

'No. He'd have it with him.'

'Thought so. His computer's gone, along with any notes he may have made.'

They went to the door.

'Could you supply me with back copies of the stories you ran on Claes Svärdendahl, Folke Allinger, and Absame the boxer?'

'They'll be archived on our website.'

'I'd like to see them in their full glory.'

'No problem.' Ljung paused. 'That was it! I knew there was something! The last time I spoke to Sami was about a fortnight ago. It was the usual; saying that everything was going fine and asking me to top up his fund. No details, of course. It's just at the end of the conversation, he suddenly said "now it's just got personal".'

Anita wandered across the bridge into Gamla Stan, intent on finding a café where she could have a look at the newspapers that Elin Ljung's nice young coffee-delivering journalist had dug out for her. The old streets were so jammed tight with noisy tourists that she nearly didn't hear her mobile phone ringing. It was Pontus Brodd.

'We've got him.'

'Who?'

'Absame. Tracked him down in Värnhem; caught up with him in *entré*.'

'Did he come quietly?'

She heard Brodd chortle at the other end of the line. 'We had to chase him all over the place. Poor old Hakim's got a lump on the side of his head the size of a... the size... well, it's big, anyhow.'

'Is he all right?' Anita asked in some alarm.

'He'll live.'

'Have you had time to talk to Absame yet?'

'No. Thought we'd let you know before we did.'

'Get what you can out of him. It's important to establish that he knew that Sami Litmanen lived in Malmö.'

'Will do.'

'Can you hold him until tomorrow? I'd like to speak to him, too. I'll be back on an early flight.'

'That shouldn't be a problem. Assaulting an officer of the Skåne County Police for starters. And we picked up the drugs he threw away when we chased him. And more good news: Hakim's found where Allinger lives. In Ystad.'

'That's excellent. We'll sort out a visit when I get back.'

'OK, Boss... sorry... Anita. Any luck up there?'

'Useful background info on Litmanen. I'm going to track down Claes Svärdendahl this afternoon. I'll fill you all in on my return. I'm afraid it'll bugger up your weekend.'

'Wasn't planning anything special.'

'Oh, and ask Bea to try and trace Litmanen's mother. She's still alive and living in Helsinki. She'll need to be told, as she's the only next of kin we're aware of. Once she's done that, get her to inform the Helsinki police. Better a home visit than an impersonal call from us.'

After she put her phone away, Anita found a relatively quiet eatery on Stora Nygatan. Though she had only planned on a coffee, the black and white checked tablecloths conjured up the thought of food. She hadn't realized how hungry she was until her eye alighted on the menu. It would be an early lunch, but she could justify it to herself because of the unearthly hour she'd had to get up. Unimaginatively, she plumped for the meatballs with potatoes and loads of lingonberry sauce. It was a detective's brain food – simple and straightforward, and it didn't interfere with the concentration.

As she tucked into her lunch, she went through the newspapers and read the stories that had broken around their three main suspects, all of whom woke up one morning to find their lives changed forever. The oldest of the stories was Folke Allinger's – NAZI MURDER PLOT UNCOVERED. The sub-heading read: *The Night of the Long Knives*, an unsubtle reference to Hitler's murder of his rival and one-time ally, Ernst Röhm, in 1934. Allinger was going to get the fake Finn to organize the stabbing of White Justice leader Hans Leonardsson so it would look like a bar brawl and not a planned assassination. Anita could read the anger and hatred in The Oligarch's words as he explained how he'd uncovered Allinger's plot, though it wasn't clear in the lead piece that Litmanen had set Allinger up. However, there was no escaping Allinger's murderous intent.

The Absame exposé was from two years ago: KNOCK OUT FOR BOXING DRUGS CHEAT. *World champion elect floored by steroid abuse* ran the gloating sub-heading. The 'World champion elect' wasn't quite true, though Absame *was* making a name for himself and held the European middleweight title. The sordid tale was more about the exploitation by Absame's trainer of a naïve immigrant with dreams of success. Absame had taken steroids without realizing the implications. He did now.

Finally, the Claes Svärdendahl sex scandal. Svärdendahl might be a horrible individual off screen and cheat on his wife with prostitutes, yet there was no legitimate reason for The Oligarch taking him down, other than the fact that he *could*. It was all rather unedifyingly voyeuristic; the details and the photos unnecessarily graphic. It wasn't Anita's idea of investigative journalism – it was pure malice. The tone of The Oligarch's work had changed dramatically between the Allinger, his first big exposé, and the Svärdendahl stories. Yet from what Elin Ljung had told her, he was now returning to his serious journalistic roots. So what had he found out about two warring companies? And what had suddenly made it 'personal' for Sami Litmanen?

CHAPTER 22

The sun had emerged from the earlier grey sky. Anita, now rather regretting having had such a large portion of meatballs, walked slowly round to the Gamla Stan underground station on Munkbroleden. She knew she should really walk to Zinkensdamm to let her food digest, and it would also give her time to collect her thoughts before trying to talk to Claes Svärdendahl, but, on the other hand, the train taking the strain was more appealing. It was only two stops – Slussen and then Zinkensdamm. She was at the entrance of the station when her mobile phone went off. She saw that it was Liv.

'Hi, how are you?' Anita asked enthusiastically. Liv was always on her conscience, and she felt herself being over-positive.

'I'm good. I hope I'm not interrupting anything.'

'No, not at all. I'm up in Stockholm on the murder case.'

'Hakim's told me about that. The Oligarch. Quite something.' Anita wondered whether she should mention that Hakim had had a run-in with an ex-professional boxer. She decided to leave that up to him, once he'd got over any bruised pride. 'You must be busy, so I'll make it quick. You asked me to look into whether there was any history or ties between Peter Uhlig and Mats Möller that might single them out as targets for the kidnappers. I'm afraid I can't find anything.' Well, it was always worth a try, thought Anita. 'However, I did find that Peter Uhlig had had a big fallout with another leading industrialist ten years ago. It was

146

at the time when the Uhlig family sold off their cement business to the Hoffberg Cement Group to concentrate on Trellogistics. Sorry, have you got time for this?'

'Yeah. Carry on.' It didn't stop Anita glancing at her watch. Her mind was in Sami Litmanen mode, though she knew she was going to have to learn to juggle the running of separate cases simultaneously.

'Hoffberg wasn't the only company in for the business. Wollstad Industries were also interested – Dag Wollstad wanted to incorporate it into his growing empire.' The name of Dag Wollstad gave Anita a start. 'When Peter Uhlig refused his offer, there developed a war of words in the press. It sounded like Dag Wollstad didn't take rejection well, so when Uhlig sold to Hoffberg for less than Wollstad's reported offer, he made a hostile bid for the remaining freight business. Uhlig managed to fight off the bid, but it left a lot of bad blood. It seems to have widened a long-standing split in the Skåne business community. Uhlig stood for the old, established companies. For stability and conservatism. For ethical business practices. Dag Wollstad was regarded as a Johnny-come-lately. Bold, brash and unscrupulous, who'd stop at nothing to get what he wanted.' That fitted the Dag Wollstad Anita had crossed swords with a few years ago. 'Some of the younger generation of entrepreneurs sided with Wollstad. Of course, Mats Möller wasn't a player then, though I suspect he'd have been in the Wollstad camp if he had been.' Anita heard a little groan at the other end of the phone. 'I'm afraid it may not be of much relevance...'

'No, no, it's interesting, Liv. Any background of this kind might be useful. Look, can you give Klara Wallen a ring and tell her what you've found out? At least we know Uhlig had an enemy, albeit one that's hiding somewhere in South America.'

After finishing the call, Anita made her way down the stairs to the underground. Two minutes later, a number 13 train pulled in. She took her seat and pondered about Dag

Wollstad's name cropping up again. Wollstad Industries was one
of Sweden's biggest and most successful groups. It incorporated
a range of diverse international enterprises, from fertilizers to
pharmaceuticals. A few years before, Anita had investigated the
murder of Dag Wollstad's son-in-law. This had led to a wider
conspiracy, where a group of powerful and wealthy people with
right-wing views were financing attacks on Malmö's ethnic
communities in an effort to cause unrest and drive them out
of the country. Specifically, they had hired a sniper, who was
responsible for a number of deaths in the city and had set his
sights on Anita and Hakim as they got closer to the truth.
Dag Wollstad, the mastermind behind the group, was tipped
off by Anita's now-dead colleague, Karl Westermark, and fled
to Bolivia, beyond the reach of the Swedish authorities. His
business empire was unaffected, as it passed into the hands of
his daughter, Kristina Ekman. Anita had worked out that she
was as culpable as her father, if not more so, and had probably
been the one who ordered the hit on Hakim and herself.
The only problem was that she had had no evidence. So, the
Wollstad family continued to make their millions, presumably
with Dag enjoying a luxurious exile on some palatial hacienda.
The trouble was that Liv's reference to Wollstad had stirred
up past injustices without being of any practical use to the
kidnapping investigation. Anita tried to bury her resentments
and concentrate on the matter in hand – Claes Svärdendahl – as
the train slipped into Zinkensdamm underground station.

Zinkensdamm was on Södermalm, which was regarded by the
press as the hipster island. A lot of beautiful people lived round
here, like the indie singer, Lykke Li. The station, like many of
those on the Stockholm metro system, had its share of artistic
creativity. The concrete wall at the exit was decorated by John
Stenborg. Anita gazed at it sceptically. It resembled a sheaf of
multi-coloured pages fluttering through the air. She was sure

it was nothing of the kind, but it was certainly compatible with the bohemian chic of the area. Anita could well imagine this particular part of the city would appeal to the self image of someone like Claes Svärdendahl, even if he was living in disgrace.

She knew Svärdendahl's apartment wasn't too far from the station. It was bright now, and she hadn't far to walk to the street where the ex-broadcaster lived, on the fourth floor of an attractive cream-stuccoed block. Anita pressed the buzzer, which helpfully had C Svärdendahl next to it; there had been no attempt to hide his identity under another name. There was no answer. Either he was out or he wasn't answering. Though the latter would be understandable, Anita had the impression that Svärdendahl wasn't the kind of man to skulk behind the sofa every time the doorbell rang. He couldn't live without some attention. The fact that he had gone berserk in *Sanningen's* offices didn't bespeak a retiring violet who felt contrition for his misdemeanours. Rather than displaying any anxiety about his sexual exploits being splashed across the front page for the nation to read and being publicly denounced for his faithlessness towards his wife, his ego seemed more preoccupied with what he perceived as unfair treatment and the stripping of the fame he felt entitled to. That's why Anita decided to wait for his return in a nearby café. It was just as well she hadn't planned to fly back that day.

Despite the lump on the side of his head and the headache he was still nursing, Hakim had insisted on being in on the interview with Absame Madar Geesi. Brodd was with him. Across the table, the ex-boxer sat sullenly. His short, black, tightly curled hair complemented his boyish looks. He'd never taken a real battering in his short career. The dark eyes might be a little glazed, but the high cheekbones and soft mouth made him undeniably striking. He was decidedly photogenic, which had helped raise his profile as much as the speed of his fists. These were curled menacingly on the table top, the blingy rings glinting in the fluorescent lighting of the interview room. Hakim watched him closely. He had empathy for the man opposite him. They were roughly the same age. Their backgrounds were similar, even if their parents came from different continents. Both were from Muslim families, both were coping with a social climate that was becoming increasingly unsympathetic to those of immigrant stock, and both were trying to make a mark in a land that was alien to their domestic cultures; yet they were now divided by a simple wooden table – and were on different sides of the law.

'You know why we pulled you in?'

Absame's stare moved from his fists to Hakim. For a second, his eyes blazed with the defiance Hakim had seen on some footage of one of his fights that he'd found on YouTube. Then the light went. He didn't speak.

'It's not the drugs. I assume that's your day job these days.' Not a flicker in return. 'It's about Sami Litmanen.' The name clearly meant nothing to Absame. 'The Oligarch.' This time there was instant recognition.

'We want to know where you were on the night of Sunday, the fourteenth of May,' cut in Brodd. 'Between, say, nine and eleven?' Absame shrugged.

Brodd looked at Absame with contempt. 'Cat got your tongue? Or don't you understand Swedish?' Hakim could have brained Brodd. 'Or is it because you went over to his apartment on Sunday night and killed him?'

Absame's face creased into an unexpected grin.

'What's so fucking funny?' Brodd was losing his temper. 'Do you think murdering someone is something to smile about?'

'I know it's not easy,' said Hakim, trying to defuse a situation that wasn't going to get them anywhere. A blundering Brodd was not what was needed; Hakim wished that Anita was with him instead. 'You've had a tough upbringing. People aren't so friendly round here when you're an outsider. I know all about that. I've gone through the same sort of shit as you. Boxing got you off the streets. You made it. You earned respect. We know how you lost that, and you have good reason to harm the man who destroyed your career. He used underhand methods.' Brodd sighed heavily, clearly unhappy that his direct approach was being usurped. Hakim ignored him. 'He got at you through your trainer. It's only natural that you'd want to get your own back.'

'Kill him, you mean,' butted in Brodd.

'What we want to know is when you discovered that The Oligarch lived here in Malmö. Did you spot him in the street? Or did someone find out for you? Someone like Dragan Mitrović? I'm sure he's got his own methods of finding things out. Maybe – and here's a thought – Mitrović had The Oligarch killed for you. You'd still be an accessory to murder, of course. You'd still go down for it.'

Absame unwound his fingers and stretched them out. Then he curled them up again into those formidable fists. Frustratingly, he just wasn't reacting any more. His facial expression was blank. He hadn't said a word. If Hakim hadn't seen him talking on television interviews, he'd be excused for thinking he was a mute.

Brodd leant over the table. 'I take it that your silence is a confession of guilt.' The same defiant look flashed for a brief moment, then was gone. Hakim hoped that Anita would have better luck cracking this one.

After another thankless ten minutes, they retreated to the corridor outside. 'I think we've got our murderer,' Brodd said confidently.

Hakim gingerly felt the side of his face. 'Now we've got to prove it.'

CHAPTER 23

Two and a half hours and three coffees later, Anita spotted Claes Svärdendahl. It was the hair that gave him away. Though she knew he was forty-one, Svärdendahl had the hair cut of a younger man – the back and sides of his head were trimmed very short, with long strands of his straw-blond top thatch swept back in a quiff. It was a fashion that she'd noticed an increasing number of footballers adopting. According to the magazine she'd read on the flight north, it was called a pompadour. Did Louis XV's mistress really look like that? Since his clean-cut television days, Svärdendahl had grown a hipster beard to go with the hairstyle. He had a tan-leather man bag slung over his shoulder.

Anita was quickly out of her seat and into the street. She caught up with Svärdendahl as he was punching in the code for his building's front door.

'Claes Svärdendahl?'

He swung round so sharply that his bag banged into Anita. 'I'm not speaking to the press,' he said aggressively.

Anita pulled out her warrant card. 'Anita Sundström, Skåne County Police.'

At the mention of Skåne, his face twitched. 'What are you doing up here?' he demanded.

'I want to talk to you about The Oligarch.'

'That's yesterday's news. I've moved on.' He pushed the

door open and strode into the corridor. Anita followed. He marched to the lift and pressed the up button.

'I need to speak to you.'

'I have nothing to say to the police. Or anyone at the moment unless it's through my agent.'

The lift doors swished open. A young couple stepped out. They averted their gaze when they saw Svärdendahl.

'Shall I ask your agent if I can speak to you about a murder case?'

Anita couldn't decide whether Svärdendahl's startled reaction was because of guilt or the fact that such a suggestion had been made in front of his neighbours. He watched nervously as the couple made their way through the front door. The girl's tinkling giggle faded as the door banged behind them and they disappeared into the street.

'You'd better come up.'

The apartment was compact in terms of floor space but seemed larger due to its high ceilings and big windows, one of which opened out onto a balcony overlooking the back of the apartment blocks opposite. It was quieter here than it would have been at the front of the building above the street. The living room was just that. Along one wall was the kitchen area while the rest of the room contained a solitary day bed covered with cushions, an upright piano and a threadbare rug that wouldn't have made the wooden floor any cosier come the winter. The one striking feature was the blue and white floor-to-ceiling porcelain stove that hugged one corner of the room, giving an indication of how old the building was – late 19th century.

When Svärdendahl noticed Anita appraising the piano, he said 'I'm renting. The guy before me was a musician. He still hasn't collected it. I'm hoping he won't. I can't play, but it helps fill the room.'

He hooked his bag over his head and put it down on the kitchen worktop. He took out a half-empty bottle of juice and a tupperware container. He opened the latter and let the contents drop into a pedal bin.

'I've just been out with the kids. My wife lets me see them once a week.' He then took a rubbery spider and a plastic snake out of the bag. 'My son Max is really into wild life. The creepier the better. His mamma hates spiders so I have to keep this one. She won't allow it in the house.' Anita didn't blame her. It was big and realistic.

Anita sat on the day bed. Svärdendahl leant back against the kitchen sink and crossed his arms. He wasn't as tall as he appeared on the television. Close up, presumably without the studio make-up, he wasn't as pretty as in the photo the team had of him on the wall back at the polishus. Now she was near enough to examine him, Anita decided that the face was too thin, the eyes too close together and the mouth too wide. Yet it was this mouth that had been the key to his smarmy popularity – the famous, mischievous, gap-toothed grin that had captivated the adoring house-bound mums and grandmothers who made up the bulk of the audience for his morning show. After his fall from grace, the same feature became a gift for cartoonists, who cruelly widened the gap between his teeth for maximum comic effect. There had been no sign of the trademark smile so far today.

'You mentioned The Oligarch and a murder case. Has the fucker killed someone this time? That guy should be behind bars,' he said with undisguised hatred.

'Can I ask you where you were last Sunday night? That's the fourteenth of May.'

Svärdendahl blinked and his eyes shifted. 'I was away.'

'Away where?'

'Not here.' He was being evasive.

'That doesn't answer my question.'

He unfolded his arms and put them behind him as though he was using the sink for support. 'If you must know, I was down in your part of the world.'

'Malmö?'

'Outside Lund. I spent the weekend there.'

Anita tensed. This was interesting. He was only a few kilometres away from the murder scene.

'And what were you doing down there?'

Svärdendahl's face coloured. 'Is that relevant?'

'Oh, yes.'

'I was at a party.'

'All weekend?'

'Yes.'

'That's one helluva party.'

'It wasn't a normal one.'

'You're going to have to be more specific. Some of the party guests may have to give you an alibi.'

'What do you mean?'

'The party? Tell me.'

Svärdendahl scratched his head nervously. 'It's nothing I'm ashamed of. It's just that if the press got hold of this, it would finish me off entirely. I'm trying to reconcile with my wife. If this got out, it would be a disaster. She'd not let me near the kids again.'

'You'd better come clean. During the time of your party, someone murdered The Oligarch in Malmö. So, you see, I need to know your movements last Sunday night.'

'Oh, Christ! I can't let this get out. I can't have your lot talking to some of the people who were there. Important people. A number from the university.' What an egotistic pain in the arse! Anita thought. All he could think about was himself and his reputation. It was as though the death of Sami Litmanen had absolutely no impact at all. Was that telling?

'Stop prevaricating! What was this party?'

'It was a sex party weekend.'

'Swingers?'

'More sadomasochistic.' Anita's heart sank. She'd rather be spared the details, though she might not be able to avoid them. 'It's all above board. Consenting adults. Since that shit exposed me in his despicable rag, I've been invited on several occasions by private groups of particular individuals to join in their activities. I'm a bit of a celebrity on that type of circuit now. I enjoy it.'

'Presumably your wife doesn't know.'

'Not her scene.'

'Did she know or suspect what you were up to before you were outed?'

'Of course not. I was good. Behaved myself most of the time. Occasionally, paid a girl up in Solna. That's how The Oligarch must have got wind of it. And then set me up.'

'You didn't take much fooling.' Svärdendahl's bashful shrug confirmed how easily he had been duped by the promises of more fame and riches. 'How come you haven't asked me about The Oligarch's murder?'

'Why should I?'

'Aren't you surprised?'

Svärdendahl gave a harsh laugh. 'Of course I'm not. There must be hundreds of people out there lining up to kill the bastard. I'm glad he's dead. Well done, whoever did it! He means nothing to me.'

'That's not quite true, is it? He must have meant something for you to storm round to *Sanningen*'s offices making all sorts of threats. You only left when they said they'd call the police.'

'I was furious. He'd destroyed everything. My career, my family. It was just malicious. I wanted to get hold of him and...'

'And what?'

'Nothing.' It struck Anita that Svärdendahl still thought what The Oligarch had done to him was totally unfair. He'd done nothing wrong. 'I'm over that now. I'm slowly trying to rebuild my life. With my wife. I'm talking to people in the business about possible projects. This will blow over and I'll be back. The public soon forgets.' Anita wasn't so sure.

'When you had no luck finding The Oligarch at the newspaper offices, did you try and track Sami Litmanen down?'

'Sami Litmanen. Was that his name? Sounds Finnish.'

'He was.'

'God, that explains a lot. Whatever he was, he was a good actor. And, no, I didn't try and find out where he was or where he lived.' Anita could tell he was lying.

'You didn't search the internet?'

'All right, all right. I did search the internet. Couldn't find anything about him. It was as though he didn't exist. If I'd known his real name, I might have had a chance. The only thing I could find was what harm he'd done to me on my Wikipedia page. Someone had enjoyed updating that.'

It was getting late by the time Anita left Claes Svärdendahl's apartment. She would have to look for somewhere cheap to spend the night before her early flight back to Malmö tomorrow. Outside in the street, she got out her mobile phone and called Hakim.

'Are you OK?' she asked immediately.

'Presumably Pontus told you,' he said with a groan. 'I'm fine. The swelling's gone down.'

'Thank goodness. Have you and Pontus interviewed Absame yet?'

'Oh, yes. We literally couldn't get a word out of him.'

The sun was still shining. A cold beer in Gamla Stan might be in order.

'You're keeping him in?'

'Yeah.'

'I'll have a go at him when I get back tomorrow.'

'Have you tracked down Claes Svärdendahl?' To Anita's relief, he sounded almost like his normal self. Was she being slowly rehabilitated into Hakim's world?

'Yes. I'm standing outside his apartment. Long chat. He was near Lund on the night of the murder.'

'Wow!'

'We need to check out his alibi.' She paused. 'I think this might be a job for Pontus.'

'He's gone home.'

'You'd better have the details then.' She proceeded to give Hakim the location of the sex party and the names Svärdendahl could remember. When she'd finished, Hakim let out a low whistle.

'I think Pontus is definitely the man for this job.'

'Thought so. I know he's not very diplomatic, but if he has a word with the hosts and establishes what went on that evening, that would be a start.'

'Given the type of activities that supposedly go on at these parties, it might be difficult to trace Svärdendahl's movements.' Hakim sounded rather appalled. 'Presumably the other guests would be preoccupied.'

'They were. Once he realized he was in the frame, he described in nauseous detail what went on in an attempt to clear himself. There are some images that I'd rather forget. The point is he'd only need about an hour to get to Västra Hamnen and back. A few lash marks on his bum isn't a good enough alibi.'

CHAPTER 24

At Arlanda, the weekday commuters were replaced by the holidaymakers and the weekenders as Anita shuffled through security. She reckoned she'd be back in Malmö before midday. As Absame was maintaining an obstinate silence, she was going to have to try and interview him as soon as she returned. That meant she wouldn't be around to meet Kevin. She sent him an apologetic SMS, which she hoped he would pick up when he landed in Copenhagen, asking him to go straight to Lasse's apartment when he arrived and she would meet him there later. A quick exchange of SMSs with Lasse confirmed that he and Jazmin would be around and happy to make Kevin at home. That pleased Anita. Lasse had missed Kevin.

Security had taken longer than she'd anticipated, and Anita had to rush to her gate just as they announced final boarding. She heard her phone going off somewhere in her black hole of a bag. She let it ring while she tried to find her boarding pass – she'd stuffed that back into her bag, too, after going through security. By the time she'd found the phone, the caller had given up. She saw it was Hakim. It could wait. She'd be seeing him in a couple of hours anyway.

The taxi dropped her off at the polishus at five minutes to twelve and she made her way straight up to her office. She tidied herself up and went to the meeting room. She hadn't seen anyone around. She'd expected Hakim and Brodd to be there.

The room was empty. As she took out her phone to call Hakim, the door opened behind her. She had a smile ready for whoever it was. But then it immediately slipped from her face. The person who had entered the room was Alice Zetterberg.

'What are you doing here?' Anita demanded as she put down her phone, Hakim's number unrung.

'Overseeing your investigations.' Anita was dumbstruck. This couldn't be happening! Crime reporter Martin Glimhall had been right.

'Who sanctioned this?'

'Commissioner Dahlbeck. I'm taking temporary charge with immediate effect.'

Had Hakim called to tip her off?

'I don't believe it. I only spoke to him the other day and he was quite happy for me to handle things while Erik Moberg's away.'

'Well obviously, he doesn't believe you're capable enough. He wanted someone more senior.'

It was her sense of superiority that really bridled Anita. One look from Zetterberg would turn anyone's milk of human kindness sour.

'I'm not accepting that. I'll go straight to the commissioner and get this sorted out.'

Zetterberg gave a mirthless snort. 'You'll have a job. Dahlbeck's just gone on two weeks' leave.' That had been another warning ignored. Moberg had told her not to trust the commissioner.

'There must be other senior people around.' Anita was just desperate now.

'You may have noticed that Malmö's got enough gang shootings, grenade attacks and burning cars at the moment to occupy a force twice our size. Besides, the commissioner regards these two cases as high priority, for differing reasons. They need someone of experience to lead them.'

Zetterberg's sarcasm only fuelled Anita's resentment. 'I've got as much experience as you have.'

'I'm already head of a section. You aren't. That says it all.'

'Shouldn't you be running your *little* Cold Case Group?'

Zetterberg brushed off the intended slight. 'I can do that as well.'

'You shouldn't spread yourself too thinly,' said Anita bitterly as she noticed that Zetterberg's stout build had thickened further since their last encounter.

'You don't have to worry about me, Anita. I can handle anything, including you.'

'Well, that's great to hear, but I've got a suspect to interview.' Anita turned back to the door.

'Absame?'

Anita swivelled back round. 'Yes.'

'He's gone.'

'Where?'

'He's been released.'

'On whose authority?'

'Mine.'

'You're not serious!'

'One of Dragan Mitrović's sharp-suited lawyers turned up this morning and got his client out.'

'This is ridiculous. He's one of our main suspects for Sami Litmanen's murder.'

'We'll get round to talking to him.'

Anita stared furiously at Zetterberg. 'I'd better go and speak to my tea... my colleagues and let them know what I found out in Stockholm.'

'They're not here either. I told them to have the weekend off and we'll start afresh on Monday.'

This was too much for Anita. She took two paces towards the door and had it half open when she heard Zetterberg shout behind her, 'If you dare walk out of here, I'll have you officially

taken off the cases. I'll have you suspended for insubordination.'
For an agonizing moment, Anita nearly carried on going. In
that instant, she couldn't have cared less. Yet something inside,
a deep sense of self-preservation, made her slam on the brakes.

'Now,' said Zetterberg, satisfied that she'd won a significant
victory, 'I want you to debrief me on both cases. Then I can
formulate a strategy over the weekend so I've got a plan of
action for *my* team on Monday. No more muddled thinking.'

Muddled my arse. Anita was about to explode again. With
great difficulty, she brought her temper under control.

Over the next hour, with as much self-control as she could
muster, Anita filled Zetterberg in. The kidnappings hadn't
produced any important leads. Two rich businessmen had been
successfully targeted. There were some connections between the
two, and they were working on the assumption that the same
gang was responsible for the snatches, as both victims had been
released in exactly the same way. The little evidence they had
appeared to point to a possible Eastern European or Russian
gang. Naturally, Zetterberg had revelled in Moberg's discomfort
at how easily the team had been duped by the gang when
delivering Uhlig's ransom; she, of course would never have
fallen for such a trick. The team felt that, like Mats Möller, Peter
Uhlig had been incarcerated in a port area. Möller had definitely
been held in Malmö. Uhlig may well have been held in the city,
too, though they hadn't yet ruled out Helsingborg or Ystad.
Uhlig himself had discounted Trelleborg as he was familiar with
the regular pattern of sounds there, including ships' horns.

'So, you haven't really got anywhere,' Zetterberg concluded.
Anita bit her tongue.

At least as far as Sami Litmanen was concerned, they had
three suspects with good motives, which Anita briefly outlined.
As for opportunity, Absame was probably in Malmö at the time
of the murder as he was the only one actually living in the city.
However, without interviewing him, it was hard to establish

whether he had an alibi or not. Zetterberg let that implied criticism pass. They'd tracked Folke Allinger down to Ystad, but hadn't had the chance to interview him yet. Claes Svärdendahl had been near Malmö on the night of the murder at a sex party outside Lund: Brodd was looking into his alibi. 'I would have thought a sex party was more your thing,' said Zetterberg unpleasantly. There it was again; the reason for their mutual hatred: Zetterberg's long-held, but erroneous, belief that her ex-husband had slept with Anita while at the Police Academy. Finally, Anita mentioned that Litmanen had been working on a current project to do with business rivals. His editor had no details other than that Litmanen had remarked that it had just 'got personal'.

'So there's a possibility that the murderer had something to do with Litmanen's ongoing investigation, though we have no idea how advanced that was,' Anita concluded.

'But we have two people that actually threatened The Oligarch in public.'

'Yes. Absame and Svärdendahl, both at the newspaper offices.'

'Well, that's a start. I think, with my guidance, we'll be able to solve these cases before the commissioner comes back off his holiday.'

CHAPTER 25

By the time Anita reached Lasse and Jazmin's small apartment in Rosengård, she still hadn't calmed down. The sight of her family only partly soothed her sense of injustice. As Anita came in, Leyla gave an excited scream of recognition. Anita scooped her up and gave her a big hug. The little girl clutched her tightly. It was such a trusting gesture in Anita's untrustworthy world. The welcome was quickly over and Leyla made it plain that she wanted down. The toddler went off to fetch a cuddly toy to show her grandmother. Jazmin's hug was next. Anita noticed over Jazmin's shoulder that she'd cleared up the living room. Anita smiled; she knew her son's partner was just as messy as she was herself. If she made this effort for her, heaven knows what she did for her own parents, whose apartment was cleaned to within an inch of its life. On second thoughts, it was probably Lasse who'd done the tidying up. She could hear laughter in the kitchen, and Lasse and Kevin emerged with beer cans in their hands. Lasse kissed her on each cheek and Kevin gave her a tentative hug, unsure where their relationship stood. She pulled him to her and it felt good to have close physical contact with him again.

After a very late lunch, Anita drove Kevin back to her apartment. They had done all the 'have a good trip?' small talk at Lasse's. They sat in silence as Malmö's Saturday-afternoon traffic ambled by. No one seemed in a hurry to get anywhere.

Kevin glanced across at Anita. To him, she was just as beautiful and as desirable as ever, though it was clear she had something on her mind. She'd been unusually quiet over lunch and had spent most of the time fussing over Leyla. Was it his return that was the problem? Was she having second thoughts about having him back? He thought it was best to broach the subject before they let things fester.

'You didn't say much back there at Lasse's. Are you OK?'

'I'm fine.' She patently wasn't. He sat back in his seat and stared at the road ahead.

They didn't speak again until she'd parked the car opposite the apartment and he'd taken out his suitcase and they'd crossed the street to the front door. She opened the door with her key and they stepped into the hallway.

'Look, Anita, if you've changed your mind about me staying here, please tell me now. I don't want–'

'Shut up, Kevin. Take me to bed – now!'

Later, over a bottle of wine which Kevin had bought duty-free at Manchester Airport, Anita began to unburden herself. Her frustration with the Zetterberg situation had built up so steadily in her mind that the only way she could think of banishing it was to take a far-from-reluctant Kevin to bed. Through the act of love-making – and it had been energetic and joyous – she had felt cleansed of the aggravation that had been eating away at her. Her final cry of pleasure had been a release of tension. As she had lain beside an exhausted Kevin, she wondered wryly if that's what primal scream therapy was all about. If it was, it had worked for about an hour. By the time she tasted her first sip of wine, the conflicting feelings of exasperation, hatred and inadequacy had resurfaced.

'It's Alice Zetterberg. She's the problem.'

'What's she got to do with the price of fish?'

'You know Erik Moberg had his heart attack? Well, I was put

in temporary charge of the team. We've got two big cases on.'

'You mentioned them. A lot of responsibility.'

'I know. It frightened the hell out of me to be honest. Then, when I was up in Stockholm, I realized that I was energized by the whole thing. At last, I could run things. I had the backing of the commissioner.' She took an inelegant slurp of her wine.

'And?'

'When I got back today, there's Alice waiting for me. The commissioner's put her in charge over me.'

'You're joking!' he said with exaggerated disbelief.

'Wish I was. You know what it's like between us. And she certainly won't have forgotten all that Ivar Hagblom business. Made her look a fool, very publicly.' The memory brought a brief smile to her lips. 'Someone like her doesn't forget. She's going to make my life a misery.'

'But you're good,' Kevin said, trying to be encouraging even if he didn't feel it. He'd come across Zetterberg and had heard enough from Anita to know that the woman could be vindictive. 'And you're strong.'

'I don't feel it at the moment.' Anita held up her nearly empty glass. Kevin refilled it. 'What's more, I can see her hindering the investigations more than helping them. She's already let one of our chief suspects go before I could talk to him.'

'Just try and carry on as though she's not there. Keep stuff back that you can use, and only reveal it when you need to. I do that sometimes when I've had a useless boss; and I've had a few.'

After another large slurp: 'Problem is Alice isn't a useless cop. If she could get over her prejudices, she would be all right. Her real weakness is that she can't think on her feet. She's inflexible. Once she's got an idea into her head... Mind you, we can all be a bit like that,' she added reflectively.

'Look, Anita. Just be professional. Don't antagonize her. And if you have to do things when she's not looking that help the investigations, do them. You'll win in the end. And, remember, if there's anything I can do...'

She suddenly felt a surge of affection for this amusing, infuriating, slightly strange-looking Englishman. She was glad he was here. 'There's one thing you can do for me. Keep this glass topped up.'

On Sunday morning, Anita left a sleeping Kevin in bed. They'd ended up having a late night. She had a quick shower and a strong coffee and left a note saying she'd be back later. They'd go out for lunch so she wouldn't have to cook. She got into her car and drove through the centre of town and out down Amiralsgatan past Folkets Park and on towards Rosengård. When she reached Apelgården, she turned off left. She brought the car to a halt in front of a block of nine-storey apartments. Other identical blocks stretched along the street, plonked there by some giant teaching his child to count. They were similar to so many unimaginative designs in Malmö. Here, the planners had at least made the effort to give the surrounding area some verdancy, with a ribbon of trees running along the entire length of the buildings and a large expanse of grass dividing them from the arboreous boundary of the adjacent Östra Kyrkogården, the cemetery where Peter Uhlig had been dumped. At this time on a Sunday morning, the only person taking advantage of the open space was a solitary dog walker.

Anita got out of her car and locked it: she wanted to make sure it was still there when she got back. She knew that Absame lived on the fourth floor of the nearest block. She reasoned that he probably felt safe now that his protector, Dragan Mitrović, had pulled him out of the police cells, and wouldn't feel the need to make himself scarce. She took the lift up to Absame's floor and stood outside his apartment door. She took a deep breath and found herself running her hand against her regulation police pistol; she had to be ready for any possible violence. She pressed the buzzer. Nothing. This time, she held her finger down continuously. No response. As she headed back towards the lift, a young black boy, about eight years old, wandered past.

'Looking for Absame?'

'Yes.'

'I saw him earlier. Had his bag with him. Gone to the gym,' he said with a broad grin. 'He's cool.'

'Do you know where the gym is?'

'On Sallerupsvägen. Opposite the school.'

'Thanks.'

'I'm going to be a boxer one day. Like Absame.'

'Good for you.'

'And then I can get me and my family out of this dump.' He was very matter-of-fact.

It was easy to park on the other side of the road from the gym as there were very few other vehicles around. The gym was on the ground floor of a 1980s block. This wasn't one of the spanking new gyms that Dragan Mitrović owned that attracted the health-obsessed professionals. This must have been the place where the youthful Absame had come to find a way out of poverty. Both the exterior and the interior had seen better days; so had the swarthy man at the desk. His wispy hair and dark stubble had that unwashed look. He was wearing an aging red tracksuit that hadn't been near a laundry room in some time. He was glued to his newspaper, and Anita could see the telltale bulge under his upper lip – snus. It wasn't just native Swedes that had the habit.

She was about to pull out her warrant card and then decided against it. No need to get his back up before she'd started.

'Is Absame in this morning?'

He didn't even glance up; just, almost imperceptibly, turned his head towards the double doors behind him.

Anita pushed her way into the gym and was met with a sickly wave of stale sweat. In the centre of the room was a boxing ring surrounded by sagging ropes. Beyond the ring, aging punch bags hung limply from the ceiling; all except one, which was being pummelled by a man in a grey hoodie top and white boxing shorts. On the flaking walls were peeling photos of famous boxers. Even she recognized Mohammed Ali. There wasn't a white face among them.

She approached Absame. His constant jabbing of the bag was accompanied by sharp bursts of breath.

'Absame Madar Geesi?'

He ignored her.

Anita took out her warrant card and flashed it at the back of Absame's head.

'Police.'

Absame stopped punching and held out his gloves to stop the swinging bag before he slowly turned round. Globules of sweat were running down his prominent cheeks. His light-grey top had turned dark with perspiration and was sticking to his chest. His proud face jerked up, and the wide, black eyes bored into her. Though the thick, padded, red-gloved hands were now dangling by his sides, she could see that they were tense, ready to strike.

'I've nothing to say to you or any cop.'

She put her warrant card away. 'That's up to you. The only problem is, if you won't speak to us, we may jump to conclusions.'

His brows furrowed. 'Conclusions?'

'That you murdered Sami Litmanen.'

'I don't know who that is.' She knew that wasn't true as Hakim and Brodd must have mentioned Litmanen's name during their abortive interview.

'You may know him better as the Kazakh fight promoter, Erkin Akhmetov. Or more likely, The Oligarch. The man who destroyed your career; the same man you threatened to kill in the offices of *Sanningen*.'

'He deserved to die.'

'Did you kill him?'

'Does herr Mitrović know you're here?'

'I thought you were a big enough boy to speak for yourself.'

'That's *no*, then.'

'Where were you on the night of the fourteenth? Last Sunday night.'

'You'll have to ask herr Mitrović.'

'Why? Are you afraid of him?'

Absame took a stride towards her. She instinctively stepped back, her eyes fixed on his gloves. His right paw was now inches from her face.

'Herr Mitrović is my boss. He's the only person who's shown me any respect.'

Though she was feeling very unsafe, her natural instinct was to continue to needle him.

'He shows so much respect for you that he has you running around town as his little drugs delivery boy. Do you beat up people who upset him, too?'

The glove pulled back and she awaited a blow to her face. She could see the fury in his eyes.

'Get out, lady cop, before I do something that you really will need to arrest me for. Just leave me alone.'

Anita retreated slowly. She wasn't going to admit that she was frightened until she'd left the building. Then she allowed herself some deep breaths. By the time she'd climbed back into her car, she felt calmer. Was Absame their killer? She was none the wiser. And if he was, it was going to be difficult to prove. The obstacle was Dragan Mitrović. He would provide Absame's alibi and a hundred convenient witnesses. Brodd was right to speculate that Mitrović had the contacts to track down Litmanen and enable Absame to carry out his revenge. After all, the murderer had smashed the lamp into Litmanen's head; nothing could have been easier for a boxer. On the other hand, Mitrović was more than capable of getting one of his thugs to do it. This wasn't going to be easy.

CHAPTER 26

'We've now ruled out Ystad and Helsingborg because of the proximity of the railway lines. I've been back to talk to Peter Uhlig, and he can't remember hearing any trains. The container areas that the kidnappers could have used are all close to the tracks. So, our best bet is still Malmö.' Klara Wallen stopped and waited for some reaction from Zetterberg. There wasn't any, so she ploughed on. 'We still haven't been able to trace either the Danish van we believe was used in the Mats Möller kidnapping or the car that they spirited Uhlig away in.'

Zetterberg sighed, so Wallen hurried on. 'The photofit of the man who waved Uhlig down hasn't produced anything from Interpol so far. We've also tried to get a description from Ann-Kristen Uhlig of the so-called policeman who stopped her outside Skårby. She apologized for not giving us a better description, but it's pretty useless. He wore a police cap and dark glasses and she was in such a state of anxiety that she really didn't pay him much attention, which was understandable in the circumstances.' Wallen nervously consulted her notes. 'No luck with the mobile phones used. And, as yet, none of the money paid out has turned up.'

'It's hardly likely to as it was in euros.'

Anita could see that Wallen wasn't sure what to say next. 'That's about it,' she concluded unconvincingly.

Zetterberg watched Wallen distractedly tidy up her notes.

'So, what you're really saying is that you are no further forward. You've achieved nothing.' Anita could see that Wallen was deflated by the putdown.

'I would say that Klara is doing a thorough, methodical job,' said Anita, defending her colleague. 'By the book.'

'You would say that. I'd say that the lack of progress says a lot about this team. A team without a rudder. But things are going to change.'

'We've done everything we could in the circumstances.'

'Like letting the Uhlig ransom money disappear under your very noses?'

Anita stared at Zetterberg in disgust. 'What do you suggest?'

'Actually, there's very little we can do now. Opportunities were missed in the early stages. The gang has carried out two successful kidnaps, so I suspect they are long gone. And if they are from Eastern Europe or Russia, there's virtually no chance of catching up with them. That doesn't mean we stop investigating, of course. For one thing, we need to reassure the business community that we are still pursuing these people and that such a thing won't happen again. Something we can't afford to do is look ineffective.'

So basically, Zetterberg was going to do nothing. Anita decided not to share her thoughts and doubts on the kidnappings at this juncture; it would be a waste of time. She was glad that Wallen hadn't mentioned Liv's research; it might turn out to be totally irrelevant. The fact that she was using an outside source would only give Zetterberg another stick to beat her with.

Zetterberg gave them all a disparaging smirk. 'Now, let's turn our attention to a case that we still have a chance of solving. I'm going to release a brief statement to the press about the murder and that we are pursuing a number of leads. I'm also going to use this to appeal to people who were in the vicinity of Litmanen's apartment to report anything they regarded as suspicious on the night in question. This should have been done before.' The implied criticism of Anita's handling of the case was clear. 'I'll mention Sami Litmanen's name but not who he was as that would spark a media frenzy.'

'That's exactly why the commissioner wanted this kept under wraps,' Anita pointed out.

'I suspect that's because he felt you didn't have the experience to handle the press in the right way.'

'Well, you didn't make such a great job of it the last time I saw you in action,' Anita couldn't resist saying. There was an intake of breath from the others.

Zetterberg just stared at Anita. Her eyes blazed. 'I don't want any of you talking to the media,' she said slowly. 'I'll deal with any enquiries, on both cases.'

After they'd recapped: 'I certainly believe,' said Zetterberg, 'that we have the three main suspects in our sights. So let's concentrate our efforts on them. All have motive, with two actually threatening Litmanen in front of witnesses. Opportunity? We know Claes Svärdendahl was nearby in Lund. I want you, Brodd, and you, Erlandsson, to follow that up. You might find mass heterosexual bonking quite an eye-opener,' she said as a snide aside to Bea Erlandsson. Bea blushed. She knew Zetterberg was getting at her sexual orientation.

'Mirza and Sundström will go down to Ystad and talk to Folke Allinger. He perhaps has the strongest motive as Litmanen effectively put him behind bars. And at the moment, we have no idea where he was at the time of the murder. But he only lives forty-five minutes away so getting to the murder scene would have been easy enough. I expect you to grill him.' Anita knew that Zetterberg was playing with them. From what she'd read about Allinger, he was not only a racist, but he'd also been described as a misogynist. A combination of her and Hakim would immediately put his back up.

'Finally, we have the boxer, Absame. This is going to be more difficult to handle as he's under the protection of Dragan

Mitrović. We'll be hard-pressed to pin anything on Absame, as Mitrović will pluck out an alibi for any occasion. So we need to try and check his movements that night. That means everywhere in Västra Hamnen during the time the murder was taking place. Check any CCTV.'

'We've already gone through virtually everything we can find,' said Hakim. 'As you can imagine, there's not much in the way of cameras in that area. No sign of any of the three suspects specifically. It was dusk around then. Civil twilight was officially 21.59 that night so it was certainly dark by the time the killer left the apartment.'

'Of course, Mitrović may have got one of his people to do the killing for Absame,' Anita pointed out. 'A way of repaying his loyalty. He made it clear that we'd have to go through Mitrović if we wanted any answers.'

Zetterberg gave her a quizzical look. 'How do you know that? I was under the impression that when he was interviewed here, he didn't say a word. Isn't that right, Pontus?' Brodd, who was also looking askance at Anita, nodded. 'So when did he make that clear?'

'He told me.'

'How the hell did he tell you?'

'Erm... I bumped into him yesterday.'

'You "bumped" into him. And where did this happen?'

'Near *entré*.' The gym was in the vague vicinity, so it was nearly true. 'He was there, so I took the opportunity to talk to him.'

'I thought I told you he was off limits at the moment.'

'I thought it was too good an opportunity to miss.'

Anita could see that Zetterberg was furious and obviously didn't believe for a moment that she had accidentally run into Absame. 'And what other gems did you pick up?'

'Nothing much,' Anita shrugged. The gesture only further infuriated Zetterberg.

'Well, make sure you don't "bump" into Absame again. I'll deal with him and Dragan Mitrović.' She didn't elaborate. 'Right, that's the suspects dealt with. Now, I spent part of yesterday at the murder scene to get an idea of the layout, etcetera. Not much there for a successful guy; he can't have been short of money in his line of work. Anyway, can I have an update from forensics?'

'Nothing that's going to help us has emerged,' said Anita staring up at the photos arrayed along the wall. They included the victim in situ as well as the rest of the living room and the office. 'The only clear prints they found in the apartment, other than Litmanen's, belonged to his cleaner. She'd been in two days before; the Friday. He was going out when she arrived. He was just back after being away for a week or so. She didn't know where he'd been. The whisky glass and the cigarette butts had his prints on them. The only other things they've managed to analyse are the torn bits of paper which were left under the drawing pins from the notice board in the apartment, but they got nothing from them. Some were from the same supply of A4 in the desk and other smaller ones were from coloured Post-it notes. The empty drawer at the bottom of the desk had been wiped clean, probably by a handkerchief, so the killer had the presence of mind to cover his tracks. Nothing on the door handles of the office or the front door either. He'd even wiped the top of the lamp, though that wouldn't have given forensics much to go on as Eva Thulin reckoned that the killer used his fist like the head of a hammer and there wouldn't be much in the way of prints from that part of the hand. She says it was a lucky first-time blow, as he wouldn't have had complete control over his aim without holding onto the lamp stand to steady it, and there's nothing to indicate that he did this. Which begs the question, other than physically covering his tracks, what was the killer trying to hide by stealing the notes on the board and whatever was in the drawer? In theory, The Oligarch had already done the damage to our three suspects.'

'Not necessarily,' said Hakim. 'Absame, for example, is tied up with Dragan Mitrović. When setting him up for his fall, Litmanen may have come across Mitrović and was now going to do an exposé on *him*. That might explain the business angle he was working on. *We* know Mitrović is not legit, but the public don't. Then again, Folke Allinger had some pretty unsavoury associates who are now involved in a legitimate political party. Again, Litmanen might have been looking into them and any dubious business connections. Not sure about Svärdendahl. Possibly his sex parties in Lund. Heaven only knows what pillars of the community might be involved in them! That would be a potent combination for a scandal sheet like *Sanningen*.'

'Quite right,' agreed Zetterberg, who was pleased to see that Anita's attempt to steer the investigation in a different direction had been countered. 'There's one other point which you've overlooked. I think the killer deliberately laid the trap which you so effectively fell into, Anita. By taking everything connected with Litmanen's current investigation, it looks like that's where the reason for the murder lies. A classic case of smoking mirrors. Take it from me, having read all the reports so far and considered what evidence has been gathered, we've got the right suspects. This is all about revenge. It's just we don't know which one is the killer.'

'So you're saying that the murder was premeditated?'

'I'm not saying that. If it was premeditated, the killer would have brought a weapon. I think whoever it was took their opportunity while Sami Litmanen was off guard.'

'It still begs the question as to why he let his killer in. That in itself is strange because not even his employer knew where he lived. He was very secretive about that, apparently. Secretive about everything. Even the mobile phone number his editor had was only to be used in emergencies. She would leave a message and he'd call back. That number hasn't been used for weeks. But surely he must have spoken to other people in the meantime.

His mother? Following up on his current investigation? I suspect he had more than one phone and if so, the killer probably took them. Yet, despite all his precautions, he let someone in,' Anita glanced up at the photo of the victim with his hands holding an invisible piece of paper, 'and he certainly can't have felt threatened as he was quite happily sitting reading something, which was later ripped out of his hand by the killer.'

'He definitely let the killer in,' conceded Zetterberg. 'I don't think it was for a cosy chat either, as indicated by the one whisky glass. If it was a planned meeting, surely the other person would have had a drink as well. So why did he let him in? Had he invited him, or did he just turn up on the doorstep? Either way, Litmanen didn't sense any danger. I think Sami Litmanen was the sort to enjoy the control he had over other people's lives. He liked to break them. Except there was one he hadn't broken. And that was the one who killed him.'

'Pontus, could you stay behind? I want a word.'

Brodd arched an eyebrow at Hakim. Was he in trouble? He hung around while the others left the room. After the door closed, Zetterberg switched on a reassuring smile. Brodd was immediately relieved.

'Nothing to worry about, Pontus. You come across as a very good officer.' Brodd tried to suppress his surprise. He'd had nothing but flack from Chief Inspector Moberg, despite being his drinking buddy, and most of the others had given him a hard time on occasions. The fact that he'd attracted such criticism through his own behaviour and misjudgements never really occurred to him. So he was immediately flattered by Zetterberg's words.

'I try my best,' he said modestly.

'Of course you do. We all do. We're a team. And that's where we appear to have a problem. We should all be pulling together in the same direction.'

'And you think we're not?'

'You heard Anita. "Bumping" into Absame. She's kidding no one. We all know that she went out of her way to find him. We have to tread a fine line with him. He has connections. Yet she must have barged in like a bull at a gate. It's going to be harder to make a case against him if he thinks he's under close police scrutiny.'

Brodd wasn't quite sure what she was getting at. He soon found out.

'Anita's a loose cannon. She undermines the rest of the team. I'm sure you can see that. Her actions could jeopardize our investigations. I don't want that happening.'

'How can you stop it?'

'By being forewarned.'

'Forewarned?'

'Yes. I want you to come and tell me whenever you think she's trying to do things on her own initiative.'

'Spy on her?'

'Oh, I wouldn't call it that. It's about keeping control. All I'm asking is that you be my eyes and ears. And if you do a good job, I'm sure Commissioner Dahlbeck will be pleased. I'll make sure that he knows you're a real team player. Think what that might do for your career.'

CHAPTER 27

The drive to Ystad was awkward. Hakim seemed lost in his own thoughts. Anita didn't want to initiate a conversation as she was still treading carefully. Instead, she put her foot down so that they'd reach the small harbour town as quickly as possible.

'I should be angry. I was at first.'

Anita squinted at the passenger seat. Hakim wasn't looking at her but straight ahead.

'Sorry?'

'Liv. I was furious at first.'

'Honestly, I still feel terrible about what happened. If I could change things now...'

'I don't mean that. I'm slowly coming to terms with that.'

Anita was puzzled. She slowed her pace; there was a lumbering truck ahead of them and no chance to pass.

'The research you've got Liv doing.'

'Ah.'

'She told me. I couldn't believe you'd asked her. I've been trying to protect her from anything to do with the job. Any reminders of what she's been through.'

Anita didn't know what to say. The passing lane opened up and she eased the car past the truck.

'But as she said, her condition is a constant reminder. She's always defended you. She likes you. And I suppose I have to thank you.'

Anita nearly swerved into the central reservation as she turned to Hakim.

'What for?'

She pulled into the inside lane and kept an even speed.

'You've given her a sense of purpose. She's loved digging around. Makes her feel useful. She has a role. She doesn't want sympathy; she wants respect. I don't think I was giving her that. I was being overprotective.'

'You love her. It's only natural.'

Hakim muttered something that she didn't quite catch. Whatever he'd said, Anita immediately felt better. Though they didn't speak again for the rest of the drive, the tension between them was starting to evaporate.

Folke Allinger lived at the top end of Ystad. The attractive town cradles the port from where ferries depart daily to Poland and the Danish island of Bornholm. Back from the harbour, colourful streets of low, traditional houses radiate from the main square before morphing into more modern estates and apartment blocks creeping sedately up the hill behind. Allinger's home was close to the ring road that encircled the landward side of the town. Within minutes, they were on a wide, pleasant road with large individual residences on one side and blocks of four semi-detached houses on the other. Some architect had had a challenge with the latter. Each pair consisting of two floors, they were built on a steep bank and were staggered like steps. Allinger lived in one of the lower houses, his aspect facing trees with a small park area beyond. Anita and Hakim descended the steep concrete steps to his front door and rang the bell.

They could smell the booze on Allinger's breath as soon as he opened the door. Anita recognized the brutish, square-jawed face and startled eyes from his photo in the meeting room, but the shaved head was now covered in long, lank hair that showed hints of grey and which partially covered up the tattoos on his thick neck. Personal grooming had gone out of the window along with personal hygiene.

'Yes?'

Anita held up her warrant card. 'Inspector Anita Sundström of the Skåne County Police. This is Inspector Hakim Mirza.' Hakim flashed his warrant card, too. He didn't bother to disguise his look of disgust.

Allinger squinted at the ID. 'Malmö? What are you doing out here?'

'We're working on a murder investigation. We'd like a few words.'

This was greeted by a snort of derision. 'Don't you read the newspapers? I may have gone to prison, but I didn't actually murder anyone.'

'Can we come in?'

Allinger hesitated. 'I don't think I want to speak to you.' He started to close the door.

'It's about the murder of the man who put you in prison.'

The door remained ajar. Then he opened it. They followed him in.

Allinger had already thrown himself down on an old, faded, brown sofa by the time they entered the open-plan living-cum-dining room. The kitchen was tucked in round a corner. The room was filthy; empty beer cans and whisky bottles, brimming ashtrays and the remains of a TV dinner being the only ornamentation. An unpleasant aroma pervaded Anita's nostrils and she hated to think what state the kitchen was in. Through the large picture window, she could see an area of decking, liberally littered with similar detritus. The ultimate in low-maintenance gardening. In the middle, a battered barbecue caked in grease sat forlornly. A huge television dominated the sitting room, and appeared to be the only thing that wasn't second hand. In one corner, there was a small, untidy bookcase. Anita couldn't help but notice the swastikas emblazoned on several of the book spines. Magazines and newspapers were strewn about the floor. Again, it didn't take much mind-stretching to guess the content. She glanced anxiously at Hakim. This was a difficult environment for him to be in. Hakim, however, seemed surprisingly calm.

Allinger rested his feet on a stained coffee table, odd socks poking out from his grey tracksuit bottoms. He leant forward and picked up a half-finished can of beer as Anita and Hakim sat down on a couple of hardback chairs. Anita shifted her backside slightly, as the chair felt sticky.

Allinger waved his can at them. 'Is this the best the Malmö police can come up with these days?'

Anita knew from Allinger's file that he was forty-six. He could have passed for ten years older. She also knew that he was unemployed. His old comrades hadn't come to his rescue when he'd come out of prison.

'We are here about the death of Sami Litmanen,' Anita began. 'You know him better as The Oligarch.'

'Someone killed him? The fucker deserved it.' There was something in Allinger's voice that made Anita think that it wasn't news to him. Yet the story wouldn't appear in the media until this evening. Zetterberg would tell the world that Mikael Nilsson's real name was Sami Litmanen, but there would be no reference to the fact that he was The Oligarch.

'We want to know where you were on the Sunday night before last. That's the fourteenth.'

'Haven't a fucking clue. Pissed in front of that, most likely.' He jerked his can in the direction of the television. 'There's not much else to do these days.'

'Except read.' This came from Hakim.

'Oh yes, I read. You should have a look at some of those books over there. Might persuade you to go back to where you came from. A certain Herr H knew how to deal with your kind. We could still learn from him. And,' looking at Anita, 'some of your lot would agree.'

Before Hakim could come up with a rejoinder to Allinger's

baiting, Anita jumped in. She didn't want the interview sidetracked by the man's loathsome politics. 'You're going to have to establish an alibi,' she said with a warning look at Hakim.

'You suggesting I killed him?'

'You've certainly got motive. And opportunity. You live near enough to Malmö.'

'I'd quite happily see him rot in hell. But there are a few others I'd put away first before I got round to him.' Anita immediately noted that he didn't question the fact that The Oligarch lived in Malmö. No one else seemed to know where Litmanen lived, except his editor.

'You're referring to Hans Leonardsson, the head honcho of White Justice?'

'Him for one. I'd have gone after him first. I think he set The Oligarch up in the first place. Got him to infiltrate the organization so he could root out his rivals.'

'You tried to do that once,' commented Hakim.

'I served my time. I could have made a difference to White Justice. Hans Leonardsson hadn't the balls to go all the way. He's now something to do with the Sweden Democrats. Gone all legit. Pathetic.'

'Why pathetic?' Hakim asked.

'Because the Sweden Democrats are pathetic. They'll never go far enough to cleanse the country of all you fucking immigrants. At least the Nordic Resistance Movement has the right idea.'

Anita could see that he was really riling Hakim. This wouldn't get them anywhere.

'Right, thank you, herr Allinger. That will be all for now.'

Hakim was bemused. 'But–'

'We'll be in touch. Maybe you can come up with a better alibi by then.'

Once outside, Anita mounted the steep steps to the car park.

'Why are we leaving?' protested Hakim.

Anita didn't answer him until she'd reached the top of the steps and was standing next to her car. 'Because we've got to try and establish that he was in Malmö that night. He knew Sami Litmanen was living in Malmö and he knew that he was dead. Of that I'm sure.'

They were standing on the foot bridge that spanned the railway line. It was a good vantage point. Just down the track was Ystad station, where passengers were boarding a train to Simrishamn, the end of the line. To their right, the town; to their left, the port, where two large ferries were berthed. Both the Polferries and Unity Line ships went to and from Swinoujscie in Poland. A smaller ferry had recently docked, and trucks were already trundling off. This was one of the five daily sailings from Rønne, the main town on the island of Bornholm. As the Simrishamn train pulled out of the station and passed under the bridge, Anita's mind briefly turned to Peter Uhlig's kidnap. She realized that Klara Wallen was right about the proximity of the railway line to the harbour. Uhlig was definite about not hearing any trains. Besides, there wasn't an obvious building around that the gang could have used.

'I want it to be him.'

She arched her head round to catch the determined expression on Hakim's face.

'Allinger?' It brought her back to a case that was solvable. 'Well, you've got a lot of work to do when we get back. He hasn't got a car registered so he either travels by train or bus. Actually, you could start here,' she said pointing to the now-empty station.

'And you're convinced he knows more than he's willing to admit?'

'Don't you? Something's not right there.'

'I'm not sure. Maybe I was letting him get under my skin.'

'He's not stupid. He knew exactly what he was doing.

Deflecting us.'

'Even if that's true, how could he have discovered where Litmanen lived? I can't see him as a sleuth. Look at the state of him. And why would Litmanen let him in?'

Anita watched a large, blue articulated truck emerge from the ferry's lower deck and ease its way up and over the ramp and onto the road that funnelled the traffic out of the port.

'I can't answer that. I have no idea why he would let his killer in. Maybe he didn't see Allinger as a threat. Maybe, as you suggested, Litmanen was looking into some of Allinger's old associates.'

'He may be turning into an alcoholic, but I reckon he'd still be as strong as a horse if he was motivated. Hatred would probably do it. I wouldn't like to see him turning up at my door at ten o'clock at night.'

'Agreed. But I do have an idea how he found out where Litmanen lived.'

'Yeah?'

'Did you clock his reference to "some of your lot would agree"?' Hakim raised his eyebrows. 'Exactly. The sad fact is that some of our colleagues still haven't adapted to the way things are in Sweden today.'

'That's putting it kindly. You don't have to tell me.'

'It wouldn't surprise me if one or two ex-members of White Justice were in the force. What if Allinger is still in touch?'

'That's entirely possible. That wouldn't explain how a Malmö cop could find Litmanen's address though.'

'Was he ever cautioned or got a ticket for something?'

'We know he didn't. There's no record of Sami Litmanen in any of the files.'

'What about Mikael Nilsson?'

CHAPTER 28

'You wouldn't believe it,' Brodd said in a way that said *he* couldn't believe it. He'd actually turned red. 'Some of the things...' Now he was lost for words. He turned to Bea Erlandsson for help, but he wasn't getting any from that quarter.

'I'm not interested in what the swingers or sex partyists or whatever they're called get up to,' said Zetterberg impatiently. 'How they get their kicks is up to them. What I want to know is what Claes Svärdendahl was doing on the night of the fourteenth.'

'Well, quite a lot as it happens. He was the celebrity guest and was in great demand. That's according to the woman who runs the parties. Though the guests are meant to be anonymous... well, he wasn't anyway. Face too well known. After that, a lot of other parts of him as well.'

'Which must mean it would be easier to track him.' Again Zetterberg showed her impatience. Brodd hesitated. He seemed to be fighting with the images in his head that their enquiries had created.

'We've managed to speak to about five of the people who were at the party so far,' said Erlandsson, who could see that Brodd was struggling. 'It took some persuading that we needed names until we said that this was a murder case and Claes Svärdendahl was a suspect. And we've still got some to track down. One of the women we spoke to admitted that she'd been

186

with Svärdendahl around half eight, near the beginning of the proceedings.'

'And there was another woman with them,' put in Brodd. 'A threesome. Handcuffs, whips, the lot.'

'They were his first appointment of the evening. She was very frank. Her husband was there, too, but he never takes part. He just likes watching his wife with other people. After Svärdendahl had finished... she used more colourful language... he left her and the other woman to carry on without him. She claims not to have seen him again. The party planner, for want of another name, Gail Goodtimes–'

'That's not her real name, by the way,' butted in Brodd.

'I didn't think it was,' huffed Zetterberg.

'She said that Svärdendahl was around before midnight. He'd tried to hit on her but she "doesn't do the guests", as she put it. He then disappeared into another room for more "romping". Again, her word. What we haven't been able to establish is what he was doing during the time between leaving the two women and when he was seen by the hostess. It may be hard to establish his exact whereabouts as there are a lot of rooms in the house – it's an old mansion – and many of the rooms were in semi-darkness. Apparently, there can be a lot of people in one room seething about, changing partners, and there are constant comings and goings.'

'More comings than goings,' Brodd grinned.

Erlandsson ignored his smutty remark. 'Most of the guests have never met each other before.'

'Total strangers,' said Brodd with amazement. 'They're just at it all night.'

'This seems to be getting us nowhere fast.' Zetterberg was chasing a quick result which would go down well with her superiors. 'OK. Follow up as many people as it takes to narrow down where Svärdendahl was between half past nine and eleven that night.'

'Presumably, they don't film their antics?' Anita enquired.

'No. Though there are a lot of swingers, some are there without the knowledge of their partners. That makes it harder for us to get them to talk.'

Zetterberg had had enough. 'Right, that's all for now.'

'What about Absame?' Anita asked.

'He'll keep,' Zetterberg said dismissively.

'But he's a real suspect.'

'I said we'll get round to him when the time's right. And leave him alone, do you understand?' Anita didn't. Why was Zetterberg so reticent?

They had already discussed Folke Allinger. Both Anita and Hakim had expressed the opinion that he knew far more about what had happened than he was letting on. However, they kept to themselves Anita's theory that a member of the force might have been in a position to tip Allinger off. It would be the sort of thing Zetterberg would make a much bigger meal of than it was worth. Hakim explained that he was going though fresh CCTV footage to see if they could place Allinger leaving Ystad and travelling to Malmö on the day of the murder. So far he hadn't found anything. Hardly surprisingly, Zetterberg was dismissive about Anita's hunch – she dealt in hard facts. Before finally packing them off like a teacher at the end of school, Zetterberg took the opportunity to admonish the team for not pulling their weight. She expected more of them.

Anita hung back. 'Yes?' Zetterberg said sharply.

'Look, Alice. The team... we are doing our best. Some of this stuff we have to shift through slowly and methodically. It's a painstaking process. That's the nature of it. It's not going to happen overnight. But we'll get there. There's no need to put everybody under undue pressure; that's all I'm saying.'

'Are you finished? No wonder you've never got anywhere in this job. What sort of career have you had? You're still just a jobbing detective. You'll never amount to anything special.

You're not focused enough, you're not tough enough and you're not professional enough. I could see that at the Police Academy. And nothing's changed. So off you go and "do your best". But in my book, sometimes doing your best isn't good enough.'

Kevin stirred from a deep sleep. As he woke, he realized he was faced with his familiar nightly dilemma – to pee or not to pee? He could roll over and try and get back to sleep or get up and stumble to the bathroom. The problem was that by the time he'd got back to bed, he would be wide awake and would often lie there for hours before drifting back into whatever strange dream awaited him. On this occasion, the call of nature won. As he eased himself as quietly as he could out of his side of the bed so as not to disturb Anita, he became aware that she wasn't there. He glanced at the digital clock: the bright red numbers proclaimed that it was 4.07. He reached the safety of the bathroom and relieved himself. Back out in the corridor, he saw that there was a light on in the living room. There was Anita on the day bed in only her knickers and T-shirt looking at something on the coffee table. As he approached her, he could see it was a photograph album.

Anita turned to him. 'I hope I didn't wake you?'

'No.' He nodded towards the album.

'It's from when I was at the Polishögskolan at Sörentorp.'

'Police Academy?'

'Yeah. In Stockholm.'

Kevin sat down beside her. He noticed a classroom photo of a very blonde girl in a T-shirt, with glasses shoved back onto her head. 'Bloody hell, is that you?'

'Yes.'

'Shit, you were gorgeous!'

'You mean I'm not now?'

'I didn't mean that,' he said hurriedly. 'You're still stunning. You look amazing.'

'Stop it before you dig yourself into a bigger hole.'

He caught her playful smile in the light of the lamp. 'It's just that I've never seen you in any photos when you were younger.' Then he saw another couple of snaps of her in her first formal uniform. The blue outfit with the white sash and belt and the police hat perched precariously on her head seemed slightly too large for her.

She noticed. 'God, I was so much thinner then. I look so young and keen. Naïve actually. The world was so full of hope. Well, my world was.'

'We all start out like that. It's our job that turns us into cynical old farts. Anyway, why the sudden urge to revisit the past? At four o'clock in the morning!'

Anita turned over a page and there were a dozen photos of young people enjoying themselves. In some they were sat around a table strewn with bottles and cans, drinking, smoking and chatting happily. In a couple, they were dancing. It was easy to pick out Anita, as she was the blondest of the group.

'This is where I met Alice Zetterberg.'

Even Kevin could spot her. She was thick-set even then with short, dark hair. On the next page, there was a photo of just Anita and Zetterberg standing together in their day-to-day uniform, each wearing cumbersome white gloves; the type traffic cops wear. Both were grinning coyly. In another shot, they were relaxing together in what appeared to be a student bedroom.

'You seem friendly enough there.'

'We were. Most of us were in student accommodation; at Kungshamra in Bergshamra. Not just the police cadets; university students, too. Alice was in the same block, so we got to know each other very quickly. She had a beaten-up old car in which she'd give me a lift to the Academy. And it was there that she hooked up with Arne.'

'Which one is he?'

Anita pointed to the group sitting on some grass with a large redbrick building behind them. All were casually dressed. 'That one,' said Anita, pointing to a young man with floppy hair with a centre parting and short sideburns. His thick eyebrows distracted attention from a prominent nose. He was holding court and the others were all looking at him. Alice Zetterberg was gazing at him like a wistful puppy. Kevin took a totally irrational dislike to him.

'Arne was fun.'

Kevin disliked him even more now.

'He was a flirt. Which I didn't mind. Thought he was a ladies' man.'

'And was he?'

'He was quite successful.'

'But not with you?'

She blew out her cheeks. 'No way!'

'So how did Zetterberg get the idea that you'd slept with him?'

'Some of us had a night out in Stockholm. Went clubbing. Alice wasn't there that night as she'd gone home for the weekend. Anyway, it ended up with me and Arne as the only ones left. We got back to our accommodation. We were both pretty pissed and we had a kiss and a cuddle. He did try to get me to go to his room but, even in that state, I knew it was wrong and I refused. No harm done, or so I thought. Then, about a week later, I started to get strange looks from some of the other cadets. It turned out that Arne had boasted about taking me to bed. Of course, it didn't take long for Alice to get wind of it. That was the end. The last couple of months of the course weren't very pleasant. Some of the other girls sided with Alice. I denied it, but no one believed me. Arne and I had been seen staggering back together, so it all fitted.'

'And sleeping with the most gorgeous girl on the course was a feather in his cap?'

'Not sure about the most gorgeous. But it did help cement

his reputation among the other boys.' She gazed at the group again. 'I only ever really kept in touch with Lennart.' She indicated a chubby young man with sandy hair sitting cross-legged. 'He didn't judge me. He was lovely. Sadly, he died a few years later in Africa. Part of an international force monitoring an election. He was shot. Wrong place, wrong time.' She sighed. 'Anyway, Alice and Arne married later and lived unhappily ever after. Well, she did. It was only a matter of time before he went off with someone else. As it turned out, it was Juni, who was in our year as well.' Anita pointed to a pretty auburn-haired girl. 'But as far as Alice is concerned, it was all my fault because I'd led her darling Arne astray in the first place.'

Kevin shifted on the day bed. He suddenly felt cold. He wasn't wearing anything. 'What made Arne go for Alice in the first place? He's not bad looking. She's not exactly Angelina Jolie.'

'Her devotion. She'd do anything for him. She was great for his ego. Isn't that what men like?'

'You don't show me any devotion.'

'What do you mean? I've let you come back despite you being a pain in the backside last time you were here.'

'You cheeky cow,' he laughed and he pushed her playfully over. The glimpse of her rounded buttocks straining against her knickers, and bare legs put an idea into his head. She sat back up, her T-shirt doing little to cover up her shapely bottom half.

'As we're now both awake,' he said, eyeing her lustfully, 'we can either go back to bed and make passionate love, or have a cup of tea.'

'That's a good idea,' she cooed. 'Lemon and ginger would be perfect.'

CHAPTER 29

The gym was busier this time late on a Wednesday afternoon. Anita wasn't quite sure what she was doing here with Zetterberg's warning still ringing in her ears. Maybe it was because of that warning. Like a recalcitrant child, she was doing the exact opposite of what she'd been told. There was little she could do about the other two suspects. Claes Svärdendahl was out of her hands. Hakim had made a breakthrough of sorts and found that Folke Allinger had boarded a midday train at Ystad heading for Malmö on the Sunday afternoon of the murder. She had left him going through CCTV footage from the Central Station, which was an obvious place to get off the train for easy access to Västra Hamnen. At least he knew what train he would be arriving on. If that proved unsuccessful, he would go through footage from the underground station at Triangeln, the stop before. Allinger's movements were now of real interest, especially as they'd found out that Mikael Nilsson, AKA Sami Litmanen, had been cautioned after an incident outside one of the city's nightclubs. He hadn't been charged, but the police had details of his Västra Hamnen address. If Allinger had a friend on the force, then he could have had access to that address, though how they had worked out the connection with The Oligarch, she had no idea. She'd visited the area of the apartment again that morning and asked around, armed with photos of Allinger, Svärdendahl and Absame. The latter two were recognized, but only because their faces had been spread all over the media. She'd had a coffee in the Italian café that Sami Litmanen had regularly breakfasted in. On the wall above Anita's table were two photographs by Mario de Basi: one of Sophia Loren, the other entitled *Italians are Flighty, Milan, 1954*. This one, depicting a woman braving the leering attentions of a crowd of men, caught Anita's eye and set off a train of thought about her role within the department. For several years, she'd felt like the woman in the photo. Her looks hadn't helped. She'd often received the wrong sort of attention: the lecherous glances, the lewd comments, the unsubtle sexual invitations and the physical groping. But what was more damaging was that she had often been sidelined because of her appearance. It was as though you couldn't have both beauty and brains. Attitudes had changed slowly over the years, though some of her male colleagues had never been able to slough off their ingrained prejudice. Yet now that the present team was predominantly female, it was a woman who was judging her by the same criterion, despite the fact that her youthful looks had waned. Zetterberg had always regarded her as a bit of fluff right from their academy days, and her unfounded jealousy had only exacerbated that opinion. Was that why she was at the gym again? To prove Zetterberg wrong? Partly. And partly because she couldn't understand why Zetterberg was reluctant to pursue a very legitimate line of enquiry.

Again, the aromatic wall of stale sweat knocked her back. Half a dozen boxers were busy pummelling their bags, and two more, both wearing padded head gear, were in the ring, sparring under the watchful gaze of Absame. None of them were white. The official Swedish attitude to professional boxing had turned it into an immigrant sport.

Anita sidled up to Absame, the ex-boxer unaware of her presence. One of the fighters was dominating his opponent, who was continually taking evasive action.

'Is he good?' she asked.

'He's got promise.' When Absame turned to see who was making the enquiry, his demeanour immediately changed. 'I thought I warned you.'

'I'm here for the boxing. Big fan of the noble art, as they call it in Britain.' She didn't know one end of a boxing glove from the other, but Kevin had given her a quick crash course with the aid of Wikipedia.

Absame's eyebrows shot up.

'Now Gennady Golovkin; he's some fighter.'

This really threw Absame. He was staggered that this female cop would know about the Kazakh boxer who was regarded as the best fighter in his division and joint holder of four boxing boards' world titles – only the WBO title was missing.

'How–'

'The most feared middleweight puncher there is. Unbeaten, too. Thirty-six fights, thirty-three knock-outs. Did a decent job on Daniel Jacobs in March. Mind you, Jacobs took him all the way. First time GGG had to go twelve rounds. But what about the Canelo Álvarez fight later this year?'

Absame gave it some thought. 'Could be close. Reckon Golovkin will shade it.'

'How do you think you'd have shaped up to him?'

Absame blinked shyly. 'Too early. I wouldn't have been ready yet.'

'The point is that you were deprived of your chance. The Oligarch pretended to be a Kazakh promoter, didn't he?'

'Yeah. Bastard said he was connected to Golovkin. That was his way in. Promised me the earth. I was conned. So was Bogdan.'

'Your trainer, Bogdan Kovač?'

'The idiot blabbed about giving me steroids. I was only on them during the early days. I was a skinny little runt to start with. Built me up. But when I realized they might be doing me harm in the long run, I stopped all that. Bogdan wasn't happy.

I think he was making money out of the steroids. Got some of the other kids onto them. I was clean when I came across that journalist bastard. Not that it mattered when he'd finished with me.'

'Is that when you fell in with Dragan Mitrović?'

The suspicion came back into his eyes. She was pushing too quickly. 'I only ask because he might have been better for your career than Kovać.'

The two boxers in the ring had stopped fighting. 'OK,' Absame called and they ducked out through the ropes.

'Herr Mitrović likes boxing. He would have been good for me. He cares about me. He was angry when my career was ruined. He was angry with Bogdan. He said Bogdan had let the Serbs in Sweden down. But it was Bogdan who taught me everything I know.'

'And he's not around anymore?'

'Disappeared. Probably pissed off back home to Serbia. And good riddance.'

Anita doubted that Bogdan Kovać had ever got as far as Serbia. That was one body that wasn't likely to turn up any time soon.

'Look, Absame, I've got to ask you where you were on the Sunday night that The Oligarch was killed. At least try and give me an alibi.'

'Ask herr Mitrović.' After opening him up, he was on the defensive again. He turned and strode off to the changing rooms.

On returning to the polishus, Anita poked her head round Hakim's door to see how he was getting on.

A boggle-eyed Hakim rubbed his eyes. 'What have you been up to?'

'Don't ask,' she said, coming in and shutting the door behind her. 'And then you won't get into trouble with Zetterberg.'

'So you've been to see Absame.'

'Is it that obvious?'

He didn't have to answer. She put a slice of sticky cake she'd picked up from ICA on the way back from the gym down in front of him. She knew Hakim had a sweet tooth.

'Thought you might need this before Ramadan starts.'

His eyes lit up. 'Thanks. Yeah, Friday. Habit, I suppose. Liv's being very good. She says she's not going to eat when I'm around during the day. When I'm out of sight, that's a different matter.'

She went to the window and peered out. The mixed weather of the last few days was beginning to settle down. It was such a relief to see the trees coming into leaf and the sun caressing the buildings on Kungsgatan. If the weather kept fine over the weekend, she'd take Kevin off for the day somewhere. Potter around southern Skåne. Find somewhere off the beaten track to have lunch.

'Oh,' said Hakim behind her, his mouth full of cake. He swallowed it before continuing. 'Pontus and Bea are rather pleased with themselves as they've found out that Claes Svärdendahl did leave his sex party at one stage. A woman saw him in the car park and get into his car. Then he drove off.' Hakim smirked. 'Apparently, she was disappointed as she wanted to... you know...'

'Bag a celebrity bonk?'

'I knew you'd have the right words. She thought it was around nine, though she couldn't be positive. She saw him again later that night, after midnight, and snared him in a corridor. Didn't bother going into one of the rooms. Up against a wall.' Anita pulled a face. 'If you want more graphic details, Pontus will happily oblige. What she did say, apart from finding his performance rather disappointing, was that she got the impression he was distracted. Needless to say, Zetterberg's all excited, and she's off to talk to him in Stockholm on Friday.'

'That'll give us a break. I'm looking forward to Friday already.'

Anita leant against the window. She could feel the warmth from the sun gently heating up her back. It felt good.

'Any luck with Allinger?'

Hakim shook his head as he wiped the last crumbs of the cake from his mouth. 'No. He definitely didn't get off at Central. I'm going through the Triangeln footage at the moment. Even if he got off there, it would be just before one. And if he went to Sami Litmanen's at around ten that night, we'll have nine hours unaccounted for. He could have been anywhere in Malmö.'

'We'll deal with that problem when you find him.' Reluctantly, she pushed herself away from her sun bath. 'Don't work too late. Go and see that lovely fiancée of yours.'

'And you've got Kevin to rush home to,' he said with a sly grin. Was she getting the old Hakim back?

'Not tonight. He's babysitting Leyla. Loves it. Besides, I'm going to check this Mikael Nilsson incident. I want to know which officers were present and if one of them could have passed on information to Allinger.'

It was after nine by the time Anita had parked her car opposite her apartment. She'd been through the system to find that Mikael Nilsson had been involved in an incident outside a Malmö restaurant two years before. He'd followed a customer out of the restaurant and an altercation had taken place. The manager had phoned the police, who had turned up just as the argument was getting physical. According to the statement Mikael Nilsson gave the two officers at the scene, the customer – one Thomas Olin – had been bad-mouthing Finns. Mikael Nilsson had taken exception to the man's views. After things had calmed down, Nilsson was let off with a caution. In the report, one of the officers had remarked that they thought it was odd that a Swede was so defensive about Finns. Anita had checked out both officers. One had since retired and the other was still based in Malmö. She wasn't sure if it was worth taking it any further given that anybody in the polishus could have accessed the file. At this moment in time, she was more interested in making herself something to eat and unwinding with a nice cup of herbal tea.

She put her key in the front door and, to her surprise, found it was unlocked. Kevin had probably forgotten when he went out. She pushed the door open and wearily headed for the kitchen. She threw her bag down on a chair and filled up the kettle. Then she opened the fridge and found that Kevin had prepared a salad for her, neatly laid out under a wrapping of cling film. What a thoughtful man. She took the plate out and put it on the table. The kettle finished boiling as she fished out a lemon and ginger teabag. She stood with the teabag in her hand, all senses alert. Had she heard a noise in the apartment? No, just her tired mind playing tricks. She took down a mug and poured the hot water onto her teabag. She inhaled the spicy aroma. There it was again! Suddenly, she had the uncomfortable feeling that she wasn't alone. Had Kevin come back early? Unlikely. If he had, he would have greeted her. Yes, she could definitely detect some movement. It was coming from the living room. A burglar? There'd been some break-ins recently in the area. She tensed and looked around for something to arm herself with – her service pistol was safely locked away in the polishus. She found a rolling pin; not much use against a determined assailant. Maybe he would be as scared as she was.

'Kevin?' she called out in the remote hope that it might be him. No answer. She tiptoed along the short corridor to the living room doorway and hovered for a moment before swinging in with the rolling pin raised above her head. There, sitting in the armchair that Kevin favoured, was a man she didn't recognize. He greeted her entrance with a smile.

'I wondered when you'd get home.'

The man was immaculately dressed in a sharp, dark-blue suit. His black shoes were polished to a mirror-like sheen. His white shirt had no tie, his only concession to modern business wear. Anita put him in his early sixties. His hair was still thick, and dyed to match his shoes. It was slicked back in a way that Hercule Poirot would approve of. But it was the face that was memorable. It was strong; the features carved from granite, the cheekbones like rocks. A livid scar cleft the right-hand side almost to the mouth, which was slightly lopsided, enabling it to move from a smile to a sneer in a flash. All this Anita took in but what transfixed her were the eyes. They were large and dark; unreadable. And they were trained on her. What was this man doing in her living room, waiting patiently for her? And how had he got in?

Which was exactly what she asked him when she had composed herself.

'It wasn't difficult,' he said with a wave of his hand. 'Please, take a seat.'

She couldn't believe that she was being asked to make herself comfortable in her own home by an intruder. Yet she did exactly that. There was something in the man's tone that brooked no argument. But it didn't stop her clinging onto the rolling pin on her lap.

'I appreciate that this is an unorthodox way of approaching you,' he said pleasantly in a thick accent that confirmed his Eastern European origins. 'More private.'

She wished that Kevin was here. 'What do you want?'

'I like getting straight to the point. I want you to leave Absame alone. You are harassing him.'

'So you must be Dragan Mitrović.'

'That was most rude of me not to introduce myself. Please forgive me.' Anita would put money on him not using that phrase to many people.

'He's a murder suspect. We need to talk to him.'

'He's not a murderer. I can find dozens of witnesses if needed.' She was sure that could easily be arranged. 'My lawyer made this clear to Acting Chief Inspector Zetterberg.' That explained a lot. So, he'd put the frighteners on her. 'Yet you seem to persist.'

'We need a solid alibi.'

Mitrović pulled out some folded papers from his inside pocket. He reached over and handed them to Anita. 'Witness statements. He was working at my club on the night of your murder. He's good at throwing out troublemakers.'

'Why didn't he just tell us?'

'He's a badly damaged boy. He took all that Oligarch business badly. Lost his confidence, his faith in human kind. At last he's found someone he can trust – my good self.' With a flourish, he put his hand on his heart. Did Mitrović stand in front of the mirror and practise talking like this? He's been watching too many gangster movies, she thought.

Anita flicked through the pieces of paper. She suspected that every name that supported Mitrović's claim that Absame was working at the club that night had a criminal record – if not in Sweden, certainly in the Balkans.

'I can tell you that Absame had no idea that this Oligarch' – he virtually spat the name out – 'was living in Malmö.'

'You like Absame?'

'Of course, he's like a son. He is loyal. I respect that.'

'You'd do anything for him?'

His smile carried no warmth. 'I do not like where this is going. I, too, did not know that the man lived here. If I had...' The implication was clear.

'Like Bogdan Kovač?'

He spread his arms wide and shrugged. She took that as a *yes*. Mitrović suddenly stood up. Anita started. She was still nervous; this was a dangerous man.

'I hope that you understand that I don't want to cause you any harm. Or your son, Lasse. Or the lovely little Leyla.' Anita's throat went dry. How did he know about her family? He didn't have to issue any further threats.

Mitrović patted down his suit jacket until he was satisfied that it was hanging perfectly.

'We'll leave you people alone if you leave my people alone. It's bad for business.' His eyes never left her. 'I will see myself out.'

Sod the herbal tea – Anita needed something stronger. Half the bottle of red had gone by time the front door opened. She jumped.

'Hi,' called Kevin. When he entered the kitchen (she couldn't bring herself to go back in the living room as she felt it had been violated), she launched herself at him, threw her arms round him and hugged him tightly.

'Heavens, I've only been gone a few hours.' He could feel her body shaking. Then she burst into tears.

He coaxed her gently into the living room and armed her with a refill of her glass. She was staring at the chair that Dragan Mitrović had been sitting in an hour before.

'There, right there,' she said, pointing in disgust. Then she took him through her ordeal.

Kevin was fuming. 'The scumbag! If I get my hands on him–'

'There's nothing you can do. There's nothing I can do.'

'He threatened a police officer and her family. Christ! Breaking and entering.'

'That's not going to bring down someone like Dragan Mitrović.' She put down her glass and clenched her hands together on her lap, turning the knuckles white. 'God, if this was some wretched thriller, I'd be the feisty cop who then kicks the baddie's ass. But it's not like that. It's my family he's threatening. I'm flesh and blood. After Westermark's crazy sister got hold of Lasse, I can't put him in danger again. Or Jazmin… or my lovely Leyla.' She was fighting back the tears.

Kevin put his arm round her shoulders.

'We'll make sure nothing happens to them,' he said soothingly. 'In order to protect them, we've got to think like cops. It all boils down to one thing – do you think Absame is the murderer? Well, two actually. Do you think Mitrović is behind it?'

CHAPTER 30

'You're looking a bit glum,' Hakim said cheerily to Anita, who was on her third coffee of the morning. After a sleepless night, she needed constant injections of caffeine.

'Bad night.' She wasn't prepared to let Hakim know about her unwanted visitor just yet.

'This might perk you up. Then again, it might not.' He was carrying an iPad. He laid it on Anita's desk. 'Recognize him?' The CCTV footage was clear. The dishevelled figure of Folke Allinger was getting off a train.

'That's not Triangeln.'

'No,' sighed Hakim. 'It's Hyllie.' Hyllie was two stops short of the Central Station and on the outskirts of Malmö. Its twin attractions were a huge shopping complex, which included the Malmö Arena; and the connection to the Öresund Bridge, and Copenhagen and Kastrup Airport on the Danish side.

'What was he doing there?' Anita muttered.

'He didn't change onto a Copenhagen-bound train. I checked that. Shopping?'

'That's very unlikely.'

'There wasn't anything on at the Arena that night, so he wasn't going to a concert.'

'At least we know he was lying about his movements.'

'Not necessarily. You asked where he was that night, not during the day.'

'You'll have to go through more CCTV to see if he got a later train into town. Sorry about that. We'll send Bea and Pontus to ask around down at Hyllie.'

'You'll have to pass that by our new boss.'

'Point. I keep trying to forget. I'll see if I can get a couple of the guys who are working with Klara's group. It's not as though they're doing much; that really is a dead end.'

Hyllie is a concrete jungle. From the miserable concrete station under the shopping complex, you emerge into more concrete, leavened with copious amounts of glass, which don't make it any less soulless. Even on sunny days, it feels chilly. Swedophiles would probably attribute it to cool Scandinavian design. Anita put it down to unsympathetic planning. The heart of Hyllie is unashamedly commercial, though blocks of housing were now mushrooming all around. Anita wasn't quite sure why anybody would want to live out here except shopaholics and those wanting easy access to Kastrup. She'd decided to come down herself, as it saved her the bother of going to Zetterberg and asking for help. It also got her out of the office. She was still troubled by last night's visit. She'd had difficulty persuading Kevin not to come into work and act as her personal bodyguard. Instead, he'd agreed to go round to Lasse and Jazmin's and keep an eye on Leyla.

Anita decided that the shops were a waste of time. Allinger didn't strike her as the type who was turned on by fashion labels. Bars and restaurants were more likely. Allinger was still hovering at the top of her own list of suspects. He had motive, and now there was opportunity. With help, he could have tracked Litmanen down. Over the years, she'd met suspects that she thought could never have committed a murder, and yet had – and plenty that seemed likely, yet hadn't. Human nature was difficult to fathom, and her instincts weren't always right. So what about Allinger? She could see him killing Litmanen. Prison had given him time to let the thought of revenge marinate. What also kept him at the top of Anita's hit list was her belief that he already knew about the murder when she and Hakim interviewed him.

Two hours later, she'd found his watering hole. According to someone behind the bar who had recognized Allinger's photo, he'd spent around three hours drinking with a friend. He'd seen them both in here before. She took the description of the other man. He was tall, about sixty, poorly dyed brown hair, with a thick moustache, wearing jeans and a white baseball cap. Oh, and he was slightly tanned. Either it was fake or he'd been somewhere in the sun recently, opined the barman. They'd consumed quite a lot of alcohol in the time, though the man in the baseball cap was buying most of the drinks. That figured. She knew the state was financing Allinger. She thanked him for his help. Just as she was leaving...

'The other guy; I think he was one of your lot.'

'One of my lot?'

'Yeah. A policeman.'

The hospital smelt like all hospitals, an antiseptic combination of hope and despair. She'd stalked the corridors in here often enough to experience both. This time she hoped that Erik Moberg was getting better and that it wouldn't be long before he returned to work. That was a thought she'd never expected to entertain.

The signs were encouraging. He was dressed. He greeted her with 'They're letting me out. Ambulance is taking me home soon.'

'That's good.'

'I should have been out of here a few days ago, but they say there were "complications". Either your heart is fucked or it's not. That's not complicated. It must be fine now, but it doesn't stop the fucking stupid dietician giving me this!' He scrunched a leaflet in his hand. 'I'm not allowed to smoke or drink. I can't even eat proper food.'

'I don't think takeaways count as proper food.'

'If you read this,' Moberg waved the leaflet under her nose, 'there's nothing left except bloody leaves.'

'It's all for the best. A healthier lifestyle might be a good thing.'

'Bollocks. I'll wither away.' Anita somehow doubted that. 'On top of that, they're threatening me with a cardiac nurse, occupational therapists, bloody physios; God knows who else. They'll have me running next. Aren't you allowed to recover in peace?'

'Do they say when you might return to work?' She tried to keep the desperation out of her voice.

'Weeks yet.' Anita's heart sank. 'And I've got a case full of damn pills. Christ! Beta-blockers, statins – whatever the hell they are – and everything else under the sun that the quacks in here reckon I need.' He sat down on the bed and it bulged under his weight. 'What I really need is some chocolate. Did you bring any?'

'Sorry.'

He tut-tutted. 'I suppose I'll have to buy my own.'

'I'm sure it's not on your list.'

'You're as bad as they are. Well, as long as you're here, at least you can update me on what's going on at work.'

Anita filled him in on both cases. He listened without interruption, which was a first in itself.

'A fellow cop?' She had finished by telling him about her most recent discovery. 'One of these ex-White Justice people?'

'I assume so. Who else would meet up with Allinger?'

'Makes me sick.' He shook his head in disbelief. 'And you've got a problem with Alice Zetterberg; I warned you the commissioner would stab you in the back. Zetterberg's a piece of work. I saw her being quoted in the press about the failed

Torquil MacLeod

ransom drop, which she conveniently distanced herself from.'

'She wasn't there at the time.'

'That's not the point,' he said angrily. 'We stick together.' He took a couple of breaths to calm himself down. 'What I can't understand is why she's not chasing Absame – or Dragan Mitrović. He's bad news. I've come across him before.'

'She obviously doesn't want to pursue that route.' She was tempted to mention Mitrović's visit, but didn't. Nor did she mention that she believed that Zetterberg had been frightened off by Mitrović's lawyer. Mitrović was exploiting her vulnerability over her family. What had he got on Zetterberg?

'I just can't work for the woman. I can't handle her.'

'You can. Just do what you always did with me.'

'And what was that?'

'Pretend to listen to my instructions then totally ignore them and do your own bloody thing.'

'Erik Moberg's out of hospital,' Anita informed Hakim, who had his feet up on his desk and his hands cupped behind his head. He looked tired.

'When will he be back?'

'Not soon enough.' Anita slumped down opposite her colleague. This was like old times again.

'Any luck down at Hyllie? I've drawn a blank here,' he said with a wave at his computer screen.

'Allinger met up with someone for a drink. He was there until about four.'

'Well, I've been through the Hyllie footage up until about seven, and there's no sign of him. So, he didn't go from your bar to the station.'

'He didn't go to another bar round there. I've been to them all, even the posh sky bar at the Malmö Arena Hotel.'

'We've still got six hours to fill in.'

'The trouble is that my helpful barman thinks that Allinger's drinking companion was a policeman.'

'Ah.'

'Ah, indeed. I've got a description. That's my next job. Find the mysterious cop, and we could be getting closer to our murderer.'

CHAPTER 31

Anita's anticipation of enjoying a Zetterberg-free Friday didn't materialize. Zetterberg was indeed flying to Stockholm to talk to Claes Svärdendahl. Anita had noticed that it was conveniently on a Friday, so she had an excuse to stay in the capital for the weekend. But rather she be there than in Malmö. Zetterberg had called Anita in for a catch-up meeting before her flight – at six in the morning. Anita dragged herself in and sat opposite Zetterberg, bleary-eyed. She knew Zetterberg had done this on purpose; they could have had this meeting last night.

Anita wasn't involved in following up on Claes Svärdendahl's movements, so she could only talk about Folke Allinger. She explained that they had traced him to Hyllie on the day of the murder and he had met up with a friend for a few drinks. Allinger had left the bar at four. As yet, there was no sign of his movements after that. The man he was drinking with was a cop called Dennis Årnell. He was on holiday but was due back on Monday. What she didn't tell Zetterberg was that Årnell had suddenly become of extreme interest to her – he had been one of the officers called to the scene of Mikael Nilsson's restaurant ruckus. Could he have worked out that Mikael Nilsson was actually The Oligarch and passed on his address to Allinger?

'Get on to him the moment he comes in. Anything else?'

'Not really, except we seem to be doing nothing about Absame.' Anita was reluctant to raise the subject as it could have dire personal consequences if they officially probed any further, but she couldn't help wondering what Zetterberg's reaction would be. Had Dragan Mitrović scared her as much as he had Anita?

'We leave Absame well alone,' she said brusquely. Mitrović had done a good job. At least Zetterberg hadn't got wind of her second visit to the gym. 'He's not a suspect at the moment.' Anita was taken aback that Zetterberg was actually dismissing the possibility. She hadn't gone as far as this before.

'And Dragan Mitrović?'

'Him too.'

Who said that intimidation doesn't work?   Then another thought occurred to Anita – what if Zetterberg had been bought off?

After such an early meeting, Anita went out and had a leisurely breakfast on Östra Förstadsgatan. She reckoned she deserved it after having to put up with the insufferable Alice Zetterberg so early in the morning. She was anticipating a quiet day and was looking forward to her trip out with Kevin tomorrow. Mitrović's threat still hung over her like a dark cloud, but if Zetterberg was determined not to pursue that avenue, then the family would be safe. Whether she could just sit back and do nothing was another thing.

She had hardly been back in her office five minutes when Klara Wallen burst through the door.

'I think there's been another snatch!'

Anita accompanied Wallen down to Drottningtorget on foot – it was only a few minutes' walk from the polishus. It was a very familiar part of town because Anita and Wallen often visited the excellent ice cream parlour whenever they needed their spirits lifting. The tree-fringed, cobbled square had been created in the early 1800s when the city's original fortifications were removed.

On the south side runs the main road leading to the centre of Malmö, with its 1960s office buildings. On the north side is a long, graceful, single-storey, yellow-stuccoed building: the old stables for the Royal Hussars, which now functions as a bar. The other two sides consist of apartments; the most graceful constructed in 1907, according to the plaque high up on the wall. It was this building that was to be the focal point of their visit, though their first port of call was one of the office blocks looking out onto the square. A woman was waiting at the entrance with a uniformed officer. In her mid-twenties, she had short ginger hair and a pallid face distorted by worry.

'This is Janet Adem,' said the officer.

'Hello, I'm Klara Wallen and this is Anita Sundström.'

'I hope I've done the right thing.'

'I'm sure you have,' said Wallen reassuringly. 'We need you to take us through exactly what you saw, Janet.'

'I work up there.' She gestured towards the building behind them. 'In an office on the third floor. I was just settling down at my desk. It overlooks the square, straight down that side,' she said, indicating the pavement outside the graceful apartment building. 'I happened to look through the window and I saw this blonde woman coming out of the far entrance of the block just down there.' She pointed towards a doorway. 'It was about ten past nine. Then this white van suddenly drove up from Norra Vallgatan over there and past that end of the Boulebar, just as she came through the door and onto the pavement. Two men in masks jumped out of the back of the van and grabbed her. I... I just couldn't believe it. It was horrible!' Adem stopped for a moment.

'It's OK, Janet. Take your time.'

'Obviously, I couldn't hear whether she was screaming, because of the double glazing... and the distance, of course, but she appeared to be crying out. She was certainly trying to resist the two men.'

'Two men?'

'I assume they were men. They were bigger than the woman. They disappeared out of sight at the back of the van. It drove off quickly and turned down Östergatan. The back doors were closed, so the men must have shoved the woman in the back and got in with her. That's when I phoned the police.'

'Did you get the number plate?'

Janet Adem shook her head in apology. 'I'm sorry.'

'Have you seen this woman before?' Anita asked. 'I mean, in the area?'

'Sorry. I've only been in the job three weeks.'

'Thank you, Janet,' said Wallen. 'This officer will take a statement.' She put a hand on the young woman's shoulder. 'You did the right thing.'

The officer took Janet Adem inside and Wallen called into the polishus to put out an alert for a white van that had recently left Drottningtorget, heading in the direction of Stortorget or Central Station. The chances of a sighting of an unmarked white van were remote, and it had had plenty of time to disappear, but she had to be seen to go through the motions. Then she and Anita walked over to the scene of the snatch and stood on the pavement where the woman had been abducted. The portal she had stepped out from was a tall, wide sunburst; the door itself one of a pair of tasteful design, the glazed insets in the wood giving the whole the appearance of German peg dolls.

'I know these apartments,' said Anita. She pointed upwards. 'The top apartment anyway. That's where Kristina Ekman lived, or lives.'

'Of course.'

Anita didn't have to explain. They had both worked on the case some years before in which Ekman's husband, the owner of an advertising agency, had been killed in his shower in this very building. The investigation had eventually led to Kristina's father, Dag Wollstad, one of the richest men in Sweden, becoming a fugitive in South America.

'Do you think it could be her? Kristina Ekman?' queried Wallen.

'Janet Adem said it was a blonde woman. And she fits the kidnappers' profile. She's as rich as Croesus. Let's go in and find out.'

An hour later, they were almost convinced that the woman who had been abducted was Kristina Ekman. None of the neighbours fitted the description of the woman briefly seen by Janet Adem; nor had there been any visitors, cleaners or delivery people coming in or out of the building at the time of the abduction. Kristina still lived in the block when she was in town, though, according to the neighbours, she was often away on the Wollstad country estate. Her children were at an international school in Switzerland. The old gentleman in the apartment below Ekman's said he'd heard someone walking around yesterday, but not this morning. He'd had his television on loudly. None of the residents had actually seen her in the last few days.

In the centre of the square, they were joined by the two uniformed officers who had been first on the scene, one of whom had taken Janet Adem's statement. A couple of people had seen the white van driving off but not the actual incident.

'Did your witnesses notice any markings on the van?' Anita asked one of the officers.

'One of them said that she thought there was no signage on it; the other didn't know.'

'Thanks. Keep asking around.'

Anita and Wallen walked at military pace back to the polishus.

'This is a bit different from the other two,' Anita said as she strode along. 'Very public.'

'That's what I was thinking,' said Wallen, trying to keep up.

'The other two snatches were done with no one else around.'

'Maybe this was the easiest place to grab her.'

'Possibly. Though, in theory, they could have stopped her on a country road. The Wollstad estate has lots of quiet lanes around it.'

'Perhaps she didn't have a fixed routine. That's what they did with Peter Uhlig: worked out his routine.'

'That's true. As soon as we get back, I'll get the number for her country place. Find out if she's there, and if she's not, warn them they might be receiving a ransom demand. And if they do, to get in touch with us straightaway.'

Alice Zetterberg was sitting on the same seat in Claes Svärdendahl's Stockholm apartment as Anita had sat on a week before. The more he talked, the more convinced she was that Svärdendahl was the killer. She had conflicting emotions. She knew he was a fatuous celebrity, yet she had always rather fancied him when she'd seen him on TV. As she grilled him about his sex party, there was a part of her wondering what it would be like to be screwed by him. She reckoned he would be good in the sack. And all this talk of sex was putting ideas into her head. She had the weekend free in Stockholm. It wouldn't be hard to pick someone up. Compensation for her frustrations over her brother-in-law, who made it obvious on her last visit that he wasn't going to stray from her dreadful, stuck-up sister. Needless to say, she wasn't staying with them this time. In fact, they didn't even know she was in the city.

'Look, I don't know what else to say. I did leave the party early on. I couldn't get a phone signal at the place and wanted to speak to the kids before they went to bed. The car park was useless, too, so I drove a kilometre or so and stopped when I got a signal. I made the call.' He felt in the back pocket of his jeans and eased out his mobile phone. He offered it to Zetterberg. 'Go on, you can check. It'll show that I'm telling the truth.'

Zetterberg took the phone and flicked through the menu until she got the calls made. Then the date. Svärdendahl had made a call at 21.13.'

'You can check the number. It's my wife's.'

'I didn't think you were together.'

'We're not. But I still have access to the kids. And I phone them regularly. It was a bit late for them and she wasn't best pleased. Nothing I do pleases her.'

'Can't blame her. Presumably it came as a shock to find she'd married a kinky sexaholic.'

He didn't rise to the bait. 'Just check it out.'

Zetterberg was staring at the phone. 'The call only lasted nine minutes, twenty-three seconds. That's not long.'

'She wanted the kids in bed. My wife.' Zetterberg noticed he never referred to her by her actual name.

'OK, this proves you made the call, but it doesn't prove where you made it from.' Svärdendahl sighed heavily. 'So what did you do then?'

'As I said, I went back to the party. To do more shagging,' he said aggressively. This woman was really getting under his skin. At least the other cop had been a lot more attractive.

'We can't find anybody to vouch for your movements during that time.'

'There were a lot of darkened rooms. We don't go round formally introducing ourselves at these things. We just get on with it. I couldn't describe all the women I fucked that night.'

'You still had time to nip down the road to Malmö, finish The Oligarch off and then get back to your sexual athletics.' She'd already got him to describe some of the things he and the other house guests had got up to.

'I'm telling you for the hundredth time, I didn't go to Malmö.' For the hundredth time, she didn't believe him.

'That's odd,' said Anita, putting down her office telephone.

Klara Wallen looked up from her paperwork. 'I've just been talking to a guy out at Kristina's Illstorp place called Lothar von Goessling.'

'German?'

'Yes. That's why we were speaking in English. His Swedish is virtually non-existent. He says he's Kristina's "companion", which I take it means boyfriend. He claims that Kristina Ekman wasn't in Malmö this morning. She's out of the country on business.'

'So who's the woman who was snatched in Drottningtorget?'

CHAPTER 32

The answer to the question that Klara Wallen had posed the day before was not a jot clearer the next morning as Anita and Kevin set out for their drive into the Scanian countryside. The description of the white van had been so vague that nothing worthwhile had been reported. A van *had* been found later, burnt out on a rural side road north of the city, but the forensic team could find no clues on their initial inspection other than that it had been white in colour. If this was the van that had been used in the abduction, then the victim could have been transferred to another vehicle. Anita, Klara and the other members of the team had spent the rest of the day down at Drottningtorget, trying to establish the identity of the blonde woman who'd been bundled into the back of the van. The trouble was, despite the time of day, they only had one witness who had seen the actual event, and that was at quite a distance – could she have been mistaken? A number of witnesses had seen a van driving away, but there was nothing unusual in that. Or could Kristina Ekman's 'companion' have assumed that she had gone abroad when in fact she'd been in Malmö all along? Maybe she hadn't told him about her real movements?

That's why Anita was incorporating a detour into their trip to include a visit to Illstorp and double-check Lothar von Goessling's story. She'd reported the incident to Zetterberg in a call to Stockholm last night. She got the impression that Alice had been drinking – it sounded as though she was in a bar. She was typically dismissive of Anita's news and, as there was no obvious candidate for the alleged abduction, Zetterberg was quite content to spend the rest of the weekend in the capital. So there was no way Anita was going to tell her about her little outing to Illstorp.

The day was fine and bright as the concrete surroundings melted away into open fields. The whole of Skåne was coming to life after months of hibernation. Brilliant yellow rape seared the landscape and through Anita's open window wafted the intense, musky smell of the flowers. Kevin, sitting beside her, was gazing intently at the passing countryside. She knew by his expression that a question was about to be sprung at her. She only hoped she could answer it.

'It always fascinates me,' he said, 'that there are so many farms dotted around, all looking virtually the same, but no villages anywhere near. At home our farms are far more random and are often based in or around a community.'

This time, Anita did have an answer.

'Rutger Macklean.'

'Rutger MacLean? Sounds Scots.'

'No, Swedish. It's got a k in there. He was a politician and land reformer. Lived at Svaneholm, a castle on the way to Ystad – quite impressive. Maybe we should go there this afternoon. Your sort of thing. He studied agriculture in various countries.'

'What time are we talking about?'

'Late 1700s, early 1800s.'

'Right.'

'Anyhow, he wanted to make his land more productive. He studied other agricultural economies, especially Denmark. He broke up the existing farms which, like yours, were often based on villages. He divided his land up between seventy-five farms, each with a new farmhouse and barn and roads connecting them all. This proved very productive; the farmers producing more from less land. The system was adopted by Skåne as a whole–'

'In 1802.'

'How on earth...?' She suddenly spied that he was fiddling with his iPhone. 'You've got your phone out!' she said in disgust. 'I try and tell you something interesting for once and you spoil it.'

Kevin was abashed. 'Sorry.'

'I should think so.' She was cross. 'What it won't tell you in Wikipedia is that it broke up communities. I feel sorry for the farmers' wives, stuck out on their own; their support networks gone. It must have been a lonely existence for many of them.'

'Like the hill farms in Cumbria.' She thought that was completely different, so she stopped talking.

After a while he announced: 'My phone is off and put away.'

'Good! You're infuriating.' Then she found she was smiling to herself.

Half an hour later, Anita turned off the main road between Tomelilla and Brösarp and they found themselves winding their way along pleasant country lanes. Another ten minutes, and Anita announced that they were there. She'd already explained the nature of their detour. Kevin was quite happy to make it if there was to be a good lunch afterwards. Anita knew they were getting close, as a mesh fence bordered the road. This was the edge of the Wollstad estate.

'What's that?'

Anita glanced over and saw a squat shape on the other side of the fencing. It moved out of the trees.

'A boar.'

'A wild boar? Fantastic! They were extinct in Britain for hundreds of years, but I think they've been reintroduced – in Gloucestershire, I believe. Not sure everybody's happy about it.'

They drove through a pair of wrought-iron gates and up a long drive. Parkland opened out on both sides. The drive curved round the edge of a large man-made lake.

'That's quite a house,' Kevin whistled.

The building resembled a château, with two elegant wings flanking the main part of the house, which was set slightly back. Over three floors, rows of dark, perfectly aligned windows set in ochre walls glinted in the sun. Anita's mind flashed back to the last time she was here; standing on the steps talking to Kristina Ekman and realizing that she was the mastermind behind the attacks by the 'Malmö Marksman', as he was dubbed by the press. Kristina was unpleasant and manipulative and, as far as Anita was concerned, a criminal. Unfortunately, she was untouchable as there was nothing against her that would stand up in a court of law. If she *had* been kidnapped, Anita wasn't going to shed any tears; it was what Kristina deserved. So why was she here? Professional pride.

The car crunched its way up to the main entrance.

'OK, I'll go inside. Don't know how long I'll be.'

'I'll be fine.'

'Don't stray too far,' Anita said severely. 'I know what you're like. I don't want you doing your famous wandering-off trick and disappearing because something's caught your eye. I want to get away from here as quickly as possible.'

'Trust me.'

She didn't.

The door was answered by the same housekeeper Anita remembered from her previous visit. She was just as brusque, and her sour demeanour didn't change any when Anita produced her warrant card.

'Malmö?' she questioned, having seen the name on Anita's ID. 'This is not your area.'

Anita explained patiently that it concerned Kristina Ekman's residence and presence in Malmö. Fru Ekman wasn't around; she was away. Anita asked if she could speak to Lothar von Goessling if he was in. He was, she grudgingly admitted. She left

Anita hanging around in the cavernous hallway with its array of coat hooks and shoe racks. When she'd visited some years before, at least she'd been treated with more courtesy and been shown into one of the reception rooms.

When Lothar von Goessling appeared, he was much younger than she had imagined; he must be a good ten years Kristina's junior. Dressed in casual clothes – tight blue jeans and an open-necked shirt that showed off his chest hair – he hadn't succumbed to a hipster beard, though the stubble was artfully crafted. The blue-black hair was long and wavy and curled over his shirt collar. The features were strong and the eyes a brilliant blue – the only concession to his Aryan blood. His smile was broad and, to Anita's eye, untroubled. He held out a hand and shook hers.

'I'm Lothar,' he said in English.

'Inspector Anita Sundström.'

'How can I help you, Inspector?'

'We spoke on the phone yesterday.'

'Of course. You were concerned about Titti.' This was the diminutive that Kristina's family knew her by. It had also been the key that had enabled Anita to unlock the mystery of Kristina's part in the 'Malmö Marksman' shootings. The German's approach was friendly, though there was no offer to talk in more conducive surroundings.

'As I said yesterday, we had a sighting of a woman of about Kristina's age outside her apartment building in Drottningtorget. At about ten minutes past nine, two masked men bundled this woman into the back of a van and drove off.' Goessling nodded in concern. 'A white van, which may or may not have been used in the kidnapping, was subsequently found burned out.'

'I appreciate your concern. I know from the press that this has happened before, with the Uhlig family and that young guy...'

'Mats Möller.'

'Exactly. I don't know who this woman is but, fortunately, it's not Titti.'

'Are you sure?'

The broad beam again. He switched it on like headlights. 'I spoke to her this morning. She was quite amused at the thought of someone wanting to abduct her.'

'It's not really something to treat lightly.'

'You're right.' He took the admonishment with a shrug.

'Where is she?'

'Switzerland. A combination of business and pleasure. Wollstad Industries has banking interests over there.' Anita was sure they did: that's probably how they funnelled money out to Dag Wollstad in South America. 'Of course, the children are at school outside Lausanne. She's taking them out for the weekend.'

'We could check that she's left the country. Flights etcetera.'

'You're awfully suspicious, Inspector,' he joked. 'But you wouldn't find Kristina flying with the hoi polloi. She uses the company plane. You can take it from me that she's safe and sound.'

There was no reason not to believe him. He was certainly unconcerned.

'Is there anything else I can help you with?'

'No, thank you.'

He showed her to the front door and gallantly opened it for her to pass through.

'Your English is very good.'

'To get on today you need good English. The international language of business. We Germans would like it otherwise...' He shrugged in acceptance of his country losing that particular battle. 'I spent a year in London working at Sotheby's. The auction house.'

'Even in Malmö, we've heard of Sotheby's. So, you collect beautiful objects?'

'What is the point of life without them?'

'Is Kristina one?'

Goessling frowned, not quite sure how to take her remark. Without responding, he followed her out to the car. There was no sign of Kevin. Goessling noticed Anita scanning the parkland and the trees beyond.

'Looking for something?'

'Someone. My companion has gone walkabout.'

'What the hell does he think he's doing?' Goessling snapped. 'You can't just wander around here.'

Anita spotted Kevin coming out of the trees. 'It's all right, he's here.'

Kevin sauntered over the grass towards them.

'Where have you been?' Goessling barked at him as he approached. 'Titti doesn't like strangers on the estate. She's very private.'

Kevin stared at Goessling in surprise.

'He's English. He can't help himself.'

'He looked upset,' said Kevin when they'd reached the gates and turned onto the road.

'These people are very precious about their property.'

'Nice property if you can get it. I found another wild boar in that bit of wood. Amazing creature. Seemed docile enough, but piss it off and I suspect it could do you some serious damage. Anyhow, how did you get on with the handsome kraut?'

'He was charming until he saw you! Actually, I got nothing. He claims that Kristina is in Switzerland visiting her kids and banking the company profits. Talked to her this morning.'

'Could be lying.'

'Why would he?'

'He might if he'd kidnapped her himself.'

CHAPTER 33

Sunday morning. Anita decided to go for a run round Pildammsparken opposite her apartment. She got up early and left a gently snoring Kevin in bed. Her runs round the park were often liberating: a great way to throw off troubled sleep and give her time to organize her thoughts for the day ahead. It was also good to get some fresh air into her lungs. She had neglected regular exercise of late and was feeling that she was putting on unwanted weight. Kevin's renewed presence in her bed had brought this home to her more forcefully. Not that the skinny sod seemed bothered by her extra pounds; he was still easily aroused. But that was probably because he was a man.

The early sun shone brightly as she pounded down the avenue of tall trees that led to the Plate, the huge circular area that was a magnet for Malmö folk during the summer months. Walkers, picnickers, or those just chilling out flocked here in the warm weather – and many events were held within its impressive barricade of beeches. At this time in the morning though, there were few people about. Another runner, a couple of dog walkers and an old man sitting on a bench with his eyes shut.

She ran a couple of circuits. The second was far slower than the first but to compensate for her legs, her mind was working overtime. Who was that woman abducted in Drottningtorget? She couldn't believe that Janet Adem had dreamt the whole thing up, but no one had come to them to report a missing person. The rural location of the burnt-out van was suspicious and didn't fit the pattern of the spate of vehicle fires that was plaguing Malmö at the moment. She had pondered Kevin's thought that Lothar von Goessling might be behind it. What would he gain? The ransom, certainly. But then, where would he go? Not easy to fade into obscurity, as he must be known in wealthy circles in both southern Sweden and Germany. A playboy with expensive tastes? If that were the case, he'd be better off sticking with Kristina Ekman. All the same, it might be worth checking out lover boy.

After a very slow third circuit, she decided to call it a day. She wiped the sweat away from her forehead. A nice shower was called for and then a leisurely breakfast. Maybe she could persuade Kevin to rustle up a full English fry-up. After her vigorous exercise, she wouldn't feel so guilty tucking into bacon, egg and sausages. She walked back along the avenue towards Roskildevägen. She was nearing the end when she stopped; a black car with smoked-glass windows was gliding along the street in her direction. She stepped behind the nearest tree trunk. She wasn't quite sure why – it was an instinctive reaction. The car slowed down to a crawl as it passed her apartment building. Then it speeded up and disappeared down the street. She was in no doubt who the car belonged to. Dragan Mitrović was keeping an eye on her.

Zetterberg hadn't arrived back from Stockholm when Anita got into work on Monday morning. But Dennis Årnell was there. The uniformed officer bounced into her office with a cheery *hello*.

'You wanted to see me, Inspector?'

Despite the obvious efforts to cover up his grey hair, and the deep tan that turned the lines on his face into dried-up river wadis, she could tell he must be near retirement age. And the stomach on him would make it hard for him to chase any criminals under seventy.

'Wherever you've been, you've certainly caught the sun.'

'Yeah. Tenerife. Lovely hotel by the beach. Great way to relax. Have to admit,' he said, taking a seat opposite Anita's desk, 'I did cheat a bit by having some tanning sessions before I went. Otherwise I'd have turned into a beetroot in no time.'

That explained the barman's description of him. 'When did you go away exactly?'

He appeared puzzled at the question but answered 'Two weeks ago. Monday. That would be the fifteenth. Why?'

'The Sunday before you left, you met up with Folke Allinger in a bar in Hyllie.'

Årnell was immediately on the defensive; the amiable demeanour gone in a trice. 'I might have.'

'I've talked to the barman who served you.'

'Big deal. I had a few drinks.'

'You know that Folke Allinger spent time in prison?'

'I thought our remit was to give people a second chance.'

'How do you know him?'

'That's my business,' he said stubbornly. Anita could tell he was angry. She had punctured his post-holiday euphoria. She was pleased.

'And it's my business when Allinger is a murder suspect.'

'Who's he meant to have murdered?'

'Sami Litmanen.' He looked at her blankly. 'The Oligarch.'

'I didn't–'

'You may have heard of the murder of Mikael Nilsson before you flew off?'

'Yes,' he said, shifting uneasily on his seat. 'I didn't connect it.' Was he lying?

'But you cautioned Mikael Nilsson in 2015.'

'Did I? I've cautioned a lot of people in the last forty years.'

'Did you realize then, or later, that this man might be The Oligarch? The man who put your drinking buddy in prison?'

'Of course I didn't.'

'I repeat, how do you know Folke Allinger?'

'We go way back.'

'To your White Justice days?'

'What do you mean?' he blustered. 'I don't... I never...' That confirmed her suspicions.

'Cut the crap. You were a member. You're not the only cop.' It deflated his indignation. 'What I want to know is why you met up with Allinger.'

He rubbed a well-tanned hand across his mouth before answering. 'I meet up with Folke about once a month. On this occasion, it was earlier than usual because I was going to be away for a fortnight. That drink was like the start of my holiday,' he added feebly.

'Tell me what happened. How long were you in the bar?'

He wasn't looking at her any more. 'Two, three hours.'

'Then what?'

'We went back to my place. I've got one of those new apartments down in Hyllie. Had a few more drinks.'

'And?'

'That's it.'

'Where did Allinger go after he left you?'

'I poured him into a taxi.'

'Why not the train?'

'He was too pissed. God knows where he would have ended up. I gave the taxi driver extra money to take him inside his house when he got to Ystad.'

'I'll need the name of the taxi firm.' He nodded.

'Folke didn't commit that murder. He was in no condition to do anything that night.'

There was nothing more to say, but it didn't stop Anita giving him a parting shot.

'It amazes me that people who join organizations like White Justice because they don't like people with different-coloured skin spend their leisure time trying to change the colour of their own.' She knew it was feeble, but it made her feel better.

An hour and a couple of phone calls later, and she had the confirmation that Folke Allinger had been deposited at his home at 19.16. The taxi driver had had to wake him up and virtually carry him into the apartment. Folke Allinger was no longer a suspect.

CHAPTER 34

Anita reported her findings on Folke Allinger to a surprisingly bleary-eyed Zetterberg at about eleven. Her boss didn't seem particularly interested as she was now convinced that Claes Svärdendahl was their man. As she left Zetterberg's office, Brodd and Erlandsson shuffled in, doubtless to be told to redouble their efforts to prove that the television presenter was not just sitting in his car phoning his young children, but actually heading off to Västra Hamnen to kill Sami Litmanen. Anita happily left them to get on with it. Time not spent in Zetterberg's company was time well spent.

After a brief chat with Hakim to let him know not to bother following up on Allinger, Anita decided to take herself out into the sunshine and find somewhere for a *fika* and a think. She found herself close to Värnhemstorget. She took her coffee out onto a pavement table. There was always a great deal of activity round the square and it was ideal for people-watching. Much of the busyness was centred around the small bus station, as green city buses snaked in and out disgorging and swallowing their passengers. A couple of dads wandered past pushing baby buggies. How times had changed. There were so many stay-at-home fathers these days that every Malmö playground had more than its fair share of men pushing their kids on swings, launching themselves at roundabouts that were going too fast or watching fearfully as their youngsters scrambled ever higher up climbing frames. Maybe Lasse should become a *lattepappa*; fathers who are never far from a cup of coffee. He disliked his low-paid job in the restaurant. He had jacked in his studies twice now – once after the wretched Rebecka dumped him and again a few months ago. The reason he gave Anita was that he wanted to spend more time with Leyla, and both working and studying didn't suit that plan. Anita hoped it wasn't an excuse to loaf around at home. Jazmin also found working in a corner shop a drudge. But she was more driven than Lasse. She wanted to work with immigrant communities but needed some qualifications to get a decent job. Anita had already offered to help them out financially if Jazmin wanted to do a course at the university. She knew Jazmin was tempted but didn't want to accept what she saw as charity. Anita was now in negotiations with Lasse's father to see if he would help out, too, but she wasn't holding her breath.

With immigrants at the forefront of her mind, she saw one that she knew loitering round the bus station. It was Absame, presumably about to make a delivery for his boss. At first she didn't move, unsure whether to go over and speak to him; Dragan Mitrović's threat still clouding her mind and her judgement. But her indecisiveness didn't last long: she found herself leaving the safety of the café table. A combination of disappointment that Folke Allinger wasn't the murderer and being unconvinced that Claes Svärdendahl was guilty persuaded her that this was the only option left at this moment in time.

Absame spotted her as she crossed over the road to the bus station. He didn't bother running. She didn't pose a threat.

'You hassling me?'

'No. I just want to satisfy myself that you aren't a killer.'

'Herr Mitrović says I'm not. He also told me that you wouldn't be bothering me no more.'

'He was wrong.'

He shook his head. 'You won't learn, lady cop, you won't learn.'

'Learn what?'

The grimace of despair was replaced by one of pity. 'My boss is a dangerous man to cross and you've pissed him off. Push him too far and...'

'And?'

'You won't be a cop no more. You won't be anything.' That left nothing to the imagination.

'Why do you work for him?'

'He looks after me. I'm just an unwanted immigrant in this country. It was OK when I was boxing fine. Everybody wanted a piece of me. But after the shit in the papers, I was nothing again. Bottom of the ladder. This may not be the sort of life God planned for me, but I've got a place to live, food to eat and money in my pocket.'

Anita didn't know what to say. She'd had similar conversations with Jazmin, and she'd been born in Sweden.

'Are you going to leave me in peace?' He tapped the pocket of his jacket. 'I've got business to transact and having a cop around puts off the punters.'

Anita walked back to the polishus with a troubled mind. There had been no point trying to nick Absame for drug dealing. That was up to the Drugs Squad to sort out. It would only antagonize Dragan Mitrović even more. She'd be lying if she said she wasn't scared; not so much for herself, more for her family. Her foremost responsibility was to protect them, and she had potentially put them in danger. After work, she'd pop over to Rosengård just to make sure everything was all right.

Further thoughts were put to the back of her mind when she ran into Klara Wallen, who was licking an ice cream. It was hot enough to justify it.

'How's things?' Anita asked.

Wallen finished a lick. 'Frustrating. We've drawn a blank on the missing woman. There's been a public appeal for witnesses.

Nothing yet.' She took another slurp of her ice cream.

They wandered over to the grassy park, the polishus looming above them. The sun made the red brickwork glow, but to Anita it was a gloomy place now Zetterberg was sitting in Chief Inspector Moberg's office.

'I wish we had more CCTV.'

'That's Sweden for you. I was talking about this to Kevin the other day. Britain is saturated with cameras, apparently. There are over six million in the country; they reckon that's one for every eleven people.'

'You're not serious!'

'Genuinely. Not that it helps Kevin much, as he has to deal with a lot of rural crime. Not many cameras out on the hills. In the cities, it's different.'

'The trouble here is getting licences to put up permanent cameras. You have to jump through so many hoops. They make it so flaming difficult. You'd think the authorities would try and make our lives easier so we can keep the streets safer – and find out who it is who's been taken in Drottningtorget.' Wallen nearly dropped the last of her ice cream in her ardour. Anita could see her point, though she was happy that Sweden hadn't descended into a snooper state like the UK.

'Has Alice Zetterberg given you any guidance on the abduction?'

'Huh! No. She's too busy trying to prove Claes Svärdendahl killed The Oligarch. Sent me away with a flea in my ear with instructions to find the "phantom woman". Her words. I think she half-believes that Janet Adem has made it all up.'

'I'm beginning to wonder.'

'And your visit to Illstorp hasn't helped as it's only proved that the woman couldn't have been Kristina Ekman.' This time, she did drop the remains of her ice cream. 'Sod it!'

They started to wander back towards the polishus.

'How are things at home?' Anita had wanted to ask for a

while without being able to find the right opportunity. She'd sensed that not all was well with Saint Rolf.

'Not good. Rolf's such a selfish bastard.' Anita almost found herself cheering. Klara was seeing the light at last. 'He has me running around like a demented flea. Do this, do that. Where's my breakfast? Where's my dinner? And he doesn't lift a finger. I've got a bloody job, too!' Her frustration was almost tangible.

They crossed the road. 'And I've got a commute. I miss Malmö. Ystad is where he comes from. It's where his ghastly family lives. And his awful friends. Not that I often meet them. He buggers off to see them at his local bar once he's scoffed down his meal.'

'Why don't you move back here? Cut out the travel. Would make your life easier.'

'I'd never get Rolf to budge.'

'You don't have to bring him.'

Wallen stopped stock-still on the pavement. She held up a hand to shield the sun from her eyes.

'Anita, do you fancy a drink after work? We haven't done that for ages.' Anita wanted to go and see Lasse and family. Wallen noticed the hesitation. 'Don't worry if you're busy.'

'It's just I was going to see Leyla.' Wallen couldn't disguise her disappointment. 'Tell you what, can we make it a bit later? I'll see them first then meet you for a drink.'

'That would be brilliant!' Klara said gratefully. 'Oh, but what about Kevin?'

Anita waved a hand. 'Don't worry about Kevin. He can look after himself tonight. But what about Rolf?'

'He can go and...' The rest was drowned out by the sound of a passing bus.

Anita and Klara Wallen walked tipsily past the Malmö Theatre. It was after eleven and the lights from the building's large windows flooded the concourse. The 'drink' had turned into a bit of a session as Klara Wallen had poured her heart out. Anita was glad that she'd managed to get to Lasse's before meeting Wallen. All seemed fine in Rosengård. Lasse had wondered why she'd asked if he'd seen any black cars with tinted windows in the street. He hadn't, and when he pressed her, she said it was to do with an ongoing investigation; said she was just curious. Anita was also grateful that after polishing off a bottle of expensive red wine at a bar, she and Klara had sensibly had a pizza to line their stomachs. Less sensibly, they'd gone through another bottle of wine. Then they'd popped into The Pickwick for a nightcap. Anita had had a beer, which wasn't necessarily a good idea – she could never remember the adage about grape before grain or the other way round. Whatever, she was probably going to suffer tomorrow. The upshot was that Anita had insisted that Wallen stay the night at Roskildevägen – and stuff Rolf. Wallen had happily agreed; the booze having given her the courage – and the nerve to answer a call from Rolf demanding to know where she was and why there hadn't been food on the table when he got home. Anita hoped that Wallen wouldn't regret telling him where he could shove his evening meal. She might end up staying more than one night.

'You've got it made, Anita,' Wallen slurred into Anita's ear.

'How?'

'You and your man. He's not around all the time. You see him when you want to and do what you want when he's not here... if you see what I mean.'

'I like that.'

'He's not demanding.'

'He's irritating.'

'But only irritating for short periods. You can keep things fresh.'

Now they'd reached Carl Gustafs väg and were waiting for the pedestrian lights to change, even though there was no traffic on the road.

'I suppose we can.' Anita was quite pleased that someone else was envious of her long-distance relationship.

'Is the sex good?'

Anita sniggered. 'Yeah. It is. And it's funny with him.'

The green man appeared and the accompanying bleeping alerted them, and they crossed over unsteadily.

'What do you mean "funny"? Weird?'

'No, ha ha funny. Makes me laugh even when we're at it sometimes. That's because he keeps talking and I have to think of imaginative ways of shutting him up.'

Wallen snorted. 'God, Rolf just humps, grunts and then falls asleep. Snores like a pig.'

'Then Kevin does have something in common with Rolf,' Anita snickered.

'But the thing is with you,' Wallen said, wagging a finger at her, 'it's not every bloody night, because your man's not there every bloody night. Maybe I'm just fed up with Rolf.'

'Do you love him?'

'I don't know.'

'Do you like him?'

'Aren't they the same?'

'You can love someone; it doesn't mean you like them.'

That led to silence as they wobbled down Roskildevägen, both women reflecting on their lots in life. It was Wallen who noticed it first.

'Look!' she shouted.

Some distance away, on the park side of the road, there was a car engulfed in flames. Anita sobered up immediately when she realized that it was her Skoda. She found herself running towards it and was oblivious to Wallen's screamed warning. She was virtually on the opposite side of the street when there was an instantaneous whoosh of flame and a thunderous crack which split the night. Anita felt her feet fly from under her and as she hit the pavement, her world went black.

CHAPTER 35

Kevin and Wallen were pictures of concern. Anita had come round after a few minutes and soon after that the paramedics were on the scene. They'd tried to persuade her to let them take her to the hospital, but after being checked over and patched up in the ambulance, all she wanted to do was to go back to her own apartment. With some reluctance, they let her have her way. She was told that if she felt sick, she should contact them immediately; she could have concussion – she promised she would. She had a couple of nasty facial cuts, a thumping headache and she felt like she was under water. Klara Wallen's warning had been all too prescient as she'd realized that the car might blow when the petrol tank caught fire. Fortunately, Anita had been far enough away from the explosion for it to cause any serious damage. She was now sitting in her living room, the window blind pulled up to show what remained of her car. Very little. The fire brigade had doused the flames and the tangle of metal that had once been her Skoda now sat forlornly between the vehicles on either side, which had both had their windows blown out.

The police, when they arrived, could only shrug. This was the seventieth car to be torched in the last few months in Malmö; Anita knew that her colleagues had been battling this plague without much success. One theory doing the rounds of the polishus was that criminals were lashing out because of recent crackdowns on organized crime and were sending out young vandals to do as much damage as possible. It tied up a lot of police man hours. The officer whom she spoke to after the incident reassured her that the culprits weren't targeting individuals as such and the arson attacks were random. It didn't make Anita feel any better. And, rubbing salt into the wound, one of the firemen had told her that it was unusual for petrol tanks to blow up and only possible if the tank was pretty much empty. Of course, she'd forgotten to fill up again. She was furious that she'd be without a car. Kevin told her not to worry – the priority was to get herself right.

It was well after one when the street was quiet once again: the police, the emergency services and the inquisitive neighbours were gone. Kevin managed to persuade Anita to come to bed. Klara Wallen had disappeared into Lasse's old room some time before, the noise of the explosion not helping her fuzzy head. Anita's brain was still addled; her headache had subsided after taking medication, but her cuts were stinging and her hearing was still muted. Her only consolation was that at least she wouldn't be kept awake by Kevin's snoring. She rolled over and snuggled up to him. She was glad he was around tonight. The incident had been dramatic and upsetting, and there was a sense of injustice about it being her car, but no life had been lost and she would mend. And her drunken chat with Klara Wallen was making her realize that maybe she had struck lucky with Kevin. Maybe they had found the perfect way to get along.

It was on the Wednesday morning that Anita was back at work. She was almost her old self again, though her hearing was still bothering her. The day before, delayed shock had kicked in and Kevin had ordered her to stay at home. But now she was anxious to get back into the fray. Little had happened on the Sami Litmanen case. Zetterberg was still convinced that Claes

Svärdendahl was still well in the frame; it was just a question of time. Zetterberg's reaction to Anita's facial injuries was also predictable: 'Been involved in another cat fight? Bound to be over a man.'

But more bad news awaited her when she got back to her office.

'I've just had forensics on about your car.' The officer who'd been called to her apartment on the night of the explosion was on the phone. 'And I don't think you're going to like what they found. It *was* targeted.'

'How could they know?'

'Someone placed a small device under the bonnet.' Anita's heart missed a beat. 'It was meant to go off when you started the car up. Fortunately for you, they wired it up wrongly and it started a fire that led to the explosion.' He finished the call by saying that there would be a thorough investigation and he would keep her in the loop. When she put the phone down, she felt sick. She could have been in the car. Kevin could have been in the car, as he used it quite a lot when she was at work. Who would have done that? Then anger began to push out the fear as she thought through who might be behind it. It was obvious. Her conversation with Absame in Värnhemstorget on Monday must have got back to Dragan Mitrović. As far as he was concerned, she had ignored his warning. And now he was carrying out his threat. This had to stop.

Anita strode down the corridor towards Erik Moberg's office. Brodd and Erlandsson were just coming out. Erlandsson pulled a face.

'I wouldn't go in there. She's not a happy woman.'

'What's up now?'

'We found someone who puts Svärdendahl at the party just before ten o'clock,' said Brodd, 'which makes it impossible for him to be at Västra Hamnen at the same time. She wasn't one of the guests, but a professional dominatrix who had been hired by the party planner to cater for specific tastes. As she was charging by the quarter hour, she kept an eye on the clock. Kinky Claes had fifteen minutes of pain at about the same time someone was lamping Litmanen.'

'So I wouldn't go in there the mood she's in,' cautioned Erlandsson.

'I don't care what mood she's in...' and she barged straight into Moberg's office.

Zetterberg's mood wasn't improved by the sight of Anita.

'What do you want?' She didn't even pretend to be civil.

'I've just found out that someone had booby-trapped my car. That person was trying to shut me up. And I know who. Dragan Mitrović.'

'And why would he do that?'

'Because I've been nosing around Absame and he doesn't like it. Either because Absame killed Litmanen or Mitrović had him murdered himself.'

'I told you to leave them well alone. Why don't you listen?'

'Oh, I've been wondering why you keep warning me off them despite Absame being an obvious suspect. I had a visit from Mitrović the other day. Broke into my apartment and threatened to do nasty things to me and my family.'

'It's your own fault.'

'I reckon he got to you first. You know as well as I do that those witness statements Mitrović gave me about Absame being at the club are junk. What did he threaten you with? What's your weakness? That's why you kept trying to keep us off their backs.'

Zetterberg sat behind Moberg's desk and shook her head slowly.

'You're a stupid bitch, Anita. What do you think I am?'

'I know exactly what you are.' Anita's blood was up now. She wasn't going to hold back. 'You're easily corruptible and you've got no scruples. You've proved that.'

'You haven't the first idea. I *know* that Absame is innocent.'

'Just because Mitrović told you he was.'

'He's got an alibi.'

'And who's given him that?'

'One of us. A cop.'

What the hell was she talking about?

Zetterberg was enjoying putting Anita on the back foot. 'One of the drugs boys is undercover in Dragan Mitrović's organization. He was with Absame when the murder was committed. They were in Trelleborg picking up a shipment of drugs at the time. That's why he avoided giving you his alibi.'

'What about Mitrović?'

'He was there, too. He didn't order any hit on Sami Litmanen.'

Anita was stunned. 'Why didn't the Drugs Squad arrest them then?' was the nearest she could get to a protest.

'They're waiting for a really big shipment to come in. You've been interfering in an important operation. You've been jeopardizing the whole thing sticking your big nose in.'

'But... but why didn't you tell me?'

'It was on a need-to-know basis and I didn't think you needed to know. My order should have been good enough.'

Anita felt foolish. And her humiliation was doubly exacerbated by her being proved wrong by Alice Zetterberg.

'As you're here, we'd better think about where we take this case next. Claes—'

'I heard.'

'Well, he's off the hook. So is Folke Allinger, and Absame was never on it, so your original list of suspects has proved to be totally useless.'

'They weren't the only leads,' said Anita, rallying. 'I did point out that there might be a tie in with whatever story Litmanen was working on. All the missing files, notes on the board. From what I remember, you dismissed that theory.'

Zetterberg wasn't going to acknowledge the point.

'You said his editor indicated that whatever he was working on had got personal.'

'Yes.'

'And what has he in the way of family?'

'As far as we've been able to establish, there's only an elderly mother in Helsinki.'

Zetterberg stood up abruptly. For a startled moment, Anita thought she was going to hit her.

'Right, get yourself up to Helsinki and find out something sodding worthwhile.'

CHAPTER 36

The next day, Anita was still more furious than frightened. She realized that Dragan Mitrović wasn't a man to make idle threats. Her chance sighting of Absame at the bus station had prompted his action. He didn't have to worry now because she didn't want to see Absame or any of Mitrović's Serbs again. If she left well alone, her family would be safe. She hadn't told Kevin about the car bomb. Partly because she didn't want to worry him, and partly to ensure he didn't do anything rash like seek out Mitrović and confront him. She was also livid that all this could have been avoided if Alice Zetterberg had told her as soon as she knew that Absame was innocent. It was Zetterberg playing with her. She'd first come across that Machiavellian side of her character at the Police Academy. Then it hadn't been so serious. This time it could have ended tragically. What also irked her was the loss of her beloved Skoda; it was the first car she'd owned that hadn't broken down every five minutes.

With the investigation going nowhere fast, matters hadn't been helped by the press conference Alice Zetterberg had held yesterday afternoon. Having previously announced that Mikael Nilsson was actually Sami Litmanen, she'd now revealed to the world that Litmanen was none other than The Oligarch. Hakim had brought in the morning newspapers, and their murder victim was on the front page of every one. Understandably, many were gloating over a rival's demise. A number were already speculating on some of the suspects that the police had already identified and now dismissed. This frenzy would continue in the coming days. Anita noticed that Zetterberg had broken the news before Commissioner Dahlbeck's return from holiday. She'd justified the announcement by saying that they were at a dead end and the investigation needed fresh impetus. She had a point, though the outcome would only put extra pressure on the team, despite Zetterberg's public assurance that they were following up a number of 'promising leads'. If nothing else, Zetterberg had got her name in all the papers and had featured on all the national and local television stations.

Anita spent her time organizing her trip to Helsinki. Her flight was confirmed for the next day and though she hadn't been able to get hold of Sami Litmanen's mother yet, she had managed to track down a journalistic colleague of his from his time in Finland. She arranged a morning meeting. She hoped it might give her some useful background information on Litmanen before he morphed into The Oligarch. She chided herself that it was the sort of checking she should have done initially instead of rushing straight off after the obvious, very public, suspects.

When the office phone rang, she hoped it might be Eila Litmanen. It turned out to be an irate Erin Ljung, the editor of *Sanningen*.

'I thought we had a deal!'

'We did,' Anita said defensively.

'So how come every damn paper has the story? Our owners are going crackers. Of all Sami's exposés, this should have been the biggest!' Anita's heart bled for the woman! She wasn't so much upset about Litmanen's death, but the missed opportunity to be the first with the news of it.

'I didn't know that the story was going to be broken like that. Otherwise I'd have alerted you,' she lied.

It didn't appease Ljung. 'It's just not on! No wonder the police are so untrustworthy.'

'I'm sorry. Look, I didn't get onto you because, as you probably realized from the press conference, there's nothing much to tell.'

'What about the "promising leads"?'

'That's what we always say.'

'What about Claes Svärdendahl?' Ljung bawled down the line. 'The fink has gone to ground completely. And Folke Allinger? Absame?'

'None of them did it.'

'Is that official?'

'You can quote a source close to the investigation,' muttered Anita reluctantly. 'Don't you dare use my name, though.'

That seemed to placate Ljung. 'OK. At least we can rubbish all the other rags' speculation pieces.'

Anita heard her shout some instructions before returning to the phone.

'Anything else I can use?'

'I don't think so at this stage.' Then Anita had a thought. 'Maybe you can help. And if it throws up any new angles, I'll make sure you get in there first.'

After a pause. 'Fair enough,' Ljung said warily.

'We need to know what the story was that Litmanen was investigating. You said it involved two well-known business companies.'

'Yes.'

'Still no idea which ones?'

'Not really, but I do know where Sami flew to in April. A list from the accounts department landed on my desk yesterday. His last receipts, for April, sent in two days before he died. He flew to Brazil on April the twelfth and was there for five days. São Paulo. Then onto Colombia. Went to a place called Armenia.'

'Like the country?'

'Yeah. Two days in Colombia. And then back here. Then he flew to Helsinki. Presumably to see his mother.'

'Brazil?' Anita's mind was buzzing. 'When he said it was household names, he did mean Swedish names, didn't he?'

'Oh, yes. This was a Swedish story.'

'So what's so important about Brazil?'

'They've got an awful lot of coffee in Brazil.'

The next call came from a neighbour of Eila Litmanen's. Eila was still in a state of shock over her son's death and wasn't well. She'd been frail and in poor health for some time and Sami's death (he was her only child) had exacerbated matters. Eila was also worried about how she was going to cope organizing a funeral – and didn't even know when the body would be transported to Finland. Would she have to pay for it? Anita tried to reassure the neighbour that the body would be released soon and to tell Eila that she was not to concern herself over the funeral costs. She was sure that *Sanningen* would pick up the bill. She would make sure they did. Eventually, they agreed that Anita was to come round to Eila's apartment tomorrow afternoon at about three, though the neighbour warned her that Eila might not be up to speaking to her. She was very up and down at the moment.

When Anita put down the phone, she prayed that Eila *was* up to it. A chat with her could be crucial. With that in mind, she didn't book a flight back the same day, as she had planned originally.

She popped her head round Hakim's door and asked if he could come to the meeting room. The board had a shorn look about it. Gone were the photos of Svärdendahl, Allinger and Absame. She presumed Zetterberg had taken them down. Under the written heading of *Suspects*, there were now no names; a depressing situation two and a half weeks after the murder.

'All set for Helsinki?'

'Yes. Eila Litmanen doesn't sound in great shape. It'll be pot luck whether I get anything out of her. But that's not what I want to talk about. I had the editor of *Sanningen* on the phone earlier.'

Hakim arched an eyebrow. 'I don't suppose she's too chuffed with Zetterberg's announcement.'

'Not exactly. She did confirm again that Litmanen was looking into warring household business names. Both Swedish companies. One new bit of information that did emerge was where he went last month. Litmanen flew to South America: first Brazil and then Colombia. He flew to São Paulo and then ended up in a town or city called Armenia in Colombia.'

'Are we looking for Swedish companies with South American connections?'

'Looks like it. Particularly Brazil. He spent five days there as opposed to two in Colombia.'

'An obvious one would be IKEA.'

'I thought of that. But as far I can see, they haven't any stores in South America. Elin Ljung did say that "they've got an awful lot of coffee in Brazil". You know, the song?' Hakim's expression was blank. She started to sing it. Still no recognition. 'The Frank Sinatra song. God, am I that ancient? The point is that she made a joke of it, but it started me thinking. According to the internet, Offesson's get the majority of their Arabica coffee beans from Brazil. They also source beans from Colombia. The rest come from East Africa.'

Hakim clicked his fingers. 'You could be right. Do you remember all those unopened packs of Offesson's coffee Litmanen had in his kitchen?'

'Not really.'

'I said it was odd that he had all the different blends. Not just one or two.'

'You're suggesting it could be part of his research?' Hakim could sense Anita's growing excitement. 'OK, I'll buy that. Offesson's could be one of the companies he was investigating.'

'Any more?'

'Not yet. That's what I want you to look into while I'm away. See who else has South American business connections, with particular emphasis on Brazil. I'd get Liv to give you a hand.'

'Liv?'

'Yes, Liv. Your bright, gifted fiancée. Get her to dig into the Offesson operation. Have they had a fallout with another company recently? Or in the past? Takeovers or hostile bids; that sort of thing. What state is the business in?'

'Very healthy, I should imagine, by the amount of advertising they do. You see signs for their coffee everywhere: *Offesson's – Start the day the Swedish way.*'

'That may be the case. But they may have upset someone along the way to success. Or gunning for a rival. It may not even be them that Sami Litmanen was investigating. Go through all the Swedish companies you can find with strong Brazilian connections, and we may find who wanted The Oligarch out of the way.'

It was there for the whole world to see. The *Sydsvenskan* newspaper lay in front of him. He had read and reread the report splashed across the front page and several inside. He knew the other newspapers were carrying similar stories. It was all over the TV and radio. The Oligarch was not only unmasked, but his murder revealed. Only he had known, albeit briefly, who Mikael Nilsson really was. Why had it taken the authorities so long for them to go public with the information? Were they that inefficient? He picked up the paper again. The police hadn't come knocking, so they obviously hadn't found a connection. That was good. A relief to a certain extent. The woman who had been talking to the press – who was that again? Inspector Alice Zetterberg. She said they were following 'promising leads'. Could one of them lead to him?

His mind sped back to that phone call. That fatal phone call he'd intercepted. And then the invitation. No, more of a threat. Come, or else! He'd soon found out that there was only an 'else'. Whatever he'd said or done, it would have all come out. He'd had to stop it.

Ever since it happened, he'd been plagued with doubts; wondering if he'd managed to cover his tracks. He'd destroyed everything he'd taken out of the apartment: the computer, the wallet, the mobile phones, the files in the desk drawer, the notes pinned to the board – even the piece of paper Nilsson had been clutching in his dead fingers.

He threw the newspaper down. All he could do now was sit tight and hold his nerve. They might never come.

CHAPTER 37

The plane left on time. Anita was settled in her seat, yawning. It had been an early start to get to Kastrup. Kevin had got up while she showered to brew her coffee. She'd turned down his offer of breakfast, saying she would grab something at the airport. The coffee wasn't right; Kevin was still learning how to make it strong enough. When the trip to Finland had been mentioned, he was keen to go with her as he'd never been to Helsinki before. She had bluntly refused. This was too important for any distractions; besides, she wanted him to keep an eye on Lasse and family just in case Mitrović thought his car bomb hadn't done the trick. Her snub hadn't dampened his enthusiasm to find out all he could about Finland's connections to Sweden. Strangely, she'd never been one for her own country's history and found far more interest in other places, particularly Britain. She'd always thought that Sweden's past was rather dull compared to the more dramatic and bloody events which had moulded the little island nation she had such affection for. However, Kevin, typically, was fascinated by Sweden's role in shaping her part of the world. After all, Finland had been ruled by the Swedes for seven centuries until it was annexed by Imperial Russia in 1809. The Finns only achieved independence in 1917. Helsinki itself had been founded by the Swedish king Gustav Vasa as a trading rival to Tallinn and the Hanseatic League across the Gulf of Finland.

Connections even lasted into the Second World War when, with the Soviet Army pushing hard at the fledgling nation's borders, over 70,000 Finnish children were evacuated to Sweden. Kevin had come up with a great deal more, but most had gone in one ear and out the other. She wouldn't have time for Finland's past – she was heading to Helsinki to catch a present-day killer.

Klara Wallen was also in work early. She'd just wanted to get out of the house. She'd had a fierce argument with Rolf the previous evening. Needless to say, he'd taken exception to her spending the night in Malmö with Anita Sundström – 'that woman's bad news'. He was furious at the thought that Anita might be stoking the fires of Klara's independence; the flames had to be extinguished before they spread. He was beginning to realize that he no longer had Klara where he wanted her: she was fighting back. She'd said some nasty things about his family; she'd never done that before. It had developed into a huge row which had resulted in Rolf storming out of the house. Klara had slept in the spare room that night and had heard Rolf stumbling back up the stairs after midnight. By then, she had a plan of action: she was going to move back to Malmö as soon as possible. First thing in the morning, she'd slipped out of the house without leaving Rolf any breakfast or explanation.

She took the call just after eight. It was from a police patrol down in Limhamn. They'd been alerted by a walker who had found a woman trussed up and tied to a bench in Limhamn cemetery. Before the officer had finished his report, she interrupted: 'Did she have a hood over her head and black gaffer tape over her mouth?' She did. 'Was she blonde?' Yes, she was.

The kidnapping! It had to be! But who was it?

The Norwegian Airways flight was only an hour and a half. The plane descended out of grey skies and a land of tall, straight pines of varying verdure came into view. Dotted in between, groups of houses became more discernible as the plane circled nearer the airport. Rain was starting to streak the window, and Anita strained to look out as she gripped her seat. She was never happy with the landing process, however often she flew. The plane banked; the landscape disappeared and she shut her eyes. She only opened them again when the plane was screeching along the tarmac and had slowed down enough to start to taxi.

Once in Vantaa Airport, her sense of direction deserted her, and she found herself wandering through a maze of long corridors in search of the train station. Eventually, she had to ask directions and was sent back virtually to where she'd started from. Fortunately, the subterranean station, at the bottom of the longest escalator she'd ever been on, was easier to navigate.

Anita now felt calmer. She was sitting on the train heading for Helsinki Central Station. The ride was as smooth as polished brass and she found it difficult to keep her eyes open. Her curiosity overcame her tiredness, however. The views from the window weren't dissimilar from those she knew from her frequent journeys to Stockholm, but the forests seemed thicker and the vegetation less varied. And there was much more water – lakes and tarns peppered the landscape and well-kept, Nordic-style houses added interest to what would otherwise have been a plethora of beautiful blandness. As she approached the city, the trees lessened and, after a spell of the usual high-rise blocks and obligatory cubes of concrete and glass, the allure of Helsinki began to play on her senses. The train rolled past the Linnanmäki Amusement Park on one side and Töölö Bay on the other as Anita glimpsed Alvar Aalto's faded marble Finlandia Hall through the rain. Within a couple of minutes, the train had slid quietly into the Central Station. On alighting, Anita slowly began to realize what an architectural gem the building was. Designed by Eliel Saarinen in the National Romanticist style, the station was completed in 1919. Passing under the huge portal archway, she took a moment to look back at the massive pink-granite splendour. Kevin would have been in heaven. She took a couple of photos to send to him, one of the building as a whole with its impressive four-sided clock tower, the other a close-up of Emil Wikström's four muscular mythical giants holding their spherical lamps, flanking the entrance. Their uncompromising stares showed that they took guarding the gateway to Helsinki very seriously.

Anita took shelter from the rain under the cover of the shopping centre opposite the station entrance. Further along, she saw a pub sign which made her smile – The Pickwick. Maybe if she had time tonight? She glanced at the clock tower. She still had an hour before her meeting. She took a few minutes to get her bearings by taking out the pocket Berlitz guide she'd bought at Kastrup. To the side of the station was a large square with a constant stream of buses trundling over its cobbles. At the far end of the square was the white-granite, red-roofed Finnish National Theatre, contrasting sharply with the gilt yellow-and-white facade of the Ateneum, the National Gallery of Art directly opposite; more of a homage to Russian architecture than Scandinavian. Scrutinizing the map, Anita worked out that Sami Litmanen's mother lived round the corner from the theatre. Anita was hoping that Litmanen's comment 'it's just got personal' would soon be explained.

Her mobile phone buzzed in her pocket. It was Hakim.

'Arrived safely?'

'Yes. Very wet at the moment,' she said, watching the rain pelting the station's watchful doorkeepers. 'Any luck?'

'Yes. You were right to get Liv involved. She's good at research. Even better than me.' Anita knew he'd never admit that in front of Liv. 'I think your coffee theory makes sense. Offessons' own plantations are in the Mogiana region. Known for its rich, red soil apparently. The area is on the border of the Minas Gerais and São Paulo states.' Anita could tell he was reading Liv's notes. 'These are north of the city of São Paulo. That probably explains why Sami Litmanen flew directly there. And the town of Armenia in Colombia is at the centre of what's called The Coffee Triangle. Offesson's don't have plantations in this region but buy from local producers.'

'That sounds interesting.'

'What's more interesting is a second São Paulo Swedish connection that Liv uncovered.' She could hear the pride in his voice. 'Trellogistics have a subsidiary company based there. Transport again. Trellogística Brasil. They are contracted by Offesson's to carry beans from the plantations to São Paulo for shipping to Europe.'

'Good work. Tell Liv I'm impressed. Anything else?'

'Not yet.'

'Keep digging. We may have our two warring companies. Is there anything shady going on? What did Litmanen discover?'

After she'd finished the call, Anita had a spring in her step, albeit a careful one to avoid the puddles.

The blonde woman sitting opposite Alice Zetterberg and Klara Wallen had already made it clear she didn't want to be there. She wanted to go home. They realized she had been through an awful ordeal. And they had established that she *was* Kristina Ekman.

'I'm sorry for what you've been through, Kristina,' said an obsequious Alice Zetterberg, 'and we'll try and keep this as brief as possible, but we've got to know exactly what happened to you. It gives us a better chance of catching the people behind this.'

'Huh! You haven't had much success so far. Look what they did to me,' she said, thrusting her wrists in their direction. Raw, red marks disfigured the delicate, smooth skin. 'This is what they did to me. Tied me to a chair for days on end. I was so frightened,' she said, biting back the tears. Zetterberg and

Wallen knew Peter Uhlig had the same abrasions

Despite the unwashed blonde hair swept back into a ponytail, the sallow complexion and the faded, smeared make-up, she still looked beautiful. She was wearing a tracksuit provided by the polishus. Wallen reckoned it wasn't the type of garment Ekman had ever worn before, or would again. She would have to wait a while longer to slip back into her designer clothes.

'They were animals!'

'Did they sexually molest you?' asked Wallen. This might be a new dimension to the kidnappers; their first woman captive.

'No. Nothing like that. Thank God! They were just horrible.'

'OK,' said Zetterberg. 'Can you take us back to the day you were abducted in Drottningtorget? Did anything unusual happen in the build-up to that day? Suspicious people hanging around near the apartment for instance.'

'No. I'd been in Malmö overnight and had my usual Friday meeting to go to in the centre of town. I came out of the building and I was aware of some vehicle driving up close by and then the next thing I knew, I'd been bundled into a van and a hood had been put over my head. I was absolutely terrified.' She stopped and bit her bottom lip.

'I know it's difficult. Just take your time.' Zetterberg wasn't used to turning on empathy, and she hoped it sounded genuine. 'Could you describe the men?'

'No. They had masks on. Then I was driven somewhere.'

'Do you have any idea how long the journey took? How long you were being driven?'

'Of course I don't! I was scared out of my mind. Do you know what I was thinking? All I could think of was my two children. What would happen to them? I wouldn't be able to protect them if something happened to me.'

'That's understandable.'

Ekman wiped away a tear in the corner of her eye with the sleeve of the tracksuit. 'I'm sorry. That's not helpful. It can't have been more than about half an hour. Maybe less, maybe a bit more.'

'You weren't moved from the van into another vehicle at any stage?'

'No.'

'We found a burnt-out van. There's a possibility it might have been the one used in your abduction. Where were you imprisoned? Was it in a room or a cellar or–'

'It was metal. Like a container.' Zetterberg and Wallen exchanged a knowing glance.

'Were you aware of your surroundings?'

'What do you mean?'

'Could you hear anything through the walls, for example? Trains, trucks, that sort of thing?'

She shook her head. 'There were certainly no trains. I could hear traffic, heavy traffic. Erm... yes... like you say, trucks.' Her eyes lit up. 'I definitely heard a ship's horn. A few times, actually.'

Anita sat in a pew and dried her glasses. The hushed ambience of the neo-classical cathedral was a much-needed antidote to the torrential rain outside and helped her to collect her thoughts. It was easy to be enraptured by the serenity of the place, and Anita particularly liked its simplicity – not too many gaudy icons or over-the-top religious paintings; just a couple of tasteful angels flanking an altarpiece depicting the death of Christ. The rest of the interior space of the domed, galleried, circular main hall was light and airy. She adjusted her watch to Helsinki time – an hour ahead of Swedish; she'd forgotten to do it on the plane. In half an hour, she was meeting Tero Rask, journalist and ex-colleague of Sami Litmanen's.

A group of Japanese tourists came in behind her, accompanied by a flapping of wet umbrellas, a whirr of cameras and an occasional squeak of excitement. The peace was broken. Anita stood up and picked up her still-wet, red hat. As she made her way back towards the entrance, her gaze was directed upwards to the beauty of the massive organ, its pipes encased in pillars and archways of red, white and gold gilt curving round the gallery above the door. She imagined the wonderful sounds it would emit in full wind, then realized that the sound she could actually hear was her phone buzzing in her pocket. She went outside and stood under the glistening white Corinthian columns before taking the phone out. It was a text from Hakim.

Woman turned up in Limhamn cemetery. Tied up same as before. Kristina Ekman!

Anita exhaled slowly. This was a turn up for the books. If the kidnap victim was Kristina Ekman after all, what was Lothar von Goessling's game? But she didn't have time to speculate further. She headed down the steep cathedral steps onto Senate Square. Her glasses were already streaked with rain again.

'We know you were held for six days. What contact did you have with the kidnappers during that time?'

Kristina Ekman held Zetterberg's gaze.

'Hardly any. I was in the bloody dark nearly all the time except for meals. Someone came in with a torch and untied me and stayed there until I'd eaten. And when I had to use a bucket to relieve myself in. The degradation. The pervert watched me.'

'Did you see their faces?'

'Always masked. It was as creepy as it was terrifying. It was not knowing what they might do next.' There was a tremble in her voice.

'Did they speak to you at all? Or did you hear them speak?'

'One of them spoke to me. Not very good Swedish. With a strong accent. More grunts really.'

'But did you ever hear them talking among themselves? Peter Uhlig thought his captors might be Russian.'

'A couple of times. The two men who grabbed me; when we were in the back of the vehicle. They certainly weren't Swedish.

I've had business dealings in Russia. Yes, I'd put my money on Russian.'

This was the confirmation they needed. It wasn't just a vague Eastern European gang; it was almost definitely Russian. Zetterberg realized that gave them something to work on.

'What was the food like?' Wallen asked.

Zetterberg gave her an astonished frown. 'What sort of question is that?'

Wallen ignored her. 'What sort of meals did they give you?'

'I don't understand.' Ekman replied.

'You know, was it carryout meals or more prepared sort of food?'

Ekman looked quizzical. 'Not very good. Pizzas, burgers... that sort of thing...' She tailed off.

'Can we get back to more important matters? We must assume that whatever ransom was demanded has been paid.'

'I wouldn't be here otherwise.'

'Yet when Inspector Sundström spoke to Lothar von Goessling at your country home, he claimed that you were away in Switzerland visiting your children, who, I believe, are at school there.'

Ekman was clearly puzzled. 'I don't know why he would say that. You mean he didn't contact you? The police weren't involved in any of this? How...?'

'We were looking for a missing woman whom we thought might be you, but Goessling changed our minds.'

Ekman's mouth dropped open. 'So you were never looking for me?'

CHAPTER 38

The Scanian landscape whizzed by in a blur of green, yellow and brown. Hakim was a city boy at heart and he was uncomfortable in swathes of open countryside. The reason for his haste was that Alice Zetterberg had told him to head across to Illstorp and talk to Lothar von Goessling before word got out that Kristina Ekman was free. Get his side of the story; specifically why he'd lied to Anita Sundström about Ekman's whereabouts. Brodd was to go with him as back-up. Hakim could think of more useful help.

Brodd was stuffing his face as usual. He'd just demolished a sandwich and was now breaking into a bar of chocolate.

'Fancy a piece?' he said, offering a chunk.

'No thanks. Wrong time of day,' said Hakim, concentrating on the road ahead.

'Wrong time of day? You mean it's not lunch?'

'It's Ramadan. We don't eat from dawn to dusk.'

'That's sounds awful. So you're having nothing from first thing until it starts going dark?'

'That's right.'

'What time can you eat then, like today?'

'After nine.'

Brodd sat back in the passenger seat and reflected on the Muslim's lot as he munched his way through half the bar.

'Wait a minute. Dawn to dusk. What about Muslims who

live in the north of the country? It hardly goes dark up there. In fact, isn't it virtually light all the time? Do they not eat?' he asked incredulously. 'They'd bloody starve.'

'I believe in places like Kiruna they're allowed to go by Stockholm time, so there's a pretend dawn and dusk, I suppose.'

'Well, that's a relief.' Brodd returned to demolishing the rest of his chocolate. It only reminded Hakim of how hungry he was. He put his foot down again. An interview with Lothar von Goessling would take his mind off his stomach.

Tero Rask was waiting for Anita in Kappeli, the great Helsinkian meeting place at the South Harbour end of the graceful, tree-lined Esplanadi Park. Dating from 1867, this large, ornamental pavilion, forged out of iron and glass, was split into two sections with a cosy bar in the middle. On one side was a swanky restaurant and on the other, a spacious café with white tables and chairs below a crystal-droplet chandelier which twinkled like a Charleston dancer's dress. The slatted-wood, domed ceiling created an airy lightness despite the gloom outside. The tall, latticed windows looked out onto the Havis Amanda fountain, its sensuous nude mermaid surrounded by four sea lions, their spouting mouths accentuating the aqueous backdrop. She took off her wet coat and hat and fluffed out her hair.

Anita reckoned Rask was about sixty. His grey hair was cropped like stubble in a wheat field. Bags under his melancholy eyes and roughly reddened cheeks testified to too much news-gathering in bars. His bulging paunch also indicated too many of the stunning cakes that were on offer at the Kappeli counter. They took their coffees and cakes – Anita thought it would be rude not to sample the local delicacies – to a cosy alcove overlooking the street. She and Rask eased themselves into the curved space, his stomach pressing against the round table top. To facilitate communication, they spoke in English.

'This is a fantastic place,' said Anita with genuine admiration.

'The rendezvous of choice. It's a great place to watch the world go by.' At the moment, the world was scurrying to get out of the rain. 'Jean Sibelius used to hang out here with all his artistic friends.' Rask gave a little chuckle. 'They were gathered here as usual one day – Aho, Leino, Gallén-Kallela among them – when Sibelius was called away to leave for Stockholm to complete a musical composition. When he returned a couple of days later, the same group were still together round the same table. One of the artists chided the famous composer: "Listen here, Jean – either you stay outside or stay inside, but stop coming in and out all the time!"'

Anita laughed at Rask's well-polished anecdote. She immediately gathered that Rask wasn't afraid of the sound of his own voice. It would make her job easier. She took a forkful of her chocolate confection.

'You weren't very forthcoming on the phone. But I checked with Martin Glimhall – I know him from way back. And he says you're OK.' He raised his cup to his lips. 'And his physical description of you was spot on, too,' Rask added with what Anita could only describe as a leery slurp. She let it pass. She got fewer compliments these days. 'Though,' he added, gesturing towards the cuts on her face, 'you seem to have been in a scrap.'

'It was a beauty treatment that went wrong.'

Rask chortled. 'I like a girl with a sense of humour.'

She opened with 'You worked with Sami Litmanen?'

'Sami? We heard about him yesterday. Shocking, absolutely shocking.' He said it so loudly that it caught the attention of nearby tables.

'I'm trying to find out about him before he came to Sweden. He was calling himself Mikael Nilsson in Sweden. But the reading public knew him as The Oligarch.'

The bags under Rask's eyes seem to droop even lower. 'We'd heard of The Oligarch, of course. But until the news came through, no one had connected the dots to Sami. How did it happen?'

'He was murdered in his apartment. We haven't released specific details with enquiries still ongoing.'

'I understand. Do you know who did it?'

'We have suspects,' she said vaguely. 'Nothing concrete yet.'

'Hence your trip over here?'

'Yes.'

'I appreciate everything is under wraps, but I was planning to do an obituary for the paper. People will want to know he's... gone.'

'That's not a problem. It's just that we can't furnish you with any specific details of the murder at the moment. Actually, your ideas for an obituary would help me. I'm trying to build up a picture of Sami Litmanen. His life before he came to Sweden.'

'If I can help.' He drained his coffee. 'But first I need something stronger. Been a bit of a shock.' With difficulty, he got to his feet. 'Can I get you a proper drink?'

'No thanks.'

A couple of minutes later, Rask returned with a large beer and a small schnapps. Anita let him settle down again before continuing.

'I'm talking to his mother later on so I'll get Sami's family background. It's his professional life that you can fill me in on. It's likely that he was killed because of his work.'

Rask shook his head sadly. 'I assumed it might be something like that. Sami sailed close to the wind at times.'

'When did you first come across him?'

'When he joined the paper as a junior reporter. I was a kind of mentor. He'd been on a couple of smaller rags before coming to us. I sort of took him under my wing; showed him the ropes. He was a quick learner. Ambitious too; a young man in a hurry to succeed. I liked his style and tenacity. He'd push that bit harder than maybe the rest of us to get a story. It impressed the bosses even if it hacked off the hacks.' This joke was accompanied by a guttural guffaw. When Anita didn't react, he said 'Isn't "hack" an expression in English for a journalist?'

'I believe so.'

Rask retreated into his beer.

'When did he start to get into investigative journalism?'

The schnapps was downed in one go. He licked his lips. 'Russia. Yeah, it was Russia. The paper sent Sami off to the Moscow bureau. That meant that he covered everything from ice hockey in St. Petersburg to conflicts in Chechnya. He was over there for about three years.'

'So his Russian was passable?'

'Fluent. Always good at languages.' That made sense as he'd successfully passed himself off as a Russian or someone from one of the satellite states.

Anita took another mouthful of the rich cake. A hidden cherry filling gave her a delightful surprise. Heaven!

'Was there any particular story that got him going?'

'Yes. It was huge when it broke here in Finland. He stumbled across a story involving a prominent Helsinki businessman who was involved with the Russian mafia. Sami exposed the fact that the Russians were using this guy's company to funnel money through to fund illegal activities around Scandinavia.'

'That was a bit dangerous.'

Rask's belly shook as he laughed, nearly upsetting his beer. 'Bloody dangerous! The paper had to pull him out of Moscow, pronto.'

Anita sipped her coffee. Perfect! Her only worry was trying to claim this lot on expenses.

'Did he carry on with the investigative journalism on his return?'

'Oh yes. Ordinary reporting went out of the window. He totally immersed himself in his work. He was good. The best. Of course, such dedication came at a cost. His marriage for starters.'

'We didn't know he was married.'

'Susanna. Pretty little thing.'

'Susanna? Doesn't sound very Finnish.'

'No, she was a Finland-Swede.'

'A Finland-Swede?'

'Yes. About five percent of the country are Finland-Swedes. Goes back to the days when your lot held sway. Seven hundred years of it. Even after we became a Russian Grand Duchy a couple of hundred years ago, Swedish was still the official language. Finnish didn't become a co-language until 1863. Even today, Finland-Swedes are treated as a pampered minority, which upsets many Finns. There's still a Swedish daily paper, *Hufvudstadsbladet*, and Swedish news and television programmes. It's even mandatory in schools. I believe English or Russian would be far more useful. But some of the young see Swedish as a way into life in other parts of Scandinavia.' He shrugged in disbelief. 'Anyway, I think Sami married Susanna *because* she was a Finland-Swede. A weird kind of status thing.'

'How do you mean?'

'Well, many of the Finland-Swedes hail from ancestors that came here from the Swedish army; soldiers were given land and tax benefits for services rendered to the Swedish king. That led to the moneyed government and intellectual classes being of Swedish origin. The old university at Turku, before it was moved to Helsinki, was a hotbed of Swedish speakers. Ironically, many of the great Finnish nationalists were Finland-Swedes, like Elias Lönnrot, whose Finnish-Swedish dictionary kick-started our own literary language; and John Ludvig Runeberg, our national poet, who wrote the words of our national anthem.'

The fire was lit in Tero Rask's eyes. It was time to steer him off cultural differences.

'Sami's scoops while he was in Helsinki: did he ever target celebrities?'

'You mean actors, singers, TV people...?' He shook his

head vigorously. 'No. He thought those types were vacuous. He wouldn't waste his time on them. He went for the corrupt, the wrongdoers. He was like a one-man crusade. Nothing got in the way. When he got his teeth into someone, he wouldn't let go. It was like he was in a different world. You could hardly talk to him. He became secretive, or security conscious anyway.'

'Why did he leave Finland?'

'He outgrew Helsinki. Too small. He loved Sweden. The idea of it, anyway. Maybe it was inspired by his mother.'

'Why his mother?'

'Oh, don't you know?'

CHAPTER 39

When Hakim and Brodd arrived at the front of the Wollstad mansion, the man they assumed to be Lothar von Goessling was pacing up and down on the lawn smoking a cigarette.

Hakim did the introduction. 'I'm Inspector Hakim Mirza and this is Inspector Pontus Brodd.'

Goessling threw away his cigarette. 'Is she safe?' he said in English.

'You mean Kristina Ekman?' said Hakim, switching to English.

'Of course I do.'

'Yes, she was left in the cemetery in Limhamn.'

'Is she OK? Physically? They haven't done anything to her?'

The sun was high in the sky now and was beating down upon them.

'She's shaken but fine.'

'I must go at once and collect her.'

'Hold on. We need to speak to you first.'

'But she'll need me.'

'We need to ask you some questions,' put in Brodd firmly. He didn't want to be left out, though his English wasn't as fluent as Hakim's. He'd decided to play bad cop if he was given the chance.

'Why did you tell Inspector Sundström that Kristina was away in Switzerland when you obviously knew that she'd been

266

kidnapped?' asked Hakim.

Goessling fished out another cigarette and lit it with a shiny, silver lighter. The expensive gold bracelet round his wrist glinted in the sun against his tanned skin. He blew a plume of smoke before answering.

'I'll never forget the moment that the call came through from the kidnappers. The ransom demand. They said that if I went to the police, Titti would be harmed.'

'Who's Titti?' Brodd asked Hakim.

'Kristina,' said Goessling with some irritation. 'The family call her Titti. I still would have contacted you, but I was persuaded not to. After all, you ballsed up the Peter Uhlig handover.'

'Who did the persuading?' queried Hakim.

'Titti's father. He didn't want to risk his daughter's life.'

'Dag Wollstad?'

'I had no one else to turn to. I'm wealthy, but I don't have a disposable four million euros.'

'The call... the ransom call... what language did they use? You don't speak Swedish, do you?'

'He started in Swedish. I knew it must be important. I just couldn't get the gist of it so he started talking in English. With an accent, like Swedes have when they speak English. Like Titti talks to me. I soon got the message.'

'So where did the ransom come from? Dag Wollstad?'

'Yes. He arranged a transfer of money to Germany. I have no idea where it came from. I flew to Frankfurt to pick it up from a bank two days ago. Cash.'

'And where did you deliver it?'

'I left it in an IKEA cool bag in Simrishamn church yesterday at four o'clock as instructed. In the third pew from the back on the left-hand side. I was to leave it under the seat.'

'Was anybody in the church at the time?'

'A couple of tourists, I think. The woman was taking a photo of one of the ships hanging from the roof.'

'And then?'

'I left. I wasn't going to hang around to see if it was picked up. Titti's life was at stake. And I didn't want them to think that the police were around.'

'Might have been better if they had been.'

'I don't think so. Now if that's all, I'm going to Malmö to collect her.' He flung away his half-smoked cigarette.

They watched Goessling stride across the grass.

'Believe him?' Hakim asked.

'Never trust a rich boy.'

Built in 1907, the art nouveau apartment block was on five floors and Eila Litmanen lived at the top. The graceful building on the corner of Mikonkatu and Railway Station Square was rendered in pink stucco and, at intervals, sported semi-circular projections from the second floor to the roof, incorporating attractive bay windows. Inside, however, the entrance hall was dark, and overwhelmed by a disproportionate amount of coloured marble – on the walls, on the floor, on the steps up to the higher levels and, most noticeable of all, on the enormous newel supporting the staircase. There was no lift.

After a gruelling climb, Anita had to pause to get her breath back. She had no idea how the old woman managed it. Eila Litmanen's neighbour, whom she'd spoken to on the phone, met her at the door. She must have been seventy at least but had the energy of a woman far younger. She introduced herself as Karita. She spoke in the accented Swedish that Anita had found difficult to follow over the phone. It was easier to decipher accompanied by vigorous hand gestures. Karita explained that Eila was ready to speak to her, but that Anita shouldn't tax her unnecessarily. She reiterated that Eila wasn't in the best of health and was understandably emotionally strained. And she tired quickly, so best keep the conversation short.

Karita took Anita through to the living room. It was an

elegant space with a high, corniced ceiling, thick walls, and quadruple-glazed windows to keep out the cold and the noise. The furniture was old-fashioned but tasteful and comfortable. Sami Litmanen had obviously spared no expense. Eila Litmanen was sitting upright in a high-backed chair. A wooden cane rested against the arm. Next to her chair was a small table with a tray on it containing a full glass of water and various bottles of pills. The wizened old lady she had expected was surprisingly tall, albeit sitting down. She had thick white hair neatly brushed back. The face was deeply lined, though Anita could see that she had once been a handsome woman. The mouth was thin and on seeing Anita enter, she dabbed nervously at the corner of her lips with a lace handkerchief. She was preparing herself for a conversation that no parent ever wants to have. Her eyes alone betrayed her sadness. Deep pools of sorrow.

'This is Inspector Anita Sundström,' said Karita. 'The Swedish police officer I told you about.'

Eila offered a bony hand; the skin stretched tightly showing a delta of veins. Anita shook it cautiously as though it might shatter at her touch. The blue dress didn't hide her thinness; it accentuated it. She must have filled it out once. Eila Litmanen was frail, though Anita could see a stoical resignation in her eyes.

'Please, Anita, sit.' She waved to the sofa opposite her chair. 'That will be all, Karita,' as though dismissing a servant.

'Of course. If you need anything, Eila...' and turning to Anita, she gave her a warning glance. 'Not too long.'

After she had gone, Eila said 'I could not do without Karita, but she does fret so. Can I get you anything? Some tea perhaps? Or some food?'

'No thanks, I'm still full of cake from Kappeli's.'

'A good choice. It has been many years since I have been there.' Her Swedish was precise, though Anita knew she wasn't a Finland-Swede from what Tero Rask had told her. Her voice was strong and clear.

'I was told by a journalistic friend of Sami's that you spent some of your childhood in Sweden.'

'Yes.' She didn't seem inclined to elaborate, though Rask had explained that Eila had been one of the huge numbers of Finnish children that had been evacuated to Sweden during the Second World War. Maybe it was a time in her life that she didn't want to remember. Anita knew that the young Finns had received a mixed reception by their Swedish hosts. Some had lived happily with sympathetic families while others had harsher tales to tell. Many didn't return to Finland until well after the war because by 1945, Finland's economy was on its knees.

'I'm so sorry about your son, fru Litmanen.'

'Did you know Sami?'

'I'm afraid not.'

'He was a lovely boy. Always good to me, especially after his father died. He did not have many friends as a child. He was reserved, like me. He did not find trusting people easy. Is that what led to his death? Did someone he did trust betray him?'

'Maybe.'

'Do not worry. I do not want to know how Sami died. Knowing he is dead is cruel enough; knowing the details of his death would be unbearable. I have already shed so many tears.'

'Fru Litmanen...'

'Call me Eila. That is my name.'

Anita watched as Eila wiped her mouth again. 'I know this is painful to talk about, but I need to ask you about the last time you saw Sami. He came here near the end of April, I believe.'

Eila nodded her head slowly. 'He did. Only for two nights. He never stayed long. Sometimes he would disappear for weeks, months, and I would not hear from him. The occasional phone call, perhaps. And then he would suddenly come and light up my day.' She stopped and picked up her glass of water; it wobbled slightly as she put it to her lips. 'Excuse me.' She put the glass down. 'He was a very generous boy. He bought me this apartment ten years ago.'

'It's beautiful.'

'He always looked out for me. His father Otso died when he was only eleven. He missed him dreadfully. Became even more introverted. Money was short then without Otso's wage coming in. I was still working as a telephonist with the Elisa Corporation. It was not highly paid. Later, I stayed on in Runeberginkatu when it was converted into the telephone museum. Life was not easy bringing up a child. No grandparents who could help. Even as a young boy, he promised to buy me somewhere nice to live when he had the money.' A hint of a smile crossed her face at the recollection.

'His own apartment in Malmö was very simple, though his work must have been well paid.'

'He has a beach house in Thailand. He would often spend time there in our winters.' That explained what his money was spent on. 'He did not like the cold, particularly after his years working in Russia.'

'Did you know much about his work as a journalist?'

'Not once he left Helsinki. I knew he must be doing well.' Eila stared round the room as though she couldn't believe how lucky she was to be living here. 'He said his work was often very secret. I do not know why he would not talk about what he did. It was just his way. Except...'

'Except?'

'The last time.'

'Did he talk about what he was working on?' Anita was trying not to press too hard.

'He wanted to talk to me about the Offesson family.'

'The coffee people?'

'Yes. You can buy their coffee in Finland, but it is not as good as Fazer's coffee here in Helsinki. You must go to the Karl Fazer Café on Kluuvikatu. And the chocolate and the cakes are splendid.'

Anita was desperate not to get side-tracked. 'What did Sami tell you about the Offesson family?'

'It was something to do with their business. In South America.' This was starting to fit in with what they had already discovered. 'It was to do with the plantations. Some company was causing problems. Disrupting the Offesson operation, he said. Corruption was involved.'

'Do you know what this other company was?' Could this be a possible breakthrough?

'He did not say, or if he did, it did not register with me.' Anita felt a sense of anticlimax.

'Was it another Swedish company?'

'Yes, I am sure it was.'

Again, Eila raised her handkerchief to her lips. This time she stifled a yawn. Her eyelids were heavy. Anita was losing her.

'Look Eila, I'll go. May I come back tomorrow?'

'I am sorry I cannot talk longer. I need to rest. Please do come back and we can talk some more. I do want to help you.'

'I know. What time?'

'Come at eleven. My health visitor comes in at ten. She will be gone by then.'

'Eleven it is.' Anita stood up and collected her bag. 'One thing puzzles me, Eila. Why did Sami want to talk to you about the Offessons?'

'Because I lived with the family during the war.'

CHAPTER 40

When Hakim and Brodd returned to headquarters, the meeting Alice Zetterberg had called was just starting. Klara Wallen and Bea Erlandsson were there plus half a dozen other officers who had been brought in to help.

'Good, you're back. What did Lothar von Goessling have to say?'

'He claims that when the ransom demand came through, he turned to Kristina's father, Dag Wollstad.'

'The fugitive?'

'Yes. He advised Lothar not to tell the police. He didn't want to risk his daughter's safety; Lothar mentioned the Peter Uhlig fiasco.'

'Before I took charge,' Zetterberg pointed out unnecessarily.

'Anyway, that's why he pretended that Kristina was safe and well. Didn't want to jeopardize the handover. The money for the ransom was four million euros–'

'The same as Peter Uhlig's. That's interesting.'

'The money was raised by Dag Wollstad. Lothar supposedly flew to Frankfurt to pick it up. That can be checked.'

'Where was the money drop off?'

'Simrishamn church. Left the ransom in an IKEA cool bag – the same as before – under a pew. Said he left. That was yesterday at four o'clock. Then Kristina is released this morning.'

'OK. We've really got a pattern here. Same M.O. as before.

Abduction followed by incarceration in a port area; the first one in a disused workshop, the other two in containers. Both Ekman and Uhlig have rope marks round their wrists. She, like Uhlig, reports hearing ships' horns and heavy traffic. Same ransom as Uhlig's; delivered in the same way – an IKEA cool bag. Same type of delivery point: a church. Same dumping of victims in cemeteries around the city in all three cases. Same type of hoods; same method of tying the victim up to a bench; same use of gaffer tape. As I say, same pattern.'

'What about the food?' Wallen asked.

'Why do you keep wittering on about the damn food? Just because Sundström mentioned it!'

'There's a point here. Peter Uhlig said he was reasonably well fed. Kristina Ekman was given takeaways, as was Mats Möller. Why are they different?'

'I have no idea. Maybe they couldn't be bothered,' she said dismissively. 'However,' she added slowly, 'we need to check out all the fast food outlets within easy reach of the harbour areas. I know you did that after the Möller business, but I'm in charge now. Ask about any customers with poor Swedish.'

'There are a lot of those in Malmö these days.'

Zetterberg ignored Brodd's comment. 'Basically, non-regulars. Obviously foreign, because we're now fairly sure of the nationality of the gang. Kristina Ekman believes that they spoke Russian. It backs up what Peter Uhlig thought his captors were speaking.'

'There must be a Swede involved,' chipped in Wallen. 'The policeman who stopped Ann-Kristen Uhlig at Skårby. The ransom demand over the phone.'

'The guy who rang through the demand to Goessling started talking in Swedish, apparently,' chimed in Brodd, 'before switching to English. Goessling doesn't speak Swedish.'

'So, they've got a local on board,' said Zetterberg. 'It makes sense. Maybe he's the one who pinpoints the targets.'

'Is he the weak link?' ventured Erlandsson. 'If he's involved in something like this, he'll probably have a criminal record. That'll be how the Russian gang recruited him.'

'That's a line of investigation. You can get on with that, Bea. The rest of us are going down to the docks. This time we're going to turn the place over.'

Anita reached Eila Litmanen's apartment just before eleven on Friday morning. She was fresh after a good night's sleep at a nearby hotel. She had resisted the temptation to visit The Pickwick pub opposite the station and had bought a cheap and hearty meal at the restaurant in the Swedish Theatre at the city end of the Esplanadi. She'd then gone to bed early after calling Kevin and then Lasse to make sure all was well in Malmö. She'd surprised herself by how much she was missing Kevin, despite the fact that she'd seen him only that morning. Maybe her feelings for him were growing deeper. She had seen enough of Helsinki to know it was Kevin country, bursting with history and extraordinary buildings. Rashly, she promised him that they would come here for a weekend break. Mind you, she'd done the same after her visit to Malta last year, and she hadn't fulfilled that promise. She'd allowed herself one indulgence this morning. Ignoring the hotel breakfast, she'd made for the sumptuous Karl Fazer Café (Fazer pronounced Fatser locally) and had had three cups of their own coffee and two cakes: one with succulent layers of chocolate and one riddled with strawberries and cream. Now she had to admit she felt a little queasy. She'd also bought some Fazer chocolates to take back for Kevin, and Jazmin who, like her, was a chocoholic. The selection for sale was so mouth-wateringly stunning that she'd taken some pictures on her phone. She would send them later.

It was Eila who opened the door to let her in. She was leaning on her cane.

'I did not tell Karita,' she said conspiratorially. 'She fusses so.'

Anita followed the old lady at a very leisurely pace into the sitting room. Today, there was an extra table in place with a coffee pot and cups and a selection of biscuits. Anita inwardly groaned. She would pay for her earlier gastronomic immoderations just by being polite.

'I thought you might like something,' Eila said as she carefully lowered herself into her chair.

'You really shouldn't have,' Anita protested. She meant it.

'I only made the coffee. Karita made the biscuits. Besides, I like to make an effort. I get so few visitors these days, except for Karita. So many are gone now. Including...' For a moment Anita thought that Eila might start to cry.

Anita did the pouring, and she left her biscuit uneaten on her old-fashioned china plate.

'You said yesterday that you spent the war with the Offesson family.'

'Yes. From 1941 until 1946.'

'Five years. That's a long time. Did you keep in touch with them?'

Eila appeared reticent. Eventually, she said 'Not really.' This struck Anita as odd. You'd expect to get close to a family over so many years.

'Was Sami interested in your time with the family?'

'He did ask.' She ventured nothing more. It was as though she'd shut the door. Anita decided that there was something she needed to unlock. She would have to take the long route.

'Tell me about the war. And what it was like in Sweden. I've seen *Mother of Mine*.' Eila looked at her uncomprehendingly. 'It's a film about a Finnish boy who is evacuated to a farm in Skåne, and the story follows him adapting to Swedish life without his mother, and the farmer's wife's slow acceptance of a child into the family home after the death of her own daughter. They eventually create a bond.'

Eila's expression showed that this hadn't been the case with her. 'The Russians invaded at the beginning of the war and took areas of the country. That was called the Winter War. But when the Continuation War came in 1941, so did the bombs on Helsinki. My mother thought it was becoming increasingly dangerous for me to be here. My father had already been called up to fight. Then one day, my mother packed a suitcase and took me to the Central Station and I was put on a train. I was so frightened and upset. I was only six. I did not understand why she had done such a thing. Did she not love me anymore?' Eila dabbed her eyes with a handkerchief, a different colour and design from the one she had used the day before.

'As you must know, most of us ended up in Sweden, though a few went to Denmark and Norway. Many of us were allocated families. Others were not so fortunate and ended up in institutions. I was fostered by the Offesson family.'

'They were rich.'

'They lived in this beautiful house in the countryside near Helsingborg. A wonderful garden, too, to play in.' She suddenly stopped.

'You must have been well looked after even if you were unhappy to be away from your mother,' said Anita, trying to keep the conversation going. There was something hidden here that she felt must be relevant.

'They were kind in their way. Well, the servants were, for I saw little of herr and fru Offesson. He was away on business much of the time. She did not have much time for the children.'

'And the children? Anders Offesson?' Eila acknowledged this with a slight raise of her eyebrows. Anita knew of Anders Offesson. He had been a great philanthropist, though he was rarely seen nowadays. She was sure that he wasn't running the business now. 'You must have gone to school. Your Swedish is very good.'

Eila summoned a wry smile. 'It was hard won. I was mocked at school for being a Finn. I was the only one there. Do people still look down on us in Sweden?'

'The jokes about drunks with knives are dying out, I'm pleased to say.'

'Is that progress?' she said wistfully. 'I was never happy there. Sweden that is. I never really settled. And I had to wait an extra year to come home. The economy here was in ruins after the war. My father survived, but had no job to come back to. Mother scraped a living. I returned to Helsinki in the autumn of 1946 when my father had at last found work. It was the happiest day of my life to be reunited with my parents. I had forgiven Mother over time. Being older, I appreciated she had sent me away for the right reasons.' Eila's right hand slipped onto the handle of her cane and she squeezed it. 'The odd thing is that I could not settle here in Finland either. Many of us returning could not. Over the years, I have been hospitalized. They say it is called mental illness. Unfortunately, I was sometimes taken away from home when Sami was growing up. It was not so bad when Otso was alive. After his death, his sister took Sami in. He resented that. His mother taken away from him. It is difficult to explain to a child that their mother is in hospital with an illness that they cannot comprehend, cannot see. An illness locked into one's head.'

Anita felt moved by the mother's anguish, still fresh after all these years.

'Sami, before he died, told the editor of his newspaper that the story he was working on, which we now know concerns the Offessons, had become personal. That was only a few days after he visited you here. Do you know what he meant? Was it the unhappiness you experienced with the family? Or the suffering you went through after you came back to Helsinki?'

Eila's wrinkled hands straightened her dress at the knees. Almost in a whisper, she said 'No. Neither of those things.'

'Eila, can you tell me?' Anita said gently. 'I want to catch the person who killed your boy. This might help me.'

Eila's eyes caught Anita's gaze and held it. There was such sadness in the old woman's lined features. She carefully wiped away the hint of a tear.

'I should not have told him.'

'Told him what, Eila?'

'About Isabell.'

'Who's Isabell?'

'Anita, promise me that you will find the person responsible for Sami's death.'

'Of course I promise. I'll do everything I can.'

Eila's fingers twined her handkerchief around as she spoke. 'Isabell was the daughter of herr and fru Offesson. Anders' younger sister. He was eight, Isabell was five. She was my only friend. I needed her, as Anders was always horrid to me. He resented me staying with the family. Once, he found the letters my mother had sent that I kept under my pillow. He burned them. He was good at making me cry. Making me feel unwanted. And pretty little Isabell would fight my battles for me. Protect me.

'One day – it was summer time – we were all sent out to play after lunch because the grown-ups wanted to relax without us pestering them. Anders was furious. He wanted to stay with the adults. I played with Isabell for a while. She was helping me to pick flowers but then she went off to find Anders. I was under one of the two oak trees in the middle of the garden. One of them had a rope ladder going up to a tree house built into the branches. I never went up as I was scared of the height. But Anders and Isabell would climb up. She had no fear. That afternoon I heard rustling above me. I glanced up. At that moment, to my horror, Isabell plunged out of the tree and fell to the ground right in front of me. It was awful.'

'How dreadful! Was she badly hurt?'

'She was dead.'

'What an appalling accident!' gasped Anita.

'It was no accident,' said Eila with a firmness that had been missing from her voice as she told her story. 'I saw Anders push her. Deliberately.'

Anita was shocked. 'What did you do?'

'What could I do? Anders said that I was not to say anything. No one would believe me, a pathetic Finnish girl. It was true. He was the adored son and family heir. My word against his. He said if I said anything, I would be taken away and put in an asylum for mad people, where I would be beaten and fed on bread and water. And I would never be allowed to see my parents again. Can you imagine what that was like for a six-year-old? After Isabell's death, the family had no time for me. It was as though I had brought them bad luck.'

'It's horrific.'

'I never told anybody what had happened, not even my husband, until I spoke to Sami that last time. All his talk of the Offessons. It just came pouring out.'

The tears were flowing now. Anita went over to Eila and put her arms around the woman's shaking body. As she tried to console her, she couldn't help thinking that she could well understand how Sami Litmanen's investigation had turned 'personal'.

On the way from Eila Litmanen's apartment, walking round the edge of Railway Station Square to catch her train to the airport, Anita phoned Hakim.

'The book... the book that was on Sami Litmanen's table?'

'I remember.'

'Did we ever find out what it was about?'

'You mean did I ever find out? Yes, I did actually. Can't remember what the title was translated as–'

'That doesn't matter. I just want to know what it was about.'

'It was to do with Finnish children that came over to Sweden during the Second World War. The translator I spoke to said it was mainly about the psychological after effects on the young evacuees. Increased mental health issues, personality disorders, substance abuse... that sort of thing. Biological consequences too – risk of heart disease, diabetes. Why? Is it relevant?'

'Oh, yes. I think I now know why Sami Litmanen was killed.'

CHAPTER 41

When Anita got back from the airport in the late afternoon, the office was deserted except for Bea Erlandsson. The young detective explained that, for the second day running, Zetterberg had everybody else out combing the harbour areas in an attempt to pinpoint exactly where Kristina Ekman had been held.

'I can see why she's doing it. The pattern of the kidnappings is virtually the same. Kristina Ekman was held in a container. Brodd rang me an hour ago to say they'd still drawn a blank. Zetterberg's going to be very unhappy.' Erlandsson gave a chuckle. 'And this will really make her day,' she said, pushing over the evening newspaper *Kvällsposten*, the Skåne edition of the national *Expressen*. Anita squinted at the headline: *WHERE'S OUR POLICE PROTECTION? ASKS KIDNAP VICTIM*. It was accompanied by a photo of a suitably anguished Kristina Ekman. She may have been though a horrific experience, but she'd still made sure she looked good for the cameras, though there was a close-up shot of her wrists for impact. Anita quickly read the article. The gist of the story was that Kristina Ekman was saying that the kidnapping of the region's wealth creators was a hijacking of the economy that she and her fellow businesspersons were helping to create, sustain and expand. It was causing commercial turmoil. It would put off investors and foreign companies who might want to set up in Skåne and generate further jobs. The police should be doing all they could to protect the region's leading employers, which, in turn, would safeguard the futures of the people of Skåne. Basically, it was an attack on the police wrapped up in the righteous indignation of a benefactor of the common working person.

'She's got a nerve,' snorted Erlandsson. 'How on earth are we meant to protect all these people? If we kept an eye on all the top business people in Skåne, we'd have no one left to do anything else. We didn't even know she'd been kidnapped until she turned up in Limhamn. Not officially, anyway.'

'Her pride's been pricked; she's been manhandled by some lower-class hoodlums and she's had to pay out money to them. That'll have hurt. She's lashing out, and we're an easy scapegoat. And Kristina's never forgiven us for going after her father.'

'He paid the ransom, you know. Four million euros, like Uhlig.'

'Makes sense. Her German playboy has the connections, though I suspect he hasn't got the money. He might be worth looking into.'

'You don't think he could have something to do with it?'

'Well... no, not really. I just didn't like him. Cop's intuition.'

'I've already checked Goessling's movements around the time of the kidnap. Said he flew to Frankfurt to pick up the ransom money from a bank over there. He did fly there and back on the days he claimed.'

'He's the sort of creep that I could see absconding with the money, but Dag Wollstad's reach is long and vengeful. He obviously paid up, or else the lovely Kristina wouldn't have been set free to slag us off.'

Anita pushed the newspaper away. She didn't really want to be around when Zetterberg saw the article. The timing was particularly bad, as Commissioner Dahlbeck would be back from his vacation on Monday. Zetterberg would have some explaining to do, though she would probably lay the blame at Anita's door somehow. Zetterberg's absence also meant that she didn't have to report on her Helsinki trip just yet. She still needed time to process the information she'd uncovered and work out how best to proceed. She wasn't a Moberg, who would just charge into the Offessons' lives demanding immediate answers. She would have to tread carefully. They were an incredibly influential family.

'Oh, Anita. There's something you might be able to advise me on. We believe that there's someone working with the kidnap gang who's local. The cop who stopped Ann-Kristen Uhlig at Skårby? The voice making the ransom demands?'

'Yeah.'

'The Russian gang, as we now think they are, will, in all likelihood, have recruited someone with local knowledge. Zetterberg's asked me to go through all our known villains to see if we have anyone who might fit the profile. But I'm having no luck. Trouble is I'm not that familiar with the scene down here.'

'You mean you haven't been around as long as I have!'

'I mean I haven't been in Malmö that long,' Erlandsson said quickly. 'And most of that time was on cold cases, not current crooks.'

'I wasn't being serious, Bea. At my great age, I should be familiar with the city's lowlife. I could look though the rogues' gallery with you. Point out possibles.'

Erlandsson sounded relieved. 'That would be brilliant, Anita.'

Anita thought for a moment. 'Actually, I can do better than that.'

'How?'

'Get it straight from the horse's mouth.'

'You're mad. Stark raving mad!'

This was Kevin's considered opinion as he sat next to Anita in a car he'd hired for a few days so that they had transport. She ignored the comment and continued to watch the gates of the large house in Limhamn. She knew he was inside and would be coming out at some stage. This was the easiest way to get to speak to Dragan Mitrović. He certainly lived in ostentatious style, itself not a Swedish trait. The gates were too ornate, the house too flamboyant, the garden too prissy; though she couldn't fault the view across the Sound with the Öresund Bridge slightly to the left and Copenhagen slightly to the right. They had been sitting there for nearly an hour. It wasn't the best way to spend a Saturday morning. Kevin had insisted on coming along once he'd realized what she was going to do. 'If he so much as lays a finger on you, I'll have him.' She appreciated the genuine concern, though Kevin's slight figure wasn't likely to put the wind up Mitrović and his thugs. He was spending most of his time playing with a new app he'd put on his phone that located commercial aeroplanes and their destinations. As they were sitting across the water from Kastrup Airport, there were hundreds of flights to check. 'Oh, that one's going to Los Angeles. Blimey, that's a long way! That incoming one we can see over there is coming from Reykjavik. Never been there. Have you?' She wasn't sure how much more of his prattle she could take before grabbing his phone and throwing it into the sea. Fortunately, there was some movement at the front of the house and a couple of minutes later, the electronic gates opened. By then, Anita had got out of the car and was firmly warning Kevin to stay put. 'I'll just look hard,' he said jokingly before adding 'Just be careful.'

The car with the smoked-glass windows Anita had spied driving past her apartment a few days before now slipped through the open gates. She walked across the road and held her hand up. The vehicle stopped as the gates closed silently behind it.

The window on the left-hand side at the back slid down. Anita went round and saw Dragan Mitrović watching her. She found it disconcerting as he was wearing expensive sun glasses and she couldn't see his eyes.

'Are you now harassing me at my home, Inspector Sundström? My wife will be watching. I don't like her to worry.'

'I'm not harassing you. I've come with news that might stop you trying to intimidate me.'

'Intimidate you?' he drawled.

'Little things like threatening my family, blowing up my car.'

'I heard about that. Unfortunate. It wasn't me.' She couldn't read his face, but she knew he was lying.

'I'm here to tell you that you and Absame are no longer considered suspects in the murder of Sami Litmanen. But don't for a minute think it has anything to do with your tactics. We're pursuing a different line of enquiry.'

'Is that official?' It wasn't. It was just that Anita knew her killer lay elsewhere.

'It's as official as it's going to get.'

'I must say I'm pleased. I always told you my boy Absame was innocent. Maybe you'll believe me next time.'

'I hope there won't be a next time.'

'Just so.' The window started to slide up.

'A minute!'

The darkened window was stopped halfway up. Anita had to cock her head to see into the car.

'I need your help.'

The window went back down again.

'My help?' he said with a hint of incredulity. 'Why should I help someone who has been falsely accusing me and one of my associates of murder?'

'I admit I was wrong... about that particular murder.' The insinuation that she might be referring to the disappearance of Absame's boxing coach Bogdan Kovać was left hanging. 'You may have read that Kristina Ekman was recently released from a kidnap situation.'

Mitrović gave an almost girlish titter. 'Oh dear; she was so horrible about the police. But she has a point. Business people of stature have to be protected.'

Anita glanced at the two hulks sitting in the front seats. 'I see you have your own protection.'

'You can never be too careful.'

'The gang behind these kidnappings. We think they're Russian. I had a feeling that you wouldn't be too happy that they're carrying out these abductions on your turf.'

Mitrović took off his sun glasses. 'I'm not. It's not good for my business or my credibility when outsiders muscle in. What makes you think they're Russian?'

'Information received,' she said noncommittally.

He shrugged.

'We think they've recruited a local. Someone who knows who to go after and where they can be found. I was hoping you might have heard who's working for them.'

Mitrović thoughtfully chewed on the end of one arm of his glasses. 'No. No one I've heard about. That does not mean they've haven't got someone from Stockholm. They're all crooks up there.'

'If you hear anything, I'd appreciate it if you'd let me know. Then we can take this gang out of the picture.'

'Of course, Inspector. I'll contact you.'

'That shouldn't be a problem; you know where I live.'

Anita drove along Strandgatan and parked near the marina. She wanted a walk. The sun was breaking through the clouds, and the chance of another fine day lay ahead. She and Kevin wandered down towards the bobbing yachts. They hadn't spoken since she'd returned to the car and told him about her exchange with Dragan Mitrović. Her mind had turned towards Sami Litmanen's killer. Last night, she'd gone home before Alice Zetterberg returned to the office. But what she couldn't

avoid was a phone call at half past nine from a distraught and
distracted boss, whom she suspected had already been drinking.
Zetterberg wasn't really interested in how Helsinki had gone,
and Anita was quite happy to keep her in the dark until she'd
decided on her next move.

'Have you seen what that cow Ekman said in the paper?'
Zetterberg almost shrieked down the line. 'How could we
protect her? We didn't even know she'd been kidnapped!' Anita
knew that wasn't entirely true. 'You should have been firmer
with Goessling. Found out that he was lying about her being in
Switzerland.' Anita was too tired to argue and let her rant on.
'Then we could have done something to catch the gang.' It had
only been a matter of time before Zetterberg was blaming her.
'It's bloody incompetence. You were involved in the Uhlig fiasco
too. What the hell am I going to tell the commissioner? He'll
go crazy. He hates this sort of crap. Someone will go down for
this, and it won't be me!' The line went dead. Anita assumed
that Alice Zetterberg would be heading for the nearest bar to
get plastered.

A number of the yachts were starting to make their way
out into the Sound; others were being prepared for an outing.
Swedes never miss the opportunity to hit the water when there's
an encouraging wind and the sun is shining. Soon the blue of the
sea would be flecked with white fluttering sails. She found that
she was holding Kevin's hand. Her first reflex was to take it away;
it's what young people do, and they weren't young anymore.
Then she stopped herself. It was nice. It was comforting. She
gave his hand a squeeze. He returned the gesture.

'Are you OK?' Kevin asked.

'Yeah. Dragan Mitrović won't be coming after us again.'

'It's the case that's on your mind. I can tell. It's the curse
of detectives. We can never leave things. We're forever asking
questions and chasing answers. Never satisfied until we get a
result. And even then we look back and question ourselves.

Could we have done it differently? Did we miss something?'

'I missed something all right. I went for the obvious in Sami Litmanen's case. All those people who'd had their lives destroyed by him. Suspects galore. I should have looked into his Finnish background earlier. I'd have found his mother's Swedish connection. If only I'd paid more attention to the book he was reading. Clues I failed to spot.'

A middle-aged couple on their boat called to each other as their slim craft moved away from its mooring. Kevin waved to them and got astonished looks back.

'You've got your suspect now. The Coffee King.'

'I definitely think it was Anders Offesson. The trouble is I've got no proof. Nothing to put him at the scene of the crime. It's not easy to barge in and accuse the head of one of Sweden's most famous families of murder. A double murder, actually. The second one to cover up the first, because I'm sure that's what this is all about. "By the way, herr Offesson, we know you killed your sister as well." It's not going to happen. We'll never get him for Isabell's killing. Even if she was willing to testify, Eila won't be regarded as a reliable witness. A frail woman in her eighties with a history of mental problems talking about an event that happened when she was six. Any decent defence lawyer would tear her apart.'

'You need a way in.'

'But how?'

Kevin was about to wave to another crew and then thought better of it.

'You should start where Litmanen began. He only found out about Anders' treatment of his mother after he'd launched his investigation into the company. What had he learned? Wasn't it two well-known companies? That's what the editor told you. Litmanen went to South America. So, we know that one is Offesson's. His mother confirmed that. But the other?'

'There is another Brazilian connection. I've just remembered.

When I spoke to Hakim in Helsinki. Liv dug it up. Trellogística Brasil. Peter Uhlig – the guy who was kidnapped. It's one of his subsidiaries. Transports the beans from the Offesson plantations.'

'Well, there's your starting point.'

'I'll give Liv a ring.'

'Find out a bit more and then approach Anders Offesson with the business angle – Sami Litmanen was investigating your company. You need some background. Then all you have to do is charm him into admitting that he's a double murderer.'

Anita flashed him a wide-eyed gape. 'I didn't realize it was that simple!'

CHAPTER 42

When Anita arrived at the polishus on Monday morning, she wondered why she hadn't been called into work over the weekend by Alice Zetterberg. The others had, and an exhausted Hakim greeted her with a wan smile.

'I hope you had a good weekend. We didn't.'

'Any developments?'

'No breakthroughs. We've exhausted the harbour areas. I've seen enough of the inside of containers to last me a lifetime. Of course, it hasn't occurred to Zetterberg that the gang may just have put the thing on the back of a truck and taken it away after use. She's all over the place. I think she's barricaded herself in Moberg's office awaiting the inevitable call from the commissioner. She's more worried about his reaction to the kidnaps because he regards them as more important people than a hated "parasite of a journalist", as she called Sami Litmanen. She's got warped priorities. The living before the dead.'

'I spoke to her on Friday night. Somehow, she'd managed to turn it into my fault. She's clearly freezing me out of the kidnappings. Suits me.'

'We're all useless, according to her. Oh, by the way, I hear you've been keeping Liv busy over the weekend.'

'Sorry about that.'

'Don't be. I wasn't around and it gave her something to do. Any luck?'

'Your girl is clever and resourceful. That's official.' Hakim couldn't hide his pleasure at the compliment. 'She's building up quite a network of financial journalists. Even made contact with one in São Paulo. All is not well in Brazil, which might explain Sami Litmanen's battling companies. You know that most of Offesson's coffee comes from Brazil and Colombia?'

'Yes, mainly Brazil.'

'Right. And that Uhlig's subsidiary firm transports the Brazilian beans to be shipped out?' Hakim nodded. 'Well, according to Liv's South American source, Trellogística Brasil has been shut down for the moment. Some irregularities. The source wasn't sure of the reason, though it could be a lack of bribes to the right people or someone wanting to take over the company using officials to put pressure on. It certainly hasn't helped Trellogistics' share price. And all this happened at exactly the same time that Uhlig was a captive.'

'Do you think Uhlig fell out with Offesson? And that the coffee people are behind this?'

'Could be. It's quite a coincidence that all this happens when Uhlig is out of the picture. He's still the main decision maker in the group.'

'You're not suggesting that the kidnappings and Litmanen's murder are linked?'

'No, I don't think so. All I'm saying is that there's a good chance that Sami Litmanen was onto something dodgy going on between Anders Offesson and Peter Uhlig. I'm sure it's a coincidence that Uhlig was kidnapped at that particular time, but the situation allowed Offesson to make his move. It's only a theory. What I *am* sure about is that Anders Offesson is our killer.'

Anita was leaving the building. It was lunch time: she was peckish and she was heading out to find something to eat. The day was blustery; the fine weather that had stretched over the weekend had now turned. It blew her hair across her face and she swept it away from her glasses. Rarely was Malmö free of wind.

'Anita!' Klara Wallen came out of the main door after her. 'Can I have a quick word?'

'Sure. I'm just going to grab some food. Want to have lunch with me?'

Wallen's eyebrows shot up. 'No chance with Zetterberg on the warpath. She's got another meeting about the kidnaps in a few minutes. Commissioner Dahlbeck's given her a right old bollocking by all accounts. Apparently, his secretary heard him shouting.'

They crossed the road and stood overlooking the canal. The water was being riffled by the wind. There weren't any pedalos out today.

'There's something on my mind that I want to run past you. There's no point talking to Zetterberg. She just gets fixated on one thing and won't listen to anything else.'

'Been there, seen that,' said Anita, resting her bottom against the railings, arms crossed.

'It's actually a point that you raised. The food that Peter Uhlig was served when he was in captivity.' This piqued Anita's interest immediately. 'When we interviewed Kristina Ekman, she said she was given fast food. So was Mats Möller. Yet Uhlig was fed things like herring, mashed potatoes, chicken, meatballs – basically, meals that have to be cooked. Are kidnappers likely to go to all that trouble, especially if they're holding someone in a semi-public area such as a harbour? You keep things tight; make life as easy as possible for yourself.'

'I understand,' nodded Anita as she swept her hair back yet again.

'The more I think about Uhlig's abduction, the more it doesn't quite add up.'

'Such as?'

'The whole handover-of-the-money business. We know the money was made available. We saw it. Then, conveniently, it disappears with the mysterious police patrol. This is after the switch of cars at the last minute; we hadn't time to put a camera in fru Uhlig's Volkswagen so we couldn't record anything. And I've looked into Trellogistics. They're not in as healthy a state as might be imagined.'

'They're having problems in Brazil, too. A subsidiary firm has been closed down. Temporarily, I think.'

'His kidnap might have been a way of releasing money that was tied up elsewhere. The board would have been obliged to cough up. I mean, what if Peter Uhlig is behind the kidnaps? A great way of raising much-needed revenue.'

'Sounds a bit implausible,' Anita said sceptically.

'I know, I know. Far-fetched. But if he's the one who set up the kidnappings, no one is going to suspect him when he's one of the victims. I mean, he was supposedly kidnapped with no one else around. A quiet country road with no witnesses. The other two were snatched in town. OK, there weren't any witnesses to Möller's either, but he was taken outside his office. The kidnappers can't have guaranteed that no one would be about.' Wallen gripped the railings with both hands, unable to direct her gaze at Anita. 'You don't think I'm daft?'

'Of course not. Makes a kind of sense.' It didn't really, yet Anita was pleased that Wallen was showing initiative. She wasn't known for thinking outside the box. Anita wanted to encourage her. 'Pursue it. My advice is to dig a bit more before you attempt to run your theory past Alice Zetterberg.'

One interesting snippet to come out of her chat with Klara Wallen was that Trellogistics might be in trouble. A quick call to Liv, who was fast becoming a business expert, confirmed that Trellogistics shares were down further. There wasn't a run on them as yet, but they were considered shaky. She'd then

called Alice Zetterberg to say that she was going out to speak
to Anders Offesson. Anita knew fine well Zetterberg was in a
meeting with the rest of the team so wouldn't answer the call;
she happily left a voice message. She knew that had she spoken
to Zetterberg, she was unlikely to have been given permission
until Commissioner Dahlbeck had been consulted. And he
wouldn't have sanctioned it without some solid evidence.

Anita drove Kevin's hire car north of Malmö, round Lund
and deep into the countryside. The landscape was mainly flat
with a patchwork of fields broken up by small woods and
copses and the usual Scanian farmhouses and occasional village.
To Anita, it wasn't as attractive as her own Österlen. She was
now in Eslöv Municipality, where the Offesson family home
was located; she'd found it via Google maps. She still wasn't
sure how she was going to approach her interview with Anders
Offesson. She'd taken the precaution of ringing ahead and
had kept the reason for her visit vague, despite the efforts of
Offesson's officious daughter-in-law to quiz her. The downside
of this strategy was that Offesson would have been forewarned;
the upside was that she was guaranteed to speak to him.

Anita had spent much of Sunday going round Västra
Hamnen with a photo of Anders Offesson to see if it jogged
any memories. The problem was the photo was out of date by
at least ten years; she couldn't find a recent one so had taken
one off the internet. The man in the picture appeared affable,
smiling into the camera. He still had a good head of greying
hair and a moustache to match. The eyes were bright, though
that might have been from the flash of the camera. The nose
was prominent, the jaw thick-set and the mouth slightly askew;
he was certainly not handsome. It was difficult to estimate his
size as he wasn't standing next to anyone. Certainly, his build
suggested he was strong enough to smash a lamp into the top of
Sami Litmanen's head. But it was hard to believe that this doyen
of the coffee dynasty, who had bequeathed millions of kronor

over the years to good causes, was a murderer.

It had taken Anita fifty minutes to reach the entrance to the Offesson estate. The lofty, wrought-iron gates punctuating a solid, high wall topped with ribbed terracotta tiles were enough to discourage any unwanted visitors. Anita spoke into an intercom and the gates opened. An avenue of limes ushered her towards the main house, where the drive divided to girdle three concentric circles of neat, low hedging, in the centre of which was a statue of a nymph. On seeing the house, Anita thought it looked very familiar. It was a cream, oblong, three-storey, Neoclassical building with a curved portico, the columns of which supported a balcony, beneath a domed rotunda incorporated into the middle section. Then it came to her – Gyllebo Castle near Simrishamn. It was almost identical and had probably been constructed at much the same time, possibly by the same architect.

Anita parked the car next to a new, green Land Rover and an older, but spacious, silver Volvo. She made her way up the steps and rang the bell. It was answered by a woman in casual slacks and a summer blouse that would have made an H&M customer blanch at the cost. The absence of lines on the woman's face did not belie her age but simply indicated the possibility of Botox. She was probably in her fifties. But it was her hair that was her most dramatic feature. Thick and black, it was fashionably unkempt, as though she'd been plugged into an electric socket.

'I'm Felicity Offesson,' the woman said, offering a hand that was manicured to perfection. The nails were a virulent shade of red.

'Anita Sundström,' said Anita, disengaging her hand from the woman's cold grasp.

'Are you sure it's Anders you want to see? Not my husband, Christer?' Her Swedish was good, though Anita now detected an American twang which she hadn't noticed when they'd talked on the phone.

'Yes.'

'I just thought... as you'd said it was to do with the business, Christer runs it now. Anders is still involved, but his poor health means he doesn't take much of an active part these days.'

The reference to Anders Offesson's health rang an alarm bell in Anita's head.

'No. I do need to speak to your father-in-law.'

'Very well. I'll take you through to the garden. He's out there. Please don't upset him. He's got a chest complaint at the moment.'

Felicity Offesson took Anita through the cavernous hallway, past a lavish staircase and down a wide corridor that led to a rear door. Outside, a carefully mown lawn, bordered on either side by splashes of radiant colour, melded seamlessly, with the aid of a cleverly designed ha-ha, into acres of rolling parkland. In the middle of the lawn, two large oak trees cast sharp shadows in the afternoon sun. Anita was taken along a stone-flagged path to an expansive patio near the far end of the house. There, sitting on a comfortable garden chair, was Anders Offesson dressed in a cream, creased-linen suit. Perched on his head was a panama hat. The spot was sheltered from the wind and a large parasol shaded him from any unwanted heat. As the two women approached the old man, Anita couldn't help her gaze straying over the lawn to the oak trees. The child's tree house was long gone.

'This is Inspector Sundström, the police officer whom I told you called.'

Anders Offesson peered up at Anita. Slowly, he stiffly rose from his chair.

'Afternoon. Take a seat.'

Anita quickly appraised his size, strength and agility. Physically, he appeared strong, but was he nimble enough to have caught Litmanen off guard? Maybe his slow movements lulled Litmanen into a false sense of security? Yet, even if he had been able to commit the murder, could he have cleaned the apartment and carried away the missing items? She doubted it.

'Shall I get drinks? Or a coffee?' enquired Felicity in a simpering voice.

'Don't bother. I'm sure the inspector won't be staying long.' Anita felt cheated. It was ironic that she was at the home of Sweden's most illustrious coffee maker and she wasn't even being allowed one.

With an arched eyebrow, Felicity left them and flounced back into the house. Offesson resumed his seat. Anita sat down.

'What do you want?' The question was abrupt. 'Felicity said it was something to do with the company. In that case, you should be talking to Christer.'

'I'm sure you still take an active interest.'

'I still own the majority shares. I attend board meetings; little else though. Christer can fill me in on any details of an evening.'

'So your son still lives at home?'

From under his panama, he gave her a dirty look before his face melted into a half smile.

'We have to fill this pile somehow,' he said, nodding towards the house behind them. 'And Christer and that wife of his will inherit it when I'm gone.'

If Anita had her way, Christer might be inheriting it rather sooner than expected.

'Do you know a man called Sami Litmanen?'

'Should I?'

'Maybe you know him by his journalistic moniker, The Oligarch.'

'Now that *is* a name I recognize. A muckraker of the highest order.'

'Many would agree with you, especially the person who killed him.'

'Am I meant to be sorry?' He dissolved into a rasping cough. He pulled out a handkerchief to cover his mouth.

Anita let the noise subside before continuing.

'At the time of his death, he was investigating your company, particularly your South American plantations.'

Offesson dabbed his mouth. 'Why would he do that?'

'I was hoping you might have an answer.'

'You're speaking to the wrong person.'

'I don't think so. I'm sure you know exactly what's going on. I know that Peter Uhlig's São Paulo truck company has been closed down for some unknown reason. That must affect your coffee production if you can't get your beans transported.'

'I admit that has caused some short-term problems. Nothing that we can't overcome.'

'But there must be something more to get The Oligarch rushing off to Brazil and Colombia. Are you putting the squeeze on Trellogistics?'

'Of course not,' he said angrily before spluttering into another coughing fit. When he came up for air, 'It's damaging our business. But it's not just that...' She could see that he was about to continue then changed his mind. After a long pause, 'Trading conditions are difficult at the moment, that's all.'

'So you can't think what his story was going to be about?'

'I'm sorry, I can't help you.' It sounded like a dismissal.

Anita didn't move. 'Did Sami Litmanen contact you directly?'

'Course not.' The denial came out too rapidly. He recovered: 'Why on earth would he?'

'Were you aware that Sami Litmanen had a personal connection to this family – to you?'

'That seems highly unlikely.'

'Eila Riihiahti.' Anders Offesson stiffened. 'The Finnish girl your family took in during the war.'

Still clutching his handkerchief, he waved his hand airily. 'Vaguely.'

'She was Litmanen's mother.'

'How extraordinary!'

'Isn't it? I spoke to her last week. She remembers you *very* well. An eight-year-old boy who bullied her; made her life a misery.'

'How ungrateful. We took her in and gave her the kind of life she couldn't possibly have had anywhere else. She came from some dreadful Helsinki slum and we gave her this,' he said, waving his hand towards the garden.

'You did. She particularly remembers the two oak trees over there. One very clearly. The one your sister Isabell was in. And she also remembers the reason for her fall.'

'You will leave, now!' Offesson barked.

'Where were you on the night of Sunday, the fourteenth of May at around ten o'clock?'

'This is outrageous! Get out of my house!'

Anita stood up. 'This isn't the last you'll hear from me.'

'Oh, yes it is! Your career is over; I'll see to that!'

CHAPTER 43

Anita made her way back through the house.

Felicity Offesson met her in the hall.

'How did you get on with the old man?'

'I'm glad he's not my father-in-law,' Anita replied in English.

A sardonic grin flickered over Felicity's face. 'A lot of people have said that since I came here. Anders isn't a great fan of us Yanks. And it doesn't help that he liked Christer's first wife. I was never going to be an adequate replacement, especially as I was the reason for the messy divorce.'

They made their way to the front door.

'Are you involved in the business?'

'I wanted to be, but Anders put a block on it.'

'So you don't know how it's going?'

'I know when things aren't going well. Christer gets moody.'

'Is he moody right now?'

Felicity furrowed her immaculately plucked eyebrows.

'Is that why you're here?'

Anita pushed open the front door. It took an effort to move the solid oak. Felicity followed her out to the top of the steps.

'In a way.'

'That explains a lot. He hasn't been himself the last two or three weeks. Introspective. I could tell he was worried. Wouldn't say what.'

When Anita reached the bottom of the steps, she called

back 'You don't happen to know what Anders was doing on the evening of May the fourteenth by any chance? It was a Sunday evening.'

Felicity took out a mobile phone from her trouser pocket and her thumbs worked the keys.

'There was a concert that night. In Lund. Brahms and Mahler, and a bit of Gershwin thrown in. That was for my benefit.'

'Your benefit?'

'Offesson's was sponsoring the event.'

'And was Anders there?'

'No. Bit embarrassing. Pleaded illness at the last minute. So Christer and I went without him.'

After Anita's visit to Anders Offesson, she went straight home. She needed time to think and to bounce a few ideas off Kevin; he was a receptive sounding board. When she arrived at the apartment, she saw him coming out of the park wheeling a buggy. Jazmin had clearly roped him in for childcare duty. Leyla gave a squeal of delight when she saw her grandmother. When they had crossed the road, Anita hoisted Leyla out of the buggy and hugged her; descending into a babble of baby language. Leyla giggled and did her usual trick of trying to grab Anita's glasses.

'Any luck?' Kevin enquired as he folded the chair up.

'I'll tell you about it after I've had a bit of a play with this gorgeous young lady.'

Jazmin turned up at six, and they had a bite to eat before she and a tired and fractious Leyla headed for home. Anita was happy to avoid the inevitable bedtime meltdown. Kevin opened a bottle of red and they retired to the living room.

'I don't usually drink on a Monday,' said Anita, happily accepting the proffered glass.

'Granny Sundström has earned it.' Kevin sat down beside

her. 'And what has Inspector Granny Sundström found out today?'

'I found out that Anders Offesson is an unpleasant man. I don't think he likes women much.'

'Is he your man?'

'He should be. He's touchy about the business, which is understandable, but he was *very* touchy when I mentioned Eila Litmanen, or Riihiahti as she was then.'

'That's understandable, too, if he did kill his sister.'

'And he doesn't have an alibi for the night Litmanen died. He pulled out of attending a concert that evening. Said he was unwell.'

'It's all adding up. Litmanen must have got him over to his apartment on some pretext. Not sure why. Maybe to make him suffer – revenge for his mum.'

'Yes. I can see that. It would explain the nature of the killing. Litmanen saying that he was going to tell the world that Offesson had committed sororicide. It fits in with it not being premeditated. Spur of the moment thing.'

Anita was staring thoughtfully into her glass.

'I sense a *but*.'

'I don't doubt he has the strength to smash the lamp into Litmanen's head, but... I'm not sure he's physically up to the rest of it. He'd have to have driven to Malmö – forty-five minutes, say. Do the deed, then collect up all the things in the apartment that the murderer took away. Drive all the way back. This is a man of eighty-four, and not in the best of health.'

'Could it have been the son?'

'Why should he do it? He didn't kill his aunt. Besides, he was at the concert with his wife.'

'So, you're back to square one.'

Anita grunted and took a long slurp of her wine.

The next morning, she knew that Alice Zetterberg would

be after her. She'd ignored several calls that Zetterberg had made to her the night before. She managed to put off going to Moberg's office until well after ten. By then, she and Hakim had gleaned some useful information.

Zetterberg was fuming, though she was trying to keep herself under control. The twitching eyes had always been a giveaway since their academy days. 'Don't you think I've got enough on my plate without getting an official complaint from Anders Offesson? And why the fuck weren't you answering your phone last night?'

'Babysitting. Didn't want it to disturb my granddaughter.' As lies go, it was at least plausible.

'Anders Offesson is a very powerful man. And you blunder in there. Any moment now, I'll get a call from Commission Dahlbeck wanting to know the reason why. You should have passed it by me first.'

'I tried to but you were busy on the Kristina Ekman case.'

'That's no excuse. You've always been insubordinate. This whole department's a mess and when I've sorted it out, if I have my way, you'll be out, too.'

'Don't you want to know why I went to see Anders Offesson?'

This took Zetterberg by surprise. 'Well?' she blustered.

'I found out in Finland that Sami Litmanen's mother lived with the Offesson family during the war.'

'So, there's a connection. But it's a hell of a jump to murdering someone.'

'Anders Offesson had a five-year-old sister, Isabell. He killed her by deliberately pushing her out of a tree. Litmanen's mother saw him do it. She was only six at the time. Anders threatened her. She was in a strange country and was frightened so she didn't say anything. She's kept it bottled up all her life – until Sami's last visit. He was already investigating Offesson's South American operation and when his mother came out with the story, that's what suddenly made the whole thing "personal" for him. I think he asked Anders Offesson over to his apartment that night. When confronted with what Litmanen knew about Isabell's death, Anders felt he had no choice but to kill him.'

'Anders Offesson must be an old man now.'

'Eighty-four,' Anita had to concede. It was an obvious flaw in her argument.

'Is he physically up to it?'

'I'm not sure.'

'Well, that doesn't sound very promising. Have you any evidence?' Zetterberg demanded.

'I've been able to get hold of the records for the Offessons' landline phone. As you can imagine, there weren't many calls on it with everybody using mobiles these days. With Hakim's help, I've traced all the numbers except one. Two incoming calls from a mystery mobile. One on May the fourth then, more significantly, a second on the afternoon of the murder ten days later. I now believe they were from Sami Litmanen's missing phone. Or one of them, anyway. We think he used different phones for different people. Offesson probably found more than one phone at the apartment.'

'Can you be sure?'

'It was a pay-as-you-go. So, no, I suppose I can't be a hundred percent sure. The point is that Anders pulled out of going to a concert in Lund that night. The Offesson company were sponsoring it so he was expected to attend.'

'You're just jumping to conclusions as usual. You're a loose cannon. And I can't afford to have people like you buggering up my team. You're on borrowed time, Anita.' She wagged a threatening finger. 'I don't want you going anywhere near Anders Offesson again unless you have real proof. And you don't make a move without my direct approval. Got it?'

CHAPTER 44

The next two days dragged for Anita and the rest of the Criminal Investigation Squad. Stung by Kristina Ekman's comments, there had been plenty of activity, yet no hint of progress. Alice Zetterberg was now virtually hiding in Moberg's office and snapping at anybody who ventured in. Anita was equally stymied. She had tried everything to connect Anders Offesson to Sami Litmanen's killing. She was sure that Litmanen had contacted him. He had no alibi for the night of the murder. Yet she had no way of proving it. With her frustration reaching boiling point, she'd left the polishus late on Wednesday afternoon and was now sitting in Erik Moberg's apartment.

Anita had never been there before. Of course, Moberg hadn't been living in Oxie that long. The apartment, in a nondescript block surrounded by nondescript houses, was the result of his last divorce. He'd lived close to Limhamn in better days. The furniture was all second hand; the good stuff had gone to the various spouses over time. It was entirely his own fault, and Anita found it hard to raise much sympathy for him on that front. But she did feel sorry for him in his current predicament. His real marriage had always been to the job, the one constant in his life – now that was under threat. He was determined to come back to work as soon as possible, which is why he seemed to perk up at Anita's visits: catching up with the case that he'd been heavily involved in before his heart attack was obviously doing him good. And Anita was also happy to see him at last taking his health seriously; he had rejected the Finnish chocolate she'd brought him. He was even off coffee and had offered her a green tea. She was impressed until twenty minutes later, when he undermined his new regime by lighting up a cigarette.

'It's extraordinary that three kidnaps later, we're no further forward,' he said, shaking his head after Anita had filled him in on the details. She noticed he'd said 'we' as though he was still fully involved in the investigation. 'I do take the point about the food. Odd, isn't it? And Wallen's angle on Peter Uhlig is interesting, too, if slightly unbelievable. Has she got any further with that?'

'Not really, though she has dug up the fact that Trellogistics are having difficulties; and not just in Brazil. Uhlig might have been tempted to raise money, though it's a strategy that could go horribly wrong.'

'It would be a helluva gamble,' Moberg said, stubbing out his cigarette decisively. 'And is the injection of the odd four million euros going to make much difference to a large organization in trouble?'

'If you do it often enough. But I know where you're coming from.'

'I must admit, sitting on the sidelines, you get a different perspective from when you're in the middle of it all. We have one kidnap in March, then suddenly two in a row in May. Why the gap?'

'Maybe some were harder to plan than others. Or the gang are getting more confident.' Anita put down her half-drunk green tea. It wasn't to her taste, and she couldn't see Moberg surviving on it for much longer. 'But yes, it's niggled me too. The first, a quick in and out. Money moved digitally. The Uhlig and Ekman operations carried out in a more traditional way. Money has to be physically accessed. That takes time. The longer you've got your captive, the greater the risks.'

'And the danger of the money drop-offs. Hell, we got done up like a kipper at Skårby. Yet you say that this German boyfriend of Kristina Ekman's just left the ransom at Simrishamn church? That would have been difficult to collect if we'd known about it and been on hand. God, I can't believe that bloody woman has turned up again.' Anita could see he was becoming agitated; he sought calmness in another cigarette. He exhaled his first puff. 'And Dag Wollstad paying up!' He allowed himself a chuckle. 'It'll be peanuts to him, but it's comforting to know it probably pissed him right off having to part with some of his precious millions for that bitch of a daughter. Couldn't have happened to a nicer pair.'

The conversation changed to life at the polishus. Anita didn't have much gossip, and she felt that she had better get going. She gathered up her bag and thanked him for the tea.

'How are you coping with Alice Zetterberg?'

'I'm not.'

'Hang in there. I'll be back before you know it. Couple of months, anyway.'

At the door, he gave her a hug. It caught her completely unawares.

'Thanks for keeping in touch. No one else has.'

'They're just busy.' The truth was that any friends that Moberg may have had had moved on or left the force. Maybe he didn't have any *real* friends, she reflected.

'And Anita. Don't let Zetterberg get to you. You're a damn good detective. I may not have shown how much I... you know what I mean.'

She didn't know where to look. 'Just come back soon,' she found herself muttering.

Pildammsparken in the early evening was a delight to the senses. Dappled sunlight twinkled through the trees, which were in early leaf, and the freshly mown grass smelt sweet. Blackbirds sang their dulcet melodies while bees droned lazily among the flowers. June was Anita's favourite month. Swedes longed for this time of year – the summers were all too short and needed to be treasured. Midsummer, when everyone threw off their inhibitions and celebrated the sun and the light, as their pagan ancestors had once done, was only three weeks away. It was still warm as Anita and Kevin sauntered round the park. Half of Malmö seemed to be there: families enjoying an after-supper walk; sweaty joggers wired up to their music; older couples arm in arm, oblivious to the activities around them; and groups of young people barbecuing on the grass. Anita and Kevin stopped by a bench and sat down. He would be leaving soon. To her amazement, she was starting to dread it. The irritation of his last stay had been replaced by a personal contentment she hadn't felt since the early days of her marriage to Björn. She squeezed his hand.

'What was that for?'

'I've got this bizarre reflex action in my hand that sometimes I can't control.'

'I'd see a doctor about that in case you do it to strangers. They might pick up the wrong signal. Whoops, there it goes again!'

They continued to sit and enjoy people-watching. Kevin's eye caught a group of students sitting on a rug. They were listening to a long-haired girl playing a guitar. Strains of the music and her gentle singing wafted across the park. The song was familiar, though Kevin couldn't put a name to it. The music set off his train of thought.

'I've been thinking about the concert in Lund. The one that Anders Offesson got out of.'

'What about it?'

'Did you check that Anders was at home when his son and daughter-in-law got back? If the murder was around ten, and

309

Anders was the killer, he would have had to look for and gather up all the things in Litmanen's apartment that might incriminate him, clean away any traces of his being there and then drive back; you estimate at least forty-five minutes. Given that it would be dark by then, add a few more minutes.'

'And your point is that he wouldn't get home until after eleven, and that the concert might have finished well before that?'

'Exactly. The chances are that if it was Anders who committed the murder, he'd reach home later than Christer and... what's her name?'

'Felicity. Of course, as they were the concert sponsors, there might have been a reception after the event.'

'Worth asking the question.' Anita had taken out her phone even before he'd finished speaking.

'Can I speak to Felicity Offesson please? It's Inspector Anita Sundström.' She turned to Kevin, who didn't understand the Swedish. 'Must be the housekeeper,' Anita whispered. 'She's getting her.'

A minute later, Felicity was on the line.

'Hello. I've just a quick question,' said Anita in English. 'It's about that concert you and your husband attended in Lund. What time did it finish?' Kevin couldn't hear what was being said so just kept his eyes on Anita, who was nodding.

'Was your father-in-law at home when you returned?'

The disappointed expression on Anita's face told him that she hadn't got the answer she was after.

'He must have been feeling better if he joined you for a nightcap?'

Anita listened and was nodding again. 'So about half ten?' Another pause as Anita continued to concentrate. Kevin noticed that her expression began to change. Something was making her sit up. 'That's very good of you, Felicity. Sorry to have disturbed you.'

Anita thoughtfully clicked to end the call and rested the phone on her lap.

'Well?'

'Remember that you suggested that *Christer* Offesson might be our man? And I pooh-poohed the idea? And he had an alibi anyway? Well, according to Felicity, he left the concert at the interval. Urgent business. Didn't reappear until after midnight.'

'And Lund is close to Malmö?'

'Twenty minutes.'

CHAPTER 45

Anita got into work early on Thursday morning. She was determined to find out all she could about Christer Offesson. As soon as Hakim appeared, she commandeered him to help. Christer was Anders' only child. Now fifty-two, he had been educated at a private school in Stockholm before studying in America, at the prestigious MIT Sloan School of Management in Cambridge, Massachusetts. Then he'd been brought into the family firm. His father had given him a thorough grounding in the world of coffee, which included a spell running one of the company's Brazilian plantations. In 2009, his father stepped aside from the day-to-day running of Offesson's, and Christer took over. Though he adopted a more cautious approach and was not as dynamic or as ruthless as Offesson Senior (this opinion garnered from a feature in *Affärsvärlden*, the long-standing weekly business publication), the company had continued to do well. However, Hakim had found a recent article with the heading: *Trouble Brewing for Coffee Giant?* which implied that profits were slipping and questions were being asked about Christer's lack of focused leadership. Christer's personal life had also run into trouble when he'd started having an affair with New York socialite Felicity Reading, the sister of one of his old classmates at business school. A messy divorce, which made headlines on both sides of the Atlantic, resulted in his first wife taking a sizeable slice

312

of his personal fortune. This might explain Anders' attitude to Felicity. The upside was that the Reading name came with big bucks from the fields of security, and health and safety. Neither marriage had produced children.

Anita felt guilty as she sipped her coffee and bit into a much-needed cinnamon bun while poor Hakim was unable to touch anything. She stared at the two recent photos of Christer Offesson they'd printed off from online magazine articles. He was unmistakably his father's son, though he wasn't as obviously imposing. He clearly cared more about his appearance. He was clean-shaven and wore his blond hair very short. The suits were expensive. He was what her mother would call 'well-groomed'.

'Right, let's go over everything again,' Anita said after licking the last crumb off her lip. 'Sami Litmanen latches onto a story of two leading Swedish companies battling it out, though we're still not sure about what. What we do know is that it's to do with South America, as he visited both Brazil and Colombia. From what Eila Litmanen told me, one of these companies is Offesson's; and Litmanen visited their coffee-growing areas. The other Swedish company we know that is definitely involved with Brazil and Offesson's is the Trellogistics subsidiary which transports Offesson's beans, among other things. We now know that Uhlig's company operation has been halted for reasons unknown. So, is it safe to assume that these are the companies Litmanen was looking at – Christer Offesson versus Peter Uhlig?'

'I think so,' Hakim agreed.

'Within this framework, we also have to assume that something dodgy has been going on. Otherwise, where's Litmanen's story?'

'Agreed.'

'Then a personal element comes into play, as confirmed by Erin Ljung at *Sanningen*. It turns out that Anders Offesson killed his sister, an event that has blighted Sami Litmanen's mother's life. So Litmanen's potential scoop turns into a mission of retribution. Maybe it can't be proved in a court of law, but that story getting into the public domain would have a dramatic effect not only on the Offesson family, but also on the business, which we now know might be experiencing difficulties. We also believe that Litmanen rang the Offesson home on two occasions, though that can't be proved without the actual phone he used. But it's highly significant that one of the calls was made on the day of the murder. Another assumption is that those calls were made to the old man. He was the target. Unfortunately, despite missing the concert, Anders wouldn't have had time to have committed the murder and get back to have a nightcap with Felicity at ten thirty, or have the physical capacity to clear the scene afterwards. So now we need to look at Christer.'

'Maybe Christer took Litmanen's call. It was on the house phone.'

'That's one possibility. Another is that Anders took the calls and then confessed to his son. Whatever, the last call seems to have involved Litmanen inviting whichever Offesson it was over to his apartment so that he could exact his revenge face to face. It's the only way I can explain how the murderer knew where Sami Litmanen lived. What we do know is that on the night, Christer left the concert at around a quarter to nine and didn't appear again until after midnight. And as we know, Västra Hamnen isn't far down the road from Lund. So, he had ample opportunity. And he also had time to dump or stash all the stuff he'd taken from the apartment before returning home after midnight.'

Hakim stretched his long legs and yawned. 'I buy all that. And the motive is–'

'Interchangeable; father and son. Except that in Christer's case, he's protecting his father's reputation as well as the company's. Remember, Litmanen's original investigation may well have exposed underhand dealings by Offesson's Coffee. That in itself could have seriously harmed the company. Throw in the killing of Isabell Offesson, and the need to murder Sami Litmanen becomes a no-brainer.'

'I like the logic. The only problem is that it's all circumstantial. We can't place Christer at the murder scene.'

'I think we've got enough to go and see him. Rattle his cage.'

'But will Zetterberg let us?'

By the time Anita had decided to go to Alice Zetterberg with what she'd got, the acting chief inspector was nowhere to be found. Brodd reckoned that she was in meetings with the commissioner. Anita had little doubt that her visit to Anders Offesson was high on the agenda. The old man's threat to finish her career might be the result. Though she could be impulsive at times, she realized that with Zetterberg, Dahlbeck and Anders Offesson, she had to be wary. Subduing her natural inclination to jump into a car and rush off and grill Christer Offesson, she waited for Zetterberg to appear. However, she spent her time wisely by finding out what Christer Offesson's movements would be over the next few hours so she would know where to track him down. The company headquarters in Helsingborg said he wasn't in and that he wasn't expected back today; they thought he might be at home. A follow-up call to the Offesson mansion revealed that he wasn't there either, though he was expected back for dinner. Anita wasn't keen on the idea of confronting Christer at home in the company of his father. She might have to wait until tomorrow and catch him in Helsingborg – if Zetterberg hadn't managed to get her suspended before then.

It was around four o'clock when she heard a commotion outside her door. She got up from her desk and went to see what was happening. Klara Wallen came rushing down the corridor.

'It's happened again! A snatch!'

'Where?'

'On Östra Förstadsgatan.'

It only took them a few minutes to get to the site of the seizure as it was only one street away from the back of the polishus. It wasn't far from where Kristina Ekman had been taken.

On the pavement, there was already a uniformed officer and a small crowd of standers-by. It wasn't long before Hakim and Erlandsson joined them. Number 26 was an angular block of five storeys. On street level, there were two commercial premises either side of the entrance; one a closed kebab shop, the other a florist's. A middle-aged woman was standing in the doorway of the florist's wringing her hands.

'I saw it all. A man came out of the front door of the apartments here and this dark blue van drove up. A couple of men... they were wearing black masks... burst out of the back of the van and grabbed him. Forced him inside and drove off down that way,' she said, pointing to Värnhemstorget.

'The same M.O.,' said Wallen

'How long ago?' asked Anita, who found herself taking charge.

'I rang the police straightaway. Ten minutes maybe.'

'Hakim. Get straight onto traffic.'

'Right away,' said Hakim, pulling out his phone.

The woman was obviously shocked. 'It was frightening. I've never seen anything like it before.'

'Can you describe this man?'

'Well built. Medium height. Short hair. Fair.'

'Have you seen him before?'

'Yes. He's come in here and bought flowers. Very well mannered. Polite.'

Wallen was writing down the names of the apartment owners listed next to the buzzer on the wall by the entrance.

'Did he live here?' Wallen asked while still writing.

'No, I don't think so. I've never seen him going out in the morning, or coming home at night. It's usually in the afternoons that I've seen him.'

'Thank you; you've been really helpful,' said Anita, patting the woman reassuringly on her arm. 'Pontus, can you take this lady's statement? Bea, you can start coordinating witness statements. Lots of people will have seen this.'

She turned to Wallen. 'Right, let's check all the apartments. That should give us a name.'

'What I can't understand,' said Wallen as she scrutinized her list, 'is kidnapping someone from here. These are just basic apartments on a busy street. No one worth four million euros is going to be living here.'

Anita buzzed into the building. There was a short passage to another door. Beyond that was a stone spiral staircase that ran up to the top floor. Next to the stairs were metal lift doors.

'You start at the bottom, I'll start at the top,' said Anita as she summoned the lift. There was room for about four people at a squeeze. This wasn't servicing luxury living.

Anita and Wallen met at the halfway landing twenty minutes later. There were four floors with two apartments on each level, and then a further apartment in the attic at the top of the stairwell.

'Everybody accounted for,' said Wallen.

'Same here,' said Anita. 'Except that top apartment. No one's in. And there isn't a name on the door.'

'So that's where the man came from?'

'Must be. According to the old fellow in the apartment just below, it's not lived in. Says this smartly dressed, middle-aged gentleman appears occasionally. Matches the florist's description. Usually afternoons. And a woman.'

'Has he seen *her*?'

'Fleetingly, a couple of times. Forties. Quite attractive. Full figure. Red hair. But he's heard her on a number of occasions.'

'Heard her? Arguing?'

'No. Screaming. Shouting. He went all round the houses

because he couldn't bring himself to say *sex*, but that's what she and the smart gentleman were up to. Old chap had to turn up the television to drown out the noises.'

Wallen shook her head. 'A love nest. A rich businessman with a love nest. Our gang must have sussed that out.'

Anita's phone went off. 'Hi, Hakim. Any joy?' After a short conversation, she looked at Wallen. 'Traffic have stopped a couple of blue vans. Not them. Hakim's now got the vehicle number plate from one of the witnesses on the street, so they know what they're looking for. Nothing yet.'

Wallen glanced at her watch. 'It's been about half an hour. Probably gone to ground by now.'

'Better wind things up quickly down here and then get back and check out who owns that top apartment. And we'd better report back to Zetterberg. I can't imagine how she's going to break this to the commissioner!'

Zetterberg had been dragged out of her meeting with Commissioner Dahlbeck to hear the news of the latest kidnap. She was almost apoplectic. This was a total nightmare. She had just spent the last two hours trying to justify what the team had been doing over the last fortnight. Dahlbeck thought of it as inaction at best; mismanagement and indolence at worst. Zetterberg had managed to put some of the blame on Moberg's original handling of the first two kidnaps and some on what she described as the 'uncontrollable' Inspector Sundström. Though Anita wasn't highly regarded by Dahlbeck – there had been too many infractions going back to the shooting of Mick Roslyn – Zetterberg hadn't avoided all the flack. Now the pressure was really on.

Zetterberg hurriedly convened a meeting in which she was updated on what had happened. Wallen told her they believed that the attic apartment was a wealthy man's love nest. The operation had been the same as Kristina Ekman's – masked men appearing from a van and grabbing someone off the street. This one had been a particularly public abduction. And at least this time they had the van's registration number. Hakim had already discovered that it had been stolen in Kalmar on the east coast on Tuesday, 23rd May; three days ago. They were trying to locate camera footage of it to see in which direction it had gone. Afterwards, Zetterberg had insisted on going down to Östra Förstadsgatan. If nothing else, she was desperate to show that she was a hands-on acting chief inspector. She rushed off with her new lapdog, Brodd.

Anita let her get on with it. Zetterberg had made it plain that she didn't really want Anita involved. There had been no chance to voice her theory about Christer Offesson. Maybe she would drive out to the Offesson home and wait for him to return. Intercept him at the gates. Not in the house. Not at this stage anyway.

She popped her head round Hakim's door. She wanted to tell him what she planned. Now that their relationship seemed to be back on an even keel, she was happy to confide in him. The truth was that she trusted his judgement. He was on the phone and she waited until he'd finished his call.

'As I won't be missed here, I thought I'd see if I can track down Christer Offesson.'

'I wouldn't bother,' said Hakim. He rubbed his forehead as though a headache was coming on.

'Think it's a bad idea?'

'I don't think you'll find him.'

'He'll turn up tonight. He's due to eat at home.'

'I doubt he'll make it. I've just found out who owns that top apartment.'

CHAPTER 46

'Christer Offesson! Please tell me you're joking!' Anita was incredulous.

'He bought the apartment two years ago,' Hakim explained. 'It wasn't through the business. He used his own name. Presumably, he chose this part of town as he would be less likely to run into his wife.'

Anita slumped down in shock. 'I can't believe our prime suspect has just been whipped away from under our very noses. The more I think about it, the more I'm convinced that Christer Offesson is our man.'

'His kidnap makes sense given the other targets. Another leading business figure. Zetterberg's going to have to warn the family that a call is imminent.'

'I can't believe all this.' Anita readjusted her glasses, which had slid down her nose. 'You don't think he's organized his own kidnap? Must have been worried after I'd talked to his father.'

'Anita, I think that's a bit fanciful. What happens when he turns up?'

'That's true.'

'I'm afraid you're going to have to talk to Zetterberg. I'll ring her now with the news it's Christer Offesson, and then you've got to let her know that the cases have just dovetailed.'

Anita groaned.

It was an hour before Zetterberg returned, and she was busy in conference with Brodd.

'What do you want?' she roared when Anita entered the meeting room.

'Christer Offesson.'

'I know it's him. Hakim phoned me. Bea's just calling to let the wife know.'

'He's now the main suspect in the Sami Litmanen killing.'

Zetterberg's expression was one of disbelief. 'I thought you said it was Anders, the old man.'

'I did. But you were right to be sceptical about his age. And I now know he couldn't have done it. He didn't have the time.'

'So what makes you think it's Christer?'

'Same reasons as the old man. But this time it was about protecting his father's reputation and that of Offesson's Coffee; I'm sure Litmanen must have had something damaging on the company as well. Christer had motive – and opportunity. He left a concert in Lund early and wasn't seen again until after midnight.'

'Proof?' Zetterberg growled in exasperation.

'I haven't found any yet. And it's not as though I can interview him!'

'This is a fucking mess. Dahlbeck'll make sure we're all in for the chop.'

Just then Klara Wallen came into the room. 'The van's been found. Abandoned on a side road near Staffanstorp. They must have switched vehicles.'

'How far out of town?'

'Roughly fifteen minutes. I'm going there now.'

'Right, I'm coming with you. Pontus, get onto forensics. I want them down there a.s.a.p..' After her recent panic and despair, Zetterberg was at last switching to decisive mode. 'And you,' she said, indicating Anita, 'can go with Hakim to the Offessons' place. They'll be getting a call soon. Get a techie

321

along to set up recording equipment.' Then, as an afterthought, 'And while you're at it, you can find some of that proof you need, so when we get Christer Offesson back, we can arrest him for murder.'

It wasn't the housekeeper that greeted Anita and Hakim, but a pale and shocked Felicity Offesson. It was a quarter past eight, and she was dressed for dinner in a knee-length, light-pink dress.

'I'm sorry,' said Anita in English.

As she spoke, another car crunched over the gravel. It was the technical back-up.

Felicity spoke mechanically as though the situation was beyond her comprehension. 'I've just had a call... a demand.'

'From the kidnappers?'

Felicity nodded.

'What have they asked for?'

'Four million euros. By next Wednesday.'

'Have they said where?'

'Where what?' she said blankly.

'Where they want the ransom money taken.'

'The man said he would ring back with the location.'

'Did he speak to you in English?'

'No. Swedish.'

A man and a woman got out of the car and started to unload equipment.

'Hakim, can you see to them? Bit late, but better do it anyway. They probably won't make contact again until the last minute.'

Anita guided Felicity down the steps and away from the house. The woman was clearly traumatized and didn't resist. They made their way across the gravel and wandered wordlessly down the lime avenue. The only sound was the crunch of their footsteps and the mellow rustling of the leaves overhead. Anita waited for Felicity to speak – she wouldn't get much out of her by pressurizing. She would talk when she was ready.

'You don't have a cigarette?'

'Sorry. Given up.'

'So have I.'

They continued on.

'Are you cold? Do you want to go back to the house?' asked Anita quietly.

Felicity stopped. She shook her head.

'Do you want to ask me anything?'

Felicity stopped walking and stood with her hands clasped, swaying gently.

'Where did they get hold of Christer? I thought the office would have contacted me; or the Helsingborg police.'

'It was in Malmö.' Felicity's head jerked up.

'Malmö? What was he doing there? I suppose it was something to do with his trip to São Paulo. He was due to fly out tomorrow morning.'

'Why was he going there?'

'He was tight-lipped about it. I gathered from Anders that it was important business he had to sort out. Something to do with distribution or some such.'

This wasn't going to be easy. 'I don't think it was to do with his trip. He came out of an apartment block on Östra Förstadsgatan.'

'Where in God's name is that?'

'Not far from our headquarters, as it happens. Your husband owns the top floor apartment.'

'I've never heard him mention it. Is it for business use?'

'I haven't been in yet but I don't think it's that sort of apartment.'

'What is it for then?'

'I think he was meeting someone.' Anita paused before adding softly 'A woman.'

Felicity's eyes widened as the inference sank in.

'The bastard!' she said through gritted teeth. 'He's been at it again.'

'Again?'

'He has previous. Hell, I'm previous. Always had a roving eye. I was his bit on the side. Never was good at keeping his dick in his pants, even after I ousted the first Mrs Offesson.' She stamped her foot on the ground. 'I bet I know who he was with.' This was the information that Anita needed. 'That red-headed bitch. Christ, he promised that was over.'

'Who are you talking about?'

'Pernilla. Pernilla Glad. She worked for Christer. She was head of international sales, which meant that she often accompanied him abroad. I got suspicious. I reckoned they were making more trips than was necessary. Checked his cell phone one night when he was sleeping. He'd been carrying on behind my back. Lovey-dovey texts.' Felicity had rapidly changed from the worried wife to the spitting-mad spouse. 'Of course, he tried to deny it when I confronted him. I told him he could forget turning her into the third Mrs Offesson and if he didn't sack her, I was going to take him for every krona he'd got. He backed down and "exit Pernilla", or so I thought.'

'It might not be her.'

'Oh, it's her. I just know. She lives in Malmö with her aging mother. That's why he'll not have gone to her place. What a complete shit!' She had now worked herself up into a fury. 'I've a good mind to let the kidnappers keep the bastard!'

CHAPTER 47

Anita hadn't got home until very late on the Thursday night. She'd updated Alice Zetterberg with news of the ransom demand and of Christer Offesson's possible mistress. Anita said she and Hakim would track Pernilla Glad down first thing in the morning. It was a straw that Zetterberg was all too keen to clutch at as nothing else had turned up on the kidnapping. She was trying to hurry through the forensics report on the dumped van.

Pernilla Glad had been easy to find – all Anita had had to do was Google, and all Pernilla's details came up: full name, age, birth date, address and size of house in square metres. It even had, helpfully: *Pernilla is unmarried/not in partnership.* Less helpfully was a list of Swedish celebrities who shared her birthday, January 8th. Kevin had been horrified yet intrigued at this amount of personal information so freely accessed. He believed in a degree of privacy, though he could see the advantages to the police – and to criminals.

Anita and Hakim drove the short distance to Rostorp early; they wanted to catch Pernilla Glad before she went to work. They turned off the main Lundavägen thoroughfare into Dahlhemsgatan and went onto the parallel Åkerögatan; a quiet residential road of neat, detached, Swedish-style houses with the upper floor nestling under the eaves. The substantial gardens were fringed by trimmed hedges or low brick walls. This was a world away from the violence and unrest in some of the other parts of the city. Glad's house was pristine. Hakim rang the bell. They heard 'I'll get it, Mamma.' from inside, and the door was opened by Pernilla Glad. There was no mistaking her. Kevin would describe her as a 'big girl'. She had a large, voluptuous figure accentuated by an expensively tailored, blue suit. Her red hair reached her shoulders and framed an attractive, freckled face. Anita certainly wouldn't have taken her for the forty-two years she knew her to be if she'd passed her in the street. She had been a successful sales executive at Offesson's, according to Hakim, and had easily found another job with an insurance firm when she'd been unceremoniously dismissed, though he suspected that Christer Offesson had used his influence. Her intelligent eyes were immediately wary, particularly when both Anita and Hakim held up their warrant cards.

'We need a word,' said Anita.

'I've got to get to work. Can this be done later?'

'I'm afraid not. It's about Christer Offesson.' Her flinch was all the confirmation they needed that they had the right woman.

'What about Christer?' There was more than a hint of anxiety in her voice.

'You heard about the man who was kidnapped in Östra Förstadsgatan yesterday afternoon?'

'It was on the television this morning. It's all over social media.'

'We haven't released his name yet, but I'm afraid it was Christer.'

The colour drained from Pernilla's already-pale face.

'Oh no! I had a nasty feeling it might be. Tried to convince myself it wasn't; that he was on his way to South America.'

'Were you with him yesterday afternoon?'

Anita could see that Glad wasn't going to protest. 'Yes.'

'What time did you leave?'

'We only had an hour. I had to go at around half past three.'

'Was Christer still there?'

'We usually give it half an hour or so before the other leaves. Christer was paranoid that Felicity would find out.'

'She knows now.'

Glad gulped.

'We need you to take us to the apartment. You got a key?'

She nodded.

As love nests go, it seemed pretty modest. Not that Anita had ever knowingly been in one before. Basically, it was a converted attic: two rooms with a small bathroom off. In the far room, two dormer windows overlooked a 1980s office block, framed in the middle distance by rooftops, above which poked out a couple of factory chimneys belching smoke and the stark, white Cementa tower on the docks. The room contained a tiny kitchenette, a small table with two wooden seats and a couple of comfortable armchairs facing an old television. In the bedroom was a king-sized bed opposite a closet with a serendipitously positioned mirrored door. There was nothing in the apartment to identify who owned or inhabited it: no photos, no pictures and no fripperies. There wasn't anything to indicate that this was a rich man's recreational pad. This was a functional space, and the function was sex.

Anita stared out of the window. 'How often did you meet up?'

'Usually once a week. Maybe twice if Felicity was away,' answered Glad matter-of-factly.

Anita was relieved that Pernilla Glad wasn't going to be awkward or obtuse. She wasn't going to have to bully or coerce her into talking. Mistresses could be unforthcoming. Luckily, Pernilla Glad had been shaken by the fact that Christer Offesson was in danger. She genuinely cared. The poor woman probably loved him. Anita couldn't make an informed judgement as to whether he was deserving of that love as she had never met their number one suspect.

'And did anybody know about this place; about your affair?'

'No. Christer bought this after I had to leave the company. We were very careful. He lost enough when his first wife divorced him.'

'Are you sure you didn't tell anyone?'

Doubt flickered across her face. 'I don't think so.'

'Someone knew. That's why he was picked up in the street outside. A vulnerable spot.'

'I honestly can't think who it might be.'

Anita swung away from the window. 'Did you meet Christer on Sunday, May the fourteenth? He left a concert in Lund early that night.'

'No. We never met at weekends. Felicity expected him to spend time at home then.' So, Glad wasn't the reason he'd slipped away from the concert. 'What has that to do with his... his kidnapping?'

'We're covering all angles. Trying to get a picture.'

Anita went back into the bedroom. Hakim was closing the closet door. He shook his head. This wasn't getting them anywhere. Anita hadn't been sure what might turn up that could connect Christer with the murder of Sami Litmanen. Nothing was the answer.

'I did meet him here the next day.' Anita and Hakim suddenly refocused. 'Actually, I was rather early. I'd had a meeting cancelled. He was a bit moody, almost as though he wasn't pleased to see me. It was the first time he'd ever been angry with me.'

'Why?' asked Anita.

'I'd picked up a shirt he'd left on the bathroom floor.'

'That's a strange thing to be annoyed about,' commented Hakim.

'He was just tetchy, I suppose. He told me he was going to throw it out.'

'Why?'

'It had a bit of blood on one of the cuffs. From a nose bleed or something.' Hakim shot Anita a telling glance. 'Said it wasn't worth washing.'

'Blood? Are you sure?'

'Yes. These things happen.'

'It must have happened when you weren't here. The nosebleed, I mean.'

'Yes, I suppose. Said he'd been here the week before. Doing some work on his own. He was under a lot of stress at work and wanted to get some peace away from the office.'

'Did he do that often?'

'I don't think so. But he had definitely been working. There was some stuff on the bed. There was a suitcase, too, that I didn't recognize.'

'What sort of stuff?'

'The usual kind of things – a laptop, files, some papers in a plastic bag. Oh, and there was a nice-looking wallet I hadn't seen before. And some mobile phones. I did think that was a bit odd, but he explained he had different phones for different contacts.'

'Like one for you, I suppose.'

She flushed.

'What did Christer do with these things?'

'He cleared them away and put them in the suitcase.' Pernilla Glad was perplexed. 'Has this to do with him being taken?'

'No. But it answers a lot of other questions.' Unwittingly, Pernilla Glad had just confirmed that her lover had killed The Oligarch.

CHAPTER 48

The whole team was gathered that afternoon, and Anita was reporting the conversation she and Hakim had had with Pernilla Glad.

'Clearly, after Christer Offesson killed Sami Litmanen on the Sunday night, he went to his attic apartment in Östra Förstadsgatan and dumped the laptop, files, etcetera – and changed his shirt. He must then have intended to come back the next day and get rid of the evidence before Pernilla turned up; except she was early. It all fits. Christer Offesson had motive: protecting his father and his company. He had opportunity: he left the concert with plenty of time to meet up with Litmanen–'

'You reckon Litmanen had asked him to his apartment?' butted in Zetterberg.

'Yes. It was Litmanen's chance to humiliate Offesson face to face. After what his mother had been put through, he couldn't resist it. I suspect that it was Anders he really wanted to see, but Christer went instead. Either to protect his father or because he was the one who'd answered Litmanen's second call. Whichever way, we can ask him when the kidnappers release him.'

'But you haven't got the evidence: the shirt, the laptop and the rest. More to the point, will Pernilla Glad stand up in court when she realizes that she's condemning her lover?'

'I don't know. Hakim took a statement which covers what she found in the apartment the day after the murder. At this stage, she doesn't appreciate the implications and she may withdraw it; especially when Offesson's lawyers get hold of her.'

Hakim followed on: 'Though we can't place Offesson at the scene of the crime, I've found CCTV footage of his car passing the Central Station at 22.57 on the Sunday night. The direction of the car suggests he was coming from Västra Hamnen and heading in the general direction of Östra Förstadsgatan. It fits in with our timeline.'

'We have enough to pull him in,' said Anita.

'OK. As soon as he appears, you can arrest him. I'll clear that with Prosecutor Blom. Just make sure you get a confession.' Zetterberg shuffled some papers before continuing: 'If we're lucky, we'll get Offesson back *and* arrest the gang when the family make the drop. No cock-ups this time. Kill two birds and all that. Presumably they can raise the money?'

'Yes,' said Anita. 'Felicity Offesson was confident that they could, though the Wednesday deadline's a bit tight.'

'Good. We'll be there when the kidnappers make their call and we'll have everyone ready to move when they give the location. And there'll be no falling for any tricks this time.'

'Have forensics come up with anything on the van?' Erlandsson asked.

'Nothing of any use. They're very professional. We've still no real idea who's behind this. All we can do is wait.'

'Klara's got a theory.'

'Have you?' Zetterberg said with some disbelief.

'Go on,' urged Anita.

Wallen cleared her throat. She started hesitantly; she didn't want to appear foolish in front of the group. 'It's Peter Uhlig.'

'You can't possibly think he's behind the whole thing,' jumped in Zetterberg.

'Just hear her out,' Anita said firmly. Zetterberg huffed.

Wallen started again. 'Trellogistics is in financial trouble. Through Anita's investigation into Sami Litmanen's death, it's emerged that a subsidiary company in Brazil was struggling. They've been shut down. That enquiry also linked Trellogistics to the Offesson coffee business.'

'So they have money problems. What big business doesn't at some point?'

Anita was about to intercede again, but Wallen continued. 'I think that maybe the kidnaps have been perpetrated not only to raise money but, with this last abduction, to deal with a business rival. I started to think about this after the Kristina Ekman kidnap; there were small things that didn't quite add up. The food for one.'

'Not that again!'

'Yes,' Wallen said more determinedly. 'Why did Uhlig get better food than the other two? That got me thinking about the actual kidnap. Möller, Ekman and Offesson were taken in very public areas; on the street, in the city. Uhlig was whisked away on some country road with no one around. Then there's the ransom money. It was convenient that we didn't see it being handed over. What if the whole episode with his daughter had been planned by the family?'

'And as far as the Ekman kidnap is concerned, they have history,' came in Anita. 'Well, Peter Uhlig and Dag Wollstad clashed ten years ago; Uhlig sold his cement business to someone else despite Wollstad offering a better price. There was also a lot of animosity twenty years back between the upstart Wollstad and the long-standing companies. The latter didn't like the way Wollstad conducted his business. The traditionalists didn't want to be tarred with the same brush. A lot of harsh things were said on both sides and Wollstad moved in on some of his rivals. What better way of getting back at Wollstad than kidnapping his daughter and getting him to pay up?'

Zetterberg was looking interested.

'And now, Christer Offesson, who just happens to be head of the company that, we believe, might be causing Uhlig problems in

South America. Offesson's could be behind Trellogística Brasil's sudden shutdown. We believe Litmanen was investigating this – that Offesson's, for whatever reason, was putting the squeeze on Trellogistics; possibly softening them up for a hostile takeover. I don't think it's any coincidence that Offesson was taken just before he was due to fly out to Brazil today.'

'There's another thing,' put in Wallen. 'We know from Kristina Ekman that she was kept in a container; the same story Uhlig told. Given that we can rely on her description, who has more access to containers in the whole of Skåne than Trellogistics? And easy access to all the ports in the area, in one of which we know Möller was held and are ninety-nine per cent sure that Ekman was held.' She shrugged. 'As I say, it's just a theory.'

Zetterberg was chewing her index finger by the time Wallen had finished. 'And his trucks go to and from Russia. All right. As we've nothing else to go on, it's worth pursuing. Do we really think Peter Uhlig is capable of organizing a kidnap gang?'

'I'm sure he could get hold of the right sort of contacts,' Wallen suggested.

'Right. I want a watch put on Uhlig. Night and day.'

And it was a night and a day later, early Saturday evening, that Anita was about to take over Hakim's shift in the Limhamn street where Peter Uhlig lived. In this affluent area, most of the houses were hidden behind high walls and security gates. She eased into Hakim's unmarked car.

'Anything?' She could see the gates of Uhlig's house further down the street. There was no other way in or out.

Hakim yawned. 'He and his wife went down to the marina for lunch. He's got a boat down there. Met up with friends. His business may be in trouble but that doesn't seem to be interfering with his weekend. Came back shortly after three and hasn't emerged since. His wife came out at around four to walk the dog. She was gone for nearly an hour.'

'I hope they haven't got anything planned for the evening. I don't fancy following them all over town.'

'Have fun.'

'Who's taking over from me?' asked Anita.

'Pontus.'

'He's keen. Didn't he do the one before you?'

'Wants to impress the "boss"; and he needs the overtime.'

Hakim's mobile phone started to ring. 'Hi Liv. I'm just finishing my surveillance shift. Anita's taking over. Look, I'll be over later. Need to change first. Be there about eight.' He listened and then swivelled round to Anita. 'She wants a word with you.' He handed over his phone.

'Hi Liv. You OK?'

'Yeah, fine. I wanted to have a quick word with you. I've found something on the net that might be of interest.'

'Concerning?'

'The kidnaps. I read this online paper called *The Local*. It's Swedish news in English. It's quite interesting to read their take on Swedish life. Anyway, they have various editions for different countries... Denmark, Norway, Switzerland, Spain. It was the French one that caught my eye. Or a story did. It was a kidnapping in Paris. A dot com millionaire was grabbed on a Friday after work and reappeared, trussed up and with a hood over his head, in Père Lachaise Cemetery on the Monday morning. He paid his own ransom via computer. All done and dusted over the weekend. Interestingly, the victim also had a Moroccan connection. Liked to holiday there. Ring any bells?'

Anita's lips flapped as she exhaled a deep breath. It certainly did ring bells. 'Do you know how much the victim paid?'

'He wasn't shy on that front. Ten million dollars.'

'And when was this?'

'Two weekends ago. He was picked up on the twenty-sixth and released on the twenty-ninth.'

'That's the same time that Kristina Ekman was a captive.' She stared out of the car windscreen. There were only a few other cars parked in the street. 'Liv, that's really good work. Thanks.'

'No problem.'

'Want to speak to Hakim again?'

'No. I'll see him later.'

The line went dead and Anita passed the phone back to Hakim. 'Liv has just made quite a discovery. We appear to be dealing with two kidnap gangs.'

'Two?'

'She's found almost an exact Mats Möller operation in France. I always had a nagging doubt about that first kidnap. Different money – dollars not euros – different type of business targeted. And Moberg wondered about the time gap afterwards and then two in quick succession. Now three, of course. They're copycat kidnaps. There's something here that's more important than ransom money going on. If it was plain extortion, then the ransoms would have been higher. I think there's an ulterior motive here. I think Klara might be right. Peter Uhlig is behind this, though I'm not entirely sure why.'

Anita was shattered by the time she opened her front door at six on Sunday morning. Her surveillance stint had been uneventful. Peter Uhlig hadn't left his house. Lights came on at dusk and the last one went out shortly after midnight. Anita had had difficulty keeping awake after her thermos of coffee had run out at three. It was even harder to keep her eyes open with no one to talk to. Normally, they would have worked in pairs, but everyone was working flat out as more cars were being set on fire and the wave of discontent was leading to inter-gang violence in the poorer parts of the city. Throw in the usual Saturday night drunkenness, and the force's resources were being stretched to breaking point.

She crept in as quietly as possible so as not to disturb Kevin. She couldn't decide whether to have a shower or just go to bed. Maybe a coffee first. She went through to the kitchen. Before she even had time to put the kettle on, her mobile sprang into action.

'Anita,' she said, suppressing a yawn.

'It's me, Bea. Go to St. Pauli Kyrkogården as quick as you can; middle section.'

'Has Christer Offesson turned up?'

'Not sure. A call's just come in. Could be. I'm at the polishus and I'm just about to go over there.'

Anita wearily grabbed the keys of Kevin's hired car and left the apartment. The drive to the cemetery didn't take long. The streets were deserted at that time on a Sunday morning. This couldn't be anything to do with Christer Offesson as she was sure that the ransom hadn't yet been paid, unless Felicity and Anders had done it secretly.

The middle section of St. Pauli Kyrkogården was situated between Sankt Knuts väg and Nöbelvägen. On the other side of Sankt Knuts väg, where Anita parked, was the north section of the cemetery, only minutes' walk away from the polishus. Anita could see why it was the perfect place to leave a kidnap victim. Despite being near the centre of town, the roads round about weren't residential. The middle section was bordered by an industrial estate on one side and a school on the other. Further cover was provided by trees lining a walkway to the chapel. Anita hurried through the gate and down the gravel path. On either side of the path were the usual multifarious plots, some flaunting an elaborate array of monuments and mausolea. Past the chapel, and Anita could see Bea Erlandsson ahead of her with two uniformed officers. Bea was talking to a tall youth who looked the worse for wear. His black hair was spiked and the crotch of his trousers was virtually below his knees. He was clutching a drinks can and appeared agitated. When Bea saw

Anita, she moved away from the youth, and exposed a figure beyond sitting on a bench. He was bound to the bench and still hooded.

'Why haven't you freed him?'

'I thought I'd better not.'

'Oh, for goodness sake,' said a tired and fractious Anita as she pushed past the young detective.

'Anita!' Erlandsson called after her. 'He's dead.'

CHAPTER 49

Half an hour later, there was quite a crowd in the vicinity of the body. Bea Erlandsson was explaining to Zetterberg that the young man, Filip Kowalski, was heading home after a late night party and had wandered through the cemetery. He found the man and took the hood off. Shocked at finding a corpse tied to a bench, he had the presence of mind to phone the police. When Bea reached the scene, she identified the victim from his photographs back at headquarters and then, wearing gloves, replaced the hood so forensics could investigate the scene properly.

The hood had now been removed and the stiff corpse untied, and Eva Thulin was busy at work with Anita in attendance. In both directions, police were combing the ground between the victim's location and the gates at either end of the cemetery.

'Couldn't the lad have found this after I'd had my breakfast?' Thulin grumbled happily. 'I was going to get breakfast in bed today because it's my birthday.'

'Happy birthday,' said Anita.

'Actually, it was yesterday, but my miserable hubby was out playing football so couldn't indulge me.' Christer Offesson was still in a sitting position. Thulin had pulled up the blood-stained shirt he was wearing and was examining his back. 'And I was on a promise this morning. Yesterday, he was too knackered after his game.'

'Too much information, Eva. What about our man here?'

'Well, the method of death is straightforward enough. Two bullets in the back.'

'Handgun?'

'Yes.'

'Interesting that they're in his back. So, it's not an execution?'

'Wouldn't have thought so. That's usually a bullet in the back of the head.'

'I wonder if he was trying to escape?'

'I can't speculate on that.'

'Maybe the shooter didn't mean to kill him. Just stop him. Christer Offesson was worth more to the kidnappers alive. Dead, he's worthless.'

'Well, accident or not, why go through all this charade again? Risk dumping the body in the middle of Malmö?'

'A warning to the next victim? Pay up or else? But they didn't give the Offessons much time to raise the cash.' There was a lot to ponder. 'Time of death?'

'Difficult to say; probably about twenty-four hours. Rigor's set in – the perps might have had a job moving him; he must already have been in a sitting position when they did. Seems they knew exactly what they were going to do with him.'

'That would mean he died within forty-eight hours of being abducted. Why wait to dump the body?'

'When it's quiet?' Eva Thulin stood back and let the photographer snap the grim scene. She waved to him to take close-ups of the victim's back. 'Now you've got two murders on your plate,' she said, peeling off her latex gloves.

'No, just the one. This was our prime suspect in the other one.'

On Monday morning, Anita felt more refreshed. After a quick meeting on returning from the cemetery with Zetterberg and the rest of the team, she had gone back home to catch up on some sleep. Zetterberg had decreed that the surveillance of Peter Uhlig was to continue, even though, because of the surveillance, he had a watertight alibi for the day Christer Offesson was killed. Of course, he could still have been behind it all. Zetterberg was flirting with the idea of hauling Uhlig in for questioning, though she'd have to run that by Prosecutor Blom. Straw poll opinion was that Offesson may have been shot while trying to get away from his captors. They desperately needed more information from forensics.

Over an evening meal the night before with Kevin, Anita had decided on her next move. First thing on Monday morning, she made three calls. The first was to Mats Möller, the second to Dragan Mitrović and the third to the polishus, which Pontus Brodd answered. Then she headed for the Central Station with Kevin in tow. She'd promised him a day out.

Brodd stuck his head round Zetterberg's door. He looked shifty.

'Yes?' Zetterberg said impatiently. She was gathering herself for a debriefing of yesterday's events with Commissioner Dahlbeck. He was in a tizzy at the thought of the scion of Sweden's most famous coffee-making dynasty lying in the mortuary in Lund – on *his* patch. Fail to solve this and the comfortable government consultancy role he was trying to line up in Stockholm would be out of the window.

'You asked me to keep an eye on Anita.'

'Yes.' She was interested now.

'She's just rung in. She's going off to Helsingborg.'

'What the hell is she going up there for?'

'Going to the Offesson head office.'

'What! I bloody didn't sanction that. Christ, that woman!'

Just then her phone rang. Commissioner Dahlbeck was ready to see her.

The train took about an hour to snake its way up through Lund, Kävlinge and Landskrona and a number of minor stations before it reached Helsingborg on the west coast of Skåne. While Kevin was staring out of the window taking in the view, Anita was deep in thought about the consequences of Christer Offesson's death. It had been an unpleasant jolt. And truly frustrating. After going all round the houses to find their killer, Offesson had been snatched from her grasp before he could be brought to justice. On reflection, she could see that they might have had difficulty getting a conviction without Pernilla Glad backing up her statement; and that wasn't guaranteed in the circumstances once Glad realized what she was being asked to do. They hadn't found the shirt or the missing items stolen from Litmanen's apartment – and they probably never would. All the same, it felt like all their hard work had come to nothing. Someone else had carried out the sentence. But who? There was uninformed speculation in the free *Metro* newspaper she'd picked up at the station. There was no way the murder of Christer Offesson could have been kept under wraps. She hadn't envied Zetterberg's task of informing the victim's father and his widow. At least she'd done it and not designated the job. Pernilla Glad would just have to find out through the media like the rest of the public.

Anita was now convinced that the Mats Möller abduction had nothing to do with the other kidnaps. Her call to Möller that morning had all but confirmed it. She knew he was reticent about saying how much had been extorted from him, so she asked him whether the ransom he paid was anywhere in the region of the dollar equivalent of four million euros. His answer was that what he paid was 'well north of that figure'. He'd also heard about what had happened in Paris and reckoned it sounded like the same gang.

So that left three copycat kidnaps, the last of which had gone wrong. Her call to Dragan Mitrović hadn't yielded any fresh information; he simply repeated his belief that the gang wasn't local, substantiated by his own enquiries. He was clearly angry that the gang was muscling in on his territory. Reading between the lines, Anita gathered that he didn't condone violence unless it was necessary to further his own strategic business plan. She'd asked if it was feasible for a wealthy businessman to bring in a professional gang to kidnap rivals. He thought it was entirely possible. It was quite common in places like the Middle East and Latin America. From the tone of his voice, she suspected that he'd been approached at some stage in his career to do something similar.

It made perfect sense that Peter Uhlig was behind these kidnaps despite the flimsy evidence being circumstantial – the fact that he had eaten herring and potatoes during his incarceration was hardly going to stand up in court. Furthermore, it was not proving easy to progress with the investigation into Trellogistics – hence Anita's visit to Helsingborg, the headquarters of the Offesson operation. Maybe there was some clue she'd pick up there that would unlock the real reason why Christer Offesson and Kristina Ekman had been kidnapped.

At Helsingborg, they exited the station through the shopping area with its impressive arched glass roof. The station abuts the shoreline, and a ferry was just leaving the harbour for its twenty minute crossing to Helsingør on the Danish side of the Sound. Järnvägsgatan opened up in front of them; the harbour on the left, and an eclectic mix of buildings lining the other side of the street. Lending sumptuous splendour to the vista was the neo-Gothic town hall with its eighty-five-metre clock tower bearing a striking resemblance to St. Mark's campanile in Venice. The size and grandeur of the building was testimony to Helsingborg's nineteenth-century prosperity.

'Hey, this is quite a place!' Kevin remarked appreciatively.

'You can have a mooch around while I investigate Offesson's.'

They turned into Stortorget which, in reality, was more of

a boulevard than a square. They carried on towards a series of old, stone arched gateways following a steep incline, at the top of which was a castellated tower.

'That's Kärnan medieval tower. On a fine day like this, you'll get great views across the Sound. You'll be able to see Helsingør Castle, what Shakespeare called Elsinore.'

'How good is that?' Kevin put the palm of his hand on his breast in a theatrical pose. 'You can be Ophelia to my Hamlet.'

'I don't think so. I'm not drowning myself for anyone, least of all you.'

'You've no soul.' Then he grinned lecherously and with a melodramatic gesture cried 'Get thee to a nunnery!'

'That would be one way of getting rid of you.' Anita was glad there weren't too many people about.

They walked a little further up the square. 'So, where are you off to?'

Anita pointed to an impressive building at the end of the street. A former bank built in the neo-classical style, this had been the Offesson headquarters since the 1930s.

Kevin gave it the once-over. 'I was expecting some big neon sign with *Offesson's* writ large. It's all very low-key and discreet. Like some of the offices in the City of London.'

'That's old money for you. Nothing too vulgar.'

'Like me.'

'Not sure about that.'

Anita was shown up a wide, sweeping staircase and into an oak-panelled room with a long table and heavy, leather-upholstered chairs. It should have reeked of coffee but reeked of understated opulence instead. Much needed illumination from long casement windows with Juliet balconies compensated for the décor. A few minutes later, a man entered the room. He must have been well into his sixties. Bald except for a halo of white fuzz, he wore a suit and tie. His face was creased in anxiety and he apologized profusely for keeping Anita waiting. He introduced himself as Bengt Månsson, the company secretary.

'Have they offered you a coffee?'

'No, I'm fine.'

As they both took seats at the end of the long table, Månsson said 'As you can imagine we're all in a state of shock. We weren't even aware Christer had been kidnapped.' His fingers ran nervously along the surface of the table like a piano player warming up for a recital.

'Christer Offesson was grabbed by a gang outside an apartment block in Östra Förstadsgatan in Malmö.'

'What was he doing there?'

'Presumably, you knew Pernilla Glad when she worked here?'

'Of course. She was very good. It was under unfortunate circumstances that she had to leave.'

'You know what they were?'

'Yes, I was aware of the personal nature of... shall we say a conflict of interest with the present fru Offesson.'

'That's a delicate way of putting it. Well, Christer was still seeing her.'

'Oh dear.'

'He was taken after meeting her at an attic apartment he owned in Östra Förstadsgatan.' Månsson's features registered disappointment that his boss had been so foolhardy. 'Was it known here that he was still seeing Pernilla Glad?'

'I certainly didn't know,' he said with exaggerated emphasis. 'That doesn't mean...' His voice tailed off.

'We're just trying to find out where the gang got their information from. Of course, they may have simply been following him and established his routine. Christer and Pernilla met regularly. But the main reason I'm here is to find out a bit more about the business.'

'What, in particular?'

'South America.' Immediately, she could see Månsson was on his guard. 'Specifically, Brazil. We understand that Trellogistics, or rather their Brazilian subsidiary, moved the coffee beans from your plantations to the port at São Paulo.'

'Correct,' he replied cautiously. 'We've had a long relationship with the company.'

'I believe that operation has been shut down, albeit not necessarily permanently.'

'Yes. It's caused huge disruption for us. We're trying to organize alternative arrangements, which, unfortunately, make everything more costly. Christer's absence at this difficult time didn't help, of course. We couldn't understand why we couldn't get hold of him over the weekend; now we know.'

'So, Trellogística Brasil shutting down is damaging your business?'

'Of course it is. If we've got beans sitting in the plantations, they're of no use unless we can get them transported. Every non-delivery costs us money. And if the beans don't arrive, then the cost of our coffee will go up and our sales will go down because we can't meet orders. It's already affecting our share price.'

'And have Trellogística given you an official explanation for the shutdown?'

'Not a satisfactory one. They blame it on local officialdom. That's one of the reasons Christer was going out to São Paulo.'

'You mentioned your share price. If that goes down, will it open you up to a potential takeover, hostile or otherwise?'

'I would hope we could fight off any unwanted interest.' Månsson's fingers stopped their nervous tapping as an unpleasant thought occurred to him. 'Without Christer, there's a vacuum in the management here. The board usually rubber-stamps his decisions. Without him... I don't know. Unless Anders can step back in. We've already got...' Månsson stopped himself abruptly.

'What?' Anita pressed.

'Nothing.'

345

'Anything you can tell me might help.'

It was too late. She got the impression that he'd said too much already.

Anita met up with Kevin in a small Italian café on a side street off Stortorget. Despite its proximity to the Offesson HQ, it served an Italian brand of coffee. She'd let Kevin prattle on for a few minutes about how much he liked the views of Helsingør and his excitement at being able to see the famous castle. She vetoed his suggestion that they jump on a ferry and have a quick look round Hamlet's home. They had to get back, but she promised that they would make a special trip before he left. Kevin looked sceptical.

She wanted his thoughts as a policeman not a history buff at that moment. She went through her conversation with Månsson.

'What if Trellogística Brasil hasn't been shut down at all and it's just a ploy by Uhlig to put pressure on Offesson's? Cutting off or cutting down their supplies. Then, on top of all that, the king-pin of the company is conveniently got out of the way – permanently as it happens – and the share price is pushed down. And then, hey presto! Trellogistics buys up Offesson's. Or more likely buys up the plantations. That's probably why Christer was flying out to Brazil to try and save the situation. His trip might have prompted the timing of the kidnap. That would mean Uhlig could hold Offesson's to ransom by controlling all their South American supply of beans. That makes sense, doesn't it?'

'I know sod all about business. However, there's a logic in what you say.'

Anita tucked into her cake with relish. She was going to have to cut back on these treats as they weren't helping her waistline.

'How does Christer Offesson's death impact on your scenario?' Kevin asked.

She thought about it for a minute. 'Probably helps, actually. If Månsson is correct, the board are rudderless without Christer.

They may be open to commercial pressure for a takeover. Månsson was a worried man and there was something he wasn't telling me. Perhaps the takeover's already started? The longer Christer's out of the picture, the more time Uhlig has to exploit the situation. Even if Anders comes back in, the damage may already have been done.'

'If that's the case, it begs the question: was Uhlig intending to kill Offesson all along?'

CHAPTER 50

It was Tuesday morning and the arrival of Eva Thulin was eagerly awaited. What had forensics come up with? Anita was hoping for some answers. She'd already spoken to Alice Zetterberg on her return from Helsingborg the day before. After Zetterberg had finished ranting at her and accusing her of 'maverick behaviour' (a description that she took exception to), Anita had managed to convey that what she had gleaned from Månsson fitted in with what they now suspected: Peter Uhlig was behind the last three kidnaps (including his own), and the Mats Möller abduction was carried out by a separate gang operating throughout Europe. This latter assumption was given further credence later in the day by the discovery of yet another similar kidnapping carried out in October last year in Turin. On the downside, the surveillance of Peter Uhlig hadn't highlighted any unusual behaviour. On Monday, he'd gone to the office at his normal time and returned home for his evening meal. Today, he'd left for work at the same time. Yesterday, there'd been a board meeting, which he'd attended. Were they discussing the takeover of Offesson's? If their theory was correct, Wallen speculated that as the final target was now dead, there was no longer any need for the kidnapping gang. They may well have been paid off by now. If that were the case, it was going to be even harder to prove Uhlig's involvement.

At that moment, Eva Thulin breezed into the meeting room.

The only member of the team missing was Erlandsson, who, with another officer drafted in to help, was sitting outside the Trellogistics headquarters in Trelleborg.

'Morning all,' Thulin said cheerily.

'What have you got?' Zetterberg wasn't in the mood for banter. She was under too much pressure.

'Well, I can confirm that Christer Offesson was shot. The two bullets–'

'Killed him. Yes, we know that. Is there anything we can use?'

Thulin gave Anita a thinly suppressed look of exasperation.

'OK. What is interesting is the weapon used. This handgun.' She held up a photograph of the weapon. 'I've spoken to a ballistics expert and the pistol is a...' She glanced down at her notes. 'Its full title is a Taurus PT-111 Millennium G2.'

'I haven't heard of that.'

'Neither had I. It's where it's from that's curious. It's of Brazilian manufacture.'

Everyone one in the room immediately grasped the significance.

'Apparently, it's used by the Brazilian police, and many of these weapons find their way into the *favelas* in Rio. According to my expert, forty percent of all guns seized by the authorities in the state of Rio de Janeiro are made by Taurus. Gangsters love them, especially this model. Light but solid. Compact. The trigger is smooth and its recoil comfortable, thanks to its grip. And as we've seen, it's highly effective.'

'How far away was the victim?' Anita asked.

'That's a good question. You speculated at the scene whether Offesson could have been escaping. Well, I thought that might be a possibility. But after examining him, I don't think so. A professional shot would only be sure of a kill at a maximum of seven metres. An amateur, considerably less. The angle of the bullets and the impacts, indicate to me that the victim was no more than two metres away from his killer.'

'Are you saying that you think it's been made to look like he was trying to escape?'

'Yes, Anita, I believe it was done to make us think exactly that, and may well have been an execution of sorts.'

This produced silence in the room. It certainly fitted in with Kevin's speculation in the café yesterday.

'Thank you, Eva. Just leave your report and I'll go through it thoroughly.' Zetterberg was dismissing Thulin.

'Just one other thing,' said Thulin, handing her file over to Zetterberg. 'Offesson's mouth. There was a tiny piece of vegetation and some earth under his top lip as though, when he was shot, he fell forward onto grass or something like that. And there was also some evidence of vegetation in his hair and on his clothing.'

After Thulin left, there was an outbreak of chatter around the room. Zetterberg had to shout to get the group's attention.

'Right, this changes a few things. Firstly, it appears our kidnap gang is likely to be from Brazil, not Russia.'

'That makes sense now,' said Wallen. 'I've had a couple of holidays in the Algarve, and Portuguese definitely has Russian-sounding inflections. In fact, the first time I turned on the television in the hotel, I thought it was a Russian programme. The snatches of conversation that Kristina Ekman heard were probably Brazilian Portuguese – must be fairly similar. And remember, it was Peter Uhlig who steered us in the Russian direction.'

'Secondly, Offesson's killing now appears deliberate. Was it planned all along? From what you found out in Helsingborg, Anita, taking Offesson out of the picture would make the company easy pickings for a predatory rival. And thirdly, the grass-stroke-vegetation. There can't be many container yards with grass in them.'

'Unless they took him somewhere else to be executed,'

suggested Hakim.

Zetterberg scanned the forensics report. 'Thulin estimates Offesson's time of death at around twenty-four to thirty hours before he was found. Maybe they didn't even bother to put him in a container.'

'If they had planned to kill him straightaway, why put in the ransom call to his wife? And why put the body in the cemetery afterwards?' Anita was pleased that Brodd was actually paying attention.

'To make everyone think that this was connected with the other kidnaps,' said Wallen, 'when, in fact, it's all to do with commerce.'

'The return of the body could be a message to the rest of the Offesson board that if they stand in the way of a takeover, they might suffer a similar fate,' said Anita. 'But one thing I still can't get my head around is why Peter Uhlig would go to all this trouble. There's something very personal going on here that we're missing.'

'Look, we could go on speculating forever and get nowhere. I think we've got to bring Uhlig in and start questioning him.' Zetterberg was being decisive.

'Will Commissioner Dahlbeck and Prosecutor Blom give you the green light?' Wallen queried.

'Just use the pretext that he's being re-interviewed in light of the latest kidnapping,' suggested Anita. 'Say we need his help. Not even a nervous commissioner can object to that.'

That evening, Anita and Kevin were sitting in the corner of The Pickwick close to the unlit fire. The leather-backed chair squeaked as Kevin sat down with two pints. He was grinning. He'd just been joking with Matt behind the bar.

'Cheers. I expect you need this,' he said before sipping his own drink.

'Yeah.' She drank gratefully.

'Have you brought Uhlig in?'

'He's coming in first thing tomorrow. Voluntarily. Of course, he doesn't suspect that we reckon he's behind the kidnappings and responsible for Christer Offesson's murder. What I can't figure out is where he had Offesson taken and where he had him killed. We don't think he did it himself. Sadly, he's not that stupid.'

'Has he got a place in the country? All you Swedes seem to have somewhere rural to escape to.'

'Except me,' she said ruefully. 'And we checked that out. He doesn't have anywhere out of town. His daughters jointly own a holiday home near Karlshamn.'

'What about that?'

'It's possible. Zetterberg's sending me there tomorrow. She wants me out of the way when she talks to Uhlig.'

They sank into silence.

'Given that Uhlig was probably lying to you, is there anything in your interview with him that gives you any clues? Inconsistencies in his story?'

'No, not really. It fits in with Mats Möller's experience. Thanks to Bernt Hägg going to the press in the first place, and then bloody Pontus filling in the gaps, all the details came out, except the ransom amount and what he ate while in captivity. The last two things are where his story falls down. Except that's not enough to convict him.'

Anita returned to her fast-disappearing pint. Kevin was going to have to order a refill pretty soon.

'There was one odd thing he came out with,' she said, holding her glass in mid air. 'The dog.'

'What dog?'

'Said he heard a dog growling.'

'Why is that odd?'

'Round a container yard? Incredibly unlikely. Stray dogs aren't a problem in Sweden.'

'A guard dog?'

'Wouldn't it bark when anything passed? Kristina Ekman didn't report any sounds of dogs. I don't know why Uhlig would mention it.'

'Maybe he did stay in a container. He would be out of sight and would look bedraggled when he was found. The same with the marks on his wrists you mentioned. Make the whole thing look realistic. He might have heard something. Could it have been anything else? Do wolves growl? I've read you have wolves wandering about Sweden. Don't they have official culls now?'

'Wolves are fairly rare in Skåne, though sheep have been attacked. But in a dock area? Highly improbable.'

'I can't think of anything else that growls except foxes. We have a real problem with them coming into towns in Britain. My sister's cat was killed by an urban fox.'

They finished their drinks.

'Another?' asked Kevin.

'Yes, please.'

He stood up and picked up the glasses with the ease and grace of an experienced waiter. He stepped towards the bar and then stopped abruptly. He returned to the table and put the glasses down with a clunk.

'There is something else that growls.'

He reached into his pocket and took out his phone. He busily clicked away until he found what he was looking for. He held the phone out to Anita so she could see the screen. 'Listen to this.'

CHAPTER 51

Anita hardly slept that night and came into work early. She and Kevin hadn't had a second pint. On the way home, Anita had rung Bea Erlandsson and asked her to do some checking for her. When she and Kevin had got back to the Roskildevägen apartment, they'd opened a bottle of red and carried on talking; batting ideas around. Eventually, Kevin went into the kitchen to make some sandwiches while Anita's mind whirled as she tried to form a coherent plan. Whatever she did, it would be without Zetterberg's knowledge at this stage. That would only spell trouble.

At ten o'clock on Wednesday morning, Brodd knocked on Zetterberg's door and entered.

'Peter Uhlig's downstairs.'

'Good.'

Brodd coughed nervously. 'I saw Anita talking to him. Showing him something on her phone.'

'What the fuck is she doing? I've had enough of this. When she gets back, I'll have her hauled up before the commissioner. At least I've got her out of the way this morning; she's off to the Uhlig daughters' holiday place over at Karlshamn today.'

'Oh, I just overheard her talking to Hakim on the way out. She's not going there.'

Anita parked Kevin's hire car at the side of the deserted road. Little traffic passed this way except to and from the big house. The only sound was the wind tugging at the trees, making the leaves rustle. She climbed over the mesh perimeter fence next to the road. Of course, Kevin had wanted to come with her. He thought it might be dangerous. She'd persuaded him that it was only a scouting mission, nothing more. What she hoped to find out, she would take back to the polishus and then they could formally move in.

She made her way carefully through the trees, twigs occasionally snapping under her feet. Each one gave her a fright. Maybe she should have let Kevin come – or Hakim. He'd advised against it but was up for being an accessory after the fact. She'd been grateful but had declined his offer – if she got this horribly wrong, he would be in the firing line along with her. As she crept stealthily on, she realized that she was coming to the edge of the wood. Through the gaps in the trees, the sweeping lawns that led up to the main house came into view. She didn't venture into the open. There was no activity that she could see, though there were a couple of large cars parked near the front door of the building.

Suddenly, there was a sound behind her. As she swung round, she whipped out her pistol and held it at arm's length, her hands trembling. There it was: the source of the noise that Uhlig had heard – a huge wild boar, snuffling aggressively, was giving her a malevolent stare. Anita didn't move. After what seemed like minutes, but could only have been seconds, the boar lost interest and slowly moved into the trees. This was where Kevin had wandered when she'd come to talk to Lothar von Goessling. He'd come across a boar and it had growled at him. That's what he'd remembered in the pub, and there it was: a video of the animal on his mobile phone. Through the metal wall of a container, to a disorientated man the sound could easily be mistaken for a dog. She'd played it to Peter Uhlig this morning and he'd confirmed that it was the sound he'd heard. And that had set off a train of thought that had brought her out to Illstorp, the home of Kristina Ekman. That day when Kevin had seen the boar, Goessling had been furious with him for wandering off – unreasonably so, she'd thought at the time. But she'd just reckoned he was being precious about his girlfriend's estate. Now she thought it was something else entirely. That's what she was here to find.

Thanks to Bea, Anita had found out an interesting fact about Kristina's toy boy. Goessling might be German, but he had a Swedish mother. All that flannel about conversing with Kristina in English was just that. He probably spoke Swedish perfectly well enough to pass as a traffic cop and phone in ransom demands.

She turned back into the trees. Kevin hadn't had time to go very far, yet he must have got near enough to something interesting to instigate Goessling's reaction. She moved deeper into the wood. She knew from the map she'd studied last night that the Wollstad estate was extensive, consisting of woodland, gardens and areas of grassland. The wild boar had free rein, though they tended to stick to the woods. After a few minutes, she hit a wide track that ran through the trees. Still with her pistol at the ready, she followed it furtively, keeping her wits about her. Soon she made out what looked like a clearing a couple of hundred metres in front of her. The light became stronger as the canopy thinned until she found herself at the edge of a large, grassy, open space – in the middle of which was something which made her heart start racing. A green metal container.

Before venturing into the open, she scanned her surroundings. The way was clear. All she could hear was the wind in the trees. She quickly crossed the grass and reached the door. She tried it. It wasn't locked and opened easily. She slipped inside, leaving the door ajar. The thin beam of light behind her showed her that the container was split into two sections. There was a door in the dividing wall. In front of her were a table and three wooden chairs. It was tidy enough, though there were a couple of empty beer cans lying on the floor. But what really grabbed her attention was what was stacked against one of the side walls: four large speakers of the kind you might see at a rock concert, and several coils of wire. So, that's how they'd created the illusion of a harbour. She felt one of the coils. She picked a piece of grass out of it. They must have surrounded the container with this sound system. No wonder the location had been impossible to find. It was nowhere near a port!

Gingerly, she opened the dividing door. She took out her phone to give herself some light. There was a metal chair in the middle of the space and a bucket in one corner. This is where Peter Uhlig and Christer Offesson must have been kept. She guessed Offesson was shot on the grass outside. She took a couple of snaps then went back and photographed the sound system. Before she left, she would take some shots of the container from the outside.

She stepped out into the light. Too late, she was aware of someone close by. Her hands went up to protect her head; then all went black.

CHAPTER 52

Anita had no idea how long she'd been out, but, however long, there'd been time to tie her hands behind her to one of the wooden chairs in the outer section of the container. She wanted to nurse her head, which was aching. The light from a lamp on top of one of the speakers hurt her eyes. Painfully, she lifted her head. A swarthy young man was pointing her own SIG Sauer pistol directly at her. He was totally relaxed and offered her a grin when she looked at him. He matched the description of the young man who had waved Peter Uhlig down.

'I'm police. You'd better let me go.'

He didn't reply; just grinned again. Maybe he didn't understand her. She tried again in English. Still he said nothing.

Then the door opened and in came Kristina Ekman and Lothar von Goessling.

'This is an unpleasant surprise,' Ekman said. She turned to Goessling. 'This woman has been causing problems for a long time.'

'Let me go,' said Anita. 'It'll only make things worse for you if you don't.'

'I have no intention of letting you go; in fact, you're not leaving here alive.'

'Killing a cop will really finish you.'

'I don't think so. No one will find a trace of you here. Lothar's already seen to your car.'

'My boss knows I'm here.'

'I don't believe you; you wouldn't have been sent on your own. No, it's time you left us – permanently. Third time lucky, I suppose.'

'What do you mean?'

'Oh, you don't know? I ordered that gunman to kill you and your Arab sidekick in Möllevångstorget all those years ago.'

'I suspected that.'

'And then there was your exploding car.' And Anita had thought it was Dragan Mitrović! 'Lothar was worried about what your English boyfriend might have seen, so we thought we'd get rid of you both. Sadly, that didn't work out quite as we'd hoped, though it seems to have left its mark on your face. Never mind, you're here now.' Her smile was as cold as ice.

Ekman nodded at the young man in the chair, whom Anita assumed was one of the Brazilians used for the kidnappings. She knew she had to play for time.

'Why?'

'Why what?'

'Why all the kidnappings?'

Ekman glanced at her gold watch.

'I really haven't got time for this.'

'Why kill Christer Offesson? Don't you want the satisfaction of telling me how clever you've been?'

'I have to admit, I'm quite intrigued as to how you stumbled onto us. I didn't think the police were that smart.'

Anita realized that she needed to convince Ekman that her colleagues were on to her and that killing one of their own would not be a good move. She tried to halt her rising panic and to think rationally. 'We're smart enough to work out that you copied the Mats Möller kidnap.'

'That's what gave me the idea. And the really clever bit was my own kidnapping. I should have been an actress. I put on a brilliant performance for the police and the press. After that, who's going to suspect little ol' me?'

'But we did suspect something wasn't right. You shouldn't have given Peter Uhlig proper food.'

It was Ekman's turn to be nonplussed. 'Why? What do you mean?'

'Kidnappers don't usually go out of their way to cook food for their captives, especially if they're supposedly holed up in some dockside container. They buy in easy rations. Takeaway meals.'

'We fed him from the house. OK, that was sloppy. I wondered why I was asked about my meals. Gave the wrong answer, didn't I?'

'We also worked out that the kidnappings weren't about the ransom money. The one thing you couldn't know, and we didn't at the time, was what Mats Möller paid out. But we now know that the gang that grabbed him extorted a lot more than four million euros. And they got their payment in dollars. You didn't know that, either.'

'Doesn't really matter in the great scheme of things. To all intents and purposes, our gang was just doing the same for less.'

'How did you know where to find Christer?'

'You mean his dismal little trysts? The police aren't the only people who carry out surveillance.'

All the time they had been talking, Anita, realizing that her tied hands were in the shadows, had been trying surreptitiously to move her wrists to loosen the rope, and now she could feel a fraction of give.

'We also worked out that the kidnappings – Uhlig's, yours, Offesson's – really had nothing to do with money. This is all about business. Or rather one particular business.' In her late-night discussion with Kevin, it hadn't taken a great leap to substitute the theory about Peter Uhlig and transfer it to Kristina Ekman and Dag Wollstad. The last she'd heard about Wollstad – and that was from Karl Westermark before he blew his brains out – was that the industrialist was in Bolivia. He must have moved. 'I take it your father's based in Brazil now. Let me guess. He bribed the authorities to shut down Trellogística. Probably when you put Peter Uhlig out of action. Similar thing with the Offesson coffee plantations?'

'Yes, Father is buying them over for a fraction of their true value. Money and threats are a good business combination in Brazil, especially with the right connections. And in Colombia, too.'

'And now you're waiting for the share price to plummet before you move in.'

'Offesson's are in a mess without Christer. Their coffee empire will be part of an obscure Brazilian conglomerate within a couple of weeks. There'll be no paper trail leading to my father.'

'And Trellogística Brasil?'

'That'll be swallowed up by the same conglomerate when the officials untie all the red tape we wound them up in.'

'Are you after Trellogistics as well?'

'It'll be taken over by Wollstad Industries soon enough.'

'I understand that. What I don't understand is why target Peter Uhlig and Christer Offesson so personally? There must be more legitimate ways of achieving what you've done.'

A thin smile crossed Ekman's lips.

'Revenge, of course. My father is a great businessman. A visionary. But he didn't come from the right background, and he didn't follow the rules. The likes of the Uhligs and the Offessons made life very difficult for him in the early years. They disliked his methods. They disliked him, full stop. They tried to thwart him at every turn. Do you know that Peter Uhlig sold his cement business to the Hoffberg Group for less than my father offered? Simply out of spite. They all used their influence to sabotage his business deals, they bad-mouthed him in business circles, and even shopped him to the tax authorities. Anders Offesson was the greatest offender. But for all their malice, they couldn't stop the rise of Wollstad Industries! And then, thanks to *you*, he's condemned to live the rest of his life in exile.' She poked Anita's shoulder viciously. 'And exile gives a man time to think, time to plot, and time to plan a day of reckoning. That's just what he's done with our help. My father and I make a great team. He provided Luis and his brothers for the kidnaps. They're experts in their field over in Rio. Then I, and Lothar, of course, did the rest.'

'We know your boyfriend was the patrol cop. And the voice phoning in the ransom demands. We checked up on his background and found his Swedish mother.'

Goessling had been looking increasingly worried as the conversation went on.

'Kristina, they know so much about us. We have to be careful.'

'Don't go all pathetic on me now!' she snapped. 'They won't be able to prove a thing.'

'I'm sure we can prove that you killed Christer Offesson,' continued Anita, who could feel a further loosening around her wrists.

'How?'

'We know he was executed. You tried to make it look like he was escaping, but the bullets were fired from close range. Lothar didn't do that very well.'

'It wasn't me! Kristina did it.'

'Shut up!'

'We also know that the gun was Brazilian.'

'Luis's brothers took their guns back to Rio on Monday. You'll have to go there to find the murder weapon.'

'And then there was the soil and the grass. They were a real giveaway.'

'The grass?'

'When you took him outside. There was earth and grass

found in Christer's mouth and hair and on his clothes. Forensics are pretty clever these days. It's amazing what they can do with soil samples. Once they match it to what you've got out there...' Anita had no idea whether that was even possible and was banking on Ekman and an increasingly fidgety Goessling not knowing either.

'You're lying.'

'Am I? Tell me, the timing of Christer's kidnap. Was it because he was about to fly out to Brazil?'

'We were always going to grab him. We had to move more quickly than we'd planned when we heard of his flight.'

'And why did you have to kill him? We were about to arrest him for The Oligarch's murder anyway.'

Ekman looked bored. 'Well, I've saved you the bother.'

Anita was still playing for time. Her wrists and fingers were aching, but the knots were beginning to unravel. 'So, why?'

Ekman took out a cigarette and lit it. All the time, her eyes never left Anita. Anita was praying that she wouldn't go round the back of the chair, so she held her gaze. She stopped all wrist movement until Ekman had started talking again.

'We'd always intended to kill Christer. It would make sure he was out of the way while Father moved in and sewed up the plantations. Killing his son would just add to Anders' hurt and humiliation. But in a feeble attempt to save himself, the fool blurted out that he'd killed The Oligarch – all that sordid business about the little girl – and that he'd done me and Father a favour. The Oligarch had spilled it all to Christer, obviously revelling in Offessons' imminent demise: the story that he'd initially uncovered was about Father's, shall we say, less-than-scrupulous transactions in South America. I don't know how he'd got onto it in the first place, but he was about to expose my father's dealings and the... "connections" that were helping him to stitch up both Uhlig and Offesson. My father has some useful but dubious friends in the *Comando Vermelho*, one of

Brazil's leading organized crime syndicates. The Oligarch's story would have finished Wollstad Industries over here in Europe. I'd be finished. Christer even tried to propose a deal. If we let him go, he promised he wouldn't stand in our way or tell the world about Father's activities. We could ensure his silent complicity because we now knew he'd killed The Oligarch. He was willing to sacrifice his company to save his life. A couple of bullets put an end to the negotiations.'

Kristina Ekman dropped her half-smoked cigarette on the floor and crushed it with her foot.

'I think that's enough. Time for you to disappear.'

'Are you sure, Kristina?' gabbled Goessling. 'If the police know all this...'

'Just do as I say. *You* don't have to shoot her. All you and Luis have to do is get rid of the body.' She came a little closer. Anita could smell her perfume. 'Father is a great admirer of the late Juan Peron. He used to have political enemies taken out by plane and dropped into the Rio Plata. They were never seen again. We can learn a lot from the South Americans. We'll do the same with you.'

The rope was nearly loose enough for Anita to wriggle her wrists free. She just needed a few moments more.

'Don't you want to know how I found out that this was where you brought your victims?'

Ekman gave a throaty laugh. 'OK, why not?'

'The wild boar.'

'Come on! Surely not!'

Anita was about to explain to give her extra precious seconds when an edgy Goessling suddenly said 'What's that?'

'What's what?' Ekman said petulantly.

'I thought I heard something.'

'Start being a man, for God's sake!'

'I'm sure I heard something.'

'Luis.' Ekman waved her thumb at the Brazilian.

Luis ambled to the door, opened it and went out. Anita strained her ears; the silence was palpable. Then a shout: 'Police!' The next moment, there was a shot, followed by another, followed by a further exchange of gun fire.

'Shit!' cried Goessling as a bullet pinged off the side of the container.

Goessling, now in a complete funk, rushed towards the door. As he pushed it wide open, he raised his arms. 'Don't shoot!'

Ekman, just behind him, pushed her boyfriend forward and slipped out of Anita's sight. Anita quickly untangled her wrists and freed her hands. She was out of the door in a flash. Outside, she could see Luis lying on the ground, clutching his thigh. Goessling was standing with arms raised shouting in Swedish that he hadn't got a weapon. Half a dozen armed police in blue paramilitary-style uniforms were pointing their Heckler & Koch submachine guns at him. Behind them, Anita could see Zetterberg and Hakim.

But Kristina Ekman wasn't there. Anita ran round to the back of the container. Here, there was another path leading into the trees. She sped down it and, round a bend, she saw a fleeing Ekman in front of her.

'Stop!' Anita yelled.

Ekman had no intention of being caught. She ran on with Anita in pursuit. Suddenly, she darted off the path into the trees. Anita followed her, pushing her way through the tangled thicket. Ekman might know the terrain, but Anita was fitter, and she was gradually closing in. Ekman was about twenty paces ahead when she ducked under a low branch and, for a moment, was out of sight. Anita reached the spot but she couldn't see Ekman anywhere. An old fallen tree trunk blocked the way. The next moment, she heard a noise behind her. Too late! A large branch, wielded by Ekman, crashed down on Anita's back. She stumbled forward, pain shooting through her shoulder. Her glasses flew off in the fall. She twisted round just as another blow rained down and caught her upraised arm. From her prone position, despite the pain, and using all her strength, Anita lunged at Ekman as she turned to run off. Her hand just barely brushed Ekman's heel but it was enough to unbalance her and she tumbled into the prostrate tree trunk.

As Anita sank back to the ground, she was aware that Ekman was still there, lying across the tree, face down. Had she cracked her head when she fell? Gingerly, Anita got to her feet. Ekman hadn't smacked her head; blood was gushing from her neck. A thin, sharp spike of wood jutting from the tree had gone straight through her jugular vein. The beautiful face was a mask of agony.

A stunned Anita staggered out of the trees, cradling her arm. In her hand, she clutched her twisted glasses. Luis was being attended to and Lothar von Goessling was being escorted away. Hakim saw her and quickly came over.

'Are you OK?'

'I'm fine, though I may have done something to my arm. Actually, I feel a bit wobbly, but I'm glad to see you lot.'

Hakim steered her towards a police car. 'You have Zetterberg to thank,' he muttered as though in apology. 'Apparently, Pontus overheard you telling me that you weren't going to Karlshamn, and rushed off to tell Zetterberg. I'm afraid I had to tell her what you were up to, and we drove out here. When we realized that something was up – we saw Lothar taking your car away – she called for armed back-up from Ystad.'

'Thank goodness for Brodd's big mouth.'

Zetterberg stalked over to the police car. 'Where's Kristina Ekman?' she demanded to know.

'Back there,' said Anita, indicating the wood. 'She won't be giving us any more trouble.'

'Hakim, go and find her.'

'It's a bit grisly,' Anita warned.

Zetterberg's gaze swept over the scene.

'I suppose I should thank you,' said Anita. 'If you'd waited five minutes longer, I'd be dead.'

Zetterberg's lip curled in distaste. 'If I'd known, I'd have waited ten.'

Anita knew she meant it.

NOTES

Finnish Wartime Refugees

During the Second World War, over 70,000 Finnish children were evacuated in the face of Soviet attacks. The first wave of refugees took place during the Winter War (1939–40) as the Finns feared that there might be a humanitarian disaster following what they believed would be the inevitable Soviet occupation. Indeed, the Soviet Union did seize parts of Finland, including some of the country's most fertile areas. With the prospect of the Soviet Union trying to annexe the whole country, the Finns became co-belligerents (as opposed to becoming a member of the AXIS powers) with Nazi Germany in the fight to regain lost territory. This became known as the Continuation War (1941–1944).

The Continuation War saw the flow of evacuated children increase, with most heading to Sweden, which was not only neutral, but also had hundreds of years of historic connections with Finland. This included children from both Finnish and Finnish-Swedish (Swedish speaking) homes. Many of the children were 'guests' of Swedish families while some of those who were ill or in poor physical condition were placed in institutions such as hospitals, sanatoria and orphanages. As one would expect, the children had mixed fortunes, though research has shown that most had later felt that the evacuation had been a positive experience.

However, when the war finished, most of the children didn't return for some time due to the poor economic conditions in a war-battered Finland and the uncertainty over the future intentions of the Soviet Union. Over 15,000 children never returned to their native land at all; many having been too young to remember their Finnish roots and having bonded with their Swedish families in the intervening years. Many were formally adopted by their Swedish families and a substantial number of

Finnish parents decided not to take their children back.

The physical and psychological effects were longer lasting for many of the returning evacuees. There was an elevated risk of heart disease and diabetes, and an earlier onset of puberty. Female evacuees were more likely to have their first child at a younger age. The psychological consequences included the increased risk of mental health issues, in particular personality disorders and substance abuse. A study by the Academy of Finland in April 2013 concluded that Finnish children sent to Sweden to avoid war suffered more than those who stayed.

To get an insight into the period, I recommend the 2005 Finnish film *Mother of Mine*, directed by Klaus Härö. It follows the life of a young Finnish boy who is taken in by a Scanian farmer and his wife during World War II. I have a personal connection with this film as Göran Brante, a friend who has been very helpful with my books over the years, plays the part of the postman delivering letters to the remote farm from the boy's mother back in Finland.

ABOUT THE AUTHOR

Torquil MacLeod was born in Edinburgh. After working in advertising agencies in Birmingham, Glasgow and Newcastle, he now lives in Cumbria with his wife, Susan, and her hens. The idea for a Scandinavian crime series came from his frequent trips to Malmö and southern Sweden to visit his elder son. He now has four grandchildren, two of whom are Swedish.

Also by Torquil MacLeod:

The Malmö Mysteries:
Meet me in Malmö
Murder in Malmö
Missing in Malmö
Midnight in Malmö
Menace in Malmö
A Malmö Midwinter (novella)

ACKNOWLEDGEMENTS

As I once forgot to mention him, I'd like to start by thanking the generous Nick Pugh of The Roundhouse for his usual eye-catching cover design. On the medical front, the Foster doctors from Gloucester, Bill, Justine and Jess, provided helpful advice yet again. If I have used it incorrectly, blame me, not them. I'd like to thank neighbour, Carol Reading, for allowing me to snoop around her containers. And her husband, Mark, who was meant to find out information about South American firearms and didn't, but still wanted a mention.

On the Swedish side; thanks go to the ever-helpful Eva Wennås Brante for introducing me to Svaneholm and Rutger Macklean. Of course, our great friend Karin Geistrand provided her usual extensive help on the police (including plundering her Police Academy photographs) and other matters over a few bottles of red wine and a visit to Simrishamn's Nordic Sea Winery. Again, it's no fault of hers that I have trampled over accepted Swedish police procedural practices.

I'd also like to mention one of my readers, John Boursy, who raised an interesting question about Ramadan in Sweden, the answer to which I've incorporated into the book. Of course, thanks to Fraser and Paula for accommodation and numerous tips on Swedish life. Thanks to Linda MacFadyen for her tireless support and her promotion of *The Malmö Mysteries*. Last but certainly not least, thanks to Susan for her editing and usual forthright suggestions.

I would also like to thank family, friends and readers for their continued encouragement.